SHIFTER
PLANET:
THE RETURN

SHIFTER PLANET:

THE RETURN

D.B. REYNOLDS

Entangled Publishing, LLC
2614 South Timberline Road
Suite 105, PMB 159
Fort Collins, CO 80525
rights@entangledpublishing.com

Amara is an imprint of Entangled Publishing, LLC.

Edited by Brenda Chin
Cover design by Sara Eirew
Cover photography by Honored_member and Kwadrat/Shutterstock

Manufactured in the United States of America

First Edition October 2019

To Roman with love.

Miss you, baby.

Chapter One

Aidan raced through the trees, his big paws skimming over rough branches, his passage nearly silent despite his nearly three hundred pounds of savage muscle and bone. They'd had a late spring snow last night, the delicate flakes melting almost as soon as they hit the ground. But up here in the treetops, there were pockets of ice melt that left wet streaks of cold along his back. He leaped for a giant grandfather tree and paused, dropping onto his belly along a wide limb, feeling the life that flowed through the tree and beyond to the entire forest.

This was his domain. The domain of every shifter on Harp. More than any other, the verdant forest band known as The Green belonged to Harp's shifters—men who could change from their human form to that of a giant hunting cat with barely a thought. Norms—that's how shifters thought of the human population of Harp who couldn't shift—sometimes asked whether shifters thought of themselves primarily as cats or humans. And, to a man, shifters would only stare blankly. There was no either-or for them. They simply were. They were shifters, and they ruled the planet. Their existence was the sole reason that humans had managed to flourish on Harp, the result of genetic manipulation designed to produce a human hybrid whom the unique planet would recognize as one of its own.

Because Harp wasn't just any planet. Harp was *aware*. Or rather, its forests were, which was the same thing. Harp's trees *sang* to those able to hear their voices. And of all the humans born on Harp, only shifters could hear that song. It was a song of abundance, telling shifters where prey could be found and which clusters of fruit trees were ripe for picking, and a song of danger, warning where predators lurked, and the many other threats that hid in the shadows. Those warnings had saved his cousin Rhodry's life not too long ago, leading an Earther woman to where he lay badly injured. Rhodry had lived and the woman had become his wife. But that was another story.

It remained that there was no greater predator on Harp than the shifters themselves. They were the apex predator on a planet where the tiniest creatures could wipe out a huge chunk of forest with a single swarm, and where giant, fanged beasts roamed the northernmost glaciers. And still, shifters ruled.

They'd made the difference between life and death when the original colonists had been on the very edge of extinction, and they continued to make it possible for humans to thrive. Their ability to commune with the forests was the key to survival on this planet. It was only natural, then, that they also dominated virtually every aspect of Harp society.

And Aidan was one of them.

Although this morning, he was feeling more cast adrift and lonely than like a ruler of the planet. It was great running through the treetops, but not as much fun as it had been to run races with his cousin Rhodry. Unfortunately, Rhodry was still in Ciudad Vaquero, Harp's capital city, which also happened to be Harp's *only* city, so most people simply called it, "the city."

Normally, not even the distance to the city would have stopped Rhodry. The miles passed swiftly in the treetops under a shifter's paws, and Rhodry had never been one to follow the rules. If they missed him at the shifters' Guild Hall in the city for a few days, who cared? Especially if it meant a chance to race with his favorite cousin. And, yes, Aidan was his favorite, despite the large number of Devlin cousins Rhodry had to choose from.

But Rhodry had a more powerful reason to remain in the city right now, and that was his wife, Amanda, who'd broken a few rules of her own to become not only the first non-shifter, but the first *female* member of the Guild. She also happened to be pregnant with twins, which was something very few people knew about yet. Her pregnancy was far enough along that they'd have to go public with it soon, but they'd wanted to wait. Twins weren't unheard of in shifter births, but these were both male, and *that* had never happened before. Besides which, Amanda wasn't Harp-born, and no one knew what risks she and her babies might face, given the relatively short period she'd had to adapt physically to the planet's environment. It had only been two years, after all. That wasn't long for a human body to adjust, especially not when one added the stress of carrying twin babies who were far from the human norm. It was one risk factor too many for Rhodry's peace of mind, so, for now, he and Amanda were both staying put in the city and maintaining a low profile.

Twins! Aidan bared his teeth in a feline grin. And not just twins, but two mini-shifters—two mini *Rhodrys*— would soon descend on Harp. The heavens shuddered at the possibility. But Aidan's grin only grew wider, startling a nearby covey of doves into a swirl of purple and green flight. He and Rhodry had been born within moments of each other, sharing a cradle, and had been inseparable from birth. They'd also been hell on their parents. If there was trouble to be found, they'd found it, and Aidan could only imagine Rhodi's sons would be the same.

It was strange to realize that Rhodry was about to become a father. It was one more responsibility in a life already chock full of the same, since he was already the de Mendoza clan chief and adviser to the planet's political leader, the *Ardrigh,* as he was known on Harp, which was old Irish Gaelic for king or ruler. It was a slight misnomer, since Harp's system more closely resembled a parliamentary government—the title was more of a nod to their Earth roots, than anything else.

For all Rhodry's new duties, however, *Aidan* wasn't feeling all that responsible. Or maybe he just didn't want to. Life was strange, but it was also—

He stilled, as all around him, the forest grew silent and alert. Beneath his paws, the grandfather tree was doing the same—listening, reaching out to the ends of the Green, searching for…what? Aidan's ears swiveled, his head turning from side to side as he searched for the cause of the forest's unease.

A heartbeat later, he saw it. A pale streak of movement where there should have been nothing but blue sky in this part of the Green, accompanied by a noise he knew well. It was similar to the roar of the shuttlecrafts that dropped through Harp's atmosphere intermittently, on the Earth fleet's regular supply run. But the last shuttle had been less than two months ago, and besides, they landed just outside the city, in an area far from this part of the forest. They were loud and stank of burning fuel and metal, only tolerated because of the benefit to Harp in terms of technology and information.

Tracking the intruder as it drew closer, he saw that, while it had the same markings as a fleet shuttle, it was a completely different kind of craft. The shuttles were small reentry vehicles sent down from a huge space-faring military vessel that traveled a regular supply route among several outlying planets. This vehicle was much larger than the shuttles, and it was not only FTL capable, but armed to the teeth.

Aidan's eyes narrowed as the craft set down in a wide-open meadow on the far side of a severe rift known as the swamp. The name came from the microclimate deep in that rift, which bisected this part of the Green in a north/south direction, beyond the mountains of Clanhome. No one lived out this way, because the swamp was nearly impassable, except for shifters who could cross above it in the trees. There was no fresh water in its depths. Its swampy environment was the result of rain and snow melt from the ridges, which sank into the deep ground and accumulated in the bottoms. Heat from the sun, intensified by the surrounding forest, created a moist, marshy environment that was a mile wide from the air, but could take weeks to cross on foot. Travelers had to go down one side, transit the muddy bottom, and then up the other side, all while dealing with the swamp's unique variety of predators. With such a small population and a vast living space, there was no reason for anyone to settle there.

Which made it all the more suspicious that an Earther craft was landing on the swamp's far side. Two years ago, Harp's people had greeted the rediscovery of their "lost colony" by a passing Earth fleet with very mixed feelings. On the one hand, they welcomed the technological advances the renewed connection with Earth provided. But on the other, they most definitely did not welcome the intrusion of Earth visitors to their planet. Harp's forests and her shifters were a secret they didn't want to share, and they didn't want anyone digging into the truth of how they'd survived that original catastrophic landing so many centuries ago.

Their reluctant welcome had been borne out when a few of the very first fleet visitors had ignored on-planet restrictions and, as a direct result, inflicted severe damage to a section of the forest—both animals and trees. Fleet command had designated Harp as a restricted planet after that, largely at the insistence of the Ardrigh, but the incident had hardened Harper attitudes even further toward Earthers. In fact, Amanda was possibly the *only* Earth-native who was now considered a Harper.

As for this rather suspect landing by an Earth craft, the secretive location itself lent credence to his suspicions. Normally, there would have been no one this far out from the city or Clanhome to witness their arrival. A shifter patrol out of Clanhome rotated this way once every two months or so, crossing the swamp through the trees, which was much faster. There was good reason to venture this far on a regular basis. Harp was a harsh planet, and one had to keep an eye out for new threats. But it was pure good luck and coincidence that Aidan happened to be here on this particular day.

He watched as a *definite* new threat settled onto the planet's surface. The noise and stink of the vehicle disturbed the Green's usual peace, but the landing place was well-chosen for all that. By avoiding any damage to the trees, themselves, the ship minimized the possibility of the forest sending out an alarm right away. Which was alarming in itself. Whoever was onboard that ship knew enough to conceal its arrival, which meant they were almost certainly up to no good. One thing he knew for sure, they had no business being way out here at the outermost edge of Harp's mountain range. *His* mountain range. The Ardrigh ruled the city, but the de Mendoza clan chief ruled the mountains, and with Rhodry gone, Aidan was his de Mendoza surrogate.

He had to find out who the hell was in that ship. Harp

was a closed planet. No one, and that meant *no one,* was permitted to land a ship here—a restriction insisted on by the Ardrigh and supposedly enforced by Earth Fleet. And that brought up yet another worrisome point—that ship sure as hell hadn't snuck through a reentry into Harp's atmosphere. The planet had a perfect, natural defense mechanism in the form of a violently destructive electromagnetic anomaly that dominated the atmosphere. Any ship making that passage was easily detectable by the fleet's science center in the city, which was partially responsible for enforcing the planet's embargo. Any ship trying to break the embargo was marked and targeted for destruction. Given the already hazardous atmosphere, it didn't take much to destroy an incoming ship. The fact that this ship had managed to evade detection and land way the hell out here, in the middle of nowhere, told Aidan that it hadn't evaded detection at all. Someone in the science center had been bought off.

He frowned. All around him, the Green remained silent, waiting. Whoever had advised the intruders had done their job well. The forest didn't see them as an immediate threat. At least, not yet. But they hadn't gone to the trouble and expense of sneaking onto the planet in order to do good works. Aidan was certain of that, but he took his cue from the trees, watching and waiting. So far, the intruders hadn't done anything but land far from the city, which was suspicious enough that he considered racing directly back to Clanhome to raise an alert. But he needed more information, and he was also reluctant to leave the ship out here alone. Even with a shifter's speed, the journey to Clanhome would take many days there and back. Who knew what damage the intruders might do in the meantime?

When the Earthers had first rediscovered Harp, more than two years ago, a handful of fleet personnel had wiped out an enormous circle of forest and razed an ancient grandfather tree nearly down to its roots. They'd paid for it with their lives in the cataclysm, but nonetheless, they'd been nothing but a small group of fools who'd thought the rules didn't apply to them. He was looking at a well-armed shipload of potential danger.

Decision made, he took off in the direction of the uninvited vessel. He'd cross the swamp and survey them first—evaluate the threat, and then, if necessary, rally some of his cousins out of Clanhome, which was a lot closer than the city. Whoever these invaders were, he was certain they'd never met a hunting party of shifters. Because if they had, they wouldn't be alive to tell of it.

Chapter Two

Rachel Fortier slumped inside the stiff confines of her fully deployed spacesuit, strapped in place by a heavy safety harness, breathing recycled air, and half dozing in boredom. She'd been trapped in her cabin, wearing the bulky suit for what felt like hours, unable to get comfortable, and waiting for the all-clear signal. Commander Ripper had blasted over the intercom, ordering everyone into their suits and warning that the ship was about to drop onto the planet, which meant transiting Harp's tricky atmosphere with its weird electromagnetic phenomenon. Rachel wasn't a physicist, but she understood enough to know that this was the most dangerous part of their trip. There was a fifty-fifty chance that their engines would simply shut down and they'd find themselves free-falling to the surface. Which was a nice way of saying they'd crash and burn...and die.

Although, she figured their odds of a safe landing were probably better than 50 percent by now. The fleet had been sending shuttles to Harp for nearly two years, and there was a fleet science center on the planet. She assumed that meant they'd been gathering data for that long, because that's what the fleet did. By now, they must have learned a thing or two about safely transiting Harp's risky atmosphere. But a forty-sixty chance of a crash-and-burn, while somewhat better, wasn't exactly comforting.

Her thoughts eased some tension she'd been feeling about their descent but did nothing to relieve the boredom. Especially now, when it seemed they'd made it through the worst part of the ride down. It had been damn rough at first, and at one point, she'd been convinced the ship was going to break apart around them. But according to the readout on her suit, that had been nearly half an hour ago, and somehow, they'd survived. There was still the occasional hard bump, but for the most part, their transit had become fairly smooth.

She was just beginning to wonder if maybe the intercom had been damaged in the descent and she was the only one still in her cabin, stewing in her spacesuit while the rest of the crew was already enjoying a hot shower, when suddenly the pitch of the engines changed. Her eyes flashed open, and she "listened" with all her senses. A second later, the ship changed angles, and she detected another shift in engine noise. Where before there'd been the typical constant roar, threaded through with a high whine that made her ears hurt, the sound had now shifted to the quieter hum associated with maneuvering control.

She'd no sooner had the thought than Ripper's voice came over the intercom, giving the all-clear to ditch their suits and move around. Rachel popped the seals on her helmet first, then hit the release on her safety harness as she sucked in a greedy lungful of the cabin's relatively fresher air. She had an arm up, smelling her pit and thinking she needed a fucking shower, when her cabin door slid open and Ripper stuck her head through with her usual disregard for privacy.

"You can ditch the suit, Fortier, but stick to your cabin for a while yet. The crew's pretty busy, and you'll only be in the way."

In the way? Fuck you very much. Ripper was gone before Rachel could voice her thoughts, for all the good it would have done. She probably wouldn't have gone wandering the damn halls, anyway. This wasn't exactly her first rodeo, and as a xenobiologist and civilian planetary specialist, her job wouldn't actually begin until the ship was settled. But she was hardly a novice when it came to space travel. She was tempted to take a stroll, just to prove she could and maybe irritate Ripper in the process. But, instead, she stripped off her sweaty clothes and took a shower, using all the water she wanted. Now that they were on-planet, there was no reason to conserve their limited supply with thimble-size showers. Harp had plenty of water, fed by underground springs that, in turn, were fed by glacial run-off from a permanently frozen polar ice cap. No planet could produce a green belt like this one without a lot of water.

She soaped up and washed away the sweat, eager now that the real mission was finally beginning. This was what scientific discovery was supposed to be, this excited anticipation of seeing and doing new things, of being on a planet where humans had been living undiscovered for half a millennium. Imagine the genetic possibilities. How big was the population, and how had they avoided destructive inbreeding? Interesting questions, but even more exciting, from her point of view, was the wildlife within the planet's green belt. They were said to be exceptionally vicious and deadly, so much so that no one was allowed to venture in among the trees without a proper escort.

That wouldn't pose a problem for her. She had as much or more expeditionary time as any crewmember on this ship and would match her experience against theirs in a heartbeat. In fact, while most of the crew were friendly enough, none of them talked much about where they'd worked before joining this mission to study Harp's animal life-forms. The only thing obvious to Rachel was that they were all former military.

Rachel's credentials, on the other hand, were an open book. She was one of the most sought-after planetary specialists in the private sector. An admitted overachiever from a family of distinguished academics going back generations, she had two PhDs—in xenobiology and chemistry—and a Doctorate in Veterinary Medicine, with an emphasis on xenomorphology. On official records, it was her scientific accomplishments that counted. But in practical terms, it was her broader, experiential credentials that made her so attractive as an expeditionary leader. She was a two-fer—a proper academic, but with all the survival skills of a military-trained planetary specialist.

She was qualified to deal with all kinds of hostile environments, had considerable experience in the same, and had assumed those two factors had influenced Guy Wolfrum's decision to hire her. That's right. Guy *fucking* Wolfrum was this mission's leader, and he'd hired *her* to study Harp's animal life, especially the huge, predatory cats who sat on top of the planet's food chain. He was a giant in the field of xenobiology and had served as Chief Science Officer on United Earth's biggest exploratory fleet, serving under Admiral Nakata. Nakata's fleet was legendary, so it had surprised a lot of people when, just under two years ago, Wolfrum had resigned his commission to live on Harp. Rumor was that he'd done it for love, and he *had* married a Harp woman. But Rachel couldn't imagine a man of his accomplishments walking away from his career if the planet hadn't also represented a truly untouched treasure trove of potential scientific discovery.

Of course, Harp was a tightly closed planet, which meant virtually no scientific data had been gathered since its rediscovery. At least, none that had been published off-planet. But she didn't believe for a minute that *Guy Wolfrum* had been sitting on his hands for nearly two years doing nothing other than enjoying the Harp version of marital bliss. Even if she couldn't share whatever she learned from this trip, or from Wolfrum himself, it represented an unequaled opportunity. A pristine planet which had somehow made life possible for humans. She was eager to finally meet the legendary scientist in person and exchange notes. All their communications thus far had, of necessity, been written, since he lived on-planet and Harp had such restrictive policies.

But while, for Rachel, it was a scientist's dream, she seemed to be the only crew member excited about it. In fact, despite their vessel's scientific designator, none of her fellow crewmen seemed to have any scientific specialties at all. There were no lab facilities on board, and her gentle prodding had produced no evidence of scientific backgrounds. In fact, if it hadn't been Guy Wolfrum himself who'd recruited her, she'd have been suspicious about their mission. As it was, she had a million questions once he finally joined them.

Assuming Ripper ever let anyone leave the damn ship.

• • •

THE PLANET HARP

Aidan lay motionless, his golden coat concealed by the dappled pattern of sunlight and cloud through the trees. Those trees were now whispering restlessly, unhappy with this metal invader in their midst. The ship hadn't done anything overtly threatening yet, and so, just as the forest didn't ring planetwide alerts about every local storm or out of control predator, the warning remained targeted at the one who could do something about it. Which was Aidan. Had he not been already on scene, the warning would have traveled farther, most likely to Clanhome.

The Green had a very symbiotic relationship with its shifters. Unlike anyone else on Harp, they weren't visitors to the planet; they were part of its ecosystem. It didn't matter that, minus a very few exceptions, every human living on Harp had been born here. Only shifters were *of* Harp, right down to their DNA. And because they were part of the planet, the Green protected them, just as it did itself. Which was why the warning would have traveled to Clanhome with its large population of shifters—both as a warning and a plea for help.

Aidan had been sitting on the same branch for hours, through a morning rainstorm and the midday clearing. But he was a born predator. He could remain still for hours more if that's what it took. He stared hard at the invading ship, taking in the smallest detail.

He'd never been on a ship in space, had never been off planet, and had no desire to do so, but that didn't mean he was ignorant. Every member of the Guild—which represented the best hunters and the sharpest minds among Harp's shifters—was well versed in the scientific facts of space travel. And their new fleet-built computing and science facility included a thoroughly updated database on the weapons and modes of transportation available to potential invaders. Shifters had a duty to protect the planet from *all* threats, and they took that duty seriously.

This ship, which had somehow snuck onto Harp and landed far away from the city, was no shuttle. Its pocked and pitted surface spoke of a hard passage through the atmosphere, just like the shuttles which visited regularly, but the engines which had finally shut down were much larger and more efficient, and, as he'd suspected, definitely faster-than-light or FTL capable. He'd been right about the weapons, too. The ship was bristling with them.

That, coupled with a landing far away from the city, added up to secrecy and collusion with someone in the science center. The question was why? Harp didn't possess any rare or valuable resources for invaders to steal. It was the reason the fleet had been so accommodating in granting them the closed planet designation. Why, then, would a bunch of Earthers—and he was assuming that's what they were, based on the ship's overall design—want to make a secret trip to Harp? There had to be something they wanted here. Something they knew Harpers wouldn't want to give up.

The answer, or at least the beginnings of an answer, lay with the people on that ship. But although he'd been watching the damn thing for hours, no one had so much as poked a nose outside. It simply sat there, under power, wasting energy it apparently had plenty of, while the sun slid down the horizon and the shade deepened among the trees. Aidan wondered if they were planning a nighttime mission, hoping to use the cover of darkness to conceal their activities. And then he wondered if they understood just how dangerous Harp was at night. Or maybe they *were* aware and were waiting for an early morning start tomorrow to pursue whatever nefarious plot had brought them here.

Or maybe not.

The forest around him grew abruptly silent a mere instant before the hiss of vacuum seals brought Aidan's big head off his paws. His eyes sharpened, his gaze on the shaded belly of the ship, where a rim of white light now outlined a slowly opening door. A ramp deployed as the hatch dropped open, and he caught a glimpse of a brightly lit interior before someone started to walk down.

His cat eyes didn't have the ability to widen in surprise, but if they did, they'd have popped out of his head. Only one person was descending to the forest floor—a lovely woman with a cap of curly, dark hair and a long, slim body. Slim, but strong, as attested by the way her formfitting pants hugged firm thighs and a flat belly, not to mention the delectable swell of her breasts beneath a snug, long-sleeved top.

"Focus, you idiot!" his own voice chided him mentally, reminding him why he was here. Not that he'd forgotten for even a minute. There was nothing wrong with admiring a fine, female form. In fact, he was something of a connoisseur of female forms, having enjoyed close, personal contact with a wide variety and on many occasions.

But not this one.

This one came from an unknown ship that had chosen to land secretly and might very well be a harbinger of more danger to come.

The woman reached the bottom of the ramp and paused, her head doing a slow turn as she scanned the trees circling the meadow, her eyes searching...for what? It was the smart thing to do in any new environment, but especially in the Green, where danger could lurk in a hundred different places. But what did this uninvited guest know about the Green? More than she should have, since she and her shipmates had known how to land without causing a crisis. But not nearly enough, he would wager, because this was the fucking *Green*. Norms who'd lived on Harp their entire lives couldn't survive out here without shifter assistance.

The woman raised a hand to one of the ramp supports and smiled as she gazed out onto the surrounding forest, her head tilted slightly. That smile did something to Aidan's gut. It wasn't the smile of an invader, of someone come to do harm, but one of delight and anticipation. As if she liked everything she was seeing and could hardly wait to explore.

He narrowed his eyes, hardening his resolve against being overly influenced by her appearance. If she'd been a man, would he still be seeing the same innocence in her expression?

Lids came down over his eyes in a long, slow blink. Yes, he thought he probably would. And that realization confused him because there was no doubt that she didn't belong here.

Heavy footsteps sounded a moment before she twisted sharply to look over her shoulder, her expression shifting to one of greater caution. More people appeared, but unlike the woman's easy stroll down the ramp, these new invaders strode toward the forest floor in a disciplined group. The woman took a sideways jump off the end of the ramp to avoid being run over, her face lightening briefly in a combination of surprise and amusement. Amusement quickly fled, replaced by bland courtesy when the leader of the new group stopped to snap out what sounded like a command. The woman nodded in agreement, but as the invaders started across the meadow, her expression was filled with rebellion.

Aidan's attention followed hers, shifting to watch the larger group. They all wore the same uniform-like grey pants and shirts with heavy boots. Their shirts bore no insignia or rank patches, but there was no doubt in his mind that these were soldiers. They moved as one, with precision and discipline, responding to the barked commands of the leader—a woman of average height, who was blocky with muscle and had her hair cut so close to her scalp that he couldn't tell what color it would be.

These soldiers were the true danger delivered by that fucking ship. Aidan didn't know how the other woman fit in, but she had to be a part of it somehow. She was on their damn crew, wasn't she?

He was torn. He desperately wanted to know more about the ship, and the woman, too. But he couldn't afford to let a pack of invading soldiers roam his planet at will. Around him, the Green had taken note of these new invaders. Where the trees initially had been cautiously watchful, there was now a shiver of foreboding and growing alarm. They remembered previous human visitors, remembered the tremendous damage a few Earthers had inflicted with a single careless act.

It was the woman who made Aidan's decision for him. With a middle-fingered salute at the departing troop, she gave a last lingering look at the forest, and then thumped back up into the ship, slapping the hatch control as soon as she'd cleared the opening.

And there went his chances of slipping onboard for a quick look around.

His head turned, his gaze easily picking out the invaders moving across the clearing with what they probably considered to be stealth. They'd reach the trees soon. There were no clear paths in that part of the forest, and the shadows beneath the trees would grow darker with every step they took, making their headlong march far more difficult. Aidan could track them easily enough, though it would be more difficult if they decided to split up. He could still do it, but it would have been easier if he'd had at least one of his cousins along.

He frowned, tempted to add his own warning to the one already humming through the trees, one which would alert his cousins to the possible danger. But he decided against it for now. Thus far, the Earthers hadn't done anything particularly threatening. He rose to his feet and made an effortless leap upward, circling around the tree until he reached the far heights of the forest, where branches were so thickly intertwined that they formed a solid road through the treetops.

With a final glance at the closed hatch of the ship, he took off after his prey.

• • •

Rachel left her cabin door a little bit open the next day as she gathered her gear, listening to her shipmates as they traveled up and down the passageway. She made no apologies for eavesdropping. It was the only way she could learn anything about their march into the forest yesterday. They may have thought they were being stealthy, but it was obvious to her that none of them were trained in wildlife observation. They'd marched away like a conquering army, probably frightening away whatever animals they'd hope to observe. And they'd left her behind, which made no sense at all. She was the xenobiologist, the only one of them, as far as she could tell, who knew anything about studying non-Earth life-forms, or *any* life-forms, for that matter. But now that they'd made planetfall, the same crew who'd been so friendly during the journey here, the ones who'd laughed over meals and sweated with her in the gym, had become studiously uncommunicative. It was as if they'd suddenly lost the ability to speak. At least to her. It was the opposite of what she usually experienced. A lot of the scientists she'd escorted in the past had been tense and even frightened during the dangerous transit to a new location, but once they landed safely, they always fell back on their scientific training and shared her enthusiasm for a new world to explore.

But not this time. With every averted glance, every unanswered question, she was more convinced that this mission was not what she'd been led to believe. Commander Ripper and her people weren't scientists of any stripe, and they weren't here for the joy of discovery. She didn't know why exactly they *were* here yet, but she was certain that it wasn't something she would have agreed to be involved in. Which made her wonder why Wolfrum had enlisted her in the first place. Had he simply needed her academic credentials to bolster his grant application? It wouldn't be the first time that someone had included names on a proposal just for the sake of appearances. But if that was case, why *her*? He was *Guy fucking Wolfrum*—he could have gotten anyone he wanted to stick their name on a proposal without the expense of flying them all the way to Harp.

She'd tried to reach Wolfrum directly. Now that they were on the same planet, with him only a few miles away, communication should have been easy. Unfortunately, there was very little that was easy about Harp. The same electromagnetic anomaly that had made their planetary descent so perilous also wreaked havoc with any kind of electronic gear, including communication devices. Nothing would work, not even a simple two-way radio.

As for anything more complex, Wolfrum's limits on what equipment she could bring along, some of which had excluded gear that she'd previously considered irreplaceable, now made sense. She'd brought her personal computer, of course. But on Wolfrum's advice, she hadn't attempted to turn it on since they'd landed. One of her fellow crewmen had ignored the warning, and his computer was now fried. Ripper had, er, *ripped* the guy a new asshole over it. Apparently, the planet's reaction would have been far more catastrophic if they hadn't been within the ship's shielding. If, for example, the errant crew member had decided to sit outside in the sunshine and type up some notes, it could have been bad. *Really* bad. Rachel had been tempted to do exactly that yesterday afternoon, when Ripper and the rest of the crew had left her alone to mind the ship. She thought it would be okay if she disabled the comm functions and only used her computer as a glorified typewriter.

Thankfully, she'd erred on the side of caution and written her notes by hand instead, saving not only her computer, but all of the research it contained. She was more than a little pissed, actually, that Wolfrum hadn't been more categorical in his warnings. Why hadn't he bothered to share his two years-worth of experience living here? Harpers would have grown up with the restrictions, but Wolfrum would have known from experience the pitfalls awaiting someone who'd grown up with Earth technology, especially when it came to scientific research.

So this morning, armed with a pad of ordinary paper and some pencils, she was heading out to take notes the old-fashioned way when the thump of boots on the metal floor of the passageway drew her attention. She paused just inside her cabin and listened. It sounded as if they were all heading out again to do whatever the hell they'd done yesterday. One thing she knew for damn sure—she was not going to be stuck babysitting the ship again. She didn't give a damn what fucking Ripper said. Now that they were on the ground, the commander had no authority over Rachel or her tasks. She'd been hired by Wolfrum to explore the planet and study its apex predators, and that's what she intended to do.

As if drawn by the thought of her name, Ripper pushed the cabin door open without even the fake courtesy of a knock, nearly running into Rachel. Putting one foot over the threshold, she said, "You're on watch again today, Fortier. Keep the hatch closed, and we'll be back before sunset." She didn't wait for a response, just dropped her hand from the door and stepped back into the passageway to follow her crew.

Rachel stepped into the hall and glared after her for all of ten seconds. "Fuck that," she muttered. Ripper was trying to sideline her for some reason, to keep her away from whatever they were doing when they marched into the shadows beneath the trees. What *were* they doing? And exactly what the galactic fuck was going on?

Well, whatever it was, it was going to stop right now. She was a scientist, and this was her mission. She'd do them the courtesy of not straying too far, just in case there was a medical emergency, especially since there wasn't a doctor among the crew. Granted, her degree was in veterinary medicine and her specialty was *xeno*biology—that is, the study of non-Earth life-forms—but critical care principles were the same for all animals. She'd treated plenty of *human* animals on her previous missions.

But that was the extent of her cooperation. She was a fully-trained, expedition-capable researcher, and it was about time she acted like one.

She waited long enough for the others to be well away from the ship, then made her way up to the bridge. The engines were all shut down; just a trickle of power remained active. Enough to keep environmental control and the various monitoring systems working. Crossing to the science station, she brought up the exterior cameras, then zoomed in on the crew as they moved into the trees on the other side of the clearing. She counted heads, making sure everyone was there, and then switched the screen back to where she'd found it, which happened to be environmental status. It was ironic, really. She hadn't been invited to the bridge even as an observer while they'd been in transit. But now that they'd made planetfall and had something else to do—presumably something they considered more important—she was suddenly good enough to be on watch. She ought to do a quick liftoff and move the shuttle to a new location, something a few miles away. That would show them. And she could do it, too. One of the courses she'd had to take in order to qualify for extraterrestrial missions was a basic course in FTL-capable ship operation and navigation. No one expected private specialists like herself to pilot a ship into battle, but if worse came to worse, she had to be able, at the very minimum, to maintain life support and send out a distress signal. Rachel could do better than that. It might take a little bit of study, given the weird dual engine setup on this ship, but she was smart and intuitive. She'd figure it out eventually. And then Ripper would come back to…nothing. The image that idea conjured up, the expression on their faces...it cheered Rachel immensely.

Unfortunately, she didn't have time to be moving ships around this morning. She wasn't writing off the possibility, but not today. Because she was going to do a little exploring of her own.

Going back to her cabin, she checked her weapons first. She was a scientist, with a duty to do no harm, but that didn't mean she couldn't defend herself. Given Harp's restriction on any kind of plasma or electronic weapon, she'd brought a double-draw crossbow along with a supply of bolts. It was small enough for her to carry easily, but modified to notch two bolts at once, each firing independently. And, as always, she had her combat knife, which was a seven-inch fixed blade of carbon steel. The knife was carried in a leather sheath on her hip, and it was something she'd included in her kit for years. One never knew when a good knife would come in handy. For this trip, she'd stowed a second knife in her boot, as well. She still felt somewhat naked without the lightweight plasma rifle she typically carried, but she was armed with the standard capture gun used to study wildlife on a variety of planets. It was loaded with powerful tranquilizer darts, although she didn't anticipate using it. Her mission on this planet was to observe only. Still, it didn't hurt to have a weapon handy. Her goal was always to avoid hostile confrontations with native species, but she'd had to defend herself more than once against a local beastie who didn't want to be observed.

Grabbing the backpack she'd already put together, she made her way down to the landing deck. The hatch opened with a rush of warm, wet air, rich with the scents of green, growing things. Rachel had traveled extensively, including to more than a few distant planets and space stations, but she didn't think she'd ever smelled anything quite so...fertile as the air on Harp.

She was smiling when she walked out from under the belly of the ship and lifted her face to the warm sunlight. There was the scent of fresh rain in the air, confirming what the sensors had already told her. It was spring in this hemisphere of the planet. The daytime temperatures should be quite warm, with some light rain, though it could still get cold enough at night to be uncomfortable without proper protection.

But while the sun felt terrific on her upraised face, time was wasting, and she had things to do. Who knew how long before Ripper and the crew came marching back? Walking to the ramp, she sealed it against casual intruders, then moved out from under the ship's belly and into the sunlight, where she turned in a full circle and looked around. There was so much to see, to study, *and* to watch out for. She found herself longing for the support of a real science team. It was unusual to have a lone researcher on such a difficult and dangerous task. She hadn't really discussed it with any of the crew but had assumed at least some of them would be assigned to share her mission, even if only to provide security. She was increasingly convinced, however, that Ripper's mission and hers had nothing in common. Whatever the commander and her crew were doing on their daily marches, it wasn't science or research.

She frowned then shook her head in dismissal. There was nothing she could do about the Ripper situation. She was here, and she was going to make the most of it. She reached down for the small nav computer she always used, but of course it wasn't there. The technological limitations of Harp didn't stop at pulsed weapons. Anything that utilized a laser was specifically prohibited on the planet. Not because they wouldn't work reliably, although they wouldn't, but because their energy could interact with the planet's atmosphere and cause catastrophic damage. Everyone on the ship had been required to view video of the devastation caused by the earliest visitors who'd chosen to ignore the prohibition. The damage was so widespread that it could be seen from space. Not even Ripper could ignore that kind of destructive potential.

Rachel slowly crossed the clearing in the opposite direction from the crew's heading, aiming for the thick trees at the clearing's edge. She'd taken only a few steps in among their crowded trunks before she had to stop because she was very simply...overwhelmed. This was heaven. A living, breathing heaven, filled with so much life! It was amazing. Everywhere she looked, there was something growing. Even the trees were a revelation. So much variety in type and size, from slender, green shoots just barely getting started, to enormous giants with trunks so thick that she was unable to walk all the way around them because of the riotous growth at their base. Vines climbed everywhere, straining for the sunlight, which was filtered and far away, barely seen through the tops of the tallest trees.

But her true fascination was with the animals that she could hear scurrying through the undergrowth and scrambling over the rough bark of the trees. The ones she could see didn't seem bothered by her at all, as if she posed no threat. That was unusual in her experience, and anything unusual only raised more questions in her researcher's mind.

A small, furry something scratched its way to the lowest branch of a nearby tree, putting it at eye level with her. She watched the little beast curiously, touching the eye shields she wore that doubled as both safety glass and sunglass, verifying they were in their proper place. The lenses had been tested against some of the most corrosive fluids in the universe. She had no reason to think Harp's poisons would be any different. She took the added precaution of pulling the gator neckline up on her shirt to cover her lower face. The fabric was similarly treated for protection.

The furry creature glared at her from green-tinted eyes, then chittered angrily and raced away, scurrying along the low branch, before leaping into the next tree. She laughed in delight, even as she automatically catalogued the interlocking limbs of the trees from the lowest to the very highest part of the forest. Her gaze dropped to the ground, with its tangled growth of vines and plants, and then back up to the treetops. She'd bet anything that the more successful animals used the trees to move quickly through the forest. And that meant the most dangerous predators, including the big cats she'd been tasked with studying, would be up there, too.

As if the idea of predators conjured them up, she suddenly had the strongest sense of being watched, a weird itch on the back of her neck, as if some great hunter was studying her with an eye toward picking the juiciest part to nibble on. She tilted her head back again, staring upward, turning in a circle as her eyes strained to see through the tangled branches. But it was impossible. She stared a while longer, then shrugged and set about her work. She wanted to get as much done as she could before the rest of them came back.

• • •

Aidan crouched down deep among the twisted branches of a great grandfather tree. The trees were increasingly uneasy about these uninvited visitors. Wordless whispers skimmed over the forest tops with a wariness that bordered on fearful. The invaders hadn't done anything outwardly hostile yet. Hadn't mistakenly blown away an entire swath of forest or even begun chopping down trees for fire or shelter. Only shifters knew which trees could be safely felled. The trees on Harp were aware. They were the lifeblood of the planet, and Harpers knew enough about the way the universe worked to understand just how unique their Green was. Which was why their forests were one of the secrets they were unwilling to share. That, and the existence of shifters.

And that's what made Aidan nervous. He didn't believe for one minute that these very militant looking invaders had come to Harp to study the foliage, but what they *had* done made no sense to him. They'd left their ship the past two mornings and marched off across the clearing, before eventually delving deep among the trees...where they'd done nothing useful at all that he could see. They'd marched around, muttered among themselves, and taken readings on some sort of handheld devices that seemed to require minimal power. Their path had been a big loop, and they'd gone around, rather than through, any obstacles they encountered, such as particularly heavy patches of undergrowth, or vines that were twisted so thickly between the trees that they were impassable.

They hadn't shot or killed anything. Although, Aidan's presence in the treetops had kept the lesser predators off their backs, so they hadn't been threatened by anything that needed killing, either. They'd taken two rest breaks during the day, eaten food from their packs both times, and then completed their loop back to the ship, where they remained until the next morning.

Aidan didn't like it, but he couldn't have said why it bothered him.

Today was looking like a repeat of the same, except for one addition. The Earther troop had marched off across the clearing again this morning, but just as he'd circled up into the trees to follow, a hydraulic hiss had pulled his attention back to the ship in time to see the hatch crack open and the ramp lower to the ground.

He paused and stared. It was the woman again. He hadn't seen her since she'd been ordered back aboard ship that first morning. Was it possible the daily marches were nothing more than an attempt to divert Harp's defenders away from this woman, who was the true threat? He frowned. The idea didn't sit right, given her interaction with the other female, who was clearly the commander of the larger troop. But these were strangers, and he might have misread that first confrontation.

He reversed course, gliding through the forest in perfect silence to take up a position above the woman. Who was she? And what the hell was she doing, smiling at that Mauden mouse as if it were a cute little pet? It might be small, but its bite contained a deadly toxin that could stop a person's heart in seconds. She'd be dead before she even knew she'd been bit.

Fortunately for her, the Mauden registered Aidan's arrival before it had a chance to do more than chitter angrily at her. And there she stood, watching the thing leap through the trees, seeming completely unaware of the danger she'd been in.

She pulled down the cloth guard she'd been wearing over her mouth. So she wasn't a complete novice when it came to protection against unknown environments. She smiled to herself—it was a lovely smile—then crouched down to pull a camera and notebook from her bag. When she did, he noted the knife sheathed at her hip, along with a tranq weapon that was a smaller version of the ones carried by her militant shipmates. He approved of the knife. It was a good weapon to have in these woods. Theoretically, the tranq gun was, too. But the sight of it sent the trees' anxiety over these visitors buzzing over his skin like an electric shock. What, exactly, were they planning to tranquilize with those weapons? And what would they do with their captives?

He sat up abruptly as the distinctive wail of a banshee scout echoed through the forest. The song of the trees warned of approaching danger at the same instant, and only minutes later, a series of escalating banshee wails replied to the scout's call, signaling the pack's race to whatever prey the scout had found for them. Aidan hesitated. The banshees were some of the deadliest creatures on Harp, especially for humans. They had the vicious, ripping teeth and long, knife-sharp claws of a carnivore, with a diet that was almost exclusively meat. If the scout had found something for them to kill…it might just be the Earther troop.

For all that they were uninvited and probably up to no good, Aidan wasn't about to abandon them to become banshee meat. On the other hand… He swung his gaze back to the lone woman on the ground below. If the pack attacked her, she wouldn't stand a chance. There had to be some way…

A solution struck him, and he started downward, lethal claws digging into the thick bark of the grandfather tree as he circled toward the lower branches, his golden hide blending perfectly in the shifting light so that he wasn't visible to the woman…until he wanted to be.

Stopping ten feet above her, he glided out onto a wide branch overlooking the section of forest where she was working and stopped. His plan involved letting her see him in all his ferocious glory, with the intention of scaring her back into the safety of her ship. But he was so taken by her serenity as she scribbled notes and took pictures of everything around her, that he crouched low and simply watched.

She was even lovelier up close, with beautiful, golden brown skin and hazel eyes that seemed to reflect the sunlight shining through the trees. She was taller than he'd first thought. Not anywhere near his own six feet, four inches, but still tall for a woman. Her hair was black with red highlights when the sun hit it, and full of curls. Her movements were confident and graceful and, despite her obvious interest in the trees and wildlife, he saw now that she wasn't foolish enough to touch anything with her bare hands. She was wearing gloves, tightfitting enough that he hadn't noticed them until he'd drawn closer.

She stiffened abruptly, her hand freezing in midair as she reached toward what she probably thought was a harmless insect. But nothing was harmless in Harp's forest. What looked like a plump worm was in reality the tentacle of a pseudo-mole, a half-rodent, half-insect creature that hid beneath the low-hanging plants near the forest floor and waited for its prey to be tempted by the worm-like free meal. It couldn't kill a human, but it would still attack, leaving a painful, stinging welt that would take days to heal.

But Aidan didn't think it was a realization of the pseudo-mole's presence that had her stopping mid-reach. She twisted around to stare almost directly up into the tree where he crouched, and then slowly stood to turn and face him. Her gorgeous eyes grew wide, and he could hear the sudden, rapid pounding of her heart, could see her muscles flexing almost involuntarily as her brain made a lightning-quick fight-or-flight calculation. If he'd been hunting her, her worst choice would have been to run. Staying put wouldn't have saved her life, either, but she might have lived a few minutes longer.

Fortunately for her, she wasn't on the menu today. He only wanted her to retreat to the safety of her ship, so that he could waste his energy running after her shipmates, in case those banshees were headed their way. But she wasn't retreating.

"Hey there, big guy," she said calmly, even as she slipped her camera and notebook into her backpack and placed a hand on the tranq gun which hung on a strap at her waist.

Big guy? What the fuck did she think he was, a giant domesticated house cat?

She took a careful step back and paused, studying him. Her heartbeat had slowed, and she smiled. "You're a pretty one, aren't you?"

He blinked slowly. *Pretty?* Okay, that was one insult too many. He growled low in his throat, a rumbling noise that rose from his chest as his lips drew back to reveal his very *un*pretty fangs.

Her heart sped into triple time, and she seemed finally to understand her danger. She still didn't turn and run, too smart or too brave to take that route. But she did edge backward toward the clearing which was a good fifteen yards behind her. The clearing was no protection. If he'd truly been hunting her, she'd have been long dead before she reached it. Luckily, his only goal was to get her out of the forest and back onto her ship. He rose to a half-crouch and took a prowling step out onto the branch, letting her see him completely, opening his mouth wide enough to bare every one of his deadly teeth.

"Okay," she whispered, as if expecting him to understand at least the intent of her words. "I get it. This is your territory, and you want me gone." She kept backing up slowly as she spoke, one hand behind her checking for obstacles, the other held low in front of her in a placating gesture. "I'm going, see?"

He dropped back to his belly, and she nodded. "That's right. I mean you no harm."

He snorted. As if she could harm him, even if she tried. Her little tranq gun might sting for a few seconds, but nothing more than that.

He rose again and padded onto a branch in the next tree over as she watched closely. "I knew it," she whispered. "You use the trees to get around. All those intersecting branches. It's like your own personal highway."

She was right, but he really needed her to stop observing and to start running away. He took another prowling step in her direction and growled, his gaze unblinking and steady.

"All right, all right," she grumbled, no longer whispering. "I'm going." She reached the edge of the clearing and glanced over her shoulder at the ship, but still didn't turn and run. Her pace quickened, but she didn't look away from him until she'd hit the shadows beneath the belly of the ship. Walking over to one of the struts, she entered a code that triggered the hatch opening and lowered the ramp.

Aidan watched the inquisitive woman board, then waited until the hatch had closed behind her, before clawing his way back to the treetops and racing off in pursuit of the larger group.

Chapter Three

The following morning, day three of their planetfall, Rachel was sitting at the desk in her cabin, taking advantage of the ship's shielding to transcribe her notes from the previous day into her personal computer while drinking coffee and munching on the sorry excuse for a fruit muffin that she'd snagged from the mess hall earlier. She'd gone there intending to sit down to a hot breakfast, only to find her shipmates gathered around one of the big tables, poring over a paper map and making plans for the new day's exploration…without her. An unexpected pang of loneliness had hit her like a fist to the gut, and her hunger had evaporated. Not wanting anyone to notice, she'd grabbed the muffin and coffee as if that had been her purpose all along, and then she'd returned to her cabin to work.

She'd just finished typing her notes and was reading them over to make certain she hadn't missed anything, when the intercom came to life and Ripper's dulcet tones ordered her to the mess hall for the day's briefing. She stared at the small speaker over her bed, half convinced she'd misheard. If there'd been briefings on the previous days, she'd never been included.

"What the hell does she want now?" Rachel muttered. She considered ignoring the order altogether, but knowing Ripper, she'd just keep squawking until Rachel showed up. It was easier simply to get it out of the way.

She saved her notes and sent a copy off to her home computer as a backup. It wouldn't go anywhere as long as they remained on the planet, but the message packet would transmit at the first beacon they encountered after leaving, whether she was onboard or not. She frowned. Of course, she'd be onboard when they left Harp. Why wouldn't she be?

Shaking away the odd thought, she stood and checked her appearance in the mirror, tucked her notebook into her pocket, and headed for the mess hall.

This should be fun.

"About time you got here, Fortier. When I give an order, I expect a prompt response."

Rachel was tempted to point out that she was not, in fact, in Ripper's chain of command. But it wasn't worth the argument, so she simply gave her a blank look and took a seat at the table, smiling her thanks at the crew members who scooted over to make room for her.

Ripper scowled at her. "Time to earn your pay, Fortier. We're going to bag one of those big cats today, and you're coming with us."

The bottom dropped out of Rachel's stomach. "Bag a cat," she repeated. "Dr. Wolfrum's briefing indicated that the specific mission of this expedition was to study the cats in place. That means we tranq and tag, take some baseline readings, and then release." Though, even as she spoke the words, she knew that wasn't what they meant to do.

"Have you seen those fuckers?" one of guys demanded.

His name was Frank White, and he was the one member of the crew—apart from Ripper—who'd been hostile to her from the very beginning. She only knew his name because it was stitched above the pocket on his shirt, as if he needed the reminder. None of the other guys had that kind of identifier.

She gave him a curious look. "I did see one, actually. Up close and personal. He's a beautiful animal."

White snorted. "Yeah, he'll make a beautiful fucking rug."

"You're planning on killing him?" she asked calmly, although she was feeling anything but calm.

"Of course not," Ripper snapped, giving White a shut-the-fuck-up glare. "These animals are far too valuable to kill."

Rachel shifted her gaze to the commander. Too valuable. She was right about that. A cat like the one she'd seen yesterday could be sold for a small fortune to private collectors and zoos. But she wasn't on this mission to capture and sell animals, and that sure as hell wasn't what Wolfrum had told her was going to happen. And where the fuck *was* Wolfrum anyway? "Have you heard from Dr. Wolfrum yet?" she asked quietly. "Will he be joining us on this *hunt*?"

"Wolfrum's scouting out more locations for us. These cats live in family groupings, but they're hard to pin down." Ripper didn't meet her eyes, focusing instead on the computer in front of her.

Rachel's thoughts were spinning like crazy, trying to come up with some way of derailing this obscene venture that they expected her to take part in. Were they out of their minds? And was Ripper telling the truth about Wolfrum knowing this was a hunt? If so, he was violating every tenet of the scientific method. He'd be kicked out of the Science Academy for this, stripped of his honors. Was that why he was keeping his distance? Plausible deniability? Something she wouldn't have if she went along with this farce. She swallowed hard, trying not to throw up. *This* was why Wolfrum, with all of his honors and prestige, had recruited her so completely out of the blue—without knowing her, without a single prior conversation. Her presence gave the expedition the imprimatur of academia, not only because of her, but because of her family's academic connections. Her parents' *and* grandparents' names carried significant weight in scientific circles, and Rachel had fallen right into his scheme.

Now she had to get out of it somehow. She would not be party to the capture of these spectacular animals, to caging them up and putting them on display. The very idea was sickening—to take them away from this endless forest, drag them halfway across the galaxy, and shove them into an enclosure a tiny fraction of the place where they'd been born. Not to mention the loss of their family group. They probably wouldn't survive a year.

But then a new, horrible, thought occurred to Rachel, making her even sicker. They wouldn't need the original animals to survive. They could simply use them to breed new ones who'd never know anything but captivity.

This couldn't be permitted to happen. It wouldn't be. Not on her watch.

"How many animals do you plan on taking?" she inquired, her cool exterior giving away none of her thoughts.

"Just one today." Ripper eyed her carefully, clearly having expected more of a protest. "There's a big golden beast that's been following us around. He keeps his distance, and I suspect that when we *do* see him, it's only because he lets us. But we can deal with that."

Rachel tilted her head. "How?"

Frank White barked a laugh. "You'll see, princess."

She raised her eyes to study his face. He was a handsome man, but there was a cruel edge to his smile that gave his words an ominous quality.

"When do we leave?"

"Fifteen minutes. We rally at the belly hatch."

Rachel stood. "I'll be there." It didn't take her long to get ready once she got back to her cabin. She'd already checked and restocked her backpack the night before, determined to go out again today and not to let that big cat scare her away this time. Though for all his growling, she'd never gotten a sense of real danger from him. That might be a case of wishful thinking on her part, but she trusted her instincts. Unfortunately, it no longer brought her any comfort. She was more afraid *for* the cat than *of* him, worried that his curiosity could be the thing that got him caught if he interacted with her shipmates the same way he had with her.

Shipmates. What a joke. She had nothing in common with Ripper and her gang. She'd known all along that they weren't researchers, but she hadn't expected this.

A sudden, loud banging on her door jerked her to her feet.

"Fortier, get your ass in gear." Ripper. Of course.

Rachel did a final check of her weapons then shouldered her pack and headed out, determined to sabotage this hunt, no matter what it cost her.

· · ·

Aidan watched from his position high above the ship as the ramp came down and the soldiers appeared for their daily march. Their actions still puzzled him. They hadn't done anything but stomp around on the previous two days. Unlike the woman, there'd been no notebooks, no photographs, and no real curiosity, either. In fact, they hadn't seemed to pay much attention to their surroundings at all. If he hadn't known better, he'd have thought they were still trying to

adapt to the gravity and atmosphere of a new planet, except
that Harp's gravity and atmosphere were almost identical to
that of Earth.

So what was their purpose on Harp? There had to be
one. They were far too disciplined and orderly to engage in
repeated, daily marches for no reason. Were they waiting for
allies to arrive? More invaders planning to sneak onto the
planet? There were those among the United Earth Fleet
who'd been unhappy with the decision to designate Harp
a closed planet. Was this new invasion the beginning of a
takeover by rebellious elements of the fleet?

Aidan stirred restlessly. He needed to get a message to
Rhodry back in the capital, but he couldn't leave yet. Not
until he had more information.

The last of the soldiers marched down the ramp, but it
didn't close as it had on the previous days. Instead, the woman
appeared, trailing behind the others and looking unhappy to
be there. She had her weapons and her backpack with her as
before, but though she was with the group, it was clear that
she wasn't *with* them.

The ramp began to close almost before she took the final
step to the ground. The sudden movement surprised her,
and she cast an angry look at the female in command of the
soldiers. That one curled her lip, snapped out an order, and
then turned and walked away without waiting for a response.
Aidan's dark-haired lovely watched her go, and for a minute
he thought she was staying behind again, but then she settled
her pack more securely on her back and hurried after the
others.

He found it all very curious, but at least today he wouldn't
have to choose between protecting the woman or following
the soldiers. Moving in absolute silence, he turned to follow
the group, sticking to the treetops, invisible from the ground.
The smaller animals in the forest around him barely noted his

passage. They knew he wasn't hunting, or at least not hunting *them,* which was all they cared about. So there was no telltale reaction from them to give away his position as he crept along the crisscrossed branches high above, his path much clearer than the one his prey had to take on the ground.

The soldiers followed the same pattern as previous days, marching in a near straight line across the clearing from where their ship had landed, heading for the deeper forest on the other side. Aidan swallowed a laugh when he heard one of the men complain about the fact that they were forced to break a new trail "every damned day," because the Green responded so quickly to the damage they caused with their blundering ways. And it was true. There should have been the beginnings of a beaten down path through the long grasses after two days of the Earthers coming and going over the same track, but it took much longer than that for a trail to form on Harp.

He took note of the soldiers' trajectory and raced ahead, so he was waiting when they reentered the forest. If they followed their previous pattern, they'd stop just short of the tree line for a water break. When they did, Aidan watched, feeling a bit smug, but he was much more interested in the fact that the dark-haired woman rested apart from the others. She didn't huddle outside the tree line, either, but walked in among the thick trunks, her fingers trailing over the bark and coming perilously close to a large insect whose hard shell blended into the bark and was covered in a very dangerous fuzz. Some people died from a simple touch. Others only developed a stinging and bloody rash, but everyone was affected to some degree. She seemed to anticipate the danger, however, lifting her hand a moment before she would have touched the insect, and he saw that she wore those thin gloves again. Even still, she let her fingers skim just above the waxy white flowers of a twisting vine, before walking a few more steps to sit on a fallen log, where she pulled out her canteen and took a long draught.

Aidan's attention skipped back to the soldiers when they stood and checked their gear, preparing to continue their march. They stowed canteens, checked straps, and…he frowned. What were they—?

Before he could finish the thought, the forest had become a war zone, as every soldier pulled an old-style automatic weapon and began firing.

• • •

Rachel screamed, not understanding what was happening. She dropped to the ground and looked around wildly, searching for the threat that had triggered such a violent reaction, some horrible beast bearing down on them in unstoppable fury. But there was nothing. It was almost as if Ripper's gang was simply shooting up the forest for kicks. But she didn't believe it. Ripper was much too by-the-book, and her people too disciplined, to do something like that. But then, what *were* they doing? And where the hell did they get those weapons?

Her first instinct was to jump up and demand that they stop shooting. But some instinct—or maybe it was her growing understanding of the kind of people they were—had her hugging the ground, her ears covered as she yelled at them to stop. Their weapons were projectile, and so didn't interact with the planet's magnetic field, but that didn't make them any less deadly. They were sub-machine guns, loaded with huge drum magazines, firing round after round, tearing up the forest and killing who knew how many animals.

She noticed Ripper standing only a few feet away, not firing, but staring up at the treetops and occasionally directing the men's fire in a certain direction. Crouching low to the ground, Rachel ran over and kicked out, plowing a foot into the commander's thigh and knocking her to one knee.

"You have to stop this!" she screamed over the sound of automatic fire. "They're killing everything in sight."

Ripper's face was only inches away, distorted in rage at Rachel's attack. She raised one arm and backhanded Rachel with the full force of her muscular body, throwing Rachel against the same log she'd been sitting on before everything went to hell. She lay there, struggling to catch her breath, staring in horror at the devastation, and convinced she was never going to make it back to the ship alive. She only hoped her final message got through to her family so that her death would have served some purpose.

Dark spots danced in front of her eyes, and she struggled to stay conscious. If they didn't kill her outright, they'd leave her here for the scavengers, maybe even that big cat she'd seen. But, no, she knew better than that. He was an alpha predator, maybe even the top of the food chain on Harp. Scavenging was beneath him.

As if she'd conjured him from her thoughts, an enormous roar shook the forest, rattling the trees and shocking even Ripper and her men into stillness. But only for a moment, as a golden blur flew from out of nowhere, an avenging demon with raking claws and a mouthful of razor-sharp teeth. He swiped at the first man as he flew by, breaking his neck with a giant paw, before grabbing a second man and closing those fearsome teeth over the back of his neck, snapping his spine with an audible crunch.

The soldiers all turned their guns on him, but he was already gone, swinging up into the trees with incredible speed, only to leap down and attack a third man before the soldiers were even aware of what he was doing. The man went down screaming, his arm torn nearly off and his neck ripped open, pumping arterial blood onto the green forest floor.

Everyone was shouting now, hoarse cries of terror and

fury as they spun about, searching for the ravening beast. They were spraying ammo wildly, and yet…

For all the gunfire and all the terrified shouts, there was a purpose to what the surviving shooters were doing. They weren't shooting into the forest any longer, not even trying to track the giant cat. Instead, they were firing almost straight up, almost as if they were *afraid* to hit him.

Rachel saw the danger and shouted a warning, hoping the beast would understand and flee before it was too late. But he couldn't hear her above the frantic gunfire, or maybe he didn't understand human words.

The cat attacked again, appearing from out of nowhere, to land on Ripper's back, bearing her to the ground with his weight, closing his teeth over her head and leaping back into the trees, dragging her with him as if she weighed nothing at all. But he never made it. Alone, he was nearly invisible, a ghost among the branches. With Ripper's body in tow, he was too visible and almost all of Ripper's surviving men abruptly switched weapons, dropping their deadly automatics and pulling tranquilizer guns, all targeting the great golden beast. Dart after dart struck the giant cat, and Rachel recognized the darts they were using. They were specially made, designed for only the biggest and most dangerous animals.

The great cat seemed to recognize the danger at last. It dropped Ripper's body and leaped for the highest branches, but the tranqs had already gone to work, dulling his senses and slowing his reaction times, making his formerly graceful movements awkward and sluggish. He froze for a single, long moment, one paw reaching for the next branch, and then he fell.

Rachel cried out as the beautiful creature crashed bonelessly from branch after branch, finally falling with a heavy thump onto the forest floor. Grabbing her backpack, she scrambled to his side, no longer worried about whether

Ripper's men wanted to kill her. The cat would die if she didn't do something quickly. The overdose of heavy-duty tranquilizer would shut down his heart, or, with him lying face down the way he was, his own weight would crush his lungs and he'd suffocate.

She knelt next to him and began yanking the darts out of his hide, her anger growing with each one she pulled. They'd clearly wanted the animal alive—why else use tranqs instead of bullets? But they'd used so many that he might die anyway.

"Help me," she demanded, struggling to roll the heavy animal onto his side.

"Fuck that," one of the men growled.

"He'll die if I don't move him, and I don't think you want that," she snapped, still yanking darts as she shoved her shoulder under the cat and tried get him onto his side.

"Do it," a rough voice ordered. She looked up to see Frank White giving her a hard stare. "He's worth nothing to us dead."

Rachel wanted to be shocked, but she wasn't. Once she'd recognized Wolfrum's deceit for what it was, she'd lost the ability to be shocked by anything about this mission.

One of the men dropped to his knees next to her, while two others each grabbed one of the cat's legs on the left side. One of them gave a count and they all pushed and pulled in unison, turning the cat onto its side.

"You'd better stop that fucking animal from dying, Fortier," White growled. "He's the only reason you're still alive."

Rachel nodded wordlessly. Like she needed him to tell her that.

She reached into her backpack for a bottle of water. Opening it, she poured some into the cat's mouth, to keep his tongue and gums moist. Next, she pulled out every syringe in her stash, and filled them to the brim with antidote for the tranq. She needed to counteract the effects right away, before—

"What are you doing?" White demanded.

She glanced up at him. "You've overdosed him. He'll die if I don't counteract the tranquilizer."

"Fuck that. He killed three of my men without breaking a sweat, and we might still lose Ripper. I don't want him coming around until he's secured onboard."

She stared at him then. Secured onboard? They must have prepared for this. Of course, they had. Which meant there was a cage, maybe more than one, designed to hold this very powerful animal. No wonder they'd kept her on the margins of the shipboard routines. They hadn't wanted her to see evidence of their true plans.

"Do you want him dead?" she asked flatly.

White glared at her, his mouth pinched tight with anger and maybe a little fear. "Keep him alive, but under. And remember, you'll be the first one he kills if he comes to."

She didn't bother to respond, but she put half the loaded syringes back into her pack. She'd need them later, because she had no intention of permitting them to leave Harp with this animal in a cage. She was going to do everything in her power to see to it that Wolfrum's hunters were shut down cold. No more animals were going to be captured on Harp, even if she had to hike to the city on her own to be sure the proper authorities knew what was going on.

Unfortunately, her best chance of achieving all of that was to go along for now.

She stroked a hand over the cat's silky, golden fur, and leaned forward to whisper in his ear. "I'm going to get you out of this, baby. Don't you worry."

Chapter Four

Amanda Sumner de Mendoza stood on the balcony of her house in the city, one hand braced on the rough bark of the wooden support post, the other rubbing her swollen belly where two tiny shifter babies were just learning to drive their momma nuts. She'd never thought of herself as particularly maternal, but now, as she tried to persuade her two little hooligans to sleep a while, she knew a fierce protectiveness that eclipsed anything she'd ever felt. She'd never thought of herself as having much of a voice, either, but apparently the twins didn't care about her voice or the words she sang. Mostly she simply hummed along with the song she heard in the trees, and that seemed to calm her two little shifters better than just about anything. Just about. Their daddy's presence, his touch on her belly when he spoke to them, that was the sure thing. The kittens knew their alpha.

She smiled, thinking that her darling Rhodry had better not get used to that kind of obedience from his offspring.

Because these babies were hers, too, and she'd had a thing against authority figures for as long as she could remember.

But for right now, they were peaceful, drinking in the ageless calm of the endless Green, the soothing rhythms of a forest in springtime. The Green always lived up to its name, but this time of year, the vast forest belt went wild with new life and growth amidst the amazing varieties of flora and fauna.

She rocked slightly from foot to foot, knowing she'd have to sit soon. She could almost feel her ankles growing puffier, the skin tightening, her feet aching. She heard Rhodry's footsteps approaching from inside and stepped back, intending to sit on the well-padded chair he'd arranged for her, when suddenly…everything changed.

She staggered, crying out in pain, as the forest screamed its agony.

"Amanda!" Rhodry was there the next instant, his powerful arms surrounding her, holding her on her feet when she would have fallen. He turned, placing his body between her and the forest, but they both knew there was no threat from that direction. Whatever was happening, it wasn't in their backyard.

"Aidan," Rhodry whispered, and she looked up at him in surprise. "Something's happened to him. Christ, I can't—"

"Shhh." It was her turn to be the protector, to soothe all *three* of the men she loved, because her babies, too, had reacted to the pain in the forest's song, something they could hear every bit as well as she and Rhodry. She sorted through that pain now, trying to make sense of it. "He's alive, Rhodi. That's what matters. And the others will have felt it, too. They'll be on their way. Don't go alone."

"I'm not leaving you, *acushla*. Who knows—"

"Am I not a member of the Guild, de Mendoza? Did I not pass the trials, same as you did? I'm *pregnant*, not paralyzed.

And it's not like you'll be leaving me all alone. There's an entire city full of people just waiting for these two little terrors to show up." Their twins weren't the first on Harp, but they were the first twin *shifters*. The few shifters previously born as part of a twin pair had all been the male half of a male/female set—with the female twin being born a "norm." Only males were shifters on Harp. In fact, the shifter trait was sex-linked, which meant the male offspring of shifters were *always* born shifter, while female offspring didn't even carry the gene. "We'll be fine," Amanda assured him.

Rhodry's arms squeezed tighter, and he shook his head.

"Rhodi, go. We're perfectly safe."

"You're right. The cousins will have heard the same thing we did," he insisted. "They'll already be on their way."

She pushed away from his chest and gazed up at him, this man she loved more than she'd ever thought possible. "Your cousins are more than capable, but Aidan will need *you*. There's no one he trusts more."

Rhodry's golden eyes had gone completely cat. They were always beautiful, but there was a wildness to them, a predatory calculation that wasn't there when he was in full human mode.

He nodded, then dropped to his knees, his hands big enough to span her growing belly as he pressed a kiss to it. "Take care of your mother, you little heathens. And be good until I get back."

Amanda would have sworn she felt the babies stiffen to attention at their alpha's command. She threaded her fingers through his long hair and laughed, her hand trailing down his broad back as he stood up. "You be good, de Mendoza," she whispered. "And come back to us."

"I love you," he growled and took her mouth in a passionate kiss that made her forget all about her swollen ankles and battered bladder.

"Love you, too," she whispered. "We'll be here waiting."

He gave her one final, hard kiss, then stepped back, stripping off his clothes as he moved. A moment later, he leaped first to the top of the bannister, and then off into the air in a swirling storm of black and gold. A huge, black hunting cat hit the soft forest floor, pausing to look up only once to where Amanda was blowing him a kiss, and then, in a haze of speed, he was gone. She heard the soft scrape of heavy claws on bark in the distance—but only because he'd let her—and then nothing.

"That's your daddy," she murmured to her twins, love in every syllable.

A soft knock prefaced the opening of a door in the room behind her. She turned, unworried, already knowing who it was.

"Cullen," she greeted him warmly. "You could have gone with Rhodry, you know. We're fine here."

He gave her a faintly insulted look. "I'm right where I need to be, lass. Aidan will have plenty of help. You only have me."

She reached up and gripped his huge shoulder. Cullen was the youngest, and biggest, of the many Devlin cousins. Rhodry had asked him to look after her when they'd first returned from their harrowing journey off the glacier nearly two years ago. They'd both been betrayed by people they should have been able to trust, and Rhodry had needed to report to the Ardrigh about just how bad things had gotten. He'd only been gone a few hours, but Cullen had taken his bodyguard duties to heart, and he was still here. Still looking after her.

She started to say something, to thank him, but a sudden movement rippled over her belly and she gripped his arm instead, her other hand pressed to the little foot stretching her skin as clearly as if she held it in the flesh.

"Amanda?" There was a note of terror in Cullen's voice that made her laugh. This giant shifter would face the hounds of hell for her, but not a pair of lively babies.

"Don't worry," she said a little breathlessly. She eased herself down onto a chair, punching the pillows until they supported her belly. "We've plenty of time before these two little troublemakers arrive."

He drew a deep breath of relief. "Right. Do you need anything? Water? Food?"

"Just some rest in the sun. The twins like it out here on the porch." Her eyes drifted shut, and she felt a soft blanket fall over her a moment before sleep claimed her.

Chapter Five

"I'm going to get you out of this, baby. Don't worry."

The woman's breath had been warm against his sensitive ears, her voice low and intimate. Nice words, but how the hell was she going to deliver?

Aidan couldn't move yet, but his senses were returning with a speed that probably would have shocked his captors. He didn't remember how he'd gotten there, but he knew where he was. He was on that damn ship. His nose was telling him that much, even without the added input of the hard floor beneath his body, the distant echo of muted voices, and the constant hum of the engine that thrummed against his returning nervous system with a unique sort of pain. He doubted his captors were aware of that, either.

He kept his eyes closed, not because he didn't want them to know he was awake, but because it made it easier for him to concentrate on the most important aspect of this whole fiasco—he could *not* permit himself to shift.

Every instinct he had was screaming at him to do just that, because shifting back and forth once or twice would heal his injuries and restore him to full, roaring strength in no time at all. But he wouldn't do it. *Couldn't.* These men, whoever they were, thought they'd captured an exotic animal. And he had to keep it that way until he figured out how to escape this clusterfuck that he'd gotten himself into.

He didn't coddle himself into believing it was bad luck or happenstance that had brought him here. This was his fuck-up. He'd made the biggest mistake that anyone could—he'd underestimated the enemy. He'd followed them back and forth for days, suspecting their motives but never believing they represented a real threat. And they'd lulled him right into their trap.

His only consolation was the certain knowledge that by now, every shifter on the planet was aware not only of his capture, but of the menace posed by the invaders. They'd made a huge mistake when they'd attacked the forest to get to him. Even trapped as he was in this metal cocoon, he could hear the trees blasting out a warning nonstop. Amanda had told him once that the trees had a special love for their shifters. Add to that the danger these Earthers had shown themselves to pose for the entire planet, and the trees' song would be one long scream of warning.

By now, his shifter cousins would be on their way out of Clanhome, and Rhodry would have launched a hunting party out of the Guild Hall, too. Aidan wasn't sure how many of the human invaders he'd killed—one or two might only have been injured. But if those bastards thought one shifter was lethal, wait until they had an entire hunting party on their asses.

He smiled inwardly. Thoughts of his cousins and impending rescue had him cracking his eyes open just enough to scan his surroundings. They'd put him in a cage. How fucking insulting was that?

But he forced himself to set aside emotion and examine

the enclosure for weakness, wanting to be sure he could break out when reinforcements arrived. There'd be a bloodbath once his Devlin cousins showed up, and he didn't want to be sitting in a damn cage like a rabbit waiting for slaughter. He wanted in on the mayhem.

What he found wasn't reassuring, however. It was a damn good cage. Whoever their source had been, whichever Harper had betrayed his own people by revealing the existence of shifters, he'd given the invaders good intel on how to contain one. Or at least, he'd given details about the big cats, which were the animal face of shifters. Aidan still wasn't convinced that the Earthers were aware of his dual nature.

His other senses told him there were no people in the immediate vicinity of his cage, so he opened his eyes enough to take in more details. Two cameras were mounted at ceiling level, one on each wall, moving in a constant 180-degree arc to cover the entire holding area. His eyes widened. There were six fucking cages here. His capture was only the beginning.

Or so they thought, he reminded himself. Their hunt, whatever its ultimate goal, was over. Their fucking lives were over. Because the safest outcome for Harp was for Aidan and his fellow shifters to leave none of their enemies alive to tell the tale. An instinctive growl rumbled up from his chest. He didn't know if they had audio on their spy cameras, but if they did…so be it. Let them recognize the beast they'd invited onto their ship.

Without warning a door opened to his left, far enough to the side that he couldn't see it without turning his head and giving away the fact that he was awake. He closed his eyes to let his other senses take over, but a moment later, he detected a familiar scent.

It was the woman. And she wasn't alone.

• • •

"Is he still alive?" Rachel hurried over to the cage. The cat should have woken by now, but she wasn't going to tell the guard that.

"That's your job, doc. It's why you're here."

"Open this damn thing," she demanded, reaching for the bars of the cage door.

"Stop," Frank White barked, coming in behind her. "Don't touch that." He tapped a keypad on the wall, entering a four-digit code when the panel came to life. "The bars are electrified."

Rachel stared in horror. "Are you trying to kill him?"

"Hell, no. He's worth too much alive. We're just making sure he can't kill *us*. Go ahead. The field's down, and the cell's open. Do your thing."

Rachel wanted to tell him where he could shove his electrical field. But while White might be the worst of the lot, the entire crew—these people she'd spent weeks with, some of whom she'd considered friends—seemed wholly unconcerned with what they'd done. Not only had they caged this magnificent animal for *money*, but they'd inflicted wanton destruction on the forest and its inhabitants in order to draw him into their trap.

She turned away without a word. Cursing Frank White might be satisfying, but it wouldn't help the cat who was her main concern. She touched one bar of the cell door carefully, not trusting that the electric field was really off. White struck her as the kind of man who'd get a kick out of shocking her, just for the fun of it.

But the bar was cold and still, so she wrapped her fingers around it and pulled the door open, going immediately to her knees next to the golden beast. He was so much bigger than she'd thought. He'd minimized his size when she'd encountered him in the forest on her own, crouching down, keeping a low profile. It was typical predatory behavior, designed to lull one's prey closer. A small thrill of excitement shivered over her nerves, despite the horrific situation. To see such a beautiful creature up close and personal was something she'd only dreamt about. It was why she'd continued her xeno-veterinarian studies well beyond what was necessary to qualify as a planetary specialist.

She rested a hand on the cat's side, soaking up the heat of his body, feeling the hard beat of his heart. Her fingers dug into his thick fur and slid all the way down his side to his hind legs. There was a wound there, with wet blood still staining the fur of his flank. The injury had probably been sustained in his headlong crash to the forest floor. She touched his leg gently, and he jerked in reaction just enough to reveal…oh yeah, definitely male.

From his watchful position on the other side of the bars, White grunted in reluctant admiration, and Rachel smiled grimly. Men and their dicks. She hoped the bastard couldn't get it up for a long time, thinking about his own inadequacies.

"You don't need to stay, White," she told him, without turning. "You guys hit him with a lot of tranq. I'm going to hydrate him some, but he'll be out for a while yet." It wasn't as if White could protect her, anyway. If the cat's ferocious assault earlier was any indication, White would be dead meat in minutes if the cat decided to attack. And she wouldn't exactly mourn his passing, either. Assuming she was around to mourn anyone. The cat had no way of knowing she hadn't been part of this unspeakable crime.

She glanced over her shoulder to see him shrug carelessly. "If you're sure. I got better things to do than watch you fondle a fucking animal."

Rachel rolled her eyes. "I'm sure. I'll lock up when I'm done."

"Yeah, right. Like I'd trust an animal lover like you with our safety. You'd probably let him out to kill us all in our sleep."

Not a bad idea, she thought, but what she said out loud was, "You're perfectly safe. He'd probably kill me to get to you, and I've no desire to die on this planet."

"Whatever. I'll check back in a few."

Rachel waited until she heard the door close behind her, then she turned and eyeballed it just to be safe. Pulling out her stethoscope, she reached over the big cat and placed the bell of her instrument over his heart, listening. But as she listened, she leaned forward and said, "I know you're awake. He's gone."

. . .

Aidan blinked a few times to moisten his eyes. The air in this damn ship was too dry. Mindful of the cameras, he didn't move other than to slide his gaze sideways to regard the woman.

"I'm Rachel, and I'm a doctor." She smiled. "I don't know how much you can understand," she murmured, clearly as mindful of the cameras as he was, "but I think you know I won't hurt you. Not like they did." She grimaced. "At least, I hope you know that. Otherwise, I'm probably on the dinner menu."

He swallowed a growl at her comment. He didn't eat people, for fuck's sake. Not even slimy bastards who deserved to die, like the ones he'd already killed. This woman, on the other hand, seemed to be a friend, but he wasn't taking anything for granted. After all, she'd arrived on his planet with the same people who'd captured him and killed who knew how many smaller animals. Not to mention the damage they'd done to the forest with their wild shooting. Not every tree on Harp was semi-sentient, but enough of them were that no one—not even the loggers who spent their lives deep in the forest—were allowed to cut down a tree without consulting a shifter first. The process was almost a ritual on Harp.

Some of the trees damaged or destroyed by these Earthers in their admittedly successful bid to capture him had been aware and linked to the grandfathers deeper in the forest. He could feel their pain even through the metal and shielding of this damn ship.

He wondered how long he'd been out. Mostly because he wanted to know how soon his cousins would descend on this fucking ship to destroy it and its whole damn crew. Except maybe the woman.

"You probably feel like crap. That's mostly the tranquilizer," she was saying.

She'd been bent over listening to his heart and lungs. Cute. He knew the workings of his body far better than she could judge with her medical devices.

"You were slightly injured, though." She slid her hand gently over his back leg.

Nice. Go a little lower, honey.

"I don't think it's broken, but...this might hurt," she warned, only a second before she pushed down on the deep gash he'd suffered when a jagged piece of branch had jammed into his flesh during his headlong crash to the forest floor.

Fuck! Had she said it *might* hurt? He growled a warning low in his throat, though he wouldn't really hurt her. Not until he knew more.

"Sorry," she said absently, not put off by his growl and not sounding sorry, either, as she continued to examine the wound. "I'm sure I saw a foreign body in the wound before. I thought I'd need to extract it, but...there's nothing there now, and this is already looking better. Remarkable. We'll just keep that to ourselves, shall we?"

Aidan grunted and moved his body slightly. She thought *that* was remarkable? Wait 'til she saw how fast he healed after the shift. She made a sound of surprise at his sudden movement, but there was no scent of fear. Apparently, she trusted him.

"What's…" she started to ask, a moment before she reached down to pick up something from the hard floor beneath his leg. There was a slight scrape of wood. "Huh. Your body must have expelled this on its own. That was fast. An adaptation to the local environment, maybe. Destroying foreign bodies to prevent infection. Fantastic," she whispered. "Hell, magnificent. You have *got* to be the apex predator around here. If you're not, I don't think I want to meet what is."

Fuck apex predator, Aidan thought viciously. *Shifters ruled the whole damn planet.* An antiseptic odor filled the air, and something cool and wet touched his side. She was cleaning his wound. How adorable. There was no bacteria on Harp that could harm him, and shifters were immune to infection. But he was enjoying her game of doctor.

He'd enjoy in a lot more in his other form. He purred to let her know how much.

She laughed. "You purred. That's so sweet."

He'd been enjoying the sound of her laugh, but scowled inwardly at the word "sweet." He wasn't *sweet*. Okay, yeah, he was charming as hell, and the ladies loved him. Huh. Maybe he was sweet.

She touched his head cautiously, slowly letting her hand settle onto the curve of his skull, as her fingers began to caress his ears lightly. "You're also beautiful."

He couldn't argue with that.

Her fingers dug into his fur, stroked all the way down his body, and back up again. "I can't let them do this." He could hear the tears in her voice, but all he could think was that he hoped to hell there wasn't audio surveillance in this damn room, because the others were dangerous. He didn't doubt they'd kill her if she caused trouble. "Don't worry. I'll work something out," she promised. "And I'll be back soon."

. . .

Rachel gathered her things into her bag, then smoothed her hand over the big cat one last time, unable to resist touching him. He was so big and silky and hot. She wanted to explore every inch of him. But time wasn't on her side. If she was going to swing a great escape for her new patient, it would have to be tonight, while everyone was off their game. The crew was still reeling from the day's events, stunned at the loss of three of their shipmates and the severe injuries to Commander Ripper. The woman wasn't dead, more's the pity, but she was out of commission for the rest of this expedition, sleeping away in one of the med chambers that would eventually diagnose and repair most of what was wrong with her. But that would take weeks.

On top of whatever grief the crew was feeling for their fellow soldiers, Ripper's absence created a huge hole in the chain of command. One of the those killed had been Ripper's executive officer, and the survivors were still struggling to decide exactly who was in charge. Or, more likely, who *wanted* to be in charge of a mission that had turned out to be far more complicated than the simple hunting trip they'd planned.

Mind you, no one had suggested aborting the mission altogether. Not yet, anyway. If they somehow managed to succeed in what, for them, had never been anything *other* than a hunt, there was simply too much money to be made. *Someone* had funded this every expensive and dangerous trip. It couldn't have been Wolfrum by himself. No one person could manage an expedition this costly. And that meant the backers, whoever they were, would reward results.

Rachel could hear the crew arguing about it down in the mess hall while she hurried back to her cabin, their voices loud enough that she didn't even have to pretend not to listen. They were all in agreement that the best course was to carry on with the original plan—a plan that, she now discovered, called for the capture of six big cats in total. The flaw in their planning was becoming glaringly obvious, however. One cat had killed three of their crew and sidelined their commander. Capturing five more was going to require significant modification of their hunting techniques. But no one seemed to know what that meant.

Rachel didn't care about their problems, however. She was no longer a part of *their* mission. She had one of her own, and it included two very simple goals. First and foremost, she had to free her furry friend from captivity. Once that was accomplished, she was determined to find Dr. Wolfrum and discover just how deeply he was implicated in this illegal hunt. That was going to take some time, however. Harp didn't have even a basic communication network, so finding Wolfrum would mean physically searching him out and confronting him directly. Only she'd have to do it on a planet where she'd never been before, with virtually no information on the massive green belt she'd have to traverse, and a weapons restriction that literally took her back to the bow and arrow stage.

Rachel had confidence in her ability as both a tracker and an explorer, however. She'd led plenty of "adventure" treks, where the thrill was to navigate a dangerous planet with primitive weapons. Not to mention the many newer planets she'd visited which restricted visitor weapons, albeit without the unique environmental dangers of Harp. But she could do it. She *would* do it. She owed it to Harp and the scientific community at large. This travesty couldn't be permitted to stand.

Back in her quarters, she locked the door then stood there a moment, looking around, inventorying everything she'd brought with her and deciding how much she could carry. She doubted she'd ever be coming back here once she left.

Most of her clothes would be left behind, of course, and she rarely brought anything on these trips that had substantial personal value. There were no good luck charms or family mementos. Everything she packed was replaceable, other than her research. But even that was securely backed up via the same beacon packets that carried her personal communications to her parents. She could be brutally efficient when she had to be. She'd take her computer when she left, because it had all her research and most of her notes thus far about the planet. She hoped to be able to access it once she reached the city, but in any event, she didn't want any of that information to fall into the enemy's hands.

She blinked, wondering when she'd begun to think of her former shipmates as "the enemy." Probably about the time they'd begun killing everything in sight, then set out to indiscriminately tranq and capture enough cats to make them all rich. Or maybe even before that, when she'd first begun to suspect that this mission was not what she'd signed up for.

"No time for this, Rache," she muttered to herself. She could navel gaze about the state of the scientific world *after* she'd freed the captured cat and made good on their escape. She glanced at the clock and brought up the outside view on her comm screen. Harp was smaller than Earth. The sun set more quickly, and the night brought absolute darkness unless one of the planet's three moons was in the sky. Tonight, it was so dark that the ship's exterior view was a nearly perfect black. She switched to infrared and couldn't help staring in wonder as the screen lit up with the wild color of multiple heat signatures inside the Green. She smiled, because all that life was on her side tonight. She'd heard Commander Ripper complaining on their first night here that the planet's teeming life-forms made the infrared view nearly useless, not to mention creepy as fuck. Rachel hoped that Ripper's observation meant that the crew no longer bothered monitoring for IR. It would make it easier for her and her patient to slip away.

While humans required special cameras to see in the night, she was absolutely convinced that the big cat they'd captured had no such need. As a scientist, she had no proof that the animal was in any way related to earth felines, but his general appearance was the same, and his eyes, in particular, were remarkably similar. She'd have bet one of her PhD's— the chemistry one, her least favorite—that her cat had the same high number of rods in his retina as an Earth feline, making his eyes extremely sensitive to low light and thus enhancing his night vision.

As a mere human, she didn't have a similar advantage, but she did have a small, but very bright, LED flashlight that she'd modified for use under similar conditions. It was no match for the cat's natural night vision, but would permit them both to make their escape without the kind of light that could give away their position.

As Rachel thought through these details, she continued sorting her supplies, separating everything into two piles— one to take and one to leave behind. Every weapon she owned—from her smallest knife, to the crossbow, and even the tranq gun—went into the "take" pile. She had no idea what she'd encounter in the forest and, while she wasn't inclined to kill native species without reason, she *was* going to defend herself as necessary against animals of every stripe, including the kind that walked on two legs.

She didn't have to worry about packing basic survival

gear. Her backpack was always ready to go, including the thin but sturdy bedroll strapped to the bottom. Tucked into the various pockets and compartments were a first aid kit, matches, and a water purifier, along with other items that she'd added over the years she'd spent trekking in wild places.

Oddly enough, one of her more peculiar habits—one she'd been teased about over the years by friends who'd thought it bordered on obsession—was finally going to come in handy on Harp. And that was using paper maps. She always carried print maps of whatever area she was about to trek. In the case of Harp, she'd printed out an orbital map that Wolfrum had sent her, showing the planet's massive green belt spreading out all around the only city. The polar caps were plain to see—one an arid desert and the other a permanent glacier—along with the northern mountains, where there was a second, smaller settlement hidden in the valleys and ravines. The detail wasn't great, since orbital maps weren't intended to be used on the ground, but Rachel had marked the intended landing site of their ship, and so figured she had enough data to find the city on her own. Her compass wouldn't work, of course—not with Harp's freaky electromagnetic field—and she didn't have a star map of this sector, which would have been very handy. But if she traveled during the day, she could use the sun's position as a directional reference.

She didn't need to look at her maps, however, to know that the planet's only city was several days' travel from her current location. She had the necessary conditioning and stamina for that kind of trek, and plenty of confidence in her own skills, but she'd nevertheless be on her own in an unfamiliar environment, which was always a risk. She already knew that all of her travel would be through the Green, and from what she'd read in the few reports and what she'd seen in her own limited explorations, there were few natural trails and no cleared roads of any kind. It would be rough travel all the way.

She slid the folder carrying the maps into a side pocket of her backpack and then quickly loaded up the rest of her gear, switching her thoughts to the more immediate problem—how to rescue the cat. The passageways to the holding pens should be mostly empty, and if not…well, frankly, she'd simply tranq anyone who got in her way, giving them a little taste of their own medicine.

Her first stop, however, would have to be the bridge. As a matter of protocol, it was manned around the clock, even when the only person available was a reluctant scientist. And while she harbored a faint hope that the survivors were all too busy licking their wounds to worry about bridge protocol, she doubted that was true. If anything, they might be even more paranoid about what might be out there, watching them. Forget the exterior cams—anyone on the bridge would raise the alarm the minute the hatch opened. So she'd have to take out whoever was on duty—hopefully by tranqing them, too—before making her way to the holding pens.

Once there, of course, she'd require the code to drop the electric field and unlock the cage. That wasn't a problem. Frank White thought he'd been so clever with his code, but it was only four digits. A smart ten-year-old could have figured out what numbers he was pushing just from watching his fingers move.

As for the cat, by now he should be fully recovered and able to walk on his own. She suspected that he'd been far more alert than he'd shown earlier, which indicated a reasonable level of intelligence. But then, he was at the top of the food chain on this very dangerous planet, so that wasn't surprising.

In fact, her biggest challenge might be securing the cooperation of the cat himself. He'd been deadly against the crew out in the forest, but before that, he'd never been anything except peaceful and curious with her. And when she'd examined him in his cage, he'd seemed to understand she was trying to help him, that she was on his side. She only hoped he still felt that way.

She zipped up the heavy pack and set it by the cabin door along with her warmest jacket. Her cabin was closest to the lower deck stairs, where the belly hatch was located. Rather than risk having one of the other crew see her sneaking along the passage in full gear, she'd free the cat from its cage and then grab her backpack and jacket on their way out. She was already wearing her heavy-duty trek boots, with their thick, ridged soles, and she'd chosen trousers and a long-sleeved stretchy top that were both the fleet's latest cold weather thermal-wear. The day had been mild, but the night would be cold. If she got too warm, she could strip off layers. It was always better to be too warm than too cold.

After a final look around the small cabin, she slowly opened her door, listening for any sign of movement. There was nothing. She poked her head out and looked quickly left and right. The passageway was empty, just as she'd hoped.

Closing the cabin door behind her, she started forward, tranq gun half-hidden against her thigh. The ship was eerily silent, nothing but the ever-present hum of the heavily shielded engine on its lowest idle. Just enough to maintain environmental controls and other necessary things, like bridge displays, interior lights, and electrified fucking cages.

She found herself tiptoeing, even though her cautious footsteps were nearly silent. As planned, she went directly to the bridge, pausing outside the open doorway to listen. A few soft pings and beeps emanated from the various instruments, but nothing out of the ordinary. She listened harder. Someone had to be there. Someone was *always* there.

Finally, she detected the soft susurration of breathing, heavy and steady. She listened a moment longer then stepped into the open doorway. It was none other than Frank White, the bastard who'd taken such pleasure in trapping her cat in a cage, who'd sprayed gunfire through centuries-old trees with an unholy grin on his face. And now there he sat, sound asleep. Poor guy, all tuckered out from killing things. Asshole.

Raising her tranq gun, she put a dart into him with no qualms at all. His only reaction was a quiet grunt when the dart hit his shoulder. She breathed a sigh of relief and went directly to the security station. The ramp code was changed automatically on a daily basis, and no one had left the ship today—not even her—which meant she didn't have the latest code. So, she updated the ramp code manually and made note of both the new code and the emergency override, which would bypass any locked door on the ship, just in case. Unless someone bothered to check, it would seem as if the code had simply updated itself as part of its regular routine. White wouldn't remember what had happened and wouldn't want to admit that he'd been too busy sleeping to know. She was about to leave after that, when one of the displays caught her eye. It was a map showing much of the same detail on Harp as her own orbital maps, except while this one indicated their own ship's location, it also showed the landing site of a second ship.

A second ship? Was that where Wolfrum was? Damn. She couldn't make a copy of the display. She didn't know the bridge controls that well and didn't have time to figure it out. The best she could do was fix the details in her head and then add the second location onto her own map once they were away and safe.

With a final, concentrated look at the console and a glance at the sleeping crew member, she made her way back to the open door, where she paused to listen before stepping into the empty passageway.

The next part of her plan all depended on the cat. If he understood that she was trying to help him escape, things would go smoothly. If not, if he decided to let loose one of his thundering roars, he could bring the entire crew down on their heads. And, of course, there was the possibility that he'd simply kill her on his way out the door.

The holding pen hatch was closed, but not locked. Rachel was the only person they might have wanted to keep the area locked against, and that was only until they'd brought the first animal onboard. Now that she had a patient, she'd be expected to spend more of her time here doing her job, which apparently was to keep this cat, and any others that followed, in good health. Oddly enough, it was close to what she'd expected to be doing on this mission, but there was a huge, perverted gap between monitoring the health of animals being studied in the wild, and animals who'd been captured and caged for money. The idea that she might have been involved in something like that, even inadvertently, made her sick to her stomach.

There was no time for weak stomachs or hesitation tonight, however. So far, she'd been lucky, finding empty passageways and a single, sleeping crewmember on the bridge. But her luck couldn't last forever.

The door to the holding pen opened smoothly as she stepped over the raised threshold and pulled the door nearly closed behind her, without latching it. It was almost perfectly dark as she groped for the pressure plate that controlled the light, with only the dim glow of the emergency panel...

She froze, heart pounding, lungs suddenly refusing to work. A low, rumbling growl filled the air, the sound speaking to the animal part of her brain that said she was about to die. She turned slowly to find two gleaming, golden eyes studying her. Their glow was so bright in the unlit room that she could make out the dark silhouette of the giant beast she was here to save.

She had a feeling her luck had just run out.

Chapter Six

Aidan blinked slowly as he studied his visitor. It was the woman. He didn't need any lights for that. He could scent her, could see her slender form in the dim light. She sucked in a startled breath, and he blinked again, knowing the effect it would have in the blackened room. Oddly, she seemed more afraid with him in a cage than when she'd blundered blithely into his forest with him only a few feet away among the trees. Her heart had kicked up, her breathing had gone shallow and rapid, and this time, he could smell her fear. But as gratifying as it was to strike terror into someone from this damn ship, he suspected that this particular someone was here to help him. And she was going to hyperventilate if she didn't calm down.

He prowled deliberately to the farthest corner of the cage and lowered himself to the cold floor, putting his head down on his paws and trying to look less intimidating. He really wasn't at his best, but he wasn't harmless, either. His shifter metabolism was still working overtime to nullify the effects of all the fucking tranquilizers they'd pumped into him. But even worse had been the attempts by the man she'd called

"White" to force him into a shift, using electrically charged rods, taunting him with threats of what they'd do to him once he was turned over to the "labs." Whether he'd intended to or not, White's hissed challenges had made it clear that the invaders not only knew about shifters, but had come to Harp for the sole purpose of capturing one and returning him to their "labs" for experimentation. That knowledge was a sharper goad that any electric prod. Aidan needed to escape and warn the others.

Unfortunately, between the repeated electrical shocks and the tranqs the man had used afterward to knock him out, he wasn't sure how long he'd been unconscious, or how long he'd been in this fucking cage. Even if he hadn't been groggy, it was difficult for him to tell time in the sterile environment of the ship.

The woman moved, reaching out a shaking hand to press a wall switch and bring up the lights. Aidan had to close his eyes against the sudden brightness. She seemed to recognize his discomfort and cursed under her breath as she dimmed the wattage way down to a more manageable level.

"Sorry about that," she muttered. She hurried over to the keypad which controlled the damn electrical charge on the cage, her fingers still shaking as they danced over the keypad in the wrong sequence. He rolled his eyes. *He* knew the code. Everything in him, every instinct, every hunger, wanted to shift to his human form and break out of this fucking place on his own. But he couldn't risk letting anyone on this ship see him shift. It would endanger everyone he loved, everything he believed in. He'd die first.

"Fuck." She cursed loudly, then immediately looked around, as if expecting the others to come rushing through the door at the sound. He could have told her there was no one close enough to hear, but her fear of discovery served his interests better, anyway. The more worried she was, the more urgently she'd get them both off this cursed ship. Because what other reason would there be for her to show up, sneaking around in the middle of the night?

"Yes," she hissed triumphantly when the dim indicator light went green and the electrical field went down. She turned to face him, her eyes wary and more than a little fearful. "Okay, big guy," she said nervously. "I don't know if you can understand me, but here's the deal. I'm here to get you out, and I'd really like for you not to kill me when I do. I know the people I work with are assholes, but I swear I didn't know what they had planned."

For someone who didn't think he understood her, she was sure talking a lot.

"You're going to need me to get off this ship, and there's something I think you can help me with once we get outside."

Aidan's gaze narrowed sharply. Was she planning on escaping into the Green, too? Was she out of her mind? She wouldn't last a day out there.

"I can't stay here," she explained. "There's a person on this planet who organized the whole mission, including getting permission to land, and I need to find him."

Aidan had to fight back a growl. As he'd suspected all along, someone on Harp had brought these invaders to their door. His mind raced with possibilities. It couldn't be a shifter. Not even the worst of them would condone capturing one of their own to be caged in a zoo, or even worse, cut up and studied. A norm might have done it, one of Harp's non-shifter population. But he couldn't see that happening. They'd have to know the Guild shifters would find out, and then their entire family would pay the price. Besides, the traitor had known how to evade the fleet's electronic surveillance in order to sneak the ship on-planet. That meant someone with access to the fleet's science center, which excluded all but a few Harp citizens, including several Guild shifters. Which took him back to all the reasons the traitor couldn't be a shifter. No, it had to be one of the Earther techs responsible for enforcing Harp's embargo. All they'd had to do was look the other way and let the invaders slip onto the planet.

He frowned. Rhodry's wife, Amanda, had full access to the center. She certainly wasn't the traitor, but she'd know how to find him. He studied the woman outside his cage. *She* already knew the traitor's name. Unfortunately, he couldn't hang around waiting on the possibility she'd just happen to mention it. He had to meet up with Rhodry and the rest of his cousins, who'd be close by now. Together, they'd deal with the ship and everyone on it.

What this woman needed to do for now was remain with the ship. She wouldn't last a day out there without him, and dying would hardly be a fit reward for his rescue. Once he and his cousins came back to deal with the others, he'd take her anywhere she wanted to go. Not only because she'd helped him, but because he'd be hunting the traitor soon, and she had the name of his prey.

Walking over to the passageway door, the woman opened it a crack and listened. He knew there was no one out there, but she seemed to gain reassurance from the act of checking, and anything that got this escape moving was fine with him.

Apparently satisfied, she walked back, whispered, "Here we go," and pressed the button. Aidan came to his feet the moment the cage door unlocked. He didn't wait to see what the woman was going to do next. Head lowered, eyes watching her for any sign of betrayal, he prowled over to the unlatched door and butted it open with his head. She was staring at him, her heart pounding so loudly that it almost hurt his sensitive ears. And yet, she was still there, her face a mask of determination trying to conceal her fear. He didn't know why she was helping him, but he remembered how she'd protested the outright slaughter in the forest. She had courage, he'd give her that. But until he truly understood her motivation, he'd reserve judgment.

She turned her back on him, walked over to the open door, and stuck her head into the passageway again. He didn't wait for the verdict this time. He knew there was no one out there, and besides, he wasn't afraid of the Earthers. If anything, he'd welcome a chance to take out a few more of them. They wouldn't catch him with their tranq guns this time, and he was no longer in a cage to be tormented with electrical prods.

These Earthers meant him and his people harm. They had no idea the hell that was about to rain down on them, but he'd be happy to give them an early taste of it if they tried to stop him from getting off this fucking ship.

He was across the holding pen in two long jumps, pushing past the woman and shoving the door wide open as he leaped out into the passageway. Ignoring her startled cry, he paused only long enough to sniff the air, and then he took off.

"Hey!" she whispered a protest as her rapid footsteps followed him down the passageway to a ladder-like set of stairs. He took the stairs in a single, long leap and raced down another passage to a closed hatch at the end of it.

The leftover scent of the forest he'd been following ended here. This had to be the belly hatch the Earthers had all used. He paced back and forth in a tight circle, while he waited for her to catch up so she could enter the code and open the damn door. He turned his head to follow her approach, growling when she didn't move fast enough to suit him.

"All right," she muttered, as she stepped up to the keypad. "How the hell do you even know this is the right exit?"

Aidan's only response was another ill-tempered growl, as he watched her key in the correct sequence. The hatch cracked open. Aiden bounded out and down the ramp before it was fully deployed, jumping the last few feet, his paws hitting the soft loam of the forest floor. The scent of the Green surrounded him, and the trees sang their joy at his freedom. Aidan's battle cry screamed into the night sky, echoed from far away by the answering howls of his cousins, as they raced to join him.

Every instinct urged him to take to the treetops and meet them, but the warrior in him prevailed. He had one more duty. The woman. He owed her a debt of gratitude for his release, but he couldn't let her follow him. She had no idea of the dangers in the Green.

...

Rachel paused long enough to close the hatch on the ship, then stepped into the darkness after the cat. And it was *dark*. There'd been a big moon in the sky earlier, but it had set before she'd tapped into the ship's exterior cameras. The cat was bounding ahead of her, racing toward the trees. He could see just fine. She didn't need any textbook to tell her that. His glowing eyes gave him away. Unfortunately, her ordinary human eyes couldn't see her own feet. She stopped dead and dug into the smallest pocket on the front of her heavy trousers for the LED flashlight, which she'd modified with thick tape, so that it gave off only the tiniest strip of light. Even so...

"Wait," she called. She had to make him stop. He'd raced down the passage so fast that she hadn't had time to stop and grab her pack. "I can't see a damn thing out here. Watch your eyes."

The beast immediately turned his head toward the trees, and it struck her again how he seemed to understand every word she said. According to the reports she'd read about Harp, the locals—who were descendants of a human colony ship—spoke the trade common language, or at least close enough to it. There'd been some drift, of course, but not enough to cause a problem in communication. So maybe the big cats had enough exposure to the human population that they understood intent, if not all the spoken words.

She frowned. That didn't jive with the briefing that Guy Wolfrum had sent her. He indicated the cats were completely wild and lived only in the most remote parts of the Green, which was why their ship had landed so far from the city. She was beginning to suspect there was a more nefarious reason for their landing choice, however. The second ship—of which she'd had no knowledge before tonight—had been assigned an equally remote landing site. But Wolfrum's report didn't line up with what she'd observed so far. There was not only the cat's response to what she said, but also his seeming ability to understand technology. He'd recognized the function of a keypad lock and had made no attempt to charge the bars of his cage, or even push against them, while they'd been actively electrified. He hadn't had to learn by being shocked even once. It was as if he'd understood Frank White's explanation of the system.

Wolfrum had made no mention of the cats' intellect, but that omission only fed her suspicions that there was a hidden agenda to this hunt. Maybe their unusual intelligence was the real reason he wanted them, and they weren't headed for private zoos at all. The military arm of the fleet would pay a fortune for an animal that could be taught to perform dangerous tasks, especially an animal that came in such a ferocious package. Hell, even she could see the possibilities. The difference was she'd never act on them.

Ahead of her, the cat abruptly turned and snarled a warning, the kind that spoke to the deepest, most primitive part of her genetic memory when men had huddled in caves while monsters prowled in the darkness. The hairs on the back on her neck stood up, and goose bumps shivered over her skin. She stared at the massive cat, his huge and very sharp teeth gleaming in the dim light, his eyes shining like golden lamps. He plainly didn't want her to follow him. Without another sound, he spun and headed for the forest, disappearing into the darkness as fast as if he'd never been drugged. As if he'd never really been there at all.

Rachel squinted after him, but her small light couldn't penetrate the shadows, and he was gone. She hadn't expected him to understand why she needed to leave the ship, much less to care, no matter how intelligent he was. But that didn't change the fact that she needed to leave. She had no doubt that White and the others would kill her when they discovered what she'd done.

Climbing back up the ramp and then the ladder, she went directly to her cabin to retrieve her backpack. A sigh escaped as the familiar weight settled on her shoulder. She understood why the cat had fled, but she'd hoped it would stick around. Not only because she didn't know where she was going, but because his presence would have driven away other wildlife in the area. It had been unreasonable for her to expect him to stay with her, however. He was a wild animal. Maybe someday their paths would cross again, and he'd remember her well enough to spare her life. But that was the most she could expect from him.

Retracing her steps, she exited the ship, and using her flashlight, moving slowly, she made her way in among the trees. She wouldn't go far tonight. Just enough to conceal her from the ship. It would have been easier if the cat had stuck close, but this wouldn't be the first time she'd trekked into a dangerous location on her own, or with others dependent on her. Although this *was* the first time she'd had anyone trying to kill her. Angry animals, yes. Homicidal people, no.

She could hear forest creatures moving about, some of them large enough that the sound of their passage made her heart skip a beat. But none of them came close. Granted, she couldn't see much beyond the slice of light right in front of her. It was possible, however, that she still carried enough of the cat's scent—the scent of an alpha predator—that it dissuaded the other animals from attacking her. It wouldn't last, but she'd take it for now. At least through the night. In the morning, she could work out a plan for the rest of her journey to where Wolfrum and the second ship waited. Or failing that, the city.

She walked for several hours, covering very little ground but moving steadily in the right direction. It would have been slow going even in daylight. There were no paths, not even an animal trail, that she could find. And the spaces between the trees were irregular and clogged with fallen logs and crisscrossed by vines. In the dark, it was nearly impossible. But her innate sense of direction kept her going, and she counted every step forward as adding to the buffer between her and her former crew.

When dawn finally eased over the horizon with a faint, pink glow, she found herself in a relatively clear space around a huge monster of a tree. The trunk was so big around that it had to be hundreds, maybe thousands, of years old. She reached out and ran her gloved hand over the rough surface, then pulled her hand back and tugged off the glove. Protocol be damned, she wanted to *feel*. The tree's surface was thick and flaked with heavy layers of bark, with channels so deep running up and down the trunk that she could fit her whole hand into some of them. Hell, she could fist her fingers and *still* fit her hand into the deepest gaps. She itched to document its existence, to take photographs and notes. But very soon White and the others would discover she was gone, and the cat with her, and they'd come after her. She had no doubt one or more of them was good enough to follow an ordinary trail on the ground, but she was a planetary specialist—an expert at moving through non-Terran environments without leaving a trace.

Sliding the backpack off her shoulders and to the ground, she crouched next to it and dug deep into the main compartment until she found what she was looking for—a tightly-rolled belt and rope contraption that very few people would recognize. It was a tree-climbing harness, and she'd included it in her gear as soon as she'd read about Harp's massive trees. To be sure, it was the simplest version she owned. Back home, she had an entire closet filled with different kinds of harnesses and equipment. But most of those would have taken up way too much room, and while they might have been safer, she really didn't need them. The trees in this area provided more than enough traction for the rope. Besides, she told herself, she'd been on the ship for too long. Her legs could use a good workout.

She undid the strap that held her regular rope to her backpack, then tied a small weight bag to the end. Looking up among the dense branches, she picked her target and executed a perfect underhand toss, slinging the weighted rope over the lowest branch and dropping it back down next to her. Moments later, she was hooked up and ascending into the canopy at a steady pace.

Stopping at the first branching, about twenty feet off the ground, Rachel stepped off and removed her climbing harness. She didn't need it to climb any farther. There were thick branches all along the trunk from this point upward, and she was tall enough to gain hand and footholds with little problem. She looked around and grinned. She *loved* these trees! Her brother would go nuts for them. Hell, her father would, too, even if his enthusiasm had more to do with research and less with climbing.

Stowing the harness in her pack, she slipped her arms into both shoulder straps, locked the waist belt and sternum strap, and started upward again. She'd find a sturdy branch to rest for a few hours, and then continue her journey. As tempting as it was to travel under cover of night, it simply wasn't practical. Unless one of Harp's larger moons decided to make an appearance, it was far too dark for her to travel in speed or safety. And if she traveled through the trees— as she'd speculated the animals must do on this planet—she could cover a lot more ground and outrun her pursuers in short order.

. . .

Aidan's ears pricked up as the song of the trees shifted and the breeze of a new morning brought him a familiar scent. His lips pulled back in a fang-baring grin. There were shifters in-bound.

His cousins were a mile or two out, on the other side of the swamp, but that was nothing for a shifter. He raced along the branches high above the steamy depths, changing his trajectory after a while to intersect with Rhodry, who was traveling alone, coming in from the city while the other cousins were arriving from Clanhome.

He and Rhodry met on the highest branches first, rubbing against each other like the huge cats they were, before plunging to the forest floor and shifting to their human forms.

"You scared the shit out of us," Rhodry growled, giving Aidan a backbreaking hug. "Amanda nearly dropped the twins on the spot."

Aidan's smile was so big that it hurt. He was full to bursting with happiness at being alive and free, and having his cousin to back him up. For the first time since his capture, he could admit to himself that he'd been fucking horrified at the specter of being studied, picked apart, and ultimately used as breeding material for whatever nightmare purposes the Earthers had in mind.

"Not hardly! Amanda's got months before those two will be ready to birth," he told Rhodry, laughing. "By that time, she'll be big as a—"

"Christ, don't say it," his cousin snapped, slapping his shoulder. "She'll kill us both."

Aidan grinned at the shifter, who was closer to him than a brother. As close as Rhodry's twin boys would be some day. He'd never doubted that his cousin would come when the humans had attacked him, just as he'd been certain that the trees would carry a warning of the invaders and his capture.

"It's fucking good to see you, cuz."

"I admit I'm a little disappointed," Rhodry said, shaking his head. "When I caught sight of that ship, I thought we'd be storming the hatches to peel you out. But here you are instead."

"Now that's an interesting story. There's a woman—"

"There's always a woman with you," Rhodry laughed. "What about her?"

"Rachel's her name, and she's the one who got me out of there."

Laughter fled as his cousin asked, "Does she know about us?"

Aidan shook his head. "*She* doesn't, but whoever brought that ship here does, and so do at least some of the crew. They meant to capture a shifter but wanted proof. They did their best to force a shift once they had me. Fortunately, it was me they grabbed, not one of the younger ones, so it didn't work."

"And the woman? Where was she for all this?"

Aidan shrugged. "Somewhere else in the ship. I don't know. She wasn't part of the torture sessions."

"Torture?" Rhodry snapped the single word, his hackles rising despite his human form.

"Some sort of electrified rod." He lifted his shirt to display a cluster of circular burn wounds on his side—not yet fully healed because his body had focused on the more dangerous injuries.

"Fuck."

"It's not as bad as it could have been. They didn't seem to want the woman to know about it, and she kept close tabs. She's a doctor of some kind. It seems they brought her along to provide medical care to their captives, but without telling her the truth of what we are. All she saw was the cat, and that's what she rescued."

Rhodry lifted his head, as if scenting the wind. "I want to hear the rest of this, but the others are close. Let's shift and intercept. You can tell us all at once, then decide what to do with this woman of yours."

Aidan opened his mouth to deny she was *his,* but he couldn't say the words. He frowned. Maybe she *was* his, but only because he felt responsible for her. He didn't get involved when it came to women, and any of his cousins would back him up on that. He loved women, and they loved him. But it was all about a good time, nothing more. The image of Rachel as he'd last seen her, glaring fiercely out into the darkness, as if daring the night to defy her, filled his mind. He smiled.

Rhodry snorted loudly. "Right. That's what I thought. Let's go. And don't let anyone else see that mooning look on your face. It's fucking embarrassing."

"Fuck you," Aidan said cheerfully, then shifted and took off before his cousin could say anything else.

The Devlin cousins were waiting when Aidan and Rhodry dropped out of the trees. They'd all pulled on the loose drawstring pants that shifters favored when roaming the Green in human form. Shifters didn't care about nudity. The shift made clothing a nuisance. But there was a logging camp not far from where they were now, and most norms didn't share the shifters' lax attitudes when it came to nudity. Shifters were all fine physical specimens, and the only rule on Harp when it came to sexual congress was consent. Everything else was free and easy. But the logging camps tended to be more conservative than Harp as a whole, and while they had no problem working with shifters to keep the forest healthy, they didn't trust them around their women.

Aidan and Rhodry quickly donned the pants their cousin Gabriel threw at them, before they were swept into a round of manly hugs. Aidan especially was pounded on the back until he could feel his bones vibrating, but he didn't complain. He'd never doubted they'd come for him, and he was as happy to see them as they were him.

"So, tell us the story," Rhodry said, automatically assuming control. Because Rhodry was more than just his cousin, he was *the* de Mendoza, clan chief of the most powerful of the mountain clans, the de facto leader of all the clans on Harp. Aidan and the others were Devlins, the largest family in the de Mendoza clan. Rhodry, too, was a Devlin, on his father's side. The de Mendoza mantle had come from his mother's line. It was complicated to outsiders, but among the clans, it was clear as a bell.

The Devlins were loyal to Rhodry as their cousin first and their clan chief second. Nothing trumped blood.

"Tell us about the woman," Gabriel called.

Aidan gave Rhodry a narrow look. "What did you tell him?"

"Ho ho! Aidan's sweet on her," someone crowed, and everyone laughed.

"There's nothing funny about what they did to the Green." Rhodry's sober words brought them all back to the reason they were here. "Nor the animals they killed. Aidan?"

Aidan nodded, abruptly as serious as the rest of them. "They were after me. Or, not me, specifically, but a shifter. And more than just one, judging by the number of cages I saw."

The cousins reacted predictably with curses and questions. Who the hell were these Earthers? And how did they know about shifters?

"I'm not sure who's behind it, although Rachel thinks she knows. Which is why I have to stick close to her after we deal with the ship."

There was another, milder round of catcalls, but then one of his cousins asked quietly, "She's one of them?"

"She came with them," Aidan admitted. "But she's not one of them. I'd swear she had no idea what they planned before they started shooting up the forest. Nor when they caged me on their damn ship."

"How'd they manage that? What weapons do they have?"

"They have two kinds of weapon. One shoots nothing but heavy-duty tranquilizer darts, that's what they used on me. But the other weapons, the ones they used to create chaos and force me to respond, those were old-fashioned projectile submachine guns. They used those to get me out into the open and didn't give a damn about the damage they did or what else they killed."

"The weapon choice indicates prior knowledge of Harp," Rhodry added.

Aidan nodded. "I made them regret their actions before I went down. I killed three of them outright, and a fourth, their leader, was so badly injured that she's useless to them."

"And your woman?" Rhodry asked.

He scowled at him, but said, "She never went along with what they planned. She was screaming her head off for them to stop when they started firing wildly, and again when they kept shooting me with tranqs. Hell, she was whispering promises to me before they even got me on the ship."

"What kind of promises?" Gabriel asked with a comically obvious leer.

"Fuck you. She promised to help me escape. Which she

did, by the way. And now she's determined to track down whoever it was that planned the mission and hired the crew, including her. She insists he's on-planet, and I need to get back before she gets tired of waiting and takes off on her own. She's not a novice when it comes to new environments, but we all know what Harp's capable of."

"All right, let's go," Rhodry decided. "We're hitting that ship this morning. They won't expect it. Aidan, did you get the ramp code?"

He nodded.

"Good. You open the hatch, then shift and join us. The rest of you shift now and stay that way."

"I have to get Rachel out of there first," Aidan said quickly. "They lost people capturing me. They'll kill her for helping me escape."

"We won't let that happen," Rhodry said confidently. "You go ahead and get her out, but I want to debrief before you whisk her away. She's our best source of intel on the enemy."

"She'll be safe at Clanhome," Gabriel offered.

"She stays with me," Aidan said. "She can help me hunt the traitor."

"Whatever you say, cuz," Gabriel agreed, exchanging an amused look with Rhodry. "All right, lads, see you on the other side." He shifted in a blur of reddish-gold fur and took to the trees with the others. In minutes, Aidan and Rhodry were alone in the small clearing.

"You like her."

Aidan shrugged. "She saved my life."

Rhodry smiled. "Yeah, but it's more than that. Let's go."

Chapter Seven

"You sure you've got the right code."

Aidan looked over at Rhodry, where they stood on a thick branch, high above the clearing where the Earthers' ship stood buttoned up tight. He didn't know if the ship's condition meant they hadn't yet discovered his escape, or if they *had* discovered it and were terrified of retribution. They had good reason for the latter. Hell was about to descend upon them.

The rest of the cousins had shifted and lay waiting for the attack to begin, but he and Rhodry remained in their human forms. Aidan, because he'd need fingers to enter the belly hatch access code and to get Rachel safely out of there. And Rhodry because, apparently, he'd become a nervous Nellie in the short time Aidan had been gone. A by-product of his impending fatherhood, perhaps.

Aidan took his eyes off the ship long enough for a quick glance at his cousin. "For the tenth time, I've got the code," he said confidently. "What's up your ass?"

Rhodry gave him a very unfriendly look. "You mean

apart from the fact that one of my favorite cousins was kidnapped by these assholes and about to be cut up in the name of science? And that I'm here instead of back home with my wife who's pregnant with twins? You mean other than that?"

"*One* of your favorite cousins? I am *the* favorite, and you know it." Aidan turned his gaze back to the ship. "When's the go-ahead?"

"We're going in now. They won't expect a daylight attack."

"They shouldn't be expecting an attack from us at all, unless they know about shifters."

Rhodry nodded. "It sure seems as if someone's been talking."

Aidan frowned. "At least some of them knew about it, that's for sure. But not Rachel. She's not a part of whatever this is."

Rhodry slanted a glance at him. "I was right. You like her."

He scowled. "We've been through this before. She has courage, and she saved my life."

"And she's quite lovely, I'd imagine."

Aidan cleared his throat. "That, too. Give the word. Let's get this done."

A small smile crossed Rhodry's face. "I've changed my mind. I'll enter the code and go in first. You come in right behind me, and—"

"Good plan, except… I'll go in first, as we discussed. I know the layout, and you're way too valuable to risk."

"That's not how it works, and you know it. Clansmen lead from the front."

"Good thing I'm a clansman, then. I have the best chance of making this work, and you know it. And if that doesn't convince you, then consider Amanda and the twins. She'll skin me alive if anything happens to you."

"That's a low blow, cuz."

"The best kind. What's the signal once I'm onboard?"

"Your lead, your choice."

Aidan thought about it. "I'd say you could wait until the screams start, but the lads might resent missing out on the fun. Let's go with a hunter's howl instead." He grinned. "That way everyone gets to play."

Rhodry studied him soberly for a long minute, and Aidan thought for sure he was going to push for a revised plan. His cousin was used to leading hunts, not following. But this one was personal to Aidan. He'd been the one captured and held in a fucking cage. Besides, only he could ensure Rachel's safety. He'd initially thought to get her out of the ship before any serious bloodshed began. But once he gave the all-clear, his cousins would attack within minutes. She'd be safer in her cabin until the fighting was over.

Also, that way, he could inflict some serious bloodshed of his own.

Rhodry gave a sharp nod. "Right. I'll have the others ready to go. He gripped Aidan's shoulder tightly. "You be careful. I'd hate having to choose a new favorite after all this time."

"Love you, too. Be ready."

• • •

Aidan scanned the ship from end to end, his study slow and deliberate. There was no sign of life that he could see. Heavy reentry shutters covered every window, which he'd expected, but there wasn't even the tiniest flicker of movement from the many sensors mounted on the bristling exterior. If not for the sound of multiple heartbeats emanating from the ship on the very edge of his enhanced hearing, he might have thought it was abandoned. If the Earthers had hoped Aidan's people would accept the ship's status at face value and go away, they didn't know much about shifter abilities. But then, that was why they'd wanted a live sample or six for their research labs, wasn't it?

He raced across the clearing in human form, happy there was no one watching from the ship to see him crouched low in the long grasses. Once beneath the ship, he straightened, not wasting any time as he strode over to the keypad next to the landing strut. He entered the code Rachel had used during his escape, half expecting it not to work. If the crew was aware of his escape—and it seemed likely they were—they'd naturally suspect Rachel, whether they had proof or not, since she'd made no secret of her feelings regarding his capture, and she'd had easy access to him. Basic security protocols would then have required them to change every code she'd had knowledge of. Even *he* knew that. And yet, the moment he tapped the final number into the keypad, the hatch opened with a loud hiss of seals, and the ramp deployed with a smooth, nearly silent glide.

He wasn't fooled by this easy entry. This was the ship's main ground-based exit. Basic security protocol would include a warning indicator on the bridge every time the ramp opened. Which meant he'd have company soon. Jumping onto the lowering ramp before it hit the ground, he ran to the base of the ladder leading up to the crew level. He paused briefly, barely breathing as he listened for the blare of an alarm, or the thunder of charging crewmen. Nothing. Death was about to roll over these invaders, and they, apparently, were going to sleep right through it. He shook his head. Rhodry and the others were waiting for his signal, but this seemed too easy. What if it was a trap?

He lifted his face and scented the air. His nostrils filled with the ship's cold, metal stink. Growling his frustration, he shifted in an instant, rolling the heavy muscles of his huge shoulders and flanks, stretching forward as he welcomed his animal self. He scented the air again, his abilities much sharper in this form, his predator's nose telling him a much more complex story. He smelled a lot of blood and other bodily fluids that spoke of injured humans. That wasn't exactly news, but the strength of the scent told him more of the ship's crew were nursing wounds than he'd thought. If so, it was just possible that they *didn't* know Aidan was gone.

Shifting back to human, he climbed the ladder in two bounds and followed Rachel's scent to her quarters at one end of the passageway. He glanced down at himself and frowned. She might be startled to find a strange, *naked* man entering her cabin. He had a speech ready about how he was there on behalf of the Ardrigh, who'd heard of the illegal hunts… But that didn't explain his absence of clothing, did it? He shrugged with a shifter's disregard for nudity. He couldn't do anything about it, and besides, if she was going to be hunting the traitor with him, she'd see him naked sooner or later anyway.

He just hoped she didn't have one of those damn tranq guns waiting when he opened the cabin door.

She didn't. Because *she* wasn't there. He had a moment of pure, unexplainable rage, wondering where she was and which of the assholes onboard she was sleeping it off with. But before he could wonder at the sheer intensity of the emotion, the full range of his senses kicked in, and he knew she wasn't *elsewhere* on the ship. She was *gone.* The overstuffed backpack she'd carried with her during her excursions into the forest was nowhere to be found, and the scent of her throughout the cabin was at least two days old. Which would put her departure on the same day as his escape. He thought back to the last time he'd seen her, standing at the foot of the hatch ramp, cautioning him about the light she was about to turn on. He'd growled a warning for her to get the fuck back onboard, and he'd left…without bothering to verify she'd obeyed his command.

"Fuck." She hadn't followed him. He'd have sensed her on his tail. But she hadn't stayed put, either. She was somewhere out in the Green on her own, but that wasn't the worst of it. Because Rachel wasn't simply in the Green, she was heading for the *swamp*. And she'd been out there alone the entire time he'd been playing games with Rhodry and deciding the best way to mount the damn assault. "*Fuck,*" he cursed again, angry at *her*, at *himself*, and especially at whoever it was that had brought all of this down on their heads.

Shifting once more, he padded out of Rachel's cabin and into the main passageway on the crew deck. He stopped there and stared, his eyes blinking slowly, taking in the tiniest sound, the faintest scent before he called his cousins to the hunt. He shook his head. These Earthers were so utterly unprepared for an attack that it almost seemed unfair. But then he remembered the animals they'd killed, the trees they'd injured and destroyed…and the very unpleasant future they'd had in mind for *him*.

All sense of fair play disappeared in a heartbeat.

These were invaders, and they needed to pay. Not only for the damage they'd already done, but for the harm they'd bring in the future if they, or any of their data, managed to escape Harp.

Ignoring the ladder, he leaped for the lower deck and the open ramp. Baring his teeth in anticipation of the coming battle, he lifted his head and *howled*. His fellow shifters, who'd been advancing through the treetops like a soft breeze, suddenly dropped to the forest floor and raced into the clearing, their passage barely stirring the long grass, as the trees whispered of vengeance and coming death. Those whispers drifted up to Aidan on the caress of a warm wind. He shifted back to human the moment Rhodry's dark head crested the ramp's opening. Shifters were vicious and uncannily strong, but they couldn't open doors. That would be left to him.

He moved fast, opening door after door, using the code that Rachel had used on the night of his escape.

His cousin Gabriel was first up the ramp, sliding past Aidan and into the first unlocked cabin, so swift and silent that Aidan might have mistaken him for a shadow. Until the screaming started. Door after door opened after that, either with Aiden's help or in response to the screams. It didn't matter which, and Aidan didn't wait to find out. Ignoring yet another ladder, he jumped through the opening to the next deck and, with the sound of screams filling the air, prowled down to the bridge, where, as luck would have it, he found Frank White all alone. The Earther hadn't raced to help his fellow crewmembers, whose screams punctuated his cowardice. Instead, he'd remained on the bridge, hiding, his back pressed against the big command console, a wicked-looking knife clenched in one meaty fist and a tranq gun in the other.

He lifted his weapons, ready to fight, and Aidan bared his teeth in a deep-throated snarl. White had been his main tormentor, the one who'd used an electric prod on him when no one was around to see. Aidan had thought at first that the Earther was using the shocks to force him to shift, but it hadn't taken long for him to recognize the truth. The man simply enjoyed causing pain, especially when his victim was unable to fight back.

Aidan lowered his head, eyes fixed on his prey, his growl a steady rumble in his chest. He wasn't going to kill Frank White in defense of the planet. This one was fucking personal. White was going to discover what happened when his victim could fight back.

Aidan's howl was a saw-toothed blade of sound ratcheting off the walls as he took a step forward and watched the Earther's face grow pale.

"You shouldn't have come back here," White blustered from a throat gone raspy with fear. "I'll kill you and that bitch, too."

Aidan's eyes never left the human coward, whose fear-sweating body took a final, jerking step back and slammed into the console. He hung there for a moment, looking around desperately as if searching for an escape that didn't exist. Aidan knew he should kill the man and be done with it, but something inside him, some predator's need, demanded more. Before the human could react, Aidan swept out a powerful paw, knocking the knife from his hand, raking four-inch-long claws across his hip on the downward stroke, ripping through skin and muscle and leaving a bloody ruin.

White screamed, his face distorted in shocked agony, but he didn't go down. He might never have faced the likes of Aidan before, but he was a hardened warrior. Using the fixed bridge chair as a flimsy barrier, he shoved away from the console, fumbled beneath it and came up firing a small plasma rifle—a weapon that should never have been brought onto the planet. Teeth bared and eyes crazed, he yelled wildly as he made a run for it, spraying fire behind him, not caring what he hit. He raced down the passageway with Aidan behind him, a laughing cackle howling from between his wide-open jaws, not trying to catch up, playing with his prey. To a point.

White couldn't be permitted to leave the ship with the plasma weapon in hand. It could do untold damage if fired outside the ship's shielding. He hit the downward ladder, clinging to his weapon, practically falling the distance to the lower deck, a shout of victory rising from his throat as he saw the open belly hatch, saw the sunlight that promised escape.

Aidan waited until the human made the jump to the ground outside, until his body hung in midair and escape seemed a breath away. And then he pounced. With thrust of his powerful hind legs, he caught the Earther mid-leap, knocking him to the ground and sending his weapon flying. Three hundred pounds of furious shifter landed on the man's back and pinned him to the ground. Aidan's claws dug into flesh and satisfaction sank into his bones as White's terror echoed through the forest, sending a message of vengeance to the trees and animals of the Green in the moment before Aidan closed his teeth over his prey's neck and snapped his spine.

He was almost disappointed when White went limp beneath him, when his heart stopped and warm blood rapidly cooled. He lifted his head and spat. He was a predator, not a cannibal. As unlikely as it might seem, he and White were both human.

Giving the dead man a dismissive flick of his paw that ripped the body's jaw open, he lifted his head and roared his victory, then turned and raced back into the ship. The screams had stopped. There was nothing but the victorious howls of his cousins echoing up and down the metal passageways. But that wasn't his target.

Shifting to human, he climbed back to the bridge and looked around. White had done a lot of damage with his stupid gun. There was still a treasure trove of information to be had here, information that Aidan could have used in his pursuit of Rachel. But it would take time to repair the bridge controls to access the ship's data, or failing that, to bypass the controls instead. Given enough time, he could do it himself—he had the equivalent of a fleet graduate degree in engineering, and like every other shifter, he'd made good use of the updated database the fleet had provided as part of their arrangement with the Ardrigh. But he didn't have that kind of time right now. Rhodry would send others to harvest what they could before the Green covered over this ship, eventually destroying it, just as it did every other invader.

There were more urgent matters at hand for Aidan, and Rachel was number one. She might think she was ready to survive Harp. She might even be right on some level. Rhodry's fleet-born wife, Amanda, had done it. But Amanda had spent months on Harp getting ready for her trial, months spent studying the planet's unique dangers and learning to use the weapons available to her. And then there were the trees. Amanda could hear Harp's trees, just as the shifters could. More than any weapon or training, it was her ability to hear the song of the trees that had made her survival possible.

As far as Aidan could tell, Rachel was as mind-deaf as any other norm, on Harp or off it. He didn't doubt she had skills, and experience with any number of deadly environments, but none of them were Harp. He had to find her before the planet itself identified her as an invader and decided it wanted her dead.

With a quick look around, he hurried back down to the crew level. He needed to consult with Rhodry.

$\cdots$

Rachel woke with a start, and not for the first time. She'd slept rough plenty of times before this, but there was rough, and then there was Harp. The tree she'd chosen was comfortable enough—the limb was wide enough, and the branching from the main trunk deep enough, that she didn't worry about falling. The tree was huge, with several other branches interlocking over her head that combined to provide protection against moisture and...other things that fell from the forest's heights. But the tree couldn't do anything about the unfamiliar noises throughout the forest—

the silent whoosh of winged predators, the deep growls of the others, and the death cries of their chosen prey. Rachel was all too aware that there were plenty of predators on Harp who considered *her* to be prey, and that, despite the comfort of her tree, she was too vulnerable. The restless night made her realize something about the years she'd spent trekking distant planets—she'd never gone solo before. Most often, she was hired as an expert guide for a select group of researchers or adventurers. But even when she'd been trekking purely for her own enjoyment, she'd gone with friends who shared her years of experience.

On Harp, she was alone. She hadn't planned it that way. Hell, she hadn't planned on setting off across the planet at all. But even then, she'd been certain her cat would hang around for the trip. She hadn't expected the wild creature to become domesticated overnight, but she had thought it would linger in her vicinity, its curiosity protecting her by coincidence rather than intent.

She rose to a crouch, swallowing a groan when her body protested, feeling aches and bruises all over from her unconventional sleeping arrangement. Sometimes interrupted sleep was worse than none at all. She tugged her pack around from where she'd been leaning against it and dug for a small bottle of water and an energy bar, which she swallowed in four dry bites. The bar was tasteless, but it was designed to give her metabolism a temporary boost while covering some basic nutritional needs. As for the water, she took only small sips, not knowing how long her limited supply would have to last. The humans on Harp would drink the same water she did, but they'd had hundreds of years to adapt to any of the planet's specific parasites or bacteria that lived in the local water supply. The last thing Rachel wanted was to spend the next few days barfing her guts up, or worse, because she hadn't properly checked her drinking water.

She had water purification tablets and a filtered canteen, but while her maps included the distant main river which ran all through the Green, they weren't detailed enough to show smaller water sources. She'd spent a good part of her sleepless hours bashing herself for not printing better maps from the ship's data. The fact that she'd never thought she'd need them was no excuse. She was the person whose job it was to be prepared for the worst. She'd failed miserably so far.

Although she *had* saved the cat. And she'd stopped the rest of them from continuing their immoral and illegal mission. Well, okay, so the cat had done that when he'd killed three crew and taken Ripper out of the picture for the duration, but she'd done her part by depriving them of their one and only test subject. The image of what they'd had planned for the magnificent creature made her literally nauseous.

The dry energy bar wasn't helping, either. She took a second tiny sip of water, just enough to wet her throat, and then another. Shoving the canteen back into her pack, she pulled out her map instead. It didn't show her anything new. The supposed location of the second ship, where she hoped to find Wolfrum, was in a nearly straight line, due west of her current position. There didn't seem to be any major obstructions between her and there, other than a dense forest filled with deadly life-forms. But Rachel was certain that, just as her map didn't show lesser water sources, it also didn't show the true topography of the Green. The planet's weird magnetic force made it nearly impossible to get an accurate read from space.

"Nothing for it, Rache," she muttered as she rose to her full height. "You always wanted to investigate new planets. Here's your chance."

Looking up, she was more convinced than ever that the sky road was the way to go. The higher one went, the more congested the branches became from tree to tree. Besides, tree climbing happened to be something she was good at. Her father had spent decades as the Research Director and Head Arborist for the Redwoods Sanctuary in old California. Rachel and her brother had grown up playing in trees that rivaled those of Harp in sheer size and age, if not in number. They'd both climbed almost before they could walk. Harp's giant trees were so old and wrinkled, with so many hand and footholds, that it was like climbing stairs. And if she stayed above the ground, she wouldn't have to worry as much about bad topography maps.

When she started her climb, the dawn was barely a hint in the sky, more shadows than light amidst the dense greenery of the forest. By noon, with the sun nearly straight up above her, she was sweating and frustrated and coming to realize that she'd had an unrealistic view of what she'd called the "sky road." She'd envisioned a nearly seamless network of interconnected branches that she could walk along like a literal road. The reality was somewhat more complicated.

She'd been right about the intertwining branches, but most of them weren't wide enough for a two-legged animal like herself to move along easily. And even when they were wide enough, they were so tangled up in each other that she'd have had to hack her way through—a job her very excellent combat knife wasn't really designed for. If she climbed even higher, the congestion was less, but the tree limbs, while sturdy, were even more narrow, and with wide gaps that required jumping. Rachel was in excellent physical condition and considered herself to be more than average athletically, but she didn't think she was up to the task of making ten-foot leaps while two hundred or more feet in the air. She was determined, not suicidal. Maybe if she'd been born on this planet, or lived here for a decade or two, she'd develop the skills necessary. But for now, the sky road was an excellent natural route, but it was designed for four-legged creatures, like her cat.

Accepting the inevitable, she started for the ground, scraping her arms and bloodying her knuckles in her impatience to get there. There was a growing sense of urgency in the back of her mind, a certainty that time was running out. She had to get to that second ship, had to find Wolfrum, before he did something even worse than capturing a lone wild animal.

Once she hit the ground, she rested just long enough for another energy bar and a sip of water. The scrapes on her forearms were bleeding beneath the long sleeves of her shirt, but she didn't want to take time to change shirts or properly bandage what were really no more than deep scratches. She'd clean them properly later, when the utter darkness of the Harp night forced her to stop. For now, she had to keep moving, had to make up for the long hours she'd spent climbing up and down and going nowhere. As for her split knuckles, they weren't even worth noticing. Every climber, whether it was trees or rocks, dealt with scrapes and scratches on their fingers and hands. It was a given.

Checking the location of the sun one more time, noting the direction of its afternoon motion, she set a punishing pace for herself. The deeper she went into the forest, the darker it became, until she walked in a permanent twilight. The sun was still overhead—she caught glimpses now and again, just enough to tell her she was moving in the right direction. But the trees were so dense, so intertwined with vines, that it was cool and shady on the forest floor. She welcomed the cooler air, but worried that it would translate into an early darkness, forcing her to stop much sooner than she would otherwise. She'd clearly been far too optimistic in judging how long her journey would take, and that was assuming—

A huge roar filled the air, so loud that the trees themselves seemed to tremble with its ferocity. Rachel didn't hesitate. She spun for the nearest tree and began climbing. Whatever that was, whatever creature had sent the entire forest into a frozen silence, she'd be better off up in the trees. The sound came again, but it was even more terrifying as human screams rose above even the thundering howls of the attacking beast. Her mind, which had been drowning in her body's adrenaline reaction the first time, was ready for it this time and she realized something. It wasn't one howl, but many, as if an entire pack of great beasts were sounding off as one. It was difficult to pinpoint the direction of the noise, but the higher she went, the easier it became. Because the growls didn't stop, and the screams only grew louder.

And then she heard the unmistakable sound of a plasma weapon being fired and her own terror grew. She'd read Admiral Nakata's official briefing on the tragedy that had caused Harp's break with the fleet. A single weapon could cause untold devastation. She waited for the explosion, but it never came. The weapon went silent, and the screams continued.

She kept climbing, frantic now to see what was happening. Finally, she was high enough to see beyond the trees, high enough that when she twisted around, following the horrific furor, she found herself looking back toward the clearing where her ship was located. Digging into her pack, she pulled out a pair of small but extremely powerful binoculars and trained them on the distant site. A sick feeling was growing in her gut. She'd suspected all along that her cat was more than a typical predator. There had to be a reason Wolfrum and his crew wanted them captured, a reason someone back on Earth was willing to pay so much money, to finance such an expensive mission, just to get their hands on even one of the big cats.

Zooming in on the ship—which was closer than she expected; she hadn't traveled nearly as far as she'd thought—

she saw two big men standing on the ramp below the belly hatch. They were only half dressed, and barely that, wearing loose drawstring trousers and nothing else. The feminine part of her appreciated the view—they were big men in excellent condition with broad chests and beautifully defined shoulders. The rest of her wanted to know who the hell they were and where had they come from. At least until three huge cats, just like *her* cat, prowled down the ramp as if they belonged there, as if…

Rachel's stomach surrendered to the horror of what she was seeing. It was only years of expeditionary experience that forced her to swallow the bile pushing its way up her throat. The big cats were looking like victorious conquerors because they *were*. The howls she'd heard, the screams…

More cats appeared, and the two men turned as if talking to the cats. Were they domesticated then? Had Ripper and her crew attacked someone's personal stretch of forest and captured not a wild animal, but someone's…guard animal? Like the giant working dogs of old earth who'd guarded the livestock herds?

But to attack the ship and kill everyone on it—because she had no doubt that everyone on that ship was dead—it seemed an extreme reaction for the capture of one animal, who'd managed to escape anyway, thanks to her.

Rachel stared through the binoculars until her eyes watered, but there were no answers. She saw a cat that might have been *hers*, but she couldn't know for sure. There were at least three others with similar coloring, or so she thought. The cats moved so swiftly through the high grasses that it was difficult to identify individuals, or even count their numbers with any surety.

Finally, she stopped trying. Putting away the binoculars, she stared at the distant ship with her own eyes, seeing nothing, trying to decide what she was feeling. She'd traveled across space with those people, spent weeks in their company. And, sure, none of them were in the running to be her best friends, but they'd been her crew.

She drew a deep breath, held it for a moment, then blew it out. It didn't help. She was going to need more than meditative breathing to deal with this one.

"This isn't your planet, Rachel," she whispered to herself. "Maybe Ripper and the others broke some religious taboo by capturing one of the cats. Maybe the locals believed the souls of their ancestors resided in the animals. Or something."

It sounded unlikely, given the background of the original colonists, but stranger things had happened. Whatever their reasons, the massacre of her former crew only added to her urgency to get to the other ship. There was nothing she could do for her crew. Their own actions had brought on their deaths. But maybe the crew of the other ship didn't have to die.

She turned and shimmied to the ground, the action almost automatic now, as if she'd been on Harp much longer than she had. She only hoped that familiarity held for the rest of her journey.

• • •

"I have to go after her." Aidan didn't look at Rhodry when he said it, his attention was on the forest, scanning the trees, listening to their song for any hint of Rachel's presence. He told himself she was okay, that she wasn't stupid, and she wasn't inexperienced. And if something *had* happened, if she'd been attacked, the forest would be singing of it. After all, killing a human—even one of the invading Earthers—was worth a note or two.

"Where's she going? Or where does she *believe* she's going, because we both know she won't get there alone."

Aidan gave his cousin a sharp look. "You think she's—"

"I don't think anything," Rhodry said quietly. "You hear the trees the same as I do."

He sighed, not at all sure that was true. Yes, he heard the trees. He'd been listening to their song all his life, from when he'd been a tiny babe, still in his mother's womb. But Rhodry was their clan leader, born to rule. Maybe he heard—

"We hear it exactly the same, Aidan," Rhodry said, as if reading his thoughts. "She can't have gone far."

Aidan grimaced. "She has some experience, but—"

"But no one's ready for the Green."

"Exactly. I think she'll head for the city. She said someone on Harp had arranged all of this." He indicated the ship and the dead bodies it now contained. "She wanted to find him and demand answers."

"No name?"

"No. That's another reason to track her down."

Rhodry nodded. "And when you find her?"

Aidan grinned. "I'll charm her into telling me what I need to know."

• • •

Darkness fell in the Green between one moment and the next. The phenomenon was mostly due to Harp's distance from its sun and a severe axial tilt, but the heavy shadows beneath the trees didn't help. Rachel knew the planet had three moons, all named after ancient Gaelic goddesses, but none of them were much help tonight. The largest of the three dwarfed the planet itself and appeared only once every few months. The second largest was a more manageable size, but she was visible only one night a month, and it wasn't tonight. The third was the smallest and most regular, rising in the sky three weeks out of every four, but at such a distance that one could be fooled into thinking she was a planet instead of a moon. The upshot of all this lunar activity was that there was no moonlight for Rachel to continue by. She could have used her LED flashlight, but she'd been walking all day over ground that was deceptively treacherous. At first glance, the forest floor was a carpet of decaying leaves and other small vegetation. In reality, that carpet concealed a myriad of burrow holes and uneven terrain, not to mention the vines that could trap an ankle in an instant. Rachel had tumbled more than once before she identified the markers of that particular vine and learned to avoid them. She was more than grateful for her sturdy hiking boots, which had seen service on several planets. They were worn to such a perfect fit on her foot and ankle that she'd had them resoled to avoid buying a new pair.

But far more taxing than the ground conditions were the trees themselves. The Green was impossibly dense in places, with heavy growth in between the trunks that was spun with such intricacy and, in its own way, beauty, that there was nothing for her to do except walk around. Which would have been simple if there'd been anything resembling a path. But there wasn't even an animal trail for her to follow.

And so when night fell, Rachel pulled the flashlight from her pocket, turned it on, and contemplated her choices. The flash illuminated an area roughly three feet in every direction. Enough to keep her company, but little else. She shined it up the nearest tree, trying to decide if she wanted to spend another night in the branches, or if she should roll out her high-tech sleeping pad and stay on the ground. Her stomach growled, deciding for her. Or more accurately, it postponed the decision in favor of food. She'd made it through the day on energy bars, which met all of her nutritional needs without even the pretense of satisfying the psychological demands of hunger. Strictly speaking, Rachel was only as hungry as was normal for dinner after a physically active day. But her brain didn't give a fuck about what her stomach had to say. She was ravenous for something more than a damn granola bar.

If she'd been on a planet she knew well, she'd have hunted, skinned, and cooked her own meal. But since Harp was a complete unknown, she stuck with the six-pack of Meals Ready to Eat, or MREs, that was a standard component of her backpack survival gear. Since the things had an expiration date that encompassed years, rather than months, the one in her pack had been there for…a while. She wasn't sure when she'd originally packed it, but she *was* certain that it was still edible. Standard operating procedure for her before setting off on any expedition, whether for a day or a month, included checking the date on her MREs. They weren't the tastiest meals in the universe, but they were hot and better than an energy bar.

Dropping her pack where she stood, she started pulling gear. First was a small laser-driven fire pack that she immediately set aside. No lasers on Harp. She knew that and thought she'd removed anything laser-related from her gear, but apparently there were a few pieces that she took so much for granted they'd slipped through.

No problem. She had old-fashioned matches, and God knew there was plenty of kindling around. And if she removed the laser mechanism, she could still use the metal box of the pack to contain her fire and prevent it from spreading to the entire forest. She set about disassembling the fire pack and was so focused on her task that she almost missed the first signs of danger.

Almost.

Like a hot breath against the back of her neck, she was suddenly aware that silence had fallen as deeply as the dark. Moving slowly, forcing herself to breathe despite the pounding of her heart, she set the fire pack down and flipped the safety strap off her belt knife. She slid the knife two inches free of its leather scabbard but didn't pull it yet. Aware of every muscle in her body, and what it would take to launch herself into action if demanded, she pulled her backpack to her side and began untying the crossbow and bolts she had secured there. The bolts came first. In a pinch, if she was forced to fight in close quarters, the heavy iron bolts could serve as weapons. The bow itself was heavy enough to use as a bludgeon, but also awkward enough to require two hands.

She'd just loosed the sheath and was working on the bow when she heard the first rustle of something big moving through the trees. She glanced up but kept working. If it was big, she'd rather shoot from a distance than fight it nose to nose.

There wasn't the slightest tremble in her fingers as she untied the final leather strap and pulled the bow free. If anything, at times like this she felt preternaturally calm, as if she'd been born to live in the wild and fight for survival. Adrenaline kicked in with a rush, making everything more clear. Her hearing was more acute, bringing into focus the soft susurration of leaves as the creature drew close. Even the shadows in the Green gained definition, painted in blacks and grays instead of a monochrome palette of darkness.

She notched first one bolt, then the second, and raised the bow, turning slightly as she tracked the animal's progress by sound. She stepped back from the tree she'd been resting against and aimed higher. The creature was right above her, if not in her tree, then very close, jumping down through the branches with no attempt at stealth, as if completely undeterred by her presence. The realization that it didn't fear her or her weapon gave her pause at last. If it hadn't learned to fear humans…

She didn't have time to finish the thought as at least three hundred pounds of something big and hairy, with a mouthful of dangerous teeth suddenly flashed through the beam of her LED, moving through the web of tree branches with a speed that belied its huge size. Without a moment's pause, it let out a deep-throated bellow, pounding its chest so hard that she could hear the impact of every fist. And a fist it was, because the creature was much like Earth's primates, with four long limbs, opposable thumbs on the hands, and long-toed feet that gripped branches nearly as well.

Rachel sucked in a shocked breath and regretted it almost immediately, nearly gagging on the animal's stink. Her eyes watered as she blinked to clear them, but she didn't need to see the creature to know she was in a fight for her life. She'd seen enough predators on enough planets to know that this one was a killer. She raised her bow. In a flash the animal moved. Faster than she could react, it threw out a long arm from several feet away and knocked the weapon from her hand, raking its claws along her forearm as it did so.

She cried out as much in shock as in pain, but she didn't cower, didn't try to escape. She knew predators, knew how they thought. If you ran, they chased. The best way to deal with them, the *only* way, if you hoped to survive, was to stand fast. The animal was blindingly quick, its attack nothing but a blur of motion. Her arm was agony, a constant shriek of pain and a distinctive heat that told her the wound might be poisoned, which left her with only one good option.

The creature opened its mouth in a cackling cry. She gripped her blade, holding it low to her side.

Confident of its victory, the creature swung to the ground and stalked closer, its eyes a nictitating gleam of green in the darkness, its arms waving back and forth in wide feints. It was playing with its food, she realized.

She watched its approach, waiting for her chance. The animal didn't know it yet, but she was no easy prey. Even so, she'd have only one shot at this, one shot at survival.

The beast slowed, some instinct warning it at the last minute that it should use caution. Rachel grinned, letting the animal see her teeth. Blunt as they were, it was a provocation to the primitive creature before her. It roared, blasting her with a wave of hot, fetid breath, and then it moved, blindingly fast. There was no time to aim, no time to consider strategy or even target. She simply reacted, stabbing out with seven inches of the best carbon steel. She didn't stop when she encountered resistance. She pushed harder until her fist slammed into a furry chest, and then she gripped the blade tighter and jammed it upward, nearly suffocated by the long hair and unbearable stench of the animal as it screeched in her ear and fought back. Its arms closed around her and squeezed. Rachel's lungs emptied, crushed beneath the pressure, as her heart fought to keep beating. Hot blood coated her hand, nearly buried along with her blade in the creature's chest, but still it kept squeezing, its arms growing tighter. She fought grimly for air but couldn't move. Her mind raced for a solution. She'd never faced a predator like this. She'd hunted before, she'd defended herself and others. But she'd never fought a battle that was life and death, never had her hand so close to the animal's heart that she could feel it beating against her own flesh.

Beating heart. She blinked in confusion as clarity slowly dawned. The creature's heart was so close. If she could just… She wrenched her left hand up between their bodies, fingers meeting on the sturdy handle of the blade. Closing her eyes as she sucked in a final desperate breath, she let go of everything except the need to survive. Both hands gripping the blade, slick fingers twisted with each other, she gave a hard, upward shove.

Blood gushed, hot and toxic, burning her skin as the animal's heart pumped ferociously, trying to function despite the fatal wound. The creature—whatever it was—slumped forward, which shoved the blade deeper into its chest, shredding more of its heart and severing critical arteries and veins. Rachel stumbled back under the weight, grunting as she hit the ground, thick roots digging into her spine as the full heft of her attacker pressed her into the dirt. She gasped for air, thinking how ironic it would be for her to have killed the animal only to have its dead carcass crush the air from her lungs.

"Oh hell no," she muttered, spitting out a mouthful of the beast's hair.

Putting her shoulder into it, she shoved up and rolled, throwing the dead animal to the ground with her on top.

"Disgusting." She fought the desire to vomit, suddenly glad she'd had so little to eat that day. She remained there for a few minutes, straddling the creature, letting fresh air fill her lungs. A sudden wracking cough reminded her that there was no such thing as fresh air within five feet of this thing, dead or alive.

Finally pushing herself upright, she staggered far enough away that she could draw breath and sank to the forest floor. She'd move in a minute. She had to get up, had to get away from the carcass. The scavengers would come soon enough, and they wouldn't be picky about whether the meat they munched was dead or alive. It was one thing to fight off a lone, big hairy thing, but it was something else entirely to survive a swarm of tiny, vicious biters. She didn't know what kind of scavengers they had on Harp, but she knew, whatever they were, she didn't want to deal with them tonight.

She peeled off her fitted, long-sleeve shirt first. It was a goner—stiff with the creature's blood, reeking of that awful stench, and irritating her skin where it made direct contact. She had a second top underneath. It was short-sleeved and not as warm, but that was okay, because the lightweight thermal jacket in her pack retained more heat than jackets twice its size. Rolling the destroyed shirt into a ball, she tossed it back on top of the carcass, where it would disintegrate as the carcass rotted. The dead animal must have a name or designator. It was too vicious a predator to have gone unnoticed. She'd have to find out what it was, so she could enter it in her notes. One didn't survive a fight like that and not make note of it.

Before pulling on the jacket, she took what was left of the water she'd been sipping during the day and poured it over her hands and arms. The blood was having a toxic effect on her skin, turning it red and itchy. Rachel hoped it was no more than that, but even a topical irritation could become serious. She followed the water with a couple of cleansing wipes and donned her jacket. The night was cold, and she still hadn't managed to eat anything.

She needed food and a fire. She needed to get moving.

She bent to pick up her backpack, swinging it up, sliding her arms into the straps and settling it on her shoulders. A sudden flash of movement in the trees made her jerk in dismay. Another one of the creatures? A mate perhaps? But, no. Rational thought defeated panic, and she remembered the stink of the dead animal when it attacked, the rustling sound it made as it slid from branch to branch through the trees.

This was different. More graceful somehow, sliding through the trees like liquid…gold. Golden fur. She searched the surrounding trees, convinced her cat was back. It had moved like that, graceful and deadly. But though she searched until her eyes burned, she didn't find him. Sighing, she settled her pack more firmly and buckled the straps, then turned her back on the dead creature and took a step…

"You can eat that, you know."

Rachel stifled a shriek of surprise and stared at the man standing just a few feet away, blocking her escape.

"They smell bad, but they taste good." He took a step

closer. "Good job taking him down, by the way. Pongos are a nasty lot. You must be stronger than you look."

Scowling inwardly at the backhanded compliment, she raised her light and flashed it in his direction, starting low as a warning, but quickly moving it up his very large body to his face. His lids closed down to almost nothing, before gradually opening to reveal gold-flecked eyes that gleamed too brightly in the glow of her light. Rachel blinked. He appeared human, but that retinal reaction wasn't quite normal. And his clothes—a lightweight tunic over similarly lightweight, loose-fitting pants and soft boots—definitely weren't fleet or any other Earth origin.

She was looking at a native of Harp, a descendent of those long-ago colonists. Simple courtesy demanded she drop her light, but she couldn't stop staring. He was good-looking, though she couldn't see many details. His hair was light, probably blond, and hung past his shoulders, which were broad and thick with muscle that even the loose tunic couldn't disguise. He was also very tall, easily over six feet, which spoke to the genetic traits of the original colonists, but also to their survival. They hadn't simply survived, they'd clearly thrived.

She tilted her head, frowning.

"I know you," she said, puzzled as to how that could be.

"Not likely, sweetheart."

She did a double take at the familiar endearment. She'd known that Harp natives spoke the trade common language, but she'd somehow expected something...different. He was right, however. There was no way she could know...

Her eyes went wide as knowledge tightened her chest. "You were at the ship," she whispered. "You killed them all."

• • •

"We delivered justice," Aidan corrected. He was grateful to Rachel for what she'd done in getting him off that ship, but he would not apologize for defending his people and his planet.

She shook her head. "You used those cats. They could have been killed, and you—"

He made a scoffing noise. "Those cats are more dangerous than any human, lass. Believe me. They were never at risk."

"But why risk them at all?"

"Because it was a cat those bastards tried to capture. Justice was theirs."

She shook her head. "There are laws against what that ship's crew did, and the fleet is responsible for Harp. They should have been turned over to—"

He interrupted her with a bark of laughter. "*Harpers* are responsible for Harp. Your fleet has no authority here. That ship was on *our* planet, killing and imprisoning *our* animals, and destroying *our* forests. It was our right to determine punishment, *our* laws, not your beloved fleet's. For all we know, the damn *fleet* was the one buying the cat they captured."

She had the grace to look uncomfortable at that. If she had any knowledge of United Earth Fleet at all, she had to know that it was a strong possibility they'd financed the hunt. She finally met his eyes, seeming more sad than angry. "But… did they have to die? I don't question your jurisdiction," she hurried to add, "and what they did, what they *planned* to do, was monstrous and unforgiveable, but—"

"There's no 'but,'" he said with a gentleness he wasn't feeling. He wanted to shout at her, to tell her that *he* was the cat they'd kidnapped, that they'd known what he was and had still intended to cage him, to force-breed him for their experiments. But he bit back the words, not willing to trust her with that much truth. "We have families living in the Green," he said instead. "Our children play here. Do you think your friends worried about them? Do you know easily someone could have been hurt with all that wild gunfire?"

She paled. "Please tell me no one was killed," she whispered.

"No *people*," he clarified. "But the Green is filled with living things, all of which are necessary to this ecosystem which, in turn, supports our continued survival. Though I doubt your friends knew or cared about that when they began their destructive campaign."

She sighed deeply, then seemed to gather her courage. "So if there was someone on Harp who'd helped the ship evade detection, and who'd known what they were going to do, you'd—"

Aidan went predator still. Fighting back a growl, he asked, "We have a traitor? Is that what you're telling me?"

"No," she insisted, biting her lip in obvious distress. "Well..." She stared at him in indecision, then sighed and said, "Yes. I think so. That's what I'm trying to find out. But if there was somebody...I mean, you must have laws. He'd go on trial. Your president—"

"Ardrigh."

"Right, your Ardrigh," she repeated, carefully pronouncing the unfamiliar word. *Ard-ree.*

"There are laws," he agreed, then gave her a smug smile. "But you're in clan territory now. The Ardrigh has no authority here."

"Clan territory? What does that mean?"

"It means the best fighters and fiercest hunters on the planet all hail from the mountain clans, and the Ardrigh is smart enough to reward our loyalty by not interfering in our affairs. It means anyone invading clan territory with an eye toward harming the forests or anyone living there, human or otherwise, will be judged by the clans, not the city."

She stared at him unhappily. "The person responsible

is more dangerous than you know. If I'm right, he's risked everything for this. He won't hesitate to kill you, and he won't care how much damage he does to Harp."

"Let us worry about that. Where is he?"

Her expression shut down. "I'll tell you. But I'm going with you."

Aidan pushed away from the tree to stare at her. "I don't think so. Time is of the essence, and you'll slow me down."

She actually appeared to be offended at that. "Well, then, I guess you'll be figuring out who he is on your own." She turned away and hefted that big pack onto her back. "Nice meeting you. Not that I did."

She would have left then, but he stopped her with a hand on her arm. She looked from his hand to his face, giving him a challenging stare, as if ready to take him on for daring to touch her. He was amused at the prospect. No question she was tough and capable. She'd taken on a pongo and survived. Sure, the animal had been a young female, but it was still impressive. But he was no mindless pongo, for fuck's sake. He was a *shifter*. She wouldn't stand a chance against him. Of course, she didn't know that. Hell, even if he'd been nothing but an ordinary human male, he still outweighed her by a good hundred pounds of mostly muscle.

"You can't stay out here alone," he said.

· · ·

Rachel gave the hand on her arm a cool look. He'd said that last as if the subject were closed. As if he'd decided, and she would obey.

Not likely. Her back stiffened, and she looked up to meet his assessing gaze. "I'll be fine," she informed him. "I have maps, I'm armed, and I have years of experience in the wild."

"Not Harp's wild, you don't. You won't last a day."

"Thanks for the vote of confidence," she said dryly, "but I've survived worse." She gave the dead animal a meaningful glance, and when he opened his mouth to argue some more, she cut him off.

"Look, the man who hired me for this mission, your traitor, has put more than *his* reputation on the line. He's put mine right there beside him. Not to mention my fucking *life*. He owes me some answers. Hell, he owes this planet more than that. I'm going to find him and demand an explanation, no matter what it takes."

"You're sure he's on Harp," the blond said, his tone calculating.

"Yes, probably in your city," she said, deliberately not mentioning the second landing site. She didn't want this guy and his people looking for that ship. It wouldn't be as simple this time. Not even the most vicious pack of giant cats would be enough. Her crew had been wounded and unprepared. If Wolfrum somehow found out the first ship had been discovered and its crew destroyed… If, for example, this hunter's clan had sent word to the Ardrigh about it… Clearly Wolfrum had connections enough to get the two ships on-planet in the first place. What if he had a spy in the Ardrigh's circle? If the second ship was armed as heavily as hers had been, they could wipe out an army of local clansmen in a matter of minutes. They wouldn't give a damn how much damage their weapons did to the Green or to Harp. Their only concern would be escape.

Rachel would have liked a companion for the journey. Particularly *this* one. It wasn't his looks, or not simply his looks, though they were fine enough. But there was something different about him that intrigued her, something more than a little bit wild that called to the adventurous part of her soul. The way his eyes glinted gold in the firelight as they studied her, following her smallest move just as a predator would.

The confidence in his big, muscled body, the grace in his every move. It made no sense, and yet, more than anything, he reminded her of the big cat who'd so captivated her that she'd been willing to risk everything to set him free.

Unfortunately, he *also* refused to see reason, despite the evidence of her abilities now stinking up the small clearing. But her mind was made up. Her ship and crew were gone, which left her only one option if she wanted the truth—find Wolfrum and demand answers, or failing that, contact the local fleet authorities. They couldn't *all* be corrupt. "I have maps. I'll be fine," she said again.

He eyed her unhappily, clearly trying to decide what to do with her, not seeming to understand that she didn't need him to do *anything*. She'd take care of herself, thank you very much. She *was* worried about the cat, though. "The cat they captured was tranquilized heavily," she said. "There might be some lingering effects, and I don't want him to get hurt because he can't defend himself or move about properly."

"The cat's fine, lass. Fully recovered and then some. He led the pack that tore that ship apart."

"I wondered. I'm glad he's recovered." She swung the backpack around and slipped her other arm into the strap. "Well, I imagine the scavengers will be homing in on this carcass soon," she said, reminding him about the dead creature, which shouldn't have *needed* any reminder. With Harp's jungle-like climate, the stench was quickly attaining unbelievable heights. "So I'm going to get going."

• • •

Aidan had no intention of letting her walk away, but he liked her spirit. "Fine, then. You lead, I'll follow. But I need to know where we're going, and what guidance you're using to get us there. This is the Green. There are no maps that give the whole truth about its dangers."

She regarded him for a long moment, as if deciding whether he could be trusted, then shrugged—not as if she'd decided, but as if she had no other choice. It was vaguely insulting and made him wonder if *she* could be trusted. What was on her precious map that she didn't want him to see? It had to be more than directions to the city, because he didn't need a fucking map to find that. Even she must understand that much. And he sure as hell didn't need some Earther woman judging his honor when he'd spent most of his life—"

"All right," she said, interrupting his private soliloquy. "I'll show you what I have, but I suspect you're right about its usefulness. It doesn't have enough detail to provide an accurate topography."

"An accurate topography," he repeated, grinning. "We're going to work great together. I can tell." He laughed at the squinty-eyed glare she gave him.

"Can we at least move away from *that* first? Unless you'd like to eat it for dinner?" she added sweetly.

He winked. "No thanks. And you're right. The scavengers are already gathering." He could hear them in the treetops and underbrush, circling. He didn't tell her that it was only *his* presence keeping them at bay. "We should head out that way," he gestured. "I'll take the lead. If it's all right with you, that is."

She rolled her eyes but turned to follow him. "I don't think we're going to work that well together at all," she muttered, no doubt thinking he couldn't hear. But he did and it made him grin. Because he had a feeling they were going to get along very well, indeed.

・・・

Rachel followed him through the nighttime forest, impressed

by the ease with which he maneuvered between trees and around obstacles as if he could see in the dark. She had her little flashlight, which she'd offered to him. His words had been polite enough, though his expression had been more amusement than gratitude.

"You keep it. I'm accustomed to the dark," he said, then turned and kept going.

Rachel swallowed her sigh. She was tired, though she'd never admit it to— She frowned. What was his name? "I'm Rachel, by the way," she said, aiming for a friendly tone.

"Aidan."

That's all he said. Just his name. He might be one hell of a good-looking man and move like a giant jungle creature, but he wasn't a great conversationalist.

"Can I ask you something?" he asked.

She was so surprised by his question that she stumbled. "Sure," she said, glad that his back was to her so he couldn't see.

He stopped and turned. "You okay?"

So much for him not seeing her tripping on her own feet. "Yeah, there's just a lot of—"

"The ground's especially uneven around here," he offered unexpectedly. No joke at her expense, not even another smug look of amusement. "And the dark doesn't help, I know. We'll travel mostly in daylight after this. But I wanted to get away from the carcass before the scavengers became impatient." He tilted his head, studying her for a moment. "Why'd you help the cat?"

Rachel blinked at the abrupt change of topic, and then asked in surprise, "How do you know I—?"

"The cats are important to us. We keep track. So, why help him?"

She looked up at him, meeting eyes that definitely weren't human norm. The pupil appeared to have changed shape as they'd moved farther into the darkness under the trees, adapting to the absence of light. It was certainly a possible evolution on a planet with minimal technology. And it would explain the ease with which he traversed the cluttered ground of the Green.

"I didn't come here to capture a trophy animal for some collector back on Earth, or to give the fleet something new to torment. I mean, yes," she amended at his doubtful look, "I was on that ship, but their mission was never mine. I was told this was for research. That we had the Ardrigh's permission to *study*, not capture, the cats. I'm a scientist, not a murderer." She looked away, then continued more subdued. "When I saw what they did, what they meant to do..." She shrugged. "I didn't sign up for that. There was no question in my mind that I had to get him out of there."

"And we're grateful you did. Like I said, the cats are important to us."

"And you're sure my cat's okay?"

He grinned crookedly. "*Your* cat?"

Rachel blushed, hoping his night vision wasn't good enough to see. "I was worried about him when he didn't come back. And then I saw the attack..."

"How *did* you see the attack?" he asked, as if it had just occurred to him. "There was no one around; I'd have known."

"There must be limits to what even *you* can do," she said, teasing him dryly. "I was roughly three-hundred yards away in a tree, using binoculars, obviously."

"Obviously. You climbed a tree?" he asked, his tone skeptical, as if that was the most unbelievable part of her explanation.

She gave him a flat look. "Yes, Aidan, I climbed a tree."

His teeth flashed in another grin, which was somehow just as charming as it was irritating.

"Your cat's fine," he said. "All the cats are fine. There

were some minor injuries in the raid, but they heal quickly."

"Oh. Well, good."

He reached out and cupped her cheek, shocking her into stillness. His hand was more than warm. It was like a brand against her skin, reminding her of something she couldn't quite place. The scientist in her registered the heat and what it might mean for his metabolism—for healing and longevity. But the woman…she caught herself rubbing her cheek against the calloused palm. She looked up and met the odd glow of his eyes. Without thinking, she took a half step closer as Aidan tipped his head down and—

She froze as loud yipping and whining erupted from behind them, like the Earth hyenas she'd seen on video, but somehow creepier. Maybe because this time she was in a dark forest along *with* them. But for all that, she was grateful for the distraction. Had she been about to kiss Aidan? Had *he* been about to kiss *her*? She swallowed, desire sliding down her throat like a hard apple.

"I'm guessing those are some of those scavengers you mentioned," she said, refusing to look at him as she needlessly adjusted the straps on her pack. "How much farther do you think we'll go tonight?"

His broad fingers brushed over her bowed head to tug on her braid, which had to be a wreck by now, what with all the climbing trees and fighting off vicious beasts. Her head came up, and she fought the urge to run a smoothing hand over it.

"Not much farther," he said. "About half a mile's walk, and we'll rest for the night."

"And in the morning?"

"We'll take a look at that map of yours. Let's hope it's good enough to give us a trail."

Chapter Eight

When Rachel woke the next morning, she was alone, nestled in the roots of one of Harp's giant trees. The ground was soft and still warm, and she remembered curling up next to Aidan during the night. He hadn't made it sexual, just two people sharing warmth on a cool night. But Rachel couldn't shake the memory of their almost kiss, and how good it had felt to be wrapped in those strong arms. For the first time since she'd discovered that Wolfrum had lied to her about everything to do with this mission, she'd slept without dreams, without waking at every small sound.

She stood abruptly, wanting to derail that line of thinking. Aidan wasn't her protector, no matter how good it felt to be around him. And he sure as hell wasn't someone she should be having romantic thoughts about. His interest in her had solely to do with what she knew about the second ship. And for her, he was simply a local guide, someone who knew the Green far better than she did and could get her where she needed to be—faster and *alive*.

She looked around, wondering where he'd gone but not

worried if he'd be back. He needed her more than she needed him. Sure, the journey to find Wolfrum would go smoother if he was with her, but she could get there on her own if she had to.

Looking for somewhere private for her morning necessities, she started away from the tree where they'd spent the night, but she hadn't gone more than a few feet before she encountered a strong scent in the air. Not bad, but not exactly good, either. She sniffed again, then walked the same distance in the other direction and found the same smell. She grinned, knowing what it was. Some animal had marked its territory all around the tree and *her,* warning other predators away. She scanned the surrounding trees looking for her golden cat. She didn't find him, but that didn't mean he wasn't there. These trees were his home, and he'd already proven he could hide in plain sight. On the other hand, the forest was remarkably still and quiet, and she wondered if the silence had to do with the cat's nearby presence. A sudden, deep-throated rumble from somewhere in the distance brought her head up, reminding her that there were a lot more predators roaming the Green than just her cat, and they weren't all likely to be as friendly.

Still needing to find a place to pee, she crossed the invisible scent line and went looking for a handy tree. It reminded her that most animals used urine for scent marking. Ick. She smelled herself discreetly but couldn't tell if she smelled any better than the cat pee. She wasn't exactly daisy fresh after the last few days of travel.

Marching thirty or so yards into the trees, paying close attention to where she was going and where she'd come from, she took care of her needs as quickly as possible, then hurried back to where Aidan had left her. She'd just freshened her hands and face with a cleansing wipe from her pack and pulled out her map, when a rush of noise had her jumping to her feet to scour the surrounding forest. The trees were so thick, and the underbrush so dense, that she couldn't see much. She looked up again and saw the branches swaying as if a wind had come up in the treetops. Or as if something was using the movement as camouflage and didn't want her to see it coming.

"Stop that, Rachel," she muttered, reining in her too vivid imagination.

"Stop what?" a deep, masculine voice asked.

She tried to conceal her jump of surprise, but from the look of amusement on Aidan's handsome face, she didn't succeed. Next time, she'd just pull her knife and throw it at him. She was damn good with her blade. And wouldn't he be surprised? She fingered the knife now as she turned to face him. Being alive and female, she couldn't help noticing that he looked way too good for someone who'd slept on the ground. Even in the dark last night, she'd been able to tell he was handsome, but with morning light filtering through the trees, she saw what a truly gorgeous male specimen he really was. The sunlight caressed the planes of his face, bringing out the almost white-blond highlights in his hair, and he was every bit as big and fit as she'd thought, with sparkling blue eyes that belied their golden gleam in the firelight and a grin that promised all sorts of wicked pleasures. She sighed.

"Talking to myself. Comes from too much time spent alone," she said, managing to keep her voice cool and unflustered.

He gave her a sample of his killer grin then tossed something in her direction. She caught it automatically. It was purple, roughly oval, and appeared to be fruit. "I'm guessing this is edible?"

"After all we've been through, you think I'd try to poison you?" He put on a hurt expression, which didn't fool her for a minute. The sparkling humor in his eyes gave it away. She liked that about him, though she'd never tell him, since his ego didn't need the stroking. But though he did what needed to be done and was, no doubt, a fierce defender of his people, he seemed more likely to laugh than to argue. She was drawn to people like that, men especially, because she was the opposite—compulsively detail-oriented and a little too serious most of the time. She attributed some of that to her job. Her clients put their lives in her hands, after all.

She frowned, reminded abruptly of her dead crew and the role Aidan had played in their deaths. She hadn't been leading their mission, hadn't been hired to keep everyone safe, but they'd all been part of the same crew. In space, you survived by sticking together.

"If I'd been on that ship when the cats attacked," she asked without warning, "would I be dead?"

He tilted his head curiously, seeming puzzled by the abrupt subject change. "No," he said after a few seconds. "The cats would have known your scent."

"All of them? Or just the one who—"

"All of them. They…communicate. You're some kind of biologist, right? You took care of the cat when it was injured. You must know about pack hunting behavior, and how predators instinctively know what each member will do. It's something like that."

"And the rest of my crew?"

He shrugged. "They were all part of the hunt that shot up the Green and killed any number of forest dwellers, before drugging and capturing the cat. They act on instinct, Rachel. And, in one way, every life on Harp is part of their pack. You threaten one, you threaten them all."

She nodded slowly. "They weren't all bad people, but they were willing to kill for money. And I'm no innocent. I know what would have happened if they'd succeeded in taking my cat back to whoever hired them. I've seen what the fleet and Earth corporations can do to an unspoiled planet." She exhaled a long, deep breath. "I can't blame your people for defending your home. I just wish it had turned out differently."

Aidan studied her for a long moment, his blue eyes coolly serious. Then he gestured at the fruit she'd forgotten she was holding and said, "You'll want to peel that first. The skin's edible, too, but it has a bitter aftertaste."

He walked into the trees a short way, back turned as he crouched down to gather his few things.

Rachel watched him go, then took out her small pocket knife and quickly peeled the fruit, making a small pile of the skin and covering it with detritus from the forest floor, before walking over to offer him a piece of the fruit. It felt like a peace offering, and maybe it was. Because she'd meant what she said. None of the crew had been friends, but she mourned their deaths. She would have fought side by side with them against an enemy. But not when it came to the ruthless destruction of a planet, and not if the job was murder for hire.

Aiden look up, his expression registering surprise at the offering. His smile was slight, but pleasure was in his voice when he said, "You're much neater than I would have been."

"It's a curse," she said, only half joking, then tasted the fruit cautiously. It was sweet but still refreshing, with the consistency of a peach from back home. She split the remaining pieces between her and Aidan, which continued to amuse him, though he winked his thanks and ate his share. She could have eaten more, but she didn't know if there *was* more. He'd only brought one piece, and besides, strange fruit could sometimes wreak havoc on an unprepared intestinal tract. She pulled out an energy bar instead. She'd never had dinner last night—her plans being interrupted by the apelike creature and then Aidan's arrival—and she was hungry. She offered Aidan a bar, too, but he declined.

"I don't know how you eat those things," he commented. "At least the ones we make have some moisture to them."

Rachel tilted her head curiously. "You make energy bars?"

"We call them trail bars but, yeah. There's a lot more fruit and honey in ours."

"That's because they don't have to last as long. These are guaranteed fresh for five years."

He made a face.

"Nobody actually likes them," she admitted. "They're meant to be nutritional, not tasty."

He laughed. "Well, when you've finished your nutrition, maybe we can look at the map. I'd like to take as much advantage of the day as possible. We can travel at night if we have to, but it'll be harder on you."

"Why not you?"

He pointed at his eyes. "I see better at night. Evolutionary adaptation."

Rachel stepped closer, intrigued by this confirmation of her observation about his eyes. "Does everyone on Harp have the same ability?"

"No. Only some of us."

She became aware of two things. One, the reluctance in his voice told her he didn't want to unravel that particular thread of conversation. Societal exclusion, maybe? The question was whether the eyes were considered a good thing or a bad thing? If he was unwilling to talk about it, however, there was no point in pushing. At least not until she got to know him better. Or until she found someone else who was willing to talk. Which brought her to the second thing.

Her curiosity about his eyes had left her standing far too close to him. He put a hand on her hip to stabilize her. She blinked in surprise at the unexpected touch, abruptly focusing on *him* instead of his retinas.

"Sorry," she murmured.

"No need," he said smoothly, and there was a trace of heat in his expression.

Her heart stuttered, but she covered up her own reaction, pulling out the used cleansing wipe that she'd balled up and shoved into her backpack and wiping fruit juice off her face and fingers. Shoving the now twice-used wipe back into her pack, she opened a different zipper pocket and retrieved her map. Unfolding it, she crouched on the ground and then looked up, inviting him to join her.

"This is an orbital map, which partly explains the bad quality. It wasn't intended to be used for ground navigation. The rest of the problem is all of this." She circled her finger, indicating the Green. "It puts out so much heat that, combined with that weird magnetic field of yours, it fucks with the instruments. I'm sure the fleet has more detailed scans, but since I'm also sure this mission wasn't authorized, they had to make do." She made a dismissive gesture.

Aidan hunched next to her, and she was exquisitely aware of how close they were. She could smell the fresh male scent of him, could feel the heat coming off his body. It seemed more than usual. "Usual" meaning the other men she'd been around, mostly the ones she'd worked with in some capacity. She'd had lovers, but nothing serious, and not for a long time, even before she'd joined Wolfrum's ill-fated mission. And certainly not since. She had a general policy against shipboard romances, though she'd never been close enough to any of Wolfrum's crew for it to matter.

Aidan studied the map, giving it a quarter turn, Rachel assumed to line it up with their current position. "You see that?" he asked softly.

Rachel gave him a sharp look. "What?"

His gaze was still on the map, but he didn't seem to be

studying it, his thoughts elsewhere. He finally stood up, paced a few feet away from her and then back, standing with both hands on his narrow hips as if trying to decide what to tell her.

She stood up to meet him. "Is the map inaccurate or—?"

"No, no. The map's fine. It's what it shows" He shook his head. "Or more likely what it doesn't."

"You're not making any sense. Just tell me."

He crouched again, pulling her with him and taking the map from her unresisting hand. "You see this?" He pointed to what looked like a particularly dense band of trees that formed a dark stripe across nearly the entire width of the Green not far from where Rachel figured they were now.

She nodded. "And there's the city." She pointed at the obvious heat signature of Harp's main population center, ignoring the tiny indicator for the second ship. Both were on the other side of the band from their current location, which seemed to be his concern. "Is that a problem?"

He snorted a laugh. "Yeah, sweetheart, that's a problem."

She turned her head and gave him a narrow-eyed glare.

He shook his head impatiently. "Okay, look, I understand your confusion. You look at this lousy map and see a bunch of trees."

"The entire Green is a bunch of trees," she snapped. "What I see there is an area of exceptional density compared to the rest of it."

"And you'd be wrong. You have something I can write with?"

Rachel produced a pencil from another pocket. Pencils were simpler and much more reliable than almost any other option.

Aidan took it without comment and began making notes. "This is us," he said, marking the map with the usual X. "This is the city." Another X, just where the ship's survey indicated it was. "But that's where your map goes wrong. Your river's all fucked up. I'm guessing your instruments are having trouble distinguishing above and below ground water, but that's not our problem. *Our* problem is right here." He made several slashing marks in that dark line of trees.

"What's that?" she asked, leaning over to study it.

"That, sweetheart, is the swamp."

Rachel ignored her gut reflex to the "sweetheart" part of his declaration and focused on the rest of it. "The swamp?" she repeated, puzzled. "There's no swamp on Harp. The geography, the climate…hell, the orbital tilt doesn't support it. You can't—" She stopped, aware he was giving her the kind of patient look one did a crazy person who was ranting nonsense. She blew out a breath. Okay, so he obviously knew more about Harp than she did. "Never mind," she said. "Please continue."

He studied her a moment longer, then said, "We do have a swamp, but maybe not the kind you're used to. Ours is a microclimate created by a deep rift that runs north/south, right where you see it there. There's no river flow, no lake, so it's not your usual freshwater swamp, but it acts like one. Rain, and some snow at the northern end, drains down from the ridges, and seeps in from ground water. Since there's no outlet, it accumulates in the deepest part of the rift and it just sits there, stewing in the heat. It's only about a mile wide as the crow flies, but neither one of us is a crow. It can take days, or even weeks, to cross. You have to go down one side, transit the swamp itself, and then up the other side. And that's just surface stuff. There are things living down there that are deadly, even by Harp standards."

Rachel scowled at the map, blaming herself for not having a better one. Sure, she hadn't planned on hiking through the Green on her own for days, or maybe even weeks. She hadn't planned on hiking anywhere that didn't involve returning to the ship at night. But she knew better than to assume the best possible conditions would prevail when visiting an unknown planet like Harp. Of course, part of her optimistic planning had been based on Wolfrum's involvement and his assurance that Harp's government had given permission for their journey. Of all the things that she might have foreseen going wrong on this trip, Wolfrum's complete betrayal of his life's work would have been the very last.

"We'll have to go around," Aidan said in disgust. "It'll take three times as long, but there's no way you'll make it—"

"No way I'll make *what*?" she demanded. "Look, buddy, I've trekked through some of the most dangerous environments in the universe. Hell, I've *guided* treks through those places. I think I can handle this one."

"No, you can't," he said bluntly. "You people never learn. Harp is unique. That's a lesson *your* fleet had to learn to *our* peril. You must have read the First Con—"

"Yes, I read Harp's First Contact report and every report filed since then. I know about the explosion, and I know your planet is deadly, but I have far more experience—"

"Those reports are limited to the parts closest to the city. They cover the smallest fraction of the Green and its dangers," he insisted, almost angrily. "You're well beyond what they deal with, and I'm telling you that you are *not* prepared."

Rachel gritted her jaw. Arrogant asshole. "I appreciate the advice," she ground out, not bothering to remind him that he hadn't actually *given* her any advice, just dire warnings. She already *knew* the facts of her predicament. She was in the middle of a wild and deadly forest that covered a full third of a planet where none of her usual navigating tech would work, where she wasn't familiar enough with the night skies to navigate by the stars—assuming she could even *see* the stars through the heavy canopy cover—and where her only weapons were a knife and crossbow. "Unfortunately, I don't have a choice. I have to get to the city."

He studied her. "I get that. But you have to listen to—"

They both turned as a wild yowl broke the morning quiet, followed by a deep, hollow thumping noise. Aidan didn't hesitate, didn't say a word. He turned to the nearest tree and, with a grace and speed Rachel had never seen in a human before, scaled the trunk so quickly that he was high among the branches only seconds after she'd registered he'd moved.

Wanting to know what was going on, she turned to the huge tree behind her, prepared to do her own climbing, but Aidan stopped her. "Don't," he whispered, his voice drifting down. Not a suggestion, but a command. Rachel narrowed her eyes, but she obeyed because he knew the Green and she didn't. She could think of ten reasons off the top of her head why she shouldn't climb, from poison to animal nests to bad guys lying in wait. She eased over to Aidan's tree and stared up into the branches, trying to find him. He had to be there, but she couldn't see any sign of him. It was as if he'd literally disappeared.

A moment later, she caught a flash of movement from the corner of her eye. She pulled her knife and spun around, only to find Aidan jumping down from a different tree, off a branch that was at least twelve feet from the ground. He landed in a graceful crouch and was immediately on his feet. Grabbing her pack, he crossed to her in three long strides and said, "We have to go."

"What? Wait." She caught the pack he threw at her and slung it over her back, settling it on her hips and fastening straps while hurrying to follow him. "Where are we going?" she demanded.

He stopped and grabbed the shoulder strap on her pack, yanking her close. "The female pongo you killed last night had a mate. He's just discovered the body, but it won't be long before he picks up our trail."

"But the one I killed was too big to be... I'd swear—"

"Don't swear, sweetheart. This is Harp. A mature female pongo is the size of a full-grown man and weighs over two-hundred pounds. A male is bigger than I am—easily three-hundred pounds and well over six feet tall on his hind legs. That thumping noise you heard was him pounding his chest in a dominance display. When we go after one that big, we do it in a pack of at least five hunters, usually more. As good as I am—and I'm a damned good hunter—I won't take him on by myself, especially not with your life in the mix. I've muddied our trail enough to slow him down, but it won't stop him."

Fuck." She frowned. "Maybe we should take a stand. Together we—"

"Stop arguing and start walking." He started off ahead of her.

"You don't have to be a dick about it," she grumbled, hurrying after him.

His soft laugh drifted back to her. "Sometimes it takes a dick to get the job done."

• • •

They'd been traveling fast and steady for a long time—Rachel could only guess at how long it had been. She hadn't thought to include a mechanical watch in her gear. But she could tell from the sun's progress through the deep tree cover, and even more by the strain on her body. She'd hydrated on the run, sharing the water in her canteen with Aidan, but her legs were beginning to tire, and she was feeling the absence of real food. The pongo she'd managed to kill had interrupted her plans to eat one of her MRE rations, and even before that, she'd been running on empty.

Aidan, of course, seemed completely unaffected by

anything so pedestrian as hunger or exhaustion. He'd set a steady pace and hadn't said a word since.

Finally, she simply had to stop. "Aidan."

He turned at once, going preternaturally still as he studied first her and then the forest all around her. "What?" he said finally, sounding puzzled.

"I need a break. Just long enough to eat something, okay?" she added immediately.

He looked like he wanted to protest, but then his mouth closed and he gave her a sharp nod. "We're nearly at the downslope for the swamp. I'll scout ahead. Try to stay alive until I get back." And just like that, he was gone.

Rachel didn't waste time glaring at his departing back. Figuring her time was limited, she studied the ground carefully, then stomped a small area with her boots just to be sure no beasties were waiting to bite her on the butt. Unfastening her backpack, she dropped it to the ground with a stifled groan then sat down next to it. Normally, she'd have taken a lot more precautions, but she figured Aidan would have warned her if there was something specific to be worried about. He might be surly, but he seemed to want her alive if for no other reason than for her knowledge of Wolfrum's scheme. Fucking Guy Wolfr—

She opened her pack, intending to gulp down an energy bar, but her hand froze mid-reach at the soft scratch of claws on bark. Hoping this might be *her* cat, she lifted only her eyes first—so as not to spook it—and then tipped her head back slowly. A giant pale-furred cat was crouched right above her, his eyes fixed on hers, unblinking and unmoving.

"Hey," she said softly. "Is that you, big guy?"

The cat's head tilted to study her curiously, and she could have sworn she saw a glint of humor in those golden eyes. But that was just her doing what she always warned her clients against, attributing human characteristics where they didn't belong.

"I guess you're all recovered, huh?" she said, still speaking softly. "I'm so glad."

The cat yawned abruptly, his mouth going wide to display an impressive set of teeth.

Rachel laughed. "Yes, you're very scary. And handsome, too."

The cat's mouth closed with an audible snap, his eyes narrowing as he studied her. Apparently, he had no sense of humor. Without warning, he stood and leaped to a higher branch, and from there to the next, and kept going. Rachel rose to lean in against the tree trunk, following his progress as far as she could before he disappeared into the forest's thick canopy. She sighed and went back to digging in her pack. She still needed to eat something before Aidan got back. She was on her second energy bar when he appeared just as silently as the cat had, dropping from branch to branch with speed and agility that shouldn't have surprised her.

He lived in this forest. It made sense that his people would have learned how to move through it quickly. There might even be some physical changes to make it possible. It was impressive—and beautiful, in its own way. *Aidan* was certainly beautiful. Watching him drop from branch to branch, the interplay of muscle and bone, the sheen of sweat on golden skin—

Her thoughts screeched to a halt. Where were his clothes?

"Everything all right?" he asked, studying her curiously as he tugged some pants from a drawstring bag around his neck that hadn't been there before, pulled them on, and then yanked a similarly made tunic over his head.

She didn't want to ask but she had to. "What happened to your clothes?"

"Ran into a Venus Vitis—a toxic vine that only grows near the swamp. It's a sure sign we're nearly there. They're clingy as hell and burn twice as badly. The only way to get rid of the spores is to strip down and start over."

"Where'd you get the fresh set?"

"Oh, we maintain emergency caches of food, clothes, and a few other supplies throughout the Green."

"Who's we? That other man who was with you when the cats attacked the ship?"

"Clansmen. And yeah, he's one of us." He produced a pair of soft boots from the same bag and put them on, too. The bag he folded into a small square, then reached out and, without asking, unzipped the side pocket on her backpack and tucked it inside, neatly zipping the pocket back up. He caught her watching. "Problem?"

"No," she said and quickly reached for her canteen, wishing she could pour it on her face to cool the heated reaction to seeing Aidan naked. She took a long drink, instead, then lowered it and said, "The cat visited me."

"Which cat?"

"My cat. The one I rescued from the ship."

He tilted his head, and his blue eyes crinkled in amusement. She hadn't noticed before, but he had gold flecks in his eyes that glinted in the scattered sunlight. She wondered if that accounted for what she'd thought was a retinal abnormality the other night. Moonlight on those gold flecks. Except there hadn't been any moonlight.

"You sure it was the same cat?" he asked. "We've got quite a few of them in the Green."

Rachel shook her head. "No, this was *my* cat. He knew me. In fact, I'm fairly sure you chased him away when you came back."

His humor seemed to grow. "What makes you think that?"

"Well, he and I were having a nice chat, then suddenly he ran off without warning, and you showed up. You do the math."

"Maybe your math doesn't work on Harp. Nothing else does."

"Math is math," she said confidently. "It's a universal constant." She began rearranging the few things she'd pulled from her backpack, then handed him the map and said, "Would you like an energy bar? I have more than enough."

"No, thanks. Is that all you're going to eat the entire trip?"

"I sure as hell hope not. But they're good on the run, like when people, and wild animals, are trying to kill you," she added dryly.

"No one's going to kill either one of us," he said darkly. He was quiet for a moment, then spoke slowly, as if thinking about his words. "Going around the swamp isn't an option anymore. That pongo won't give up. Our best chance is to head directly down. He won't follow us there, which should tell you just how dangerous the swamp dwellers are."

"You'll get no argument from me. I never wanted to go around anyway. It adds too much time to the trip, and I need to reach the city."

He gave her a narrow-eyed look. "It won't be easy or fast. We'll have to go down one side, traverse the depths, then climb back out the other side, which is a lot harder than it sounds. It's hot and humid, it stinks to high heaven, and it breeds deadly creatures that live nowhere else on the planet."

She tilted her head back against the tree, staring up through the canopy and thinking. "Have you ever tried going up instead of down?"

She'd half expected him to laugh, but he didn't. "You mean take to the trees?"

She nodded. "I don't know about Harp, but I've visited other rainforests where certain animal species never touch the ground until they die. The canopy here seems fairly dense, and several of your tree varieties are way sturdier than the typical rainforest. Their branches must—"

"You ever climb a tree before, Rachel?" he interrupted to ask. "Not the one in your childhood yard. I'm talking about a monster of a tree that soars hundreds of feet into the air."

"As a matter of fact, I have," she said mildly. Did he think Harp was the only planet in the universe that had giant-size trees? She was *so* going to enjoy shoving that superior attitude of his right back in his face. But for now, she had to stay on track. "Are you saying you haven't?" she asked in the same unruffled tone, mostly to irritate him. Because she'd seen him move through the trees, so *obviously* he could climb.

He laughed, which she hadn't expected. "I've climbed a tree or two," he said smugly. "But here's the problem. All those animals you're talking about who live in the trees and use the tree road to get around? They have four legs. Sometimes with four sets of digits and four opposable thumbs, with claws all around. And they almost always have a prehensile tail. You have any of those?"

"No," she said quietly, then flashed him a challenging look. "Do you?"

He gave her a funny look, holding her gaze for a beat too long before looking back at the map. "We'll take on the downslope today, but just enough to dissuade our furry friend. We'll stop early after that. I don't want to go any farther than we have to after sundown. It's dark enough in there. We don't need to add to it. Tomorrow morning, we'll hit the serious downslope. It's going to be rough going," he said, folding the map and handing it back to her. "I hope you're as good as you say you are."

Rachel was readying a snappy comeback as she put away the map, when the trees above them were suddenly filled with a wave of screeching monkey-like creatures. She knew what that meant. Instantly alert, she glanced at Aidan for a decision. This was his world, his monkeys.

"Let's move," he said, grabbing her hand and pulling her to her feet. "You go ahead, a straight line on this heading. I'll hang back—"

"Hell, no," she snapped. "We both go, or we both stay and fight."

For a moment, she thought his temper was going to blow. He was clearly accustomed to being obeyed. But for all that she accepted his greater experience with this planet, she had her own experience with surviving as *a team*. And she was tired of being treated like some silly woman he needed to protect. Fuck that. He'd told her no one was dying on this trip, and she was going to do her part to make sure that was true.

Aidan glared at her, and she could almost hear the argument going on his head. He finally made the smart decision, but she could tell what it cost him. "Fine," he growled. "Run. I'll be right behind you."

She hesitated only a moment, not trusting his word. But, in the final analysis, she had no choice. It wasn't as if she could knock him over the head and carry him on her shoulders. She was strong, but not that strong. She might have laughed at the image that conjured if she hadn't already turned to run.

· · ·

Aidan let Rachel get a few strides ahead, enough that if the pongo caught up to them, he'd be the creature's only target. He'd lied when he told her he'd never taken down a big pongo on his own. He had, of course. Most of the patrols he did in and around Clanhome were solitary. When he encountered a threat, he didn't have time to race home, gather a hunting party, and race back. He was Rhodry's second in the clans, a seasoned member of the shifters' Guild, and one of the best hunters on Harp. When he encountered a threat, he dealt with it.

But he didn't bring fragile females with him on patrol. Especially not an Earther female with lickable golden skin and black curls that tumbled like a shining wave over her shoulders. He didn't doubt she could be fierce. Her stubbornness alone would drive most men mad. And her courage was unquestionable. She'd risked everything to free him from that damn cage. But the only ones equipped to do battle with Harp's predators were its bigger predators. And when it came to pongos, that meant shifters.

He would survive a confrontation with a pongo, but he didn't know if Rachel would. Pongos were smart enough to recognize the weakest member of their prey and take advantage. The creature wouldn't attack Aidan. It would go after Rachel and possibly hurt her badly before Aidan managed to force it to deal with him instead. And he wasn't willing to take that risk.

Rachel glanced over her shoulder, scowling when she saw he'd dropped back, slowing her own pace, until he caught up. *Fine, then,* he thought. She'd simply have to go faster. "Pick up the pace, sweetheart. I'm rather fond of my ass."

She did something unexpected then. She laughed and started running faster.

Aidan lost a piece of his heart at that moment. He'd been with many women in his life. Harp had few sexual restrictions, and shifters were always sought after as lovers. He'd also been blessed with an abundant charm that women seemed to enjoy, unlike Rhodry who leaned more toward a gloomy disposition. It was amazing, really, that his cousin had managed to persuade a beautiful and strong woman like Amanda to marry him. He chuckled to himself because, as unlikely as it might seem, what with Amanda being an Earther, those two had been made for each other.

But despite Aidan's vast experience and charm, he'd never trekked the Green with *any* woman, much less one who wore her courage as boldly as her weapons. Rachel hadn't been afraid of the Green, and she hadn't underestimated the dangers, no matter how much he accused her of it. She'd recognized her own ignorance when it came to Harp's wildlife, but she'd been willing to risk it anyway. Not for money or profit, but because someone she'd trusted had betrayed everything she believed in, and she was determined to make him pay. It was a matter of personal honor, and that was something Aidan understood.

And so he ran with her, only a few steps behind, his senses tuned to every twist of the pongo's body as it crashed through the trees in pursuit. Oddly enough, by running on the ground, they had the slight advantage in this area. The trees overhead were far more tangled with vines than in other parts of the Green. Vines that started their lives on the warm, moist slopes leading down to the swamp, but quickly spread to the sturdy trees in the higher parts of the Green where sunlight was more plentiful and there were plenty of small animals to trap in their webs. Because the vines that grew out of the swamp—the Venus Vitis he'd lied to Rachel about encountering, when, in fact, he'd been playing cat with her— were more akin to spider webs. They trapped unwary prey and sucked them dry.

All of that meant the pongo was encountering far more resistance in the trees then he and Rachel were on the ground.

"Slow down a bit, lass," he called. "The ground drops fast and with little warning," he explained, when he came up beside her. They walked a few paces with Rachel still in the lead, checking every step before putting her weight on it but making good time for all that. He was beginning to believe her claims of survival experience. Not that he'd ever admit to doubting them.

She stopped abruptly. He felt more than saw her put a testing foot down and immediately shift her weight to her back foot. "Aidan."

He crouched next to her and sniffed, detecting the delightful bouquet of rotting vegetation that drifted up near the ground. Rachel went to one knee next to him and did her own sniffing. She tilted her head, then sniffed again, before looking up at him. "I don't smell anything."

"It's faint. You have to know what to look for."

She studied him. "You were also born on Harp. I know several geneticists who'd give their firstborn child to take a look at your DNA."

He gave her the kind of cold glare that would have sent most norms running in the other direction. "No one's going to be studying my DNA."

"I didn't say they were *going* to," she responded absently, her attention moving to the terrain ahead of them.

She'd barely noticed the glare. Which only made him want her more. He was a cat, and she intrigued him.

"I said they'd like to. I have no intention of helping the people behind this commit whatever crimes they had planned." She pointed slightly to the left of their position. "That way?"

Aidan was impressed. "That way," he confirmed. "The footing will get steadily worse as we descend. At some point, vines will become a serious problem. They start climbing mid-slope, but anything deeper than that and they're all over the ground. Keep your knife handy."

"Always," she said and started forward.

Chapter Nine

Amanda leaned against the huge tree, one palm flat against the coarse surface, fingers digging deep into the thick ridges that marked the many centuries the grandfather had stood watch over Harp. No one knew for sure how old the forests of the Green were—thousands of years, rather than hundreds. But those trees, the oldest of the old, remained hidden in the depths of the Green, standing vigil over a planet that had changed and grown around them.

The real question was when the forest had become… Sentient was too strong a word, but it was something close. The Green was absolutely aware and very active in defense of the planet and every creature that dwelled within its shadows, including a nearly endless variety of vicious and unpredictable killers. Shifters sat at the top of those killers now, but they'd only been around for the last five hundred or so years, and it was partly the Green's sentience that had driven the colonists' scientists to such desperation that they'd created shifters.

Leaving one hand on the tree's rough bark, she rubbed her belly with the other, feeling her babies reach out to match her touch. "That's right, you little hooligans," she told them. "You're clever, but we're ready for you. Your daddy's a badass, never forget it."

The Green hummed its delight beneath her fingers, making her laugh out loud. Ever since she'd gotten pregnant, the trees had sent her nothing but joy every time she touched them. It didn't matter what else was going on in the Green, what alarms Rhodry or the others might be responding to. The Green was thrilled with her coming babies, and it let her know.

She'd wondered, at first, if other women on Harp experienced the same thing, but then it had hit her. She was the first, the *very* first, woman in Harp's history capable of hearing the trees' song, at least as far as anyone knew. She suspected her unexpected ability had to do with her father, whom she'd never met but who—she'd recently learned—had been an earth witch on his home planet. Apparently, he'd been able to make things grow—sort of a green thumb times a thousand.

Amanda would have liked to discuss all of this with her mother, who was Chief Medical Officer onboard one of Earth Fleet's largest armadas, but the unique nature of the Green, and the very existence of shifters, was a secret that Harp had no intention of sharing with anyone. Especially not the fleet.

She stroked her belly again, letting the ancient tree's life force calm her little wild ones, connecting them to the vast Green that would be their home. "Don't you worry, babies," she murmured. "You're safe as safe can be, even when your daddy's not here. Because your momma's a badass, too."

Though, that didn't mean that all three of them didn't miss Rhodry when he was gone. His seniority in the Guild, coupled with his informal advisory role with Ardrigh Cristobal, had kept him away from home too often lately. Few people knew it yet, but as soon as their little shifters were born, she and Rhodry would be moving permanently back to the mountains of Clanhome where their children could grow up surrounded by cousins, just as Rhodry had. Family was everything to the clan. Besides, there were plenty of other powerful shifters who could manage the Guild and advise Cristobal. It was time for them to step up.

In fact, once Rhodry returned from checking in with Aidan, they'd be making a long-planned visit to Clanhome to finalize plans for the move. They'd be traveling by hovercraft—which she'd been forced to acknowledge was necessary, given the distance and her *temporarily* diminished physical abilities, which privately drove her a little crazy. And she still didn't know any details about the latest crisis. She had her connection to the trees and so knew that Aidan was all right, and Rhodry was on his way home. But she wouldn't know what the threat had been until he returned.

The trees' song changed abruptly, turning all sunny and happy. Amanda smiled. She didn't have to wonder who was coming. She looked up with a bright smile for Cullen.

"Come to fetch us home, Cullen?"

He grinned. They both knew he'd been lurking close by the whole time. He hated it when she wandered off alone. He trusted her abilities and especially trusted the Green's protection of her, but he was never far away, either. He stayed out of sight and pretended she didn't know, but she always did. "Your mother sent a message," he said, as if that were the reason he'd found her.

"What'd she say?" she asked.

"Well, I don't know, do I, lass? I'm not in the habit of reading other people's mail."

She laughed and hooked her hand through his arm as

they walked back to the Guild Hall and the house nearby that she and Rhodry had built. "Any word from Rhodry?" she asked. She'd discovered that the shifter network was sometimes more finely tuned than hers. Maybe it was years of practice, or maybe just because the cousins had all grown up together, their minds connected virtually from birth.

"He's close."

"Hear that, babies?" she said, resting a hand on the swell of her belly.

"You think they can hear you?" he asked curiously.

"Of course. Just like they hear the Green's song, and Rhodry, too."

He thought about it while they climbed the stairs of the house. "You don't let Rhodry sing to them, do you? He has a terrible voice."

She laughed. "That's what he says. He leaves the singing to me." She picked up the envelope with her mother's message as she passed the small table just inside the main room, then she sank onto the couch. Shoving a pillow behind her back, she slipped a finger under the sealed envelope flap and said, "Let's see what Grandma has to say."

"Elise says she's much too young to be called that." Cullen's somewhat scolding tone didn't surprise Amanda.

Men had always liked her mother. Elise was beautiful and charming, and delicate enough that men instantly wanted to protect her. But Cullen mostly liked her because she always fed him when she came to visit. He was a big guy and, according to Rhodry, young enough that he was still growing. He wouldn't get any taller, but apparently his muscles still had some bulking up to do. She couldn't imagine how big he'd be when he finished, but it didn't matter because he'd still be Cullen—dangerous as hell and viciously devoted to Rhodry and her. And now, to their children.

Amanda read the short message and didn't know whether

she wanted to wince or smile. Maybe a little of both. "She's coming to visit."

Cullen brightened predictably, but he didn't have to deal with the implications of her visit. Amanda was always happy to see her mother, but this time… Elise was about to become a grandmother to two little shifters, and there was no way in hell Amanda would be able to keep the secret of shifters' existence from her any longer. She'd have to be told, but she'd also have to be sworn to secrecy. No one else could know. Not fleet, not Elise's vice-admiral boyfriend, *no one.*

Amanda sighed, but a moment later, the trees' song changed in a way that was just for her. She started to get up, but Cullen beat her to it, opening the balcony door just as Rhodry came into view, going from the trees to the balcony and into the room in two graceful leaps. He shifted almost immediately, grabbing the drawstring pants Cullen tossed at him, pulling them on with a grin as he walked over to the couch.

"*Acushla.*"

Amanda's heart swelled at the familiar endearment, and she fought back tears—stupid pregnancy hormones—as she grinned back up at him. God, she loved this man. And her babies did, too. Whether they were responding to *her* feelings or to the sound of their father's voice, she didn't know, but they were wide awake and knocking on her belly as if to get his attention.

He sat next to her and smoothed one big hand over their rowdy twins while pulling her into a kiss with the other. "I missed you," he murmured against her lips. "Are you all right?"

"We're fine. How's Aidan?"

"Falling in love."

"Again?" she asked skeptically, while from across the room Cullen made a dismissive noise.

Rhodry laughed, and the babies bounced happily at the sound. She groaned and muttered, "Stop it, you two."

He smiled, feeling the twins' movement beneath his hand. "I think Aidan might be serious this time."

"I'll believe that when I see it," Cullen muttered.

Amanda was inclined to go along with him. She didn't know Aidan as well as either one of the two men, but in the time she *had* known him, he'd always had at least two women vying for his affection, and frequently more than that. The idea that he'd finally met someone he was *serious* about? That barely computed.

Rhodry kissed the side of her forehead, his expression abruptly serious. "Unfortunately, we have much bigger problems than Aidan's love life. An Earther ship snuck onto the planet somehow—"

Cullen cursed as Amanda said, "That shouldn't be possible."

"No, it shouldn't, but it happened, and it gets worse. They landed far enough away from both the city and Clanhome that no one would notice, took out machine guns, and shot up the Green. They waited until Aidan showed up to fight them off, then they captured and caged him."

Cullen growled his curse this time, the sound of an enraged beast.

Rhodry nodded in his direction. "We think that was their goal. They wanted a cat, and they wanted him alive."

"I'm assuming you didn't leave any of them alive, since the Green's calmed down. Mostly, anyway. How'd you get Aidan out?" Amanda asked. She felt nothing for whoever had been on that ship. They'd broken the fleet's embargo and Harp law in pursuit of profit, and they'd paid the price. There was only one reason to capture a great hunting beast like the ones which shifters resembled in their cat forms, and that was to sell them to a zoo or someone's private collection for display and breeding. The only other reason would be if they'd somehow discovered the truth about the existence of shifters. But if anyone at fleet had learned about *that*, they wouldn't be sending a single privateer to sneak onto the planet. They'd be invading.

"You'd be right about the crew's fate," Rhodry agreed. "But Aidan had already escaped. Thanks to the new love of his life."

"The woman was that far out? Is she with a logging family? You *know* how much they hate shifters."

"Even better. She was a scientist onboard the ship. She's from Earth."

• • •

THE SWAMP

Rachel had experienced some unpleasant ecosystems in her explorations, but nothing compared to Harp's swamp. The damn thing shouldn't even exist for all the reasons she'd told Aidan, but she was beginning to realize that when it came to Harp, few of the established scientific rules seemed to matter. His explanation for the swamp's existence made a kind of sense, but only on Harp. And regardless of whether it *should* be there or not, it most definitely was. They'd gone steadily downslope for about fifteen yards, and she could smell the rot that Aidan had picked up from the top. She still couldn't figure out how he'd done that. There'd been a slight breeze blowing *toward* the hidden rift that should have made it impossible. But, apparently, not for Aidan. She'd been joking about the DNA sharing, but she really did believe he displayed some serious genetic mutations that had probably made it possible for his ancestors to survive. He was fascinating, and not only because of his DNA.

He was, unfortunately, just her type—physically big guys

who were not only super smart, but also tough and strong enough to match, or exceed, her skills when it came to survival trekking. Brains were a must, but so was a love for exploration. From the little she'd seen, she already knew that Harp was unique enough for a lifetime of new challenges and discoveries. She just had to keep her heart out of the mix. Because as much as she was attracted to Aidan, there was another way he was her type. That easy charm seemed to go hand in hand with the kind of men she found attractive, but it was like a fatal flaw. She'd been all but engaged to such a man once. A beautiful man, a wonderful lover. He'd been smart and full of adventure, an expedition guide like herself. She'd been madly in love, convinced she'd found the perfect man to share her life with. Until she'd discovered he had a lover on every planet he visited who believed the same. It had been a hard lesson, but she'd learned it. Men like that—handsome, charming to everyone they met—should never be trusted with a woman's heart. They loved the chase too much to ever settle for just one.

And why was she wasting brainpower thinking about broken hearts? If she didn't focus on the ground underfoot, she was going to end up with a broken ankle, which would be far more painful and possibly fatal. And then, she'd have to deal with Aidan's irritation at having to slow down because of it. As it was, the skin on her arms remained red and irritated, like a bad sunburn, from exposure to the pongo's blood. She didn't need to add any more injuries to the mix. On Wolfrum's advice—perhaps the one honest thing he'd told her—she'd taken a prophylactic round of broad-spectrum antibiotics and had another full round in her pack. But a truly serious injury could leave her vulnerable enough that infection could take hold. A hot, wet place like this was undoubtedly teeming with bacteria. Who knew if Earth meds could deal with it? Far better to avoid breaking her ankle in the first place.

"Not much farther now," Aidan murmured. They'd both begun speaking softly since beginning their descent. There was something about this place that made one want to keep a low profile—a sense of opportunistic predators lurking, waiting for prey unwary enough to draw attention.

"I'm guessing there'll be no camp?" she asked. More likely they'd simply hunker down and wait out the night. *A fire was unlikely*, she thought. It would draw too much attention. Same would go for the smell of any hot food. She thought about how long he'd said it would take to cross to the other side. It was going to be a dreary few days…or maybe weeks.

Aidan touched her shoulder, indicating she should pause. She stopped in place, waiting. In the short distance they'd come, she'd already learned several hazards of the swamp, including a muddy mound of what he'd told her were tiny, biting insects that found the smallest gaps in your clothing and were nearly impossible to get rid of once they'd burrowed their way in.

She followed his gaze as he looked around in the dying light. It was already so dark where they were that she was maneuvering mostly by feel. She longed for her little flashlight but knew it would only attract insects of almost every variety. She wanted to ask what he was looking for but waited to see, instead. His gaze settled on a sturdy-looking tree about twenty feet to their right. She'd noticed, before it became too dark to see, that the farther they descended, the more slender the trees became. Looking up, she saw the crisscrossed branches she'd come to expect of the Green, but she could tell that these would never support her weight. Maybe if she'd been four-legged, as Aidan had noted, so that she could distribute her weight differently, they might have held. But not in her bipedal human form.

"You sure you can climb?" he whispered.

She wanted to grab him by the shirt and snarl at him.

Yes, she sure as hell could fucking climb. But they were both under stress, so she sucked in a breath and simply nodded. "I can climb."

She could barely see his face, but his eyes had taken on that same glow, so she saw it when he winked at her. He'd been teasing her. There they were, heading for this swamp he'd given her such dire warnings about, and he was still laying on the charm. She didn't know if that made her like him more or less.

Oh, what the fuck. She was an idiot because it definitely made her like him more.

Taking her hand and holding it close, he guided her over to the tree he'd selected and indicated she should climb.

She gave him a skeptical look. "And you'll be right behind me."

"Right on your very fine ass," he assured her, laughing when she punched his gut. A gut which was hard as a fucking rock. "Climb," he said seriously.

So, she climbed. And apparently impressed her Harp companion.

"Where'd you learn to climb like that?" he asked, settling down next to her on a broad branch. She couldn't help noticing that he'd positioned himself between her and anything that might come at them from the front. With the trunk at her back and a second broad branch overhead, they were as protected as they could be.

"My father was Research Director at the Redwoods Sanctuary in old California when I was growing up. My brother and I spent most of our childhood climbing trees as big or bigger than these."

"I've seen pictures of those in the old archives. Do they still exist on Earth?"

She nodded. "In the Sanctuary, but nowhere else. Even there, the number is far fewer, but it's better than it would have been if the state hadn't taken action early on. They're a national treasure." She shivered unexpectedly. "Did the temperature just drop?"

He leaned back and wrapped an arm around her shoulders, pulling her into the heat of his body. "It happens on the slopes after sunset when the day's heat rushes to escape the deep rift. It never comes from as deep as the swamp itself, but the slopes can get cool."

"This is the freakiest planet," she grumbled, hugging her arms and grateful for his warmth. "Aren't you cold?"

He shrugged. "I don't get cold."

"Not ever?"

"Sometimes in the snow. And don't even mention my DNA."

She laughed. "I wasn't going to. That's a simple adaptation. Everyone does that."

"Sleep," he ordered.

"We can trade off watch shifts. How long does night last?"

"That's not necessary. I'm a light sleeper. If anything comes within ten feet of us, I'll know it."

"Another adaptation, Aidan?"

"Absolutely. I'm a hunter. We sleep in the wild as often as in our beds."

"Tell me about these hunters," she murmured, her eyes closing. It had been a long, tiring day. "Is it a family thing? A professional guild? What?"

"A little of both. Go to sleep."

"You're very secretive." She surrendered to sleep almost before the last word left her lips, and the last thing she remembered was the touch of Aidan's lips on the top of her head.

• • •

The next morning Rachel was convinced she must have imagined that kiss because the Aidan who'd held her while she slept had been replaced by his drill-sergeant alter ego. He'd woken her at the precise moment the sun hit their tree. Although to say it hit their tree would be a gross exaggeration. A pale facsimile of sunshine barely brushed the treetops above them. She knew it was sunrise more by the change in the sounds of the forest than the tiny bit of brightened light around them.

"Grab your energy bar, lass. It's time to move."

"Good morning to you, too," she muttered. "Can I pee first?"

He laughed. "Sure. I wouldn't recommend squatting too close to the ground, though. You never know what might poke its head out and take a bite."

"Thank you for that vivid picture, but I'm fully aware of the precautions one must take when peeing in the wild."

"Only for women."

"Oh ho, is that what they've told you? I've been on planets where things will reach out, take a bite, and climb right up your dick."

He jerked in shock, and Rachel would have sworn she heard a gasp, although he'd no doubt deny it. *She* wasn't that discreet. She laughed, and he poked her in the side. "Are you serious?"

She lowered herself the final few feet to the ground, watchful for unpleasant surprises. "Hell, yeah, I am," she told him, checking the ground around her. "It's most unpleasant getting them out, too. Had it happen to a guy I dated a few times."

"So much for that romance, I'd imagine."

"He wasn't feeling amorous for months after, that's for sure. But we were over before it happened."

"How come?" Aidan didn't bother with caution. He

jumped directly from the branch where they'd slept to stand next to her. Rachel stared up, measuring the distance. It had to be fifteen feet, maybe more. And yet he'd landed as light as a cat.

"I travel a lot, which means I'm gone a lot. He wanted someone more available."

He hummed wordlessly.

"What about the women here on Harp?" she asked.

"Well, they don't travel," he said, laughing.

"You're evading the question."

He shrugged. "It's different here. Nobody lives far from family. The only ones who travel any distance are the loggers, and their families travel with them."

"And the hunters, I'd imagine," Rachel said, stepping behind a tree where hopefully he couldn't watch her squat. She'd have liked to go out of hearing distance, as well, but that was pure vanity. Everyone pees. Far better to have your companions listen to you pee, than to be so far away that they can't help you if a monster attacked.

"Some of us travel the Green a lot," he conceded. "Some remain close to home."

Rachel pulled up her pants. This was about the time in any expedition where she began longing for a hot shower. She sighed, knowing it would probably be weeks before that happened. The best she could hope for until then would be a quick dip in a cold stream.

"You ready to move?" he asked, standing right in front of her when she rounded her tree.

She gazed up at him and saw the slight crinkling of his eyes. He'd done that on purpose. *Ah, Aidan,* she thought. *Payback's gonna be a bitch.* She smiled sweetly and said, "I'm ready. Do you want an energy bar?"

He gave her a suspicious look but asked, "How many of those things do you have left?"

Rachel reached into her pack and counted. "Ten."

"All right, yeah, I'll take one. But we're having meat for lunch and dinner."

"Cooked meat?" Not all cultures cooked their protein.

"Unless you'd prefer it raw?" he asked curiously.

"No, no. Just checking."

"Can we start walking now?"

She rolled her eyes. Like *she* was the reason they were still standing there.

"Walk where I walk," he cautioned.

Rachel nodded as she settled her backpack once more. She'd done this so many times on so many planets that she barely noticed the weight anymore. She followed Aidan downward, keeping her eye on his footsteps but pausing to scan the rest of their surroundings, too. The tree canopy didn't seem that much thicker than it had above, but it grew increasingly dark as they descended, as if the sun couldn't penetrate the deep crevice in the earth. She thought it possible there'd be an hour every day when the sun was directly above and shining into the deep, narrow rift, but no more than that. Her foot slipped, but she caught herself easily. This wasn't the first treacherous ground she'd had to navigate, but she had to admit that Harp's swamp had little to recommend it. The slope was slick with rotting vegetation and probably equally rotting animal matter, and the stench was unbelievable. It surrounded them like a heavy wet blanket, as if particles of the rot were floating in the air, landing on her clothes, her exposed skin…her hair. She found herself wishing she'd worn a hat.

The morning passed without incident. Aidan walked with confidence, seeming to know where to step to avoid whatever swamp hazards lay in wait. In fact, Rachel was beginning to think he'd exaggerated the dangers, hoping to scare her off from going after Wolfrum altogether. They'd seen so little wildlife that she wondered what he planned to hunt down for that promised hot lunch. Her stomach growled on cue, and she looked up to ask him about it, when he abruptly lost his footing and flew several feet downslope.

Rachel's first reaction was shock. Every experienced trekker she knew tripped and stumbled on occasion, including her. But not Aidan. She'd never seen him so much as take a misstep. Every foot he placed, every hand when he climbed, was perfectly balanced and exactly where it needed to be. Her instincts were screaming something was wrong before he'd hit the ground.

Aidan shouted a warning, but she'd already seen it. He hadn't fallen. There was a giant snakelike thing wrapped around his leg and moving rapidly up to squeeze his torso. One of his arms was still free, and he had his knife out, stabbing at any part of the creature he could reach. But it wasn't going to be enough. It was a monster snake, several times wider around than Rachel, its body coiling up to tighten around Aidan's chest. It would squeeze the life out of him, shutting down his lungs, his heart. Already she could hear him straining to draw enough breath to curse, could see the power in his thrusts weakening.

Rachel put away her own belt knife. She'd grabbed it instinctively, but it wouldn't even irritate the giant snake. Dropping her pack to the ground, she yanked at the straps holding her crossbow, nocked two bolts, and slipped two more into her belt. Doing a quick eyeball assessment of the snake's body, which was twisting in the undergrowth as it fought to control Aidan, she took a few experimental steps forward and stopped, but the creature ignored her. She walked closer.

"Rachel," Aidan wheezed. "Stay back." He was on the ground now, still slashing but growing weaker.

She ignored him, just as the snake was ignoring her. It was in full-on attack mode, totally focused on disabling its prey—which happened to be Aidan—before eating him whole. Stepping carefully—a misstep here could be fatal for both of them—she said softly, "Aidan."

He looked up and met her eyes, then glanced at the crossbow and shook his head. "No," he said in warning.

She smiled. "Trust me." Cocking the crossbow and hoping this damn creature really was a snake, she drew a deep breath, slid her foot forward…and nearly went down as a length of the thick body whipped against her leg. "Fuck."

"Rachel," Aidan growled.

She ignored him. This damn snake was *not* going to defeat her, and it was sure as hell not going to kill Aidan. He was far too much alive to die. Switching her gaze from the twisting coils to her feet, to the snake's head, and back again, she glided cautiously over the slick ground until she came within touching distance. The snake's eyes were closed, all of its energy and instincts focused on crushing its prey. Planting both feet, she placed the point of the bolt precisely above and between the creature's closed eyes and let fly from only inches away.

The bolt hit with a dull thud, smashing the skull with an audible crack. The snake seemed to reel, its head waving loosely, eyes flickering in her direction. But it wasn't dead, and she didn't hesitate. Reptile brains were tiny. Aiming for the green fluid dripping out of the crack in the skull, and hoping her memory of reptile brains was accurate, she fired the second bolt, then pulled out her boot knife, prepared to dig around in the creature's skull if that's what it took to finish it off.

The massive body collapsed in a slow wave, filling the air with a slithering rush of sound until, finally, the coils surrounding Aidan relaxed. He staggered slightly but didn't fall, grabbing her instead and running uphill, dragging her with him until they hit the nearest tree.

"Climb," he ordered, his voice still strained, as if his lungs weren't yet working fully.

"Aidan," she protested, but he gripped her around the waist and lifted her until she could grab the first low branch.

"Climb, damn it."

Not understanding, but infected by the urgency in his voice, she slung the crossbow awkwardly over her shoulder and climbed.

"Keeping going." He was right behind her, his hand on her thigh, as if ready to give her a push.

"Aidan, what—?"

"Higher."

Hearing the strain in his voice, she twisted to look back at him. Those gold flecks in his eyes were too bright in the dark shadows of the downslope, the muscles on his arms flexing visibly beneath the thin tunic.

She levered herself onto a thick branch—twenty feet up and big enough to hold both of them—and stopped. She wanted to know what was happening. The damn snake was dead. What could possibly—? She looked down and gagged. Something was eating the snake from the inside out. The skin split wide open to disgorge a black swarm of beetle-like creatures that quickly covered the carcass. And they just kept coming.

"What the hell is that?" Rachel whispered.

"Snipes," Aidan said from where he was perched right next to her. "They have a symbiotic relationship with the python. They keep its gut clean of bones and other indigestibles, until it dies. And then their eggs hatch and their population multiplies over and over. The dead snake feeds their offspring, and they go looking for a new host. And they're not picky about what they eat in the meantime. Everything and anything becomes food, including half-dead hunters and pretty Earthers with fancy crossbows."

Rachel smiled at the description then elbowed him gently. "You weren't half dead. More like two-thirds."

• • •

Aidan chuckled, though the whole situation grated. If he'd been alone, he'd have shifted and the damn python would have been *his* lunch, instead of the other way around. He'd been moments away from saying the hell with it and shifting anyway. There was no way in hell that they were going to finish this mission without Rachel learning about shifters, anyway. So why the fuck should he have to wrestle with a damn python while it choked the breath out of him?

"Thanks for the vote of confidence," he told her lightly. "And thanks for killing that fucker. How'd you know where to shoot? Their brains aren't exactly a big target." He had to admit he was impressed. She'd been cool as a breeze off the glacier.

"I'm a xeno-vet, remember?" she told him. "Reptiles all over the universe seem to share certain anatomical characteristics, including their tiny brains. I took a chance that this guy was a reptile. Looks can be deceiving."

No shit, Aidan thought. Wait until she set her xeno-vet eyes on a shifter. They both watched in silence as the voracious snipes reduced the python to a pile of dried skin and loose bone and then marched away to find some other host.

"Wow," Rachel whispered.

"Yep. We should move on. I want to stop for lunch, but… not here."

She laughed. "Worried you're still on the menu?" She climbed from the tree with impressive skill, jumping the last few feet.

He followed and then started away. "Sweetheart, on

Harp everyone is always on the menu." Except for shifters, he wanted to add. There were very few creatures on Harp who would attack a shifter and even fewer who'd survive the encounter. He was still irritated as hell that he'd gotten caught the way he had. If any of his cousins learned of it, he'd never hear the end of their jokes. What still really pissed him off, though, was that he'd had to hold back his shift. Normally, he'd never have attempted the swamp in human form. Hell, *normally,* he'd never have been on the ground at all. He'd have climbed a tree and run over the top of the damn thing.

But then there was Rachel. Who else would make sure she reached the end of her stubborn journey to the city alive? Okay, so any number of his cousins would probably volunteer. Hell, Gabriel already had. But that wasn't happening. Aidan was her cat, even if she didn't know it yet. And she was his... something. He didn't know yet exactly what she was to him. Only that she was his to protect. And, yeah, she actually had damn good survival skills all on her own. That had been a neat trick with the snake. He'd never thought of it. But then he'd never had to because he was a *fucking shifter!* And that brought him right back to all the reasons he was pissed as hell.

Movement overhead caught his attention. Time for lunch.

Casting his eye about as they walked, he found what he was looking for. Whatever geological forces had created the rift that the swamp called home, the process had left behind enormous boulders scattered at random along both slopes and piled in the center. The rocks were sometimes infested with a variety of small life-forms, or covered over by vegetation, but occasionally there'd be one which stuck out enough to get a little more sunshine, a little less moisture. If one had to make camp on the ground, those were the most likely spots for it.

"Over there," he told Rachel now, nodding in the direction of the rock cluster. "It's as safe as anywhere else.

You make camp, and I'll hunt lunch."

"Wait." Rachel put a hand on his arm before he could swing into the trees and away. "Shouldn't we stay together?"

"We are together. I'm not going far."

She frowned. "What are you—?"

At that moment, a pack of cebas swarmed by overhead, their passage marked only by the swoosh of movement through the trees. The swamp version of a banshee, the cebas were eerily silent. The only time they vocalized at all was during mating season, when the males fought for breeding rights. And then the sound was a hoarse grunt, barely discernible beyond a few yards, nothing like the loud chittering of the banshee, which could carry for miles. The other distinguishing aspect of the ceba was less charming. Cebas were green. Not because they'd been born that way, but because they were true swamp-dwellers, their fur covered in green moss. They were slimy on the outside, but very tasty on the inside.

In answer to Rachel's question, Aidan pointed upward.

"What are those things?" She squinted. "Creepy."

"Tasty," he corrected.

She opened her mouth as if to object, but then blew out a resigned breath. "Can I make a fire?"

"Absolutely. Make it a small one and confine it to the rock." He swung up into the nearest tree. "This won't take long."

Aidan felt almost guilty at the freedom zinging through his veins as he climbed into the canopy. It had nothing to do with Rachel and everything to do with who he was. He was a shifter, and it was suffocating to be confined in his human form. He was as much man as cat, but the cat lived closer to nature, with fewer rules. Shedding his clothes and boots, he tied them into a bundle and stashed them in a tree fork. Then, with a yowling call to remind the swamp dwellers who ruled the planet, he went hunting.

Rachel looked up as the eerie howl of a big cat sent a shiver of excitement skating over her nerves. Forgetting the small fire she'd been coaxing into life, she searched the surrounding canopy, hoping for a glimpse of her cat. Had he followed them into the swamp? There was no doubt in her mind that, as apex predators, the big cats wouldn't have to worry about things like giant, beetle-filled snakes. Between her work and university, she'd seen a lot of different life-forms, including a lot of symbiotic relationships, but the image of those beetles eating their way out of the snake like a glistening black wave to swarm over its carcass still made her shudder. Not because she cared about the snake, but because it was all too easy to imagine the tiny black things swarming over her instead.

She spat a wordless sound of disgust before turning back to her tiny fire, which she'd ignored and was threatening to go out. Aidan had said he'd be quick, and the last thing she wanted was for him to come back and find her obsessing about dead snakes, or worse, daydreaming about a certain golden cat. He seemed to find her obsession with the beast intensely amusing. But it was perfectly natural for her to be concerned about the animal's continuing health. She was a doctor, after all. And he'd been her patient, albeit an unwilling one.

Besides, Aidan had said the cats were important on Harp, so she was, in some small way, making up for the sins of her shipmates. The thought made her frown because the most important thing she could do for the cats was to find that second ship and stop them before they could launch a second brutal attack on the Harp wildlife, the cats specifically. She felt slightly guilty keeping the existence of the second ship from Aidan thus far. At some point, she was going to have to tell him. How else would she explain her sudden desire to break off and travel away from the city she'd been so eager to reach?

She sighed.

"How's that fire going, hunter?"

Rachel spun. Her first reaction was to wonder how the hell such a huge man moved so quietly. Her second pleasure that he'd called her "hunter." But then he dropped a gutted, skinned, and headless *something* next to her fire, and pleasure took a hike.

She studied the carcass and thought it was probably a banshee—those mammalian, monkey-like creatures which ran in packs on Harp—but then she saw the bands of green fur circling its wrists and ankles, along with the matching green skin. She leaned closer. Unusual coloring like that was frequently a function of diet. She thought it must be specific to the swamp, because in her admittedly limited experience with life-forms on Harp, she hadn't seen green skin on any other mammals. She jerked back when the green seemed to be sliding off the fur and onto the feet, with the consistency of thick sludge. Curious but, given her recent beetle experience, also cautious, she reached into her pack for a small magnifier, leaned in for a closer look…and wished she hadn't.

"Does everything here have something crawling on it?" she muttered. She hadn't really expected Aidan to hear her, but of course, he did.

"Pretty much, lass. Life finds a way, right? Isn't that what you scientists say?"

She glanced up from where she was once again leaning over and studying the creeping army of tiny, wriggling worms. "Does that hold true all over Harp?"

"No," he admitted. "Just here in the swamp. Makes for interesting eats."

She gave him a dry look. If he was trying to shock her delicate senses, he had the wrong woman. She'd eaten far less appetizing things than a few green worms. "Do we eat the worms?"

He actually appeared revolted by the idea, but then he grinned. "Hell, no. I just left them on there for you to see."

"That's so sweet," she cooed. "What's it called? I like to know what I'm eating."

"A ceba. His pack swung overhead a ways back, before we stopped."

Rachel nodded, remembering the silent creatures. "Do I need to set up a spit?"

Aidan gave her a surprised look. What? Did he think she brought a personal chef along when she trekked?

"No," he said finally. "I'll chop this bad boy into pieces, and we'll roast him on skewers. They're not that meaty, but it's tender." He picked up the creature and walked a little way off. After several whacks of his knife, he tossed several bits farther away and then returned with a pile of boneless lengths of meat layered neatly on a large green leaf.

Understanding what he had in mind, Rachel had already stripped the leaves off several skinny sticks. Taking the meat, she skewered it onto the sticks and placed them over the fire, bracing them with small stones.

Aidan had gone off to clean his hands and blade, using more of the same big leaves, but now he returned, settling next to her with their backs against a chunk of rock that had been sliced cleanly in half several millennia ago.

"Do I need to worry about something unpleasant crawling out from under this rock?" she asked, reaching out to turn the skewers.

He laughed. "Probably. But since there's no place in this damn swamp where that's not true, you might as well be comfortable."

She smiled but didn't say anything.

"You surprise me," he said.

She glanced over. "How?"

"You're tougher than I'd expected from an Earther."

"Have you met a lot of Earthers?"

"A few. Mostly the few fleet personnel who rotate in and out, manning the science center. Though, after this little trick, I doubt Ardrigh Cristobal will permit even that much access to continue. We can handle the facility ourselves by now."

"What are they like? The fleet types who run the center, I mean?" She was thinking that at least one of them had to have been in on Wolfrum's scheme. If not actively participating, then at least looking the other way.

Aidan shrugged. "They're rarely seen. They arrive by shuttle, march to the science center, and that's it. They don't mingle."

"What a waste," she said, shaking her head in disbelief. "Is that what you thought I'd do? I mean, how the hell did you think I was going to get back to the city without...*mingling*?"

"I figured I'd escort you gently to Clanhome and you'd wait there in comfort until the Guild or Cristobal sent a hover to fetch you."

Rachel didn't know whether to be insulted or amused, so she went with curiosity instead. "You have hovercraft here?"

"Two. They're solar-powered, kept in the city, and used only in emergencies."

She checked the meat, wanting it cooked through—take that, you fucking worms—but not dried into chunks of jerky. "So, if I'm not a dainty maiden waiting for rescue...what am I?" she asked, pulling the first skewers off and passing one to Aidan.

"Oh, now you're just fishing for compliments."

She laughed, then took a bite of the meat and chewed. "This isn't bad," she admitted. "It could use some salt, but I've had a lot worse."

The silence was companionable as they sat on the rock and finished their lunch, such as it was. The absence of fresh produce was one thing Rachel had always despised about trekking. She always became a temporary vegetarian when she returned from a long trip, though not for long. She was a carnivore through and through.

Aidan rose to a crouch and started breaking down their fire pit, such as it was. "You finished eating?" he asked. When she nodded, he took the leftover meat, wrapped it in yet another giant leaf, and then double wrapped it, using a second leaf. "Okay if I put this in your pack?"

Rachel pulled her pack over and opened an outside pocket which had an insulated lining for just that sort of thing.

Aidan peered inside. "I'm beginning to think you really do have experience in the wild," he said, tucking the meat away then zipping the pocket closed.

"I'm trying not to be insulted by that comment."

"Try harder. It was a compliment."

She scoffed. "Your compliments need work."

He offered a hand to pull her to her feet and used too much strength. She crashed into his chest, and for a moment, their bodies were perfectly aligned, his hand holding hers behind her back, her other hand on his waist for balance. Rachel's breath caught as her nipples hardened against his chest. Aidan's arm tightened, and she looked up to meet his gold-flecked eyes, stunned by the wave of pure, unadulterated lust that hung in the air between them. She swallowed the knot in her throat, reminding herself that this wasn't the time or place.

His eyes filled with the same knowledge. He gave her a lopsided grin that held a promise for the future and then released her to stand on her own.

"Will we make the bottom before nightfall?" she asked, securing her various bits of gear and weapons in their proper places. The last thing one wanted was to be searching for the right knife in an emergency. Or to see the heat in his eyes right now.

Aidan shook himself from head to toe. It was such an *animal* thing to do that it caught her attention. *He was so much a part of the Green*, she thought. She wondered how much time he spent in the wild. Did he ever go home to stay? Or was he just a visitor there?

"We'll make the swamp itself tomorrow afternoon if we're lucky. For now, we'll travel as far as we can before darkfall, then rest. Daylight gets shorter the deeper we go. By the time we hit bottom, we won't see more than an hour of light in the middle of the day."

"We'll cross in the dark?" she asked, not happy about the prospect.

He nodded. "No choice."

Rachel drew a deep breath and returned his nod. She'd faced worse and survived. She'd do it again. "Let's go."

• • •

They slept in the trees that night. Aidan told Rachel again that a watch wasn't necessary, that he'd wake in time to catch any intruder. But that was no longer true. He had no intention of sleeping. The swamp was a strange fucking place. Even he didn't know every creature that lived there, and he spent more time patrolling this sector of the Green than any other shifter, including his many cousins. The deeper they went, the weirder the life-forms. He had to fight the urge to shift; his cat was clawing to get out, his instincts recognizing the danger. There was no threat in the Green that he couldn't fight better in his shifted form, but Rachel didn't know about shifters, and it wasn't up to Aidan to tell her. There was only one Earther who knew Harp's biggest secret, and that was Amanda, Rhodry's wife. She'd earned her place on Harp with blood, sweat, and plain damned courage. He'd told

Rachel that she wasn't what he'd expected of an Earther in this situation. What he *hadn't* told her was that she reminded him of Amanda. No hysterics, no waiting for someone else to solve the latest crisis. Just a cool head and an even cooler hand with that crossbow. Nothing fazed her.

He grinned. Nothing except the sexual tension between them. He'd seen her look of panic when they'd had their *moment* earlier. If they'd been in the regular part of Green, their evening would have turned out very differently.

Movement rippled in the trees all around them, and he raised his head, listening. What he wouldn't give for a big pack of noisy banshee right about now. Those damn cebas made for a tasty meal, but they were shit when it came to a decent warning system. He'd been catching whispers from the trees for hours now, even before they'd stopped for the night.

There was one other thing about the swamp that he hadn't mentioned to Rachel, because it was something only shifters would understand, and that was the trees in the swamp—they were…sicker somehow, although that wasn't the right word. The deeper one went into the rift, the less *connected* the trees were until, at the very bottom, there was no song at all. The Green was working steadily to "heal" this deformity, but progress was crushingly slow. Harp had existed for millennia before the colonists had crashed here, and the Green had yet to gather the swamp into its healthy fold.

For a shifter like Aidan, that sickness meant he couldn't reliably count on the trees for information and warning. He could tell there was something *wrong*. Something big that these trees couldn't convey. But he couldn't make anything more of it. It made him wonder if he and Rhodry had missed a member of Rachel's crew when they'd cleared out the ship. Had someone been hiding? If so, they'd been locked so securely that not a scent, not a sound had given them away. It was damn difficult to fool a shifter's senses. Not impossible, but… Aidan didn't believe it. If a crew member had been missed it was because he hadn't been on the ship during the attack. He could ask Rachel how many people had been onboard, but what was the point? She'd only become suspicious and concerned, and it wouldn't change anything. If someone was on their tail, he'd deal with them. Assuming the swamp didn't do it for him.

She stirred next to him, scowling in her sleep at the rough bark against her cheek. He smiled and tugged her gently against his side. She sighed and relaxed against him, letting her cheek rest on his shoulder instead. He dropped a kiss on her head then leaned back, wide awake. He could go days without sleep when necessary. Enough to get them out of this damn swamp and back onto dry land.

• • •

Two days later, they faced the swamp. In her mind, Rachel had lumped the downslope in with the swamp proper, figuring it would simply be more of the same, but with water. More sticky hot air that clung to every inch of exposed skin and stank like several somethings had died recently. More slick mucky vegetation underfoot and more roots to twist an unwary ankle or hide a vicious little beast with teeth half the size of its body. She'd been thankful ten times over for the sturdy mid-calf hiking boots she'd dragged halfway across the universe. She'd never imagined the swamp could be worse than the downslope.

Now, surrounded by a morning darkness that was nearly as deep as the night, she stared at the stagnant water with its coating of fluorescing green slime and knew she'd been wrong.

"That's the most disgusting thing I've seen in…forever, I

think. And that's saying something."

Next to her, Aidan laughed. Nothing seemed to bother him. He didn't think she knew, but he hadn't slept since they'd set foot on the downslope. You'd never know it to look at him. He must have incredible endurance. More of that "hunter" discipline, she imagined. She had a lot of questions about that. So many that she was itching to make a list. But then he'd just ask her what she was writing, and she'd have to tell him. Because she couldn't tell him any more lies. The *big* lie—that she was going to the city—was like a rock in her stomach.

Or maybe in her heart, because she *liked* him. Apart from the undeniable lust that sparked between them at the *most* inconvenient times, she liked him. She wished she'd never kept the truth of the second ship from him in the first place. Her reasoning at the time, that she didn't want Aidan or any of his people to get hurt, seemed ridiculous now. She'd only spent a few days with him, but she recognized a soldier when she saw one. He might call himself a hunter, and maybe he was that, too. But he was a warrior, and probably far more capable than she was of dealing with Wolfrum and his team. What had she thought, anyway? That she'd walk up to Wolfrum and talk him out of his scandalous plan? Fuck. Just thinking about the whole situation made her head hurt. She kept circling around and around with what-ifs, and all of them ended with Aidan hating her. And that made her heart hurt.

"Do we make a raft?" she asked, determined not to think about anything but getting out of this damn swamp. The rest would wait.

He snorted. "You wish. I'm afraid not."

She shot him a disbelieving look. "Really? Why not—"

"You start chopping down trees for a raft, and you're only going to bring a whole new crop of misery onto our heads.

There are a lot of things living in those trees. Hell, half of them will stick onto the wood after you build the raft and feast on you all the way across."

She sighed. "How deep is it?"

"If we're careful where we cross?" He glanced down at her boots, then grinned. "Too deep."

She glared. "What about you, tough guy? You telling me you're going to barefoot across that thing?"

He made a dismissive noise. "Am I suicidal?" His hand shot out and snagged one of the big-toothed rodents who'd been stupid enough to try and sneak from one tree to the next while Aidan was standing there. *Evolution at work*, she thought, as he tossed the unfortunate creature into the water. It uttered its death scream a second before it was swallowed by a bubbling froth of water and feeding frenzy, as what seemed like a thousand, sharp-toothed creatures fought over the body.

"What the fuck?" she whispered.

"They're called cucas," Aiden said. "Don't ask me why. I don't know." He tugged on a hanging vine, yanking it free of the trunk that it twisted around, then, letting his full weight rest on it, tested its strength. He handed it over to her, showing her how to coil it around her hand and into her fist. "Don't fall."

Rachel looked up with a narrow-eyed glare and snarled at him.

He grinned. She sounded like the tiniest baby shifter kitten when she did that.

"Maybe you should go first."

"Not likely," he dismissed. "If I fall, you'll just use the distraction to swing yourself to safety."

She laughed. The truth was, and they both knew it, that if either of them fell, the other would risk their life in a vain and probably suicidal attempt at rescue.

With a final testing tug on the vine, she set her eyes on the opposite bank, took a running start down the slope, and flew over the water, her knees tucked up beneath her as if expecting the cucas to leap out of the water and bite her feet. Aidan watched, admiring her courage along with her form. Although she had very trim legs beneath her sensible cargo pants, he thought her ass was a far more bitable target.

She hit the opposite bank with a whoop of success and then promptly fell on said bitable ass. Aidan had done the same on his first crossing when he'd been fifteen and still in training. The ground on the opposite bank was just as soft and twisted with undergrowth as this one, which made for an awkward landing.

"You okay?" he called.

Rachel was on her feet and already scanning the ground and trees, looking for threats. She hadn't even tried to brush off the mud and slime that coated the back of her hands, which, oddly enough, made him think better of her. It would have been a pointless task, as well as a waste of energy, and she was professional enough to know that. She looked up at his call and gave him a grinning thumbs-up.

Aidan laughed, thinking he might be in love. He knew for damn sure he was in lust. But right now, they had to get away from this fucking swamp before the sun rose enough to warm the water. Because as dangerous as the cucas were, they were far from the deadliest thing living in there.

"Heads up!" he called and swung over the water with practiced ease.

"You want to hold up here long enough to grab some—"

"No." Uncoiling the vine from his wrist, he turned and urged her ahead of him. "Let's move."

Rachel took one look at his face and didn't hesitate. She started climbing the upslope with grim determination. "I'm sure you'll tell me why we're in such a hurry. Being as I'm your partner and all."

Aidan felt the slight shift in warmth that told him the sun was rising as much as it ever did this deep in the rift. Catching up to Rachel, he looped an arm around her waist and powered them both another five yards up the slope until they reached a tree thick enough to provide some concealment. Shoving her behind the tree, he wrapped his arms around her and bent his head to whisper in her ear. "Watch."

As if waiting for his command, the sun beamed down through the tangled trees to touch directly on the water, which lost its neon green slick and became a dull, muddy brown. Steam soon became visible—a few wisps dancing over the surface to begin with, quickly becoming graceful ghosts. A single plopping sound, as if something had dropped into the water—though the truth was quite different—was the first sign.

Rachel's head tilted. "What was—? Oh shit. What the fuck…?"

Aiden grinned at her reaction, only able to do so because they were well out of the danger zone. "We don't even have a name for it. It's just the swamp monster." He watched the huge creature dash with surprising speed out of the water, its six legs churning up the opposite slope, where it gobbled up a trio of rodents as they raced away. The monster chewed with great deliberation, its mouth so big that it was as if its head simply cracked open to reveal a set of deadly teeth and a gaping throat.

"The sun triggers it?" Rachel whispered, as if afraid to draw the creature's attention.

"The sun's warmth," he clarified. "We think it goes into a kind of cold stasis the rest of the time, although 'cold' is a relative term down here."

"Is it like this all year round?"

He nodded. "With some time variation, yes. It always

emerges with the sunlight, but we've never been able to match a schedule to its retreat. That's why I didn't want to cross in the afternoon."

"What's it doing now?" she asked, leaning forward to catch every detail.

Aidan almost groaned at the press of her ass against his groin. "The rodents were a snack. Watch this," he murmured. The monster flexed its legs slowly, as if stretching, and then rolled its head back until it was studying the tops of the trees. With no warning, it suddenly shot forward and slammed itself against the base of a slender tree. There was a crashing noise overhead, and then one of the green-furred cebas fell almost right into the creature's waiting maw. Its jaws snapped shut with a crunch of bone and a thin cry which was the only sound he'd ever heard a ceba make. Still chewing, its belly already growing fat, the swamp monster slowly turned and lumbered back to the waterline to digest its food. Its clawed feet dug in, anchoring itself in the mud, its solid black eyes going cloudy beneath a pale, nictitating eyelid as it soaked up the fragile sunlight.

"Wow," Rachel breathed, her body still. "I mean, disgusting, but...wow."

Aidan trusted she meant the swamp monster and not his body, which was not immune to the firm swell of her ass. He inched back. This was not the time or place, and he had no interest in tormenting himself.

"Yeah. If you could stand the conditions down here, you could spend a lifetime studying the swamp."

"If you could stand it," she repeated. "Not for me, thanks."

He chuckled. "I thought you were all about research."

She shook her head. "I'm also all about breathing. The air down here is so thick with foreign particles... I don't want to think about what's already taking up residence in my lungs.

Speaking of which, can we start climbing out now?"

"Sure. I thought you'd want to see our monster first."

"You were right." She turned to look up at him, still standing far too close. "Thanks."

Aidan met the sincere look in her eyes and felt an awkwardness that he hadn't experienced in years. He didn't get flustered around women. Quite the opposite. He was more accustomed to *causing* the fluster.

"You're welcome," he muttered, then turned and backed away. "We should move. There's still a way to go before we're in the clear."

• • •

Rachel followed Aidan as they climbed the upslope of the swamp. They spent most of their time bent over, using their hands as much as their feet, but she didn't mind, eager to leave the swamp and its monster behind.

She blushed, remembering other things about their morning monster viewing. Like the raw strength of Aidan's arms when he'd dragged her behind that tree, and the press of his body as they'd stood there watching. *All* of his body. She hadn't missed the hard length of his erection against her butt. How could she? He was barely dressed in that thin tunic and pants he wore all the time.

Unfortunately, the swamp picked that moment to show its teeth one last time. She was digging her fingers into the slope as she'd done a hundred times already, gripping the slick undergrowth and looking for a handhold. But this time, the undergrowth fought back.

"Fuck!"

• • •

Aidan heard Rachel curse. She'd been swearing under her

breath for most of the morning, but this one was different. There was pain and—panic. He spun. If he'd learned one thing about Rachel, it was that she didn't panic. Sliding down on his heels, he uttered his own curse. She was on her knees, one hand still gripping a sturdy, green tree trunk. But her other hand was in the air, half swallowed by what looked like a snake, but was actually an insect. Its many legs were waving wildly in the air, its teeth sunk into the flesh of her hand. Rachel reached for its mouth, fingers poised to grip the jaw and force it open.

"Don't!" he shouted, when she went to pull the partially opened jaw off her arm. He skidded next to her and grabbed the writhing insect with one hand and her wrist with the other. "This is a rizer," he said, trying to distract her with facts. "Its bite is rear-facing, three rows of teeth. If you try to pull it off like that, you'll only dig the teeth in deeper."

She stopped in mid-motion, but now he could see a faint tremble in her arm. "I think… There's…" She swallowed slowly, as if it hurt. "Heat," she said finally. "I think it's—"

"Poisonous," he finished for her. If she was sensing heat, the paralyzing agent in the rizer's bite was already pumping into her muscles. "It's a paralytic," he explained, replacing her hand with his much larger one on the creature's jaw. "Let go, sweetheart. Let me do it."

Her hand fell away. "How serious?" she asked, meeting his gaze evenly, despite what had to be significant pain. He'd been bitten by a rizer. He knew exactly how bad the pain was.

He gripped the insect's jaw and squeezed with shifter strength, breaking the joint and backing its teeth out of her flesh. He tossed the thrashing bug down the hill. With its jaw broken, the rizer's life expectancy was no more than a few minutes, but Aidan didn't care. That was life on Harp. He was far more concerned about Rachel, who was staring at him as if he held the answers.

He pulled her into his arms. "It's okay, Rachel. I know it hurts like hell, but slender as you are, you're still much bigger than its usual prey."

She laughed weakly.

"You'll lose the arm—"

"What?" she rasped, pulling back to stare at him.

"*Use* of the arm," he amended quickly. At her disbelieving look, he amended that even further, saying very clearly, "Temporary use of the arm. *Very* temporary."

She blew out a relieved breath and rested her forehead on his shoulder. "How long?" Her voice was stronger, but still not fully restored.

"Let me see." He held the wounded arm in both hands, gently squeezing muscles, trying to determine how deeply the rizer's poison had penetrated. She never uttered a sound, other than giving a startled hiss when he felt along her forearm, closest to the bite.

"Should you cut it open? Try to drain it?" she asked.

He shook his head. "The poison is too thin, disperses too quickly. We'd only open you up to infection. Speaking of which, do you have antibiotics in that giant bag of yours?"

She nodded. "Ointment and capsules. In a zipper compartment just inside the main pack."

He dragged the pack closer and found a small plastic bag that held the antibiotics. Popping two of the capsules from their blister pack, he handed them to her along with the canteen. She downed them obediently then watched as he cleaned the bite with some antiseptic wipes from the same compartment of her pack. He smeared ointment on the rows of tiny puncture wounds and then pressed a stick-on bandage to it, reinforcing it with a pressurized wrap. It was a little bit of overkill, but they still had a long way to climb out of this fucking swamp, and Rachel was going to need the use of both hands.

"How's the pain?" he asked, watching her eyes for the truth.

"Much better," she lied.

"Uh-huh. Can you flex your fingers?"

She tried and failed. "Fuck," she muttered.

"Totally expected," he assured her. "It's too soon. How about the arm? Can you bend your elbow?"

It took her a few seconds, as if the nerves weren't getting the message, but then her arm bent, and she shot him a triumphant grin. *Little victories,* he thought, and smiled back at her. "That's actually better than I expected. Why don't we break early, have some lunch? By the time we're ready to head out, you should have most of your hand back."

"I wish you'd stop saying it like that," she grumbled. "I keep waiting for my fucking arm to fall off."

He laughed. "Sorry. I forget you're not from around here."

Her smile was pleased, and he realized he'd paid her a compliment—an Earther woman who fit right into the Green. What he didn't tell her was that they wouldn't be heading out until morning, because the rizer's poison wasn't quite finished with her yet. She was still in for a miserable night.

Chapter Ten

Aidan cursed as he held Rachel's shivering body, sweat soaking her face and into her hair, her shirt already drenched. He wished for a cool cloth to wipe her forehead, like his mother had done for him when he'd been small. But their supply of drinking water was already low, and he sure as hell wasn't going to use swamp water on her. Besides, while it might have soothed for a minute or two, it wouldn't have done much good. She didn't have a fever or an infection. He'd given her another dose of antibiotics to make sure of that, just because the rizer's mouth was filthy. But what was making her sick was a reaction to the poison itself, her body rejecting the alien venom. And it *was* alien. Rizer was the one venom that no one and nothing on Harp had managed to develop a resistance to, not even shifters.

Rachel's eyes opened as another wave of tremors shook her hard enough that he had to tighten his hold to keep her securely against his chest.

"You lied," she rasped. "You said I'd be better after lunch." She licked dry lips, and he offered her the bottle of water for a tiny sip, then smeared her lips with a moisturizing salve he'd found in her pack.

"I said you'd be better by the time we headed out. I didn't say when."

Her eyes closed as she drifted back to sleep, but there was the slightest smile curving her lips.

• • •

Rachel stifled a groan when she woke the next morning. Everything ached. Everything. She hadn't felt this bad in… Fuck that. She'd *never* felt this bad. It was as if a herd of something with big feet had stomped over her body and left her in a bog. Because it wasn't enough that she felt like shit, she also stank. It had to be pretty bad when she could smell herself, given her present surroundings. She refused to open her eyes, hoping she was still dreaming, that they were actually out of the swamp and back in the leafy sunshine of the Green itself.

"Nope, it's not a dream. You really are waking up to the most charming man on Harp, who's already hunted and cooked breakfast."

She gave in and started to sit up, fighting the urge to bat away his hands when Aidan reached out to help her. She had to admit she wasn't at her best, and his arm did feel good around her, comforting in its solid strength. She had a vague memory of him holding her through the worst of the night, too.

"Thank you," she said.

"You should taste the breakfast first."

She smiled. "That's not what I'm thanking you for."

He hugged her gently. "I know. Here." He handed her more of the antibiotics and water.

Rachel was thirsty, but she drank only the minimum

necessary, knowing their water supply was still short. Taking back the canteen, he then offered her a piece of what she recognized as ceba meat. She wrinkled her nose. "I should probably stick with one of my energy bars."

He grunted. "Nice try. You need protein first—real energy, not sugar. You can have one of your dry-as-dust bars for dessert."

"Who put you in charge?" she grumbled, but took the small piece of meat, knowing he was right. She ate doggedly, ignoring the unfamiliar taste. It was energy, nothing more. But she still declined a second slice. "I'm full. Honest."

Aidan laughed. "You want dessert?" He held out the energy bar.

She shook her head. "I'll save that for later. I need to—" She rolled to her knees, hoping she wouldn't embarrass herself if she tried to stand, pretending not to see his outstretched hand, ready to catch her if she fell. Not likely. She'd survived worse than a giant bug bite in the past, and she was sure Harp had even worse to offer in the future.

"Don't go too far," Aidan cautioned. "I've seen women pee before, you know."

Rachel nodded. She was sure he had. In fact, she was sure there was very little about a woman that Aidan hadn't seen. Once the necessities were taken care of and her clothes restored to their proper order, Rachel returned to what passed for a campsite in the swamp.

He looked up, his gold-flecked eyes searching her face. "Are you good to head out?"

"I'm ready. It was a bad night," she acknowledged, "but the clock is ticking, and I don't give up that easily. Let's go."

He studied her for a moment, then said, "You set the pace."

Rachel agreed. She'd have done the same thing—hell, she *had* done the same thing when a member of her party had been injured. You either traveled as a team, or you didn't travel. She reached for her pack, looked up when Aidan would have taken it from her.

"That thing weighs a ton," he said dryly. "I'll carry it today."

She shook her head. "And if we were on a stroll in paradise, I might let you. But you're the one who insisted there's always some new threat lurking on Harp. I'll carry the pack. You can be the muscle."

He muttered something about a "stubborn woman" but handed over the pack and didn't even try to help her put it on, which she perversely appreciated.

"The air will get fresher the higher we go today," he said from behind her as she started climbing.

She dug her toe in and pushed herself high enough to scramble for the next handhold. "It sure as hell can't get worse."

Almost before the words were out of her mouth, she wanted to take them back. The universe was a trickster with an infinite playbook. It was never a good idea to tempt its imagination.

. . .

Aidan reached overhead and gripped a low-hanging branch, pulling himself up the damn slope with pure muscle power. Rachel was ahead of him, setting the pace. They had to keep going at least until they left the swamp behind. After that. Well, he knew she wanted to reach the city and whoever it was that had hired her. He was anxious to find the asshole, too. But as remarkable as she was, and as determined, she risked more by pushing too hard. In fact, he intended for them to head for Clanhome. She could rest there while Aidan and the others tracked down the traitor. Assuming she'd tell him the traitor's name. She hadn't yet because she was convinced he'd go after asshole without her. Which he would. He and his cousins could shift and get there in half the time it would take her.

He growled low in his throat, loud enough that ahead of him, Rachel froze, moving only to give him a questioning look over her shoulder. He shook his head. "Just me," he said, smiling. "I missed a branch and nearly fell."

She studied him with hazel eyes that saw too much, before giving him a silent nod and continuing her climb. He had no doubt that she understood there was more to Harp than he was telling her, but she hadn't worked out what yet. She never would. There might be several forms of genetically modified humans out there—mostly created to deal with the unfriendly conditions in space—but he could guarantee she'd never seen a shifter among them. He and his shifter brethren were one of a kind. The scientific records of their genetic mods and births had been destroyed, lest anyone, like Earth fleet, think to breed up a shifter crop of their own. Harp's shifters remembered their own history. They knew how easily norms dismissed anything other than perfectly human as *less than*. Less than human, less than worthy of life and freedom. And shifters were not about to become the fleet's newest super-soldier slaves.

His thoughts slammed to a halt as he caught a wisp of unease among the trees. The closer they drew to the upper edge of the rift, the stronger the link between the local trees and the Green beyond, and what they were whispering wasn't good. It was the same as he'd sensed earlier, before they'd hit the swamp bottom, that feeling of something *wrong,* something big, that even the trees couldn't explain.

He threw his head back and scented the air, wishing he could shift. Every one of his senses was sharper in his animal form, not to mention he could have climbed into the treetops to search out whoever was on their trail. Because he had no doubt that the invader the trees were sensing was after him and Rachel.

Shaking his head in disgust, he looked up and realized she had gotten at least twenty yards ahead of him, which was too far. He'd taken his first, hurried step to catch up with her when the swamp went dead silent. Animals large and small had gone quiet, hiding in their nests and burrows, while the trees' confusing song had become a litany of warning.

Damn it.

"Rachel." That was all he said, just her name. And that's all it took. In an instant, her crossbow was in her hand and she was nocking a pair of bolts, her head turning left and right as she searched for the threat.

"What is it?" she murmured, eyes straining to see in the twilight dimness of the swamp's upslope.

His nostrils flared, and his eyes changed, becoming catlike, enhancing his vision. If the danger was close enough to make the swamp dwellers hide, it was close enough for him to scent. He blinked in surprise. "Pongo," he murmured, half in disbelief. He'd never heard of a pongo descending into the swamp for any reason. It was the reason they'd taken this route in the first place.

"The same one?" she asked in a tight whisper.

He shook his head but said, "It has to be. Keep going."

"No!" she said immediately. "I'm not leaving you—"

"No one's leaving anyone. We're both getting the hell off this slope. We can't fight it here." It was a lie, but he needed her safe…and far enough away that he could shift and deal with this fucking pongo on his own terms.

"Fine," she said, stubborn as ever. "You lead the way."

"Rachel, damn it—"

Three hundred pounds of pongo swung through the air from twenty feet away to land on Aidan in a whirlwind of sharp teeth and deadly intent. Claws raked his back, and the animal's fetid breath, reeking of dead flesh, overwhelmed his senses, making his eyes water and his gorge rise. "Rachel, leave your pack and go!" he shouted as he reached overhead and dug his fingers into the thick pelt, feeling claws dig deep gouges into his flesh as he tossed the pongo over his head and to the ground in front of him. It was a big monster, old and wily enough to have followed them through the swamp, to wait until the conditions favored its victory, with Rachel sick and Aidan stuck in his human form. The beast couldn't have understood why, but he'd have scented out the fact that Aidan hadn't shifted in days.

He glanced up to see Rachel had dropped her pack, but the infernal woman wasn't leaving. She didn't understand that she put him in more danger by staying. As long as she was there, he couldn't shift.

"Go!" he bellowed, putting into it all the dominance of his shifter nature, the force of will that made him one of the most powerful of his generation.

The pongo leaped into the air, deadly clawed hands and feet all reaching for him, when suddenly it gave Aidan a look of raw animal cunning and twisted about in midair. Hitting the ground, it raced upslope, heading for Rachel.

Aidan threw back his head and *roared,* and then with a roll of sensation that encompassed every cell in his body, he shifted.

· · ·

Rachel jerked as a tremendous roar vibrated through the thick air. It was a terrifying sound, the challenge of an enraged beast. She spun in a circle, fearing some new threat had emerged from the swamp. But what she saw made her forget everything else.

One moment Aidan was facing off against the enraged pongo, and the next he'd vanished in a spinning storm of golden sparks. And what emerged from the storm was...her eyes went wide...*her cat.*

The pongo, which had been charging uphill, reversed course, jumped ten yards through the air, and landed on her cat's back, its teeth buried in the cat's neck. She gave an enraged yell and lifted her bow.

• • •

Aidan heard Rachel's scream, but he couldn't help her if he didn't stay alive. Understanding its danger as soon as he shifted, the huge pongo had spun away from Rachel and closed on him instead, reaching out to wrap powerful arms around him, digging in its claws as if to anchor itself to his body. Aidan yowled in rage and pain, but he *finally* had the only weapons he needed to win—his teeth, his claws, and his experience. He twisted and rolled, using his weight as a weapon, slamming the beast to the ground. With a loud grunt, the pongo released its hold as Aidan's move crushed the air out of its lungs. But only for an instant. The animal jumped back to its feet and leaped for the trees, but Aidan anticipated the move and jumped faster. Landing on the pongo's back, he sank vicious fangs into its neck and hung on, burying his foreclaws into the beast like hooks, while the deadly claws on his back feet dug in, over and over, ripping out great, bloody chunks of flesh and guts, finding vital organs and tearing at those with equal fervor.

And that quickly, the tide of battle shifted, with the pongo fighting for its life, its deep howl of defiance becoming a high-pitched bark of fear that was music to Aidan's ears. He bit down harder into the ruin of the pongo's neck, tearing through flesh until his jaws closed around the hard ridge of its spine. The vertebrae shattered with a satisfying crunch as the pongo went limp, and Aidan raised his head in a bloody roar of victory. The triumphant howl echoed through a swamp, traveling to the depths of the rift, terrifying prey who had never heard the sound before. Finally kicking aside the lifeless body as the red haze of battle lust receded from his vision, he remembered Rachel. He turned and saw her standing strong, crossbow in hand, staring at him in wonder, but with a fine dose of anger mixed in.

"Aidan?" she asked, as if testing the concept.

He dropped to the ground with a groan of pain. He'd won the battle, but the damn pongo had done some damage. Several ribs were broken and there were deep wounds all along his left side and flank. He knew he should shift to jumpstart the healing, but first he was going to lie there for a moment and catch his breath.

"Aidan," Rachel said again, softer and from much closer, he realized as he felt her gentle hand on his injured side. "You've been keeping secrets," she murmured, already digging into her pack for first aid supplies.

He could have told her it wasn't necessary, that shifters were resistant to pretty much everything on Harp, and that all he really had to do was shift a few times to heal most of his injuries. But he was enjoying the attention too much. Plus, as soon as he took on his human form, he'd have to answer questions. Right now, he could simply lie there and be petted.

"I can't believe you let me treat you like a big kitty cat," she scolded as she poured water over his bloody flank. "Oh, baby," she said softly.

There was so much tenderness, so much empathy in those two words, that Aidan wanted to roll in the scent of her.

"You have some broken ribs here," she murmured, pressing gently.

He lifted his head to snarl at her. That hurt. He wanted to

go back to the gentle strokes and soft words.

"Don't you snarl at me," she snapped. "I'm trying to help you *again*, even though you've been lying to me this whole time."

Aidan needed to shift to accelerate his healing. He couldn't keep her safe when he couldn't even breathe without pain. On the other hand, if he shifted to human, he'd have to explain everything to Rachel, and he wasn't ready to have *that* conversation. That left only one option. Taking the coward's way out, he closed his eyes, drew a deep breath, and shifted in a whirlwind of golden sparks, taking on his human form just briefly, before shifting back once more to his cat.

• • •

"Shit!" Rachel froze, staring down at the giant cat. No, this wasn't a cat, it was *Aidan*. Part of her was pissed and a little wounded that he'd kept such an enormous secret from her after all they'd been through. She'd taken care of him when he'd been drugged and abused on the ship. She'd gone against her own crew to get him out of that cage and… She struggled for breath as the true enormity of Wolfrum's crime hit her. He *knew* about this. He had to. She'd wondered why he'd go to such lengths to capture an animal for some perverted collector's private zoo. Why he'd risk his reputation, his entire life's work!

But *this*. My God, the military would pay a damn fortune for a soldier like Aidan. A shifter, for fuck's sake! The scientist in her shoved to the forefront, demanding to know how it was even possible. It couldn't be a spontaneous adaption. It was too huge.

She looked down at the sleeping cat and wanted to shake him awake and demand answers. But this was Aidan, and he'd risked his life to defend her. She sighed and settled in next to him, stroking her hand over his flank. She pressed gently on his injured ribs, wanting to know if—

She jerked her hand up when the big cat grumbled at her touch and shoved his head into her lap, demanding attention. Rachel froze with her hand in midair, then smiled. There was no doubt this was Aidan. She shifted her hand to his big head, rubbing around his ears and stroking down over his neck and shoulders in a careful, repetitive pattern. He sighed lustily and relaxed beneath her hand, his breathing deep and regular.

Rachel shrugged. He'd watched over her last night, and now it was her turn. He could sleep and heal while she kept watch. As she sat there, every sense finely tuned, hyperalert to any sign of danger, she thought about Wolfrum. How did that kind of man—a decorated fleet officer, one of the most highly regarded scientists in his field, given award after award for research and discovery—how did such a man fall so low as to contemplate capturing *human beings* for slavery and experimentation? Because she *knew* what the fleet would do if they got their hands on someone like Aidan. They wouldn't see the beauty of the animal or the magnificent human adaptability—they'd see a super soldier, a weapon. They'd break him down to his DNA, figure out a way to breed a new crop of shifters with all the aggression and fearlessness but without the alpha characteristics that would make them too hard to control. And they wouldn't stop with one shifter. They'd take over the planet. There'd be no more closed status for Harp. Oh, it would be closed, but not for anyone's protection. The military would want its secrets all for themselves.

She squeezed her eyes shut, thinking miserably. She had to tell Aidan about the second ship now. No more lies about heading to the city to meet Wolfrum. She'd kept silent for fear of what Wolfrum and the second crew might do if they were cornered, the people they'd kill, the animals they'd butcher. But now she understood what she'd seen when the cats had attacked her ship. She'd thought it had been wild cats against a wounded and unprepared ship's crew. And afterward, when Aidan had claimed the entire crew had been killed, she hadn't been convinced. There was simply no way a bunch of wild animals could defeat her heavily-armed shipmates. But now, after witnessing the fight she'd just seen between Aidan and the enormous apelike pongo, the viciousness of the battle he'd won… She imagined a dozen or more Aidans against her Earther crewmates. They wouldn't have known what was hitting them. They'd have been torn apart. It was obvious that Harp and its shifters could take care of themselves, but now they needed to know the face of their enemy. And *she* had to tell them.

Chapter Eleven

"No wonder you're always half dressed."

Aidan paused in pulling on his tunic and turned to face Rachel. He'd woken to find her dozing next to him, one arm draped protectively over his back. It had touched something deep inside, created a tight feeling in his chest that he'd never felt before and wasn't sure he wanted to feel now. But he couldn't deny the connection between them. From the very beginning, when her fellow Earthers had dragged him half conscious onto their ship, she hadn't seemed to recognize the danger he posed to her. Or maybe she'd had the right of it, because as satisfying as it had been to slaughter her crew, he'd never once considered attacking *her*.

Earlier, he'd wanted to put his arms around her and hold her close. But he hadn't been sure how she'd react to waking next to a naked man instead of a cuddly big cat. So he'd forced himself to slide out from under her grasp, moving one muscle at a time so as not to disturb her. She was safe as long as he was in the vicinity, so there was no need to clutch her to his chest, no matter how tempting the idea was.

He studied her now, trying to gauge her reaction to his big reveal. Shit. Rhodry was going to kill him when he found out. But that was in the future. Right now, he had to deal with Rachel.

"Shifters don't worry much about being naked, but others do," he explained. "We can't drag a full set of clothes around with us, so we cache these throughout the Green." He shrugged. "There's none in the swamp, though, and this is my last pair. So, if I have to shift again…" He grinned, then stilled, waiting for her response.

"Don't bother on my account," she said dryly. "I enjoy the view. And don't pretend you don't know how good you look."

His grin widened. "I try."

She rolled her eyes, then sighed, her expression grim. "We have to talk."

"About this," he asked, gesturing at himself. "Nothing I can do about it, sweetheart."

"No, not that. Although, you must know I have questions. And I *still* can't believe you didn't tell me, but…there's something more important, something you need to know about Wolfrum."

Aiden stilled. "Wolfrum?" he repeated. "You mean Guy Wolfrum?"

She nodded. "He's your traitor."

Aidan wanted to be shocked, but he wasn't. There'd always been something off about the Earther scientist, something that had offended shifter sensibilities like a piece of bad meat. Rhodry hadn't trusted him, nor had Amanda. Her instincts had weighed heavily on Rhodry's opinion, of course, but they'd carried weight with Aidan and the other shifters, too. She'd proven herself too many times, both during the Guild trials and after, proven her intellect and abilities, not to mention the strength of her connection to the

Green. Plus, she'd served with Wolfrum on the Earther ship. If she sensed something suspicious about him, they had to listen.

Aidan finished pulling on his tunic. "Tell me," he said, but she wouldn't look at him. He hadn't known her long, but long enough to know that wasn't typical for her. She was nothing if not forthright, sometimes defiantly so. The news about Wolfrum was bad enough, even if it wasn't a complete surprise. That she wouldn't meet his gaze meant there was more, and maybe worse.

"What is it, Rachel?"

She sighed, and when she finally looked up, her face was lined with misery and…guilt?

"You need to know," she said as she drew closer, stopping a few feet away as if unsure of her welcome. "Fuck. There's a second ship, Aidan. I think that's where Wolfrum is."

Aidan stared. "A second ship?"

Rachel nodded, then crouched down to dig her damn map out of her backpack. He watched her in disbelief. She'd been lying to him all along about going to the city to confront Wolfrum. She wasn't trying to get to the city, she was trying to find the second ship.

"So what was your plan?" he asked. "Unless Wolfrum's somehow managed to land his ship in the middle of Ciudad Vaquero, you were never going to the city. So how'd you plan to get there? And why didn't you tell me the truth?" He was angry at her deception, but even more at her betrayal. They'd fought and survived together. He'd started to think there was something more between them, more than traveling companions, more even than friends. She'd been lying to him all along, keeping the truth about the threat to *his* people from him.

There were tears in her eyes when she met his stare. "It sounds stupid now, but I swear I thought Wolfrum would kill you if I told you where they were. I knew you'd go after him, and I was sure Wolfrum would butcher you and the other hunters."

"Shifters," he growled. "We're called shifters."

She nodded. "But don't you see, this is so much worse now. Wolfrum knows what you are. That's why he wanted you, why he wants you, still. And by now, he must know that the first ship failed. They had to have some way of signaling each other. Radios wouldn't work, but flares would, or who the hell knows what else? If Wolfrum knows, or even suspects, the first ship is dead, he'll also know that you and the other shifters are the ones who took it out, and that he's finished, in every way that counts. He's betrayed not only Harp, but everything on which he built his career.

"He has one last chance to gain something out of this venture, and that's to capture a shifter and get it to his buyer. But he'll be desperate by now. There's nothing he won't do."

Aidan clenched his jaw, knowing she was right. He had to get word to Clanhome, and to Rhodry in the city. "Show me where it is," he growled.

"I'm sorry," she said earnestly.

He just grunted and jerked his chin at the map.

She lowered her head, chin hitting her chest, eyes closed in resignation. She hung there a long moment then unfolded her map and smoothed it out on the back of her pack. "Here," she said and looked up expectantly, almost challenging him to join her.

He crouched next to her without a word.

"Okay." She glanced up once, as if fixing the location of the sun in the sky, and then rotated the map slightly.

Aidan didn't need to check the sun. He reached out and turned the map to the proper position.

"Ah," she said, seeming to understand. "*This* is where we are now." She pointed. "And this…" She slid her finger in a westerly direction and slightly north, closer to the mountains and Clanhome. "This is the second landing site."

Aidan studied the map, fixing the site in his head, recalling everything he knew about the area. Wolfrum, the bastard, had chosen well for both ships. He'd picked two remote landing spots, both far from the city. They were on opposite sides of Clanhome, but still in clan territory, guaranteeing the presence of shifter patrols who would respond to an attack like the one that had brought Aidan out of hiding, bringing Wolfrum's prey right to him.

"There're no settlements out there," he muttered, thinking out loud. "No lumber camps that I know of." He frowned. The first site had been completely remote and unsettled, but there was something about this second site that was striking a nerve. "Right," he breathed, as it finally hit him. "Cristobal," he said.

Rachel raised her head in surprise. "Your Ardrigh?"

Aidan nodded, still not looking at her. "His family has an old hunting lodge out there."

"Will he be there now?"

"Doubtful. I've never known him to use it. His grandfather only built it to piss off the clans."

"If he's there, will he be alone?"

"Hell, no. He'll have a whole hunting party with him. All shifters."

She frowned. "Wolfrum wouldn't be stupid enough to go after the Ardrigh, would he?"

"Fuck if I know. He's *your* guy, not mine."

She glared, eyes flashing and cheeks flushed hotly. "Fuck you. I'm trying to help."

"If you were really trying—"

"I explained why I didn't tell you about the second ship. I was trying to save lives, including yours. And it's not as if you've been forthcoming. You had a big fucking secret of your own."

"I had a damn good reason for keeping the existence of shifters a secret, which is proved by the fact that *your* people are here trying to cage us like animals!"

"They are not *my* people!" She jumped to her feet, matching his glare. "I did everything I could to sabotage their mission. And if you'd told me the truth about *your* people," she added, her voice rising along with her anger, "I'd have told *you* the truth about the other ship from the very beginning!"

Aidan stared at her, breathing hard. He was furious…and more turned on by this woman than he'd ever been in his life. She was beautiful. Forget the weight she'd lost over the days of their trek through the swamp, forget the dirt on her cheek, and the blood on her arm. She was fierce and determined and spitting mad. And she had a point.

He closed the distance between them with a single step, slipped an arm around her waist and tugged her against his chest. Her eyes widened in alarm and then heated with a desire that matched his own. They'd been building toward this for a long time, longer than she even knew. He lowered his head and kissed her.

• • •

Rachel didn't know what to think. When he'd slung an arm around her and yanked her forward, she'd been alarmed. He was so much bigger than she was. He could easily overpower her, and even though she had a knife, she wasn't sure she could use it on him. They'd been through too much together. But when her body collided with his, when her breasts were crushed against his hard chest…she looked up and saw the desire in his eyes and every sexual instinct she possessed came alive. The simmering hunger that had been building between them for days, stoked by every casual touch, every comforting embrace, burst into a raging flame.

Aidan bent his head to kiss her, his mouth unexpectedly gentle, barely touching at first, a soft brush of lips. But when she rose up to meet him, his arm tightened, pulling her onto her toes as he claimed her mouth for his own, his lips firm and demanding, his tongue sliding between her teeth to explore every inch, twisting sensuously around her tongue and then pulling out to stab in and out in a way that caused an ache between her thighs. She lifted her arms around his neck, wanting more, feeling the firm press of his erection behind the thin fabric of his pants, wrapping one leg around his thigh to better rub herself against him, putting the hard length of him between her legs, right where she needed him.

Aidan groaned against her mouth, his fingers digging into her lower back as he held her in place, his cock stroking between her thighs. Rachel grabbed the back of his tunic and pulled, wanting bare skin—

Something heavy crashed onto the forest floor right next to them, so close that its fur brushed against Rachel's bare arm. Aidan acted before she had a chance to figure out what it was, whipping her around and into the curve of his body, dropping them both to the ground as the trees above them shook as if a violent wind had dipped out of the sky. Debris rained down all around, dead leaves and branches, rock-hard berries that were stinging pellets against her hands where they clutched Aidan close.

"What the fuck?" she asked, breathlessly.

"Cebas," Aidan said, laughter in his voice. "Paying us back for hunting and killing them these last few days."

"Fuckers."

He kissed her briefly, then sighed. "I can't believe I'm saying this, but… This isn't the time or place, sweetheart. We need to get out of this fucking swamp."

She echoed his sigh and brushed something wiggly from

his shoulder, wondering what the hell she'd been thinking. Had she actually expected to have sex on this slimy, swampy hillside? "Hell," she said grumpily, "one look at your naked butt and the swamp monster would climb this fucking hill to take a bite."

He laughed, his eyes more gold than blue as they caught a stray streak of sunshine. "Come on," he said, jumping to his feet with a catlike grace that made a lot more sense now that she knew what he was. "Let's climb this last bit of hillside and get some fresh air and real sunshine for a change. There's a lively stream not too far from the top. The water's cold, but there's a good-sized pool that's shallow enough to warm up a bit in the sunlight. We can get naked and wash off the muck." He pulled her to her feet, yanked her against his body, and growled, "And finish what we started." He kissed her hard and fast then set her on her feet, not letting go of her until she was steady. "You ready?" he asked.

She snorted at the stupid question, patted his cheek, then grabbed her pack and started climbing.

• • •

It took the better part of the day to finally climb out of the rift, leaving the swamp and its treacherous slopes behind. Aidan would have liked another hour or two of sunshine before they stopped for the night. They were back in the Green itself, which meant the foliage was increasingly thick and the canopy similarly dense. It also meant that before long he'd be able to send a warning to Rhodry and the other cousins using the trees' song. The song wasn't a message line. He wouldn't be able to go into detail. But he could alert them to the existence of danger, and they were smart enough to make the connection between the invaders and a new threat. Especially since he was the one ringing the alarm. They all knew he was with Rachel, the woman from the ship.

His thoughts were interrupted by Rachel's curse when her foot caught on something in the nearly lightless night. He could operate just fine with the minimal glow from Banba, the smallest and most distant of Harp's moons. But Rachel couldn't. Even with him taking the lead, forging a trail through the thick brush and cutting away thick vines that blocked their path, her steps had grown slower and more cautious as the sky darkened. In the end, there was no point in pushing it. They were both exhausted after more than a week of daily fights with swamp dwellers, tasteless meals, and too little sleep. It made more sense to stop early enough to have a decent meal and make a comfortable camp.

"Can you smell it, Rachel?" he asked, turning his head slightly so she could hear him without the need to raise his voice. The Green might be better than the swamp, but it was still a dangerous place. If he'd been alone, he'd have climbed a tree and fuck anyone or anything that tried to stop him. But he wasn't taking any chances with Rachel along. It was better not to draw unnecessary attention to two weary travelers.

She inhaled softly in response to his question and surprised him by saying, "Moving water."

He grinned, oddly proud of her skill in the wild. As if he'd had anything at all to do with it. "It's a very small branch of the Leeward Stream," he confirmed.

"Is that the main east/west river?"

"'Main' is a relative term. It's not all that big. Nothing like the rivers you have on Earth, but it doesn't need to be. There aren't that many of us. It's run-off from the glacier, as much underground as not. By the time it hits the center of the Green, it runs as low as two feet and as high as eight, depending on the season, until it's finally swallowed up by the southern desert. What you're smelling now is one of the irregular creeks that feed the swamp. It's running high right now, which is good for us. Within a month, it'll be mostly mud."

"Will we reach it in time to wash up before sunset?"

For the first time, he caught a tired note in her question. Despite his misgivings about Rachel's fitness for travel through the Green, he had to admit she'd done better than most Harp natives. She couldn't match his skill, but she didn't have his inborn advantages. It helped to be able to turn into a giant hunting cat. And then there was the Green, which was once again a steady and soothing song in his head, now that they'd climbed out of that damn rift. Someday, not in his lifetime, the Green would conquer the swamp, and even the swamp monster would be happier.

"With luck, we'll not only wash up, but we should be able to catch our dinner. There's always a stray silver or five who gets confused and ends up in the wrong creek. How good are you at cleaning fish?"

She snorted. "I'm assuming silvers are fish, or fish-like. As long as I get to eat it, I can clean and cook anything."

"You cook?"

She laughed. "Don't sound so excited. I cook over a campfire. Back home, my parents' cook fixes care packages for me. All I have to do is heat them up."

"It's not so different here. When I'm in Clanhome, I eat mostly in Devlin house. We shifters provide the meat, others prepare the meals."

"Devlin house?"

"Our clan house. Devlin is the largest of the clans, but we're sworn to de Mendoza, which is our oldest clan. The head of de Mendoza is the leader of all Clanhome. My cousin Rhodry is the current de Mendoza. He comes to it from his mother's side. His father was a Devlin."

"His father's dead?"

"Aye. An accident when Rhodry was just a lad. He and

his mother moved into Devlin house after that, even though her father was still the de Mendoza and still alive. Mean bastard of an old man."

"And your parents?"

"Alive and well, as are my five sisters, two brothers, and more cousins than I can count. No one crosses the Devlins. We're a tight bunch, and there's a lot of us."

"Are you all shifters?"

"Most of the lads."

She caught up and pulled him to a stop. "None of the women?" she asked, looking up at him curiously.

He tipped his head to one side, thinking. Since she knew shifters existed, which was Harp's biggest secret, was there any reason not to tell her that the trait was sex-linked? Rachel wasn't stupid. She'd figure it out for herself once she reached Clanhome, where she'd be surrounded by shifters. She was bound to notice they were all male, so he might as well tell her. He scowled at the sudden image of Rachel surrounded by his many alpha male cousins.

"The trait is sex-linked," he told her. "A shifter's sons will always be shifters. His daughters won't even carry the gene."

"Really?" She turned and started walking again. "I wonder how the founding colonists worked that out."

"I don't think anyone knows. The records were destroyed."

"So you said. I'm not sure I believe you, but that's all right. Harp's entitled to her secrets."

He caught up and wrapped an arm around her waist, lifting her off her feet a moment before she would have kicked a zillah nest, nearly invisible in the twilight of dusk.

"What?" she asked, then looked down. "What the hell is that?"

"Zillah lizard. They burrow into the ground for their nests. Our footsteps stirred them up."

"Are they poisonous?"

"No, just disgusting once they reproduce."

"Huh. You can put me down now."

Aidan blinked in surprise and set her on her feet, carefully away from the zillah. He hadn't been consciously aware that he was still holding her. "There's a good spot about thirty feet that way," he said, guiding her to the left of their path. "You can't see it from here, but the bathing pool I told you about is there, and at the bend in the creek, you can usually snag some silvers. Use your flashlight."

"It won't hurt your night vision?"

"I'm not that delicate."

She gave a breathy laugh as if she didn't believe him, but dug out her small LED light and turned it on, aiming it just ahead of her feet. Aidan followed slowly, drinking in the song of the trees like a man who'd been dying of thirst. It was something he'd never been without, a call he'd first heard in his mother's womb. He listened now, reaching far beyond their current location, searching for any hint that the second ship had attacked the Green, certain the trees' agony would carry to every shifter on the planet.

He found nothing, which meant there was still time to stop Wolfrum from carrying out his sick plans. He glanced ahead to where Rachel had found the camping spot he'd indicated. She'd already dropped her pack and was sitting on the ground untying her boots. His awareness already mingled with that of the trees, he reached out, searching for some sign of his cousins, or any shifter, really. He found no one, but sent the warning anyway, hoping someone would be close enough to hear it.

"God, that feels good."

He turned his head at the sound of Rachel's quiet exclamation, watching as she tugged off her socks and began rubbing her feet.

"I hope you're right about this place," she called softly, without looking up. "If I wake up with disgusting bugs in my boots, I'm dumping them on *your* head."

Aidan laughed as he walked closer to where she sat. "I'll be your—" The breath ran out of him as she pulled her shirt off over her head then stood and shimmied out her pants and panties in a single move. Her bra followed, joining the pile of clothes on top of her pack. She was gorgeous—her body long and sleek with muscle, her ass a round temptation, her full breasts tipped with dark nipples that puckered in the night air like rosy berries waiting to be bitten. He stared wordlessly until she shot him a glance over her shoulder.

"I thought shifters didn't have a problem with nudity."

Aidan's heart kicked back into action at the challenge in her words. "We don't." He stripped off his tunic and reached for the tie on his pants, only to pause again as he watched her step slowly into the bathing pool, his shifter eyes seeing every delicious detail as the water lapped over her legs, her ass, dripping off her breasts as she ducked under and then sat on a rocky ledge beneath the water and gave a pleasured sigh.

Aidan cleared his throat softly and reminded himself that he was the charming cousin, the one who had plenty of experience with women. Dropping his pants and kicking off the soft boots, he closed the distance to the pool. His vanity demanded he hesitate on the edge long enough to catch Rachel's admiring scan of his body, her gaze sliding up over his hips and chest, then dropping back down to where his penis jutted hard and heavy between his legs. His cock jerked to attention, reacting to the hunger in her face. Her gaze shot up to meet his, and he had to fight back a groan when she licked her lips nervously.

"Fuck me," he whispered and stepped down into the pool

Rachel's gaze was still locked on his face. "Okay," she whispered back.

Aidan dropped to the deepest part of the pool then reached out and snagged her around the waist, pulling her off the ledge and into his arms. "You weren't supposed to hear that," he grumbled.

She laughed. "Does that mean the invitation doesn't stand?"

"Hell, no." He kissed her then. Not a promise for the future kind of a kiss, like he'd given her before. This was passion and lust and demand. He crushed her lips against his, feeling her breasts against his naked chest, those lushly hard nipples scraping his skin like twin pebbles. He dropped a hand down to the swell of her ass and pressed her naked body against him, rubbing his cock between her legs, feeling the heat of her pussy despite the cool water. "Rachel…" It was the last warning he was going to give her.

"Yes," she whispered. She slid her arms around his neck, and her thighs opened as she wrapped her legs around his hips.

"Damn." Aidan had fucked a lot of women. Sex was accepted on Harp, even encouraged among young people. But it had never felt like this. He slid his cock into Rachel's body and couldn't hold back a groan of pleasure. She was hot and slick and tight, her sheath gripping his length, caressing it with intimate ripples. He pushed deep inside her, not stopping until he was fully buried in her delicious heat. He held there a moment, relishing the sensation, and then began to move, one hand palming her firm ass, holding her in place as his cock glided in and out on the satiny cream of her arousal. He bit hard on her lower lip, drinking in her small cry of desire as his lips traveled over her jaw and down to her neck. He bit her again, branding her, sucking her skin between his lips until he was certain he'd leave a mark, and then licking his way back to her mouth.

"Bastard," she muttered, biting his lips before he could

kiss her.

"What?" he asked, pretending innocence as his cock continued to thrust in and out, never stopping its rhythm.

She smiled against his lips, then shifted one of her legs higher on his hips, holding him more tightly, meeting every thrust of his cock with one of her own, their bodies grinding against each other with every hungry plunge. Her sweet mouth trailed over his jaw with tiny bites, her teeth closing teasingly over the lobe of his ear, then gliding down to his neck where she licked and kissed in time with the press of her hips, lulling him into a sensuous rhythm until her teeth closed down hard over the pulse point in his neck.

Several things happened at once.

His cock bucked hard at the erotic pain, feeling the pulsing pleasure of his climax building in his balls, even as Rachel moaned softly.

"Aidan," she whispered and pressed herself against him as her pussy flooded with juices. Her whisper became a desperate cry as her body clamped down hard, squeezing and releasing his cock, like a thousand tiny fingers massaging him, caressing him, pulling him deeper into the seductive heat of her body. Her cries became more frantic as his thrusts sped up, his own climax an overwhelming pressure as he continued to fuck her, loving the feel of her slick tissues, not wanting it to end.

He took her mouth in a desperate, passionate kiss, their tongues tangling, teeth clashing, until his body surrendered. He lifted his head and howled as he climaxed, the heat of his release an overwhelming pleasure as Rachel's cries joined his, her pussy clamping down on him in another orgasm until all they could do was hold onto each other in desperate desire.

• • •

Rachel clung to Aidan, her arms around his neck, her legs locked around his hips. His cock was still flexing inside her, her pussy shivering every time the hard length of him moved. Hard? How could he still be hard after all that? She tensed her hips experimentally, moving the tiniest bit, and was reward with his groan. She kissed his neck, licking the bite mark she'd left there. She didn't know how things worked on Harp, but she hadn't missed the fact that he'd blatantly marked *her*. She wanted it clear that the claiming went both ways. Aidan was hers.

Her stomach clenched with something close to fear. Her feelings for him went beyond fantastic sex. Beyond even the closeness that developed when two people survived a life-threatening challenge together. She'd felt that before. She'd even had sex with partners who'd gone through it with her. This was more. And it terrified her, so she pretended it wasn't happening.

Arching her back, she slid her pussy along Aidan's cock, until his big hand closed over her butt and pressed, holding himself deep inside her.

"Be a good girl," he muttered.

"Fuck good."

He laughed. "I should have known you'd want to be in charge." He pulled out and immediately thrust deep inside her. He was so damn big. Thick and long and hard. "Not this time, sweetheart." He tightened his arms around her, one hand on her butt, the other arm holding her shoulders so she couldn't move, as he slid slowly in and out of her pussy. His eyes never left hers, flickering gold in the dim light, making her feel as if he saw far more than she wanted him to. She wanted to look away, to close her eyes against an intimacy that made her heart race with fear, but she was no coward. She forced herself to meet the demand in his gaze, to acknowledge that this was more than sex, more than the release of adrenaline.

A shiver of pleasure tightened her abdomen as her pussy clenched around his erection. Rachel tried to move, to ease the ache of desire, but Aidan wouldn't let her. His gaze narrowed, his lids lowering over those golden eyes as he continued to fuck her, slowly, luxuriously, gliding on the slick juices of her growing arousal. Her fingers tightened on his shoulders, short nails digging into his flesh.

"Aidan," she whispered, pleading for release.

He lowered his head and kissed her, one hand gripping the back of her neck, as he began thrusting harder, faster.

She kissed him back, biting, her fingers twisted in his long hair. A second orgasm swept over her, bowing her back as he crushed her against his chest, her cries meeting his groan as the sudden rush of his climax filled her with heat.

Rachel lowered her head to his shoulder. He still hadn't released her. Their hearts were pounding against each other, chests heaving as they struggled to breathe. His hold loosened, leaving her breasts to rub against his chest, the scrape of her hard nipples over his skin sending a fresh wave of pleasure rippling through her body.

She and Aidan groaned in unison, then laughed. "Someday, sweetheart," he murmured against her ear. "When we're not worn out from surviving the swamp, or racing across the Green to save Harp…someday, I'll have you in my bed with all the time in the world to make love to you."

Rachel shivered as his warm breath floated over her skin. It was too easy to picture that someday. To imagine Aidan, golden skin gleaming over powerful muscles, his eyes dancing with mischief and desire as he spread her legs and… She forced the image away, her body already rubbing against his like a wanton thing.

"Is that a date?" she asked, trying to break the unbearable weight of the moment.

"Not a date," he growled. "A promise."

She shivered again. Aidan slipped an arm under her legs and stood. "The water's cold," he growled. "You need to warm up."

Rachel couldn't remember the last time she'd been carried by a man. Had she ever been? And yet Aidan held her with such ease as he stepped out of the water and over to the small, cleared area where they'd left their things. It felt perfectly natural, her arms around his neck, her head on his shoulder. "Do you have clean clothes?" he asked quietly. "If not, I can find a cache—"

"I have clothes," she said, kissing his jaw. She felt his grin against her lips.

"I like you like this, all sweet and soft."

She bit him. "Don't get used to it."

He laughed and set her on her feet. "You get dressed. I'll get the fire started."

"What about you?" she asked. "Don't you need clothes?"

"Not really. I thought I'd wear fur tonight. It'll keep us both warm."

Rachel's eyes widened. She was both intrigued and excited. She remembered the big, warm cat she'd treated on the ship. The lush thickness of his fur beneath her fingers, the deep thud of his heart. "Can we do that?"

He shrugged and said, "Why not? It's still me."

"Do you prefer one form over the other?"

• • •

Aidan didn't answer right away. *Did* he prefer one form over the other? Shifters rarely thought about it. They were the same person, no matter what form they wore. It wasn't as if they lost themselves to their animal, or vice versa. On the other hand, there was no doubt that each form had its benefits and drawbacks.

"Well," he said thoughtfully, "the ability to talk is nice."

She laughed in a way that made him think his answer had surprised her. "I guess it would be," she conceded at last. "But with your cat… You're so wild. It must be freeing."

"It's spectacular, but it has its limits."

He could see the curious tilt of her head as she studied him. "Like what?" she asked.

"Sex, for one." If he'd hoped to shock her, he failed miserably. He was the one shocked when she asked her next question.

"You don't have sex while you're shifted?" She spoke without stuttering, without embarrassment. She was a scientist, and he was her subject.

Shit. Why did he ever start this?

"Well, for one thing, I like women in my bed. So, unless my lover is into bestiality, sex in my cat form is a no-go. In fact, it's definitely a no-go, because *I'm* not into it."

"Right, no female shifters," she said thoughtfully, ignoring his whole dissertation on bestiality, as if he hadn't even mentioned it. How the hell had he gotten into this discussion? "Fascinating."

"Yeah. That's the word I'd use. 'Fascinating,'" he said dryly.

She laughed. "You're embarrassed."

"Am not."

"Okay," she agreed, but he could still hear the laughter in her voice.

He gave her a narrow look and said, "You start the fire and I'll catch some fish."

• • •

Rachel couldn't contain her amusement. The big bad shifter was embarrassed, and all because she'd asked some straightforward questions. Logical questions. Did he prefer one form over the other? Was one the real him, and the other simply a mask that he put on for convenience? After all, *she* wasn't the one who'd raised the subject of bestiality. Her grin was huge as she gave him a little salute then turned to get the fire going. She pulled on her spare set of clean clothes first. Aidan might be accustomed to roaming around naked, but she wasn't. It had nothing to do with nudity and everything to do with creepy crawly things that liked to sneak into places on the human body where she'd really rather not have them. She'd just gotten the flames going well and was working on stripping down some sticks to use as skewers for the fish, when Aidan reappeared. She stood to meet him, already pulling her knife, intending to fulfill her promise to clean his catch, but the two large, silver-scaled fish which he laid by the fire had already been gutted and washed.

"Hey, that was *my* job," she said, looking up at him, trying to ignore the fact that he was gorgeously naked.

His gold-flecked eyes danced with knowledge of her reaction, his expression one of pure male satisfaction. "Silvers are easy. I'll let you do the gutting when we're deep in the Green and I'm hunting with my teeth instead of my hands."

If he was trying to disgust her, he failed. Rachel had dressed more than her share of all manner of beasts. Plenty of her clients in the past had enjoyed the hunt, but not what came after. In her book, you ate what you killed, or you gave it to someone else who would.

"I'll look forward to both. Seeing you hunt, and me dressing the game," she clarified at his questioning look.

Aidan wrapped a big hand around her neck and pulled her in for a long, wet kiss. "You are not what I expected, Earther woman."

"You're not the first person I've surprised. And you're freezing," she said, her arms circling his waist. "Put on some clothes." It was an exaggeration. His skin was slightly cooler than his usual furnace-like heat, but it was an excuse to get some clothes on him. He was simply too tempting, and they needed to eat. Regrettably, one could not live on spectacular sex alone.

His chuckle said he knew what she was doing, but he went along with it, pressing a quick kiss to her lips before strolling over to where he'd dropped another of those cached clothing packs the shifters seemed to leave around the Green.

"You guys have those everywhere?"

"No, just the places we travel a lot. This one and the one on the other side of the swamp are kept stocked because we usually take the tree road, which means we always travel shifted." He pulled on the pants first, then the tunic, but shoved the boots back inside the drawstring bag.

"How do they get re-supplied?"

Dropping a small package of trail mix bars next to the fire, he said, "When we check into Clanhome after a patrol, we make note of any caches we used. The next patrol resupplies. Most of the year, the ones out here don't get used much, but there's a logging crew that rotates out this way, and they're fussy about naked shifters hanging around. Don't want to tempt their women," he added, grinning.

That attitude made perfect sense to Rachel, but she didn't say so. He didn't need his ego getting any bigger than it was. She finished skewering the fish and set them on the spit she'd set up over the flames, then picked up her empty canteen. "Is this water drinkable?"

He nodded. "This far from the glacier, it is."

"No weird parasites to worry about?"

He paused. "I don't think so. As far as I know the fleet personnel manning the science center drink the local water with no enhancements. And it all comes from the same place. Come on, I'll walk with you, keep you from falling on your ass in the dark."

She flicked on her LED, sorely tempted to flash it in his eyes, but she'd regret it if some new threat appeared out of the forest while he was blinded by her light.

He caught the look on her face and laughed, coming very close and leaning down to whisper in her ear. "It's not that I doubt your skills, sweetheart, it's just that I'm very fond of your ass."

She pushed him away, trying not to laugh. He was too charming by half. Shoving two of the empty bottles at his chest, she said, "Fine, you can come. But I lead."

"That's all right. I have excellent night vision, and I don't mind the view."

"You always carry salt with you?" Aidan asked, nearly an hour later as he finished the last of the fish and dropped the remnants into the fire.

"Sure, and pepper, too. That's the minimum necessary for a tasty dish, according to Evelyn."

"Evelyn?"

"My parents' cook. They loved us, but they were way more invested in their work than their children. Evelyn saved my brother and me from starvation."

"My compliments to Evelyn then, the next time you see her." He added that last casually, waiting for her response, wondering if she planned to rush back to Earth on the next shuttle, a possibility that had him fighting back a growl. He paused, surprised by his own reaction. He didn't do long-term with women. Hell, he barely did short-term. So what the hell did he care if Rachel went home? After all, her life was out there, visiting exotic places and finding new ways to risk her life. He knocked the two forked spit sticks into the fire.

Rachel looked up in surprise. "We could have used those in the morning." There was a question in her voice.

He shrugged. "It's not like there's a shortage of wood."

She eyed him a moment longer, then said quietly, "You should go ahead, Aidan."

"What?"

"You need to warn your people about Wolfrum and the second ship, and you'll travel a lot faster without me."

He studied her. "Are you trying to get rid of me?"

She snorted. "Like I could. No, I'm serious. You're too polite to say it, but I slow you down."

It was his turn to snort. "I'm not too polite. You *are* slower than I am, but so is more than half the population of Harp. That doesn't mean I leave them behind because it's more convenient."

"We're not talking convenience. This is life or death. Damn it, Aidan, they put you in a cage, *knowing* you were human. And now that the first hunt failed, Wolfrum will be all the more determined to make sure their second hunt succeeds. He won't care who gets hurt. You and I are the only ones who know everything, and *you're* the only one who can stop him."

"I'm not leaving you alone out here." He knew she was right, but, damn it, he didn't want her to end up dead because of it.

"Don't insult me," she snapped. "Maybe you could get away with that macho crap before, but you've seen what I'm capable of now. I can handle the Green for a few days on my own."

"And what about the rizer bite that almost killed you?"

"Okay, what about the damn giant snake that almost killed you?" she countered angrily.

"I could have handled it," he grumbled.

"And I could have handled the rizer bite!" Her voice gentled. "Don't get me wrong, it was a lot better with you there, but I would have survived on my own if I'd had to."

Aidan stared at the fire, not happy with the way this conversation was going. He kept lumping her in with most of the norms he knew. And not just the women, either. Most of the non-shifter population, male and female both, rarely ventured more than a hundred yards into the Green surrounding the city. They'd been raised with warnings about its dangers and were happy to leave it to shifters, while shifters considered the Green their private realm, and so were happy to keep it that way.

On the other hand, he had to admit that Rachel didn't fit the typical "norm" description. To be honest, she reminded him a hell of a lot more of Rhodry's Earther wife, Amanda, who'd come here with the fleet and broken every stereotype of what a woman and a norm could accomplish, if she was willing to fight for it. Some shifters had worried that Amanda's success in becoming the first woman *and* the first norm to ever pass the exceedingly dangerous Shifter Guild trials would start an avalanche of norms wanting to try their hand at the same. That had been two years ago, and not a single norm had signed up.

Now there was Rachel, and damn if he didn't think Rachel could pass the trials if she tried. That didn't mean he *wanted* her to try. Amanda had nearly died. And he knew what Rachel would say to that.

"Two more days," he said finally. "I want you farther away from that fucking cesspool. *And*," he continued, when she opened her mouth to comment—whether it was to agree or disagree, he didn't know—"I'll find one of my cousins to escort you, to make sure you're safe."

She rolled her eyes.

"Look, I know you're tough, but at a minimum the cousins can show you the fastest way to get where we're going. And if we need to get a message to you, it'll be faster if he's with you."

She frowned thoughtfully. "Why would he make a message faster?"

Aidan struggled with what to say. She knew about shifters, but he hadn't told her about the trees' song, the life blood of every shifter. Not even *Harp-born* norms could hear that song. "We travel a lot faster through the trees, and with our enhanced senses, we can find each other more easily."

She gave him a searching look, but eventually said, "You'll do what you want anyway. As long as you take off to warn your people, I'm good with it. I wouldn't mind meeting some of your cousins."

Aidan narrowed his eyes, wondering what she meant by that. Maybe he should send a cousin with the warning, while he doubled back— Oh fuck, no. What was he thinking? Was he actually afraid Rachel would prefer one of his cousins over *him*? Or, even worse, that she'd take up with one of them, because he was gone a few days? Or, worst of all, why did he care?

"They're good lads," he agreed, trying not to growl. "We should shut this down now," he said, pointing at the fire. "You okay with banking it for the night?"

She chuckled. "Are you suggesting I'm afraid of the dark? You're batting a thousand tonight, kitty cat."

He was across the fire in an instant, had her off the ground and in his arms a second later, her back to his chest. "I don't know what *batting* is, sweetheart," he whispered against her ear, satisfied at the shiver of awareness that shook her slender form. "But I'm no kitty cat." He spun her around and kissed her, biting her lower lip and taking advantage of her gasp to slip his tongue between her teeth, tightening his hold until there wasn't the smallest distance between them, her breasts crushed against his chest, his already stiffening shaft pressed against her belly.

"The fire," she pulled back to say breathlessly.

"I've got the fire." He kicked dirt over the stone circle, dousing the remaining flames. Darkness swallowed them whole.

Rachel's fingers tightened on his shirt. "I can't see a thing."

"I can." He swung her into his arms, ignoring her soft protest, and carried her over to where they'd laid out their few things, including her bedroll. Aidan didn't usually need a bedroll, and he wouldn't need one tonight, either. Rachel's would do for what he had planned, and after that, he'd shift for the night.

"You need to stop carrying me everywhere."

"It's more efficient."

"Bullshit. You just like to seem all macho."

"I'm the apex predator on this planet. I *am* all macho."

"Hmmm. Okay, put me down now."

He laughed and set her down next to her bedroll. "Have your eyes adjusted yet?"

She looked around. "Yes," she said, sounding surprised. "There's more light tonight."

He nodded. "Eriu is in the sky. She's our second moon and only rises one night a month. She'll be gone tomorrow."

"And the third moon?"

"Fodla. She only shows her face once every seven months, but we have a festival whenever she does. She's nearly as bright as the sun."

"Sounds beautiful. You think I'll see it?"

He regarded her a moment, then said, "Depends on how long you'll be here." He knelt and began dragging her bedroll into place.

"Let me," she said, taking the lightweight bedroll, which was zippered like a sleeping bag, and unzipping it all the way along the side. "It'll be tight, but there's room for both of us."

Aidan let Rachel slide into the sleeping bag first, since he wouldn't be staying. Once she was asleep, he'd shift, and they'd both sleep warmer. But he didn't intend to let her sleep just yet. They'd fucked earlier, in the pool, but he wanted more. The memory of her naked in the moonlight—so beautiful, so unabashedly sexual—had him going instantly hard. And all their talk of future moonrises and the possibility of Rachel being gone before she could see them... It made him want to have her as many times as he could while she was still here, as if he could store up her scent, her taste, the slick feel of her around his cock, for when she was no longer here.

He frowned. That idea was too pathetic for him. He wanted to fuck a beautiful, willing woman who was about to share a tiny bedroll with him. He didn't need any more reason than that.

Sliding into the bedroll after Rachel, he put his arm around her waist and snugged her up against his body, then bent to kiss the soft spot just below her ear. She shivered and reached back, threading her fingers through his hair, holding him in place.

"Tired?" he murmured.

He felt her cheeks move into a smile. "Not that tired." She pushed her tight ass against his groin, moaning when she encountered his fully erect cock. Aidan slipped his hand into her pants, over her belly and between her thighs, dipping one finger between the smooth lips of her sex and into her pussy, finding her already slick and aroused. She hissed out a breath and thrust against his hand. She was so wet and so fucking hot. He added a second finger, plunging deep inside, pressing the heel of his hand against her clit, as he fucked her with his fingers, holding her tightly against his chest as she bucked against his hold.

"Aidan," she gasped, her fingers so tight in his hair that he thought she'd rip his roots out. "Let me—" Her words broke off as he ground her clit beneath his thumb. She cried out in shock and then pleasure as she was thrown into a hard, fast climax that had her straining against his hold before she collapsed against him, trembling. "Fuck," she breathed.

Aidan's cock was painfully hard, aching to plunge into that soaking wet pussy. Removing his fingers from inside her, he dragged them over her still-sensitive clit, and then raised them deliberately to her mouth, sliding them between her lips until he felt her tongue wrap around his fingers and lick away every trace. He growled, imagining how it would be to have her tongue wrapped around his cock instead.

Something inside him snapped. Kneeling on the bedroll, he grabbed Rachel's pants and, taking her panties at the same time, stripped them down her long legs and off. He took a moment to admire her pretty pussy, so silky and smooth, then gave in to temptation and slipped one finger between her outer lips, stroking her creamy slit and smiling when she thrust against his hand with a hungry moan.

"I want those gorgeous breasts," he murmured and began to push up her shirt.

But Rachel clearly wanted more. Sitting up, she tugged her stretchy shirt over her head, followed by the tight-fitting bra, leaving her gloriously naked.

Aidan took a moment to admire the beauty before him, then bent over and closed his mouth over her nipple, feeling it plump into hardness against his tongue. He bit down just enough to be felt, enough that she cried out and bucked beneath him, and then he released the nipple with a final swirl of his tongue and moved to give her other breast the same lavish attention.

Rachel was breathing hard, one hand curved around his neck where he was bent to her breast, but with the other hand, she was pushing against the loose waistband of his pants, her fingers open wide as she stroked over his groin, straining to reach his cock.

Aidan yanked his tunic off and shimmied out of his pants, his hands spreading her legs while he was still kicking the pants from around his ankles. He heard the fabric tear and didn't care. Shoving Rachel's knees up, pressing them wide, he slammed his cock deep into her body. She was ready for him, her pussy slick with satiny cream, her sheath like a hot, tight glove all around his thickness, but still he paused for a moment, giving her time to adjust to him. Her hands ran down his back in an almost soothing motion, before her fingers dug into his ass and she flexed her hips pushing herself against him.

Aidan ground his groin against hers and then pulled his cock completely out of her pussy, holding it just outside her opening, feeling her wet heat against the tip of his cock as he dipped in and out, until she snarled his name.

"Aidan."

He smiled at the demand in her voice and held himself apart for a moment longer, then plunged his cock into her pussy and began thrusting in and out, fucking her hard, hearing her helpless cries as his cock stretched her wide, her inner muscles grasping at his thickness, the tissues hot and slick. Aidan leaned down enough to take her mouth in a savage kiss, growling when she responded in kind, their mouths crushed against each other, teeth clashing. And all the while, his cock was slamming into her, while her nails dug into his shoulders and her hips lifted, meeting his thrusts.

He knew the moment Rachel's climax began to build. Felt her muscles tense, the rush of wet heat that flooded her pussy a moment before her sheath clamped down on his cock and she bit his shoulder to muffle her scream. Aidan had thought to ride her orgasm out, to fuck her arousal soaked pussy until she came a second time. But the feel of her around him as she climaxed, the clench and heat of her pussy, the erotic pain of her teeth in his muscle, sent him over the edge.

He exploded with a roar of pleasure, his own release thundering down his cock, Rachel's sweet body squeezing his shaft, caressing him into surrendering every drop until he was drained dry.

Aidan collapsed onto Rachel, then immediately rolled them both so she was on top. Reaching over, he pulled the flap of the bedroll over her bare back, and then both of them simply breathed. His heart was pounding, matched only by the thump of Rachel's heart against his chest. He licked away the sweat on her neck, then kissed her there.

She stirred, wiggling slightly, his cock still half erect against her soaking wet sex.

He hummed in deep pleasure, and she raised her head, eyeing him in the darkness, though even with Eriu in the sky he was sure she couldn't see his face. "Is sexual energy some kind of shifter trait?" she asked suspiciously.

He grinned. "No, just an Aidan trait."

She *tsk*ed. "I can't believe you said that," she said, then paused. "On second thought, I can."

He stroked his fingers through her hair, which she'd left unbound after their bath. "You should get dressed. You can never count on a peaceful night in the Green. I don't want you fighting a hycat with no clothes on."

"Me neither. What's a hycat?"

"One of our uglier predators. They're usually found north of here, but if they scent something tasty enough, they'll extend their range." He winked, making his meaning clear.

"Is that real?"

He laughed. "Aye, but they prefer much colder weather, so I think you're safe."

"You guys have a catalog of the various life-forms in the Green? It seems endless, and they're all mean. Don't you have any friendly animals?"

Aidan thought about her question. They did have such a

catalog, but it wasn't something they shared with just anyone. The Shifters Guild maintained the listing for their own purposes, mostly to educate future members, or those who hoped to be. He wasn't aware of a single instance when they'd shared it with anyone else.

"The rabbits are friendly. And also, delicious. But you won't have any fuzzy little animals coming to eat out of your hand if I'm around. They recognize what I am."

"Huh." She covered a yawn with the back of her hand. "I need to clean up before I put my clothes on." She said it accusingly, as if the stickiness coating her thighs was his fault.

He grinned. "I'll help."

"*That* won't help at all," she grumbled, but she was smiling when she said it. "Come on, you can get dressed, too."

"No need. I'll sleep shifted. It'll keep the beasties away."

• • •

The cleanup went quickly, and before long Rachel was fully dressed and sitting on her bedroll, excited and alert as she waited for Aidan to shift. "Can you slow it down?" she asked.

Aidan chuckled. "Ah, no. I make the decision to shift, but after that nature takes over."

"I wonder if… No," she muttered, "digital cameras wouldn't work here, too dependent on electronics. Maybe I could find an old video camera, with film, and slow it down. I wonder if that—"

"Rachel."

She looked up.

"No one's going to be filming shit."

"Oh." She tipped her head from side to side. "Of course not. I understand. It was just a thought, kind of automatic."

"Uh huh." A heartbeat later, he was shifting. There was no buildup, no magical incantation, not even a grunt. Just one moment he was a man and the next, in a whirlwind of golden sparks, he was a gorgeous cat.

Rachel didn't say anything, but her mind was whirling with theories and possibilities. The golden sparks didn't make scientific sense. She'd bet anything that, if she *did* ever manage to get the transformation on video, a frame by frame playback would show a lot more happening than just a pretty light show. Aidan interrupted her thoughts, shoving his big head against her belly to get her moving toward the bedroll.

She hugged him—half because he was a big, beautiful cat and she simply loved the idea that she *could,* and half to irritate him—then scooted into the bedroll and held up the top flap in invitation.

Aidan studied her, his unblinking eyes gleaming a brilliant gold in the dark, and then he padded over and sank onto the bedroll with the giant kitty cat version of a long-suffering sigh. Rachel draped her arm over his back, snuggling close to his warmth, and despite the hard ground, the deadly forest, and the looming threat of Wolfrum and his killers, she fell instantly, deeply asleep.

Chapter Twelve

They traveled quickly the next morning, taking advantage of the clean sunlight filtering through the trees, after so many days spent in the permanent twilight of the swamp. After a brief shift back to human to discuss their route for the day, Aidan had returned to his cat form and stayed that way. Rachel knew he was there only because he was so convinced she'd never survive without him, but most of the time, she couldn't see or hear him. He would suddenly appear on a branch ahead of her or pad into sight on the ground, his movements completely silent. She was intensely curious about where he went when he disappeared, how far he ranged ahead of her, and how he got there. Did he remain always in the treetops? Did he double back to check their back trail? Was he hunting? She toyed with the idea of putting a spotter on him somewhere. She had several of the small tracker-dots in her pack. She used them when guiding groups of researchers who frequently had more enthusiasm than common sense, sticking dots on the ones who tended to wander so she could round up any lost sheep more easily.

She wasn't sure they'd work on Harp. Besides which, she doubted Aidan would agree to being spotted. He sure as hell wouldn't appreciate being lumped in with lost sheep. The very idea made her laugh, which she quickly swallowed just in case the big bad shifter happened to be lurking nearby and wanted to know what she was laughing about.

They walked steadily through the day, driven by the knowledge that the second ship was out there plotting who knew what kind of disaster. Aidan seemed convinced that they hadn't attacked yet, though he didn't share his reasons why. Rachel assumed it had something to do with the behavior of the other animals, small signs that, having spent his life in the Green, he could read. She only knew that Wolfrum would be desperate for the second ship to succeed. If the wholesale slaughter her crewmates had committed was considered a rational first attempt, she could only imagine what a desperate Wolfrum would try now.

She bit into one of Aidan's sticky sweet trail bars that probably had more sugar in a single bar than she'd eaten in the last six months. Maybe longer. But they'd barely stopped all day, and she needed the short-term energy fix that sugar provided. Aidan, on the other hand, could probably go days without rest, maybe snatching some bloody dinner on the fly. That was an advantage she'd bet shifters simply took for granted, that they could gulp down a tasty rabbit and keep going. No need to make a fire to cook or stay warm.

She eyed his broad back where he was walking ahead of her in his human form for a change. And what a fine form it was. Her thighs clenched, remembering what it was like to have him between her legs, buried deep in her body.

"When did you say your third moon rises next? Fodla," she clarified, recalling the name of Harp's biggest satellite. "I'm looking forward to it," she said with deliberate casualness.

He shot a brief glance over his shoulder. "Not for four

months. You planning on being here that long?"

She planned on being on Harp a lot longer than that, especially now that she'd learned about shifters. Where had they come from? Aidan was every bit as human as she was. She had very personal proof of that, but there was also the fact that shifters had offspring with non-shifter females. The basic rule of biology was that if you could breed, you were the same species. But there had to be other genes in there, too. Where had *they* come from? And how the hell had the colonists' geneticists made the blend work? She couldn't ask Aidan. He was very touchy on the subject of shifter origins and existence, and she couldn't blame him, especially given recent events. She herself had little love for the fleet science labs and would never trust them with anything she learned about Harp or its shifters. But Aidan wouldn't believe her, so she said only, "I'm a xenobiologist. There's a lot to study here."

He grunted wordlessly and kept walking, while she grinned in sudden realization. Aidan had a healthy ego. Hell, he had a healthy everything, but it was his ego that amused her the most. He didn't want her to stay for science, he wanted her to stay for *him*. Even if it was only for a brief romance. Although something told her it would take a lot more than that to get Aidan out of her system. There was a strong attraction between them. She couldn't deny it. She didn't *want* to deny it. She'd have to be dead not to desire him based purely on his physical beauty. But it was more than that. He was confident and possessive, irritatingly protective, and all the other things you'd expect in an alpha male. But he was also charming, funny, and irreverent, qualities she personally found very attractive in a man. She'd grown up in a household steeped in the stuffy politics of academia. Her parents were brilliant and loving, but laughter was not something that was often a part of their household. By the time Rachel had gone off to university, she'd been starved for meaningless chatter, for a lighthearted story about something *funny* that happened during their day's work. Hell, she would have been happy to hear some gossip about who was fucking whom just for the sake of sex, rather than to get ahead.

She'd bet *Aidan* had never fucked anyone solely for their political connections.

"Are you watching my ass?" he called back, proving her point. Such utter masculine confidence.

"Maybe," she admitted.

He laughed, and she felt the warmth of it all the way to her soul. *That's* what she wanted in her life. She tried to imagine what it would be like to live in a house filled with that kind of joy and couldn't do it. But she knew she wanted to.

"Do you know—?" she began to ask, but he shut her down.

"Shh," he hissed. "I'm listening."

She scowled at his back, not sure if he really *was* listening, or if he simply didn't want to answer any more of her questions. "I was just thinking—"

"Try to think more quietly," he muttered, and she almost threw something at him.

She picked up a short piece of log that would do nicely. Good heft, well balanced.

"You'd never land the blow."

She wanted to try, just to prove him wrong, but he was right, and she knew it. So what the hell? She'd only look like an idiot. She set the log down quietly, making a scuffing noise with her foot to cover the movement.

"Good choice."

God, he was irritating. But the scientist in her couldn't help marveling at the incredible senses he must possess to be so exquisitely aware of his surroundings. She didn't want to dissect him—that was barbaric—but she wouldn't mind running a few cooperative tests. She wondered if he'd agree—

Her thoughts stuttered to a halt as they emerged into an open space with such a clear view of the late afternoon sun that the temperature seemed ten degrees warmer from one step to the next. There was a small hut on the opposite side of the clearing, and… She smelled the water before she heard it. Fresh water. A lot more than the small stream of the previous night, and moving fast.

Aidan didn't slow, but walked directly to the hut. Reaching high over his head—well above the reach of most adults, including Rachel—he retrieved an ordinary metal key and slipped it into the lock.

She followed him inside, noting the hut's sturdy construction and thick insulation. From the outside, it looked like an ordinary, almost primitive, travelers' hut, but it was more. The shelves were stacked with plain tunics, pants, and soft boots, like those Aidan wore, and there was an insulated food container, which opened with a hiss of escaping air to reveal more of the sugary trail bars, along with what looked like dried fruit and other prepared food stuffs, though she didn't see any preserved meat or fish. This hut had been built with shifters in mind.

"Can anyone use this place? Or only shifters?"

Aidan gave her a curious look. "Why would you think that?"

"Please," she said dryly. "I may not have your superb senses, but I'm not blind."

He grinned, probably at the compliment to his senses— there was that healthy ego. "Anyone can use it," he said. "But it's rare that anyone other than shifters gets this far into the Green."

"Rare, but not never?"

He gave her a searching look, then shrugged and said, "You're here, aren't you?" He grabbed a thick bedroll and tossed it onto the floor. "We'll rest here until morning. There's only the floor, but—"

"I've slept in worse conditions. I can hear the river nearby. It sounds bigger than the one last night."

He nodded. "We've reached the Leeward Stream. You'll want to be careful. This time of year, the spring run-off makes it fast and deep. And no bathing in it, either. It'll be freezing cold. In fact, let me fetch the water for us, because I don't fancy having to dive in to save your shapely ass from drowning."

She narrowed her eyes at him. "Make sure *you* don't fall in, because I'll be too busy filing my nails to save you."

He leaned toward her with a laugh and would have kissed her, but she drew back with a squinty-eyed look of warning. Which only made him laugh harder as he grabbed a wooden bucket and headed outside.

• • •

Dinner was a cold affair that night. There was no need of a fire for warmth inside the hut, and they were both more interested in sleep than a hot meal. Aidan knew that Rachel thought he was tireless, and he didn't mind fostering that perception. But while shifters had a lot better stamina than norms, and he could function for days without sleep if he had to, the last few days had taken more than the usual toll on him. He'd slept well the previous night, but between the ordeal on the ship, and then the battle to get them both through the swamp alive, his energy was running as low as he could remember it ever being. A second night's rest would go a long way to restoring his strength, something he was going to need over the next few days as he raced first to warn Clanhome, and then to find the second ship before they did any more damage to his planet.

Rachel hadn't noticed, but the key hadn't been the only thing hidden in the cubby above the door. His cousins had left a message for him, as well. They'd come and gone the previous day, making sure the hut was fully stocked and letting him know that Rhodry was in Clanhome with Amanda, and that they were alerted to the possibility that the crisis wasn't over. They'd known he'd head for the hut on his way to take Rachel to the city. What they didn't know yet was that he wasn't going to the city. Still, he welcomed the news that Rhodry was at Clanhome.

The trees had grown increasingly restive since they'd emerged from the swamp. It wasn't yet the kind of shocked fear there'd been after the Earthers from the first ship had attacked the Green and taken him prisoner, but more a sense of dread. Had the second ship done something to heighten the trees' alarm in the two days since he and Rachel had escaped the swamp? And what about the possibility that Cristobal was a target? Historically, the clans were no great friends of the Ardrigh's and vice versa. Long ago, Rhodry's de Mendoza grandfather had tried to seize the throne from *Cristobal's* much older grandfather. He'd failed, but the attempt had solidified the break between the clans and the Ardrigh. They understood the role Cristobal played in maintaining order and stability on Harp, but if he died, no matter who caused it, it could set off a whole new dynastic battle, thus reigniting hostilities that Rhodry was working so hard to end once and for all. And if that happened, shifters would die on both sides.

Aidan lay on the hut floor, his arms around Rachel where she lay curled against him, and listened hard to the trees' whispering, searching for something specific that would answer his questions. But there was nothing except an overwhelming sense of impending disaster. There were times when Aidan would have traded all the protection afforded by Harp's atmospheric anomaly for a simple two-way radio.

"Is something wrong?"

Rachel's softly voiced question surprised him. He'd thought she was asleep, exhausted from their long day. Not for the first time, he realized he'd underestimated her. Amanda would have chided him for letting stereotypes influence his perceptions. But he didn't need a lecture from her to be disappointed in himself. He'd been raised in the clans, among women who were far tougher and more capable than their city sisters. There was no place in the mountains for a woman who sat and waited for a man to solve her problems.

On the other hand, he couldn't exactly tell Rachel how he knew something was wrong, beyond the suspicions they already shared. Shifters weren't Harp's only secret. The Green itself, with its network of semi-sentient trees that sang to each other, was perhaps the most important secret of all. The Earthers would swarm the planet if they knew about it, destroying in their zeal the very thing that they claimed to study.

"My cousins left a message," he said finally. "There's something ominous happening farther north. Details are sparse, but it seems likely your fr—that is, the other ship has made itself known."

"No more waiting, Aidan," she said urgently, pushing up onto one elbow. "You have to go on without me. I know you don't think so, but I'll be fine. I've done this before."

"Not here, you haven't."

"Damn it, this isn't the only place in the universe with—"

"Rachel," he said, and she must have heard something in his voice, because her protest died. "I don't doubt your skill, but you don't know Harp. You don't know how close our ancestors came to dying before they figured out how to survive here, and they were colonists, prepared for the worst. Promise me you'll wait here until one of my cousins arrives."

"Aidan—"

"Promise or I won't go."

She punched his gut. "That's blackmail."

He squeezed her tightly. "Promise, Rachel."

"Fine. Asshole."

He sighed in relief, then dipped his head to kiss the soft skin below her ear. "Sleep while you can. We're both going to need it."

• • •

It was still dark when Aidan shook Rachel awake. She scrubbed her face with some of the cold water left from the night before, then stepped outside to see he'd lit a small fire.

"Tea," he said, handing her a battered metal cup. "And there's fish on the fire. I caught it this morning."

Rachel took the cup carefully, sliding her sleeve down over her fingers against the heat of the metal. The hot liquid was welcome, and he'd added a lot of something sweet, like honey. She crouched down to the fire and pulled a piece of white flesh off the fish roasting there.

Aidan was sitting perfectly still, his gaze distant, and his head lifted, as if listening to something she couldn't hear. Using his shifter senses, she assumed. She waited, taking the opportunity to study him unawares. Without his natural charisma working to charm anyone within reach, he seemed oddly *more*, rather than less. More handsome, more *dangerous*. His big personality was just a cover for something even more deadly than his charm.

He returned to himself from one breath to the next. His posture relaxed and he turned to her with a smile. "Did you ask me something?"

She walked around and crouched next to him. Threading her fingers through his hair, she leaned in and kissed him then pressed her forehead against his. "You need to go, Aidan. I'll be fine."

Aidan realized something as he stood and pulled Rachel into his arms. Early on, he'd dismissed her claims of experience in the wild, but she was as good a partner as he'd ever had. They'd fought their way through the swamp, side by side. Had each other's backs more than once. Saved each other's lives. He *knew* she'd be all right without him, that whichever cousin he dispatched would keep her safe, and if not, she'd damn well take care of herself.

For all that, he hated to leave her. "Give me a kiss," he demanded.

She raised her face with a grin, and he kissed her thoroughly, gratified to see she was more than a little breathless when they finally broke apart.

"I need to shift," he said, almost reluctantly.

She nodded and stepped back.

He cupped her face with both hands and kissed her again. "Don't die," he ordered. And then he shifted and leaped for the trees.

• • •

Rachel would never get tired of seeing that. Aidan's shift was a beautiful sight in and of itself, with the concealing swirl of light and shadow. But when it was over, a magnificent hunting beast stood before her, and it was everything she could do not to reach out and stroke his golden fur. She knew exactly how soft he felt, how the individual hairs glided like silk through her fingers. But while he'd welcomed her stroking when they lay next to each other, petting him *now* like a big tabby cat didn't seem…appropriate. Respectful.

She sighed inwardly. Being a responsible scientist was a pain in the ass sometimes.

It was too late, anyway. Aidan was already nothing but a blur of pale, golden fur as he launched himself into the nearest tree—a standing jump of at least twenty feet straight up. He didn't make a sound, either, not even when all three hundred plus pounds of him landed on a thick tree branch, or when his sharp claws dug into the bark and he began climbing for the treetops.

Fast, quiet, and deadly.

She watched until there was nothing to see, until her eyes watered from searching, and then lingered longer to listen. The Green was eerily silent. Nothing moved. No rustle of leaves up above, no scratching of claws in the dirt, not even the frantic peep of some small prey. She nodded to herself, then walked slowly back to the hut to wait, closing the door behind her. Once inside, she did a quiet inventory of her pack, checking her medical supplies, re-stocking the nutrition bars they'd eaten, with trail bars from the hut's supplies. Those had seemed too sweet at first, but she'd begun to prefer the shifter version over her own, once her palate adjusted, admitting that the fruit and honey made them much tastier.

She also packed an extra set of clothes for Aidan. She only wished the hut supplies included clothes something closer to her size. The ones she had on were hopelessly stained, and the ones in her pack, while they'd been rinsed thoroughly, were even worse. Under normal circumstances, she'd have tossed every bit of it into the rag pile. But that wasn't an option. She wasn't a small woman, but it seemed shifters were uniformly big men, and their spare clothing came in only one size—too big. But it wasn't as if this was the first time she'd been dirty on a trek. She grabbed an extra tunic, anyway, thinking she could use it as a nightgown someday. A memento of her time on Harp. The thought made her sad, that someday she'd leave Harp, and Aidan, far behind.

Shaking the thought away, she shoved the tunic deep

inside and leaned the resupplied pack against the wall. She checked her weapons next. She'd never seen Aidan carry anything more than a knife, but it seemed as if some shifters carried bows. Either that or they stocked the hut with other travelers in mind, because there was a good supply of arrows in one corner. None of them would fit her crossbow, unfortunately. She still had a few bolts remaining, she'd just have to make them count.

Taking a few more minutes, she used her LED flash to check her map one more time, then folded it away, opened the door a crack and peered out, listening as much as looking. Satisfied, she grabbed her empty canteen and made the trip down to the water's edge, where she lay on her belly to fill it from the fast-moving Leeward Stream. The stream's bank was muddy, but she didn't care. She'd be a lot muddier before the day was over, and that was assuming it was a good day. There were a lot worse things she could be covered with.

Pushing to her feet, she walked back to the hut, where she paused for a moment, once again searching the trees, listening for movement. The eerie silence that had surrounded Aidan's departure was gone, replaced by the familiar sound of every tropical forest environment she'd ever visited. Oh, sure, there were differences. Every forest was unique, with its own prey, its own predators. But they were never silent unless an apex predator was on the prowl. The noise told her that he was well and truly gone, that he hadn't done a sneaky double back to be sure she stayed put.

Smiling, she went back to the hut one last time, pulled on her jacket, stowed the canteen in her pack, then picked it up and walked outside. Using the key that Aidan had returned to the ledge above the door—like he thought she hadn't noticed?—she locked the door and replaced the key, then shouldered her pack and headed out. A quick look at the map told her the second landing site was several days' walk away, and rather than wait for Aidan's cousin to come all the way to the hut, she figured to meet him along the trail, saving them both some time. She knew Harp was dangerous, and she'd never have started off on her own at night, but she had confidence in her own skills. A confidence backed up by experience in some of the most dangerous environments in known space. And, knowing Aidan even as little as she did, she knew his cousin—who would, of course, be a shifter, and thus able to travel much faster than she could—would no doubt meet her before the sun passed its zenith. And if she was wrong? If Aidan's request was delayed? Then, she'd climb a tree and hunker down for the night. It wouldn't be the first or the last time that she'd gone without sleep on a trek.

But the one thing she wasn't willing to risk was missing the opportunity to confront Guy Wolfrum. He'd violated every tenet of scientific discovery, betrayed every researcher who'd ever worked with him, looked up to him. But more than that, he'd made *her* complicit in this most heinous crime, and she wanted to know why. She *demanded* it.

Checking the position of the sun, she turned in a northwesterly direction and started walking.

Chapter Thirteen

Aidan raced along the intertwined branches of the tree road high up in the Green's canopy, his paws barely touching the wood. He'd run all the previous day and through the night, driven by a sense of urgency that had no words. The Green's warning was muted, almost puzzled, as if the trees couldn't make sense of whatever the Earthers were doing, but his instincts were screaming, telling him that the Green's confusion was even more ominous. Maybe it was because he had more information, because he knew something that the trees, for all their semi-sentient awareness, couldn't possibly understand. He knew about Wolfrum's presence and what it meant for shifters. He knew what that ship was really after and what they'd do to get it. What if this second ship had mounted a new weapon? Something targeted at the forest? The Green was a unique living force, but there was so little technology on Harp. If the Earthers were smart, they'd just sit there, not taking any offensive action, until they were ready to launch a truly devastating attack. By the time the trees blasted out a warning, it would be too late. Of course, the people on that ship shouldn't know about the Green's unique nature, but if Wolfrum was there, and if he knew about shifters, he could easily know about the Green, too.

If Aidan's reasoning was correct, then time was running out. He had to get to Rhodry and rally a shifter force to stop the second ship before it could launch whatever attack they had planned. He had to warn Clanhome, had to make sure that every shifter on every patrol was accounted for. And if there was any chance that Cristobal was in the area, he had to be found and warned.

And *then* they'd eliminate the threat once and for all. No second chances. Not for anyone on that ship, but especially not for Wolfrum.

All of his senses pricked abruptly with the awareness of another shifter nearby. Without slowing, he changed trajectory to cross paths, knowing the other shifter would be doing the same. He sensed his cousin Santino before he saw him, relieved that it was one of his blood cousins, rather than a shifter from one of the many extended clan families who were honorary relations. Santino was a younger cousin on his father's side, which made him a Devlin. He'd passed his Guild trials a few years back but had only recently been allowed to run patrols alone.

Aidan slowed as they drew closer. As the younger shifter, Santino would find him, not the other way around. And besides, he didn't want to be panting for breath like an old man when they met.

Santino shifted mid-jump between one tree and the next, coming to a stop next to Aidan with a grin. "Aidan! I'm glad to see you're still in one piece. Rumor has it you were nearly made a rug on some Earther's hearth."

Aidan scowled. Where the fuck had that come from?

"Who the fuck told you that?"

Santino stilled, as if hearing something other than the expected embarrassment in Aidan's voice. "Aidan?"

"Something's going on, something bad. I need to get to Rhodry, but first—"

"He's at Clanhome," Santino said eagerly. "He and Amanda both, because of her—"

"Yeah, I get the picture. They're still there?"

Santino nodded. "Staying a few days, I think. Do you want me to—"

"I'll head for Clanhome. I need you to follow my back trail and escort a woman—

Santino opened his mouth to protest, but Aidan cut him off.

"It's not what you think. You know about the ship we destroyed?"

His cousin nodded.

"So then, you know there was a woman, a scientist who helped me escape."

Another nod.

"She took off before we attacked the ship. We didn't know why, but since she saved my life, I wasn't going to let her die in the swamp. I caught up with her, and what she told me is far more serious than Rhodry or anyone else knows. There's not only a second ship, but that asshole Wolfrum's involved. I had to leave her on her own to make time, but—"

"You left a woman out there alone? An Earther? Are you crazy?"

Aidan glared. "Shut up and listen. Her name's Rachel, and she's damn good in the wild, nearly as good as Amanda. Speaking of which, don't mention Amanda's pregnant. She and Rhodry don't want that news getting off-planet as long as they can stop it."

"She hasn't told her family yet?" Santino asked.

"Not yet, but that's not the biggest worry. It's that damn fleet. If they find out she's pregnant, they'll want all manner of tests on the babes. Their scientists have been lobbying for a full DNA registry of Harpers since they first landed two years ago. That's bad enough, but with Rhodry being the twins' father, there's no way in hell we can let anyone get at them. Or Amanda, for that matter."

"Isn't her mother some big fleet scientist?"

"Yes, but Amanda seems confident that Dr. Sumner will keep the secret. It's the rest of fleet, and whomever *they* might tell, that's the problem."

"And you think this Rachel can't be trusted?"

"I didn't say that. But it's not my decision, either. The bottom line is I don't want her wandering the Green alone any longer than necessary. You're going to find her and escort her to that second ship."

"Where—?"

"She knows where it is." He saw the frustration on Santino's face and understood. It probably seemed like a task for someone younger, someone less skilled, while the serious stuff would be happening around Aidan and Rhodry. "Tino," he said, gripping his cousin's shoulder and using his family nickname, "it's critical that Rachel get there quickly and in one piece. She knows the ship *and* Wolfrum better than we do."

Santino met his gaze, then gave him a somber nod. "I'll get her there. How long ago—"

"I left yesterday morning, this same time. Follow my back trail, but stay sharp. I told her to wait for you at the Leeward Stream hut, just this side of the swamp, but she's skilled and more accustomed to being in charge than taking orders. She might have started after me on her own by now."

Santino's grin returned. "A woman who doesn't follow your every command? The Aidan charm must be slipping."

"And you're an idiot. Fortunately, you're a good tracker. Go."

His cousin raised two fingers to his forehead in a snappy salute then shifted and took off, following Aidan's path back up and into the canopy.

Aidan didn't waste any time. He shifted, too, and headed directly for Clanhome.

Two hours later, he swept through the outer perimeter of Clanhome, bypassing the patrols without a word, knowing they'd recognize him. His passage, as abrupt and uncharacteristic as it was, triggered an alarm. Two shifters soon paced him. One was his oldest brother, Gabriel, and the other a shifter his own age who'd married into the clans. Gabriel, at least, knew him well enough to read the urgency in his race through the trees, and bounded out in front to steer him toward the house that Rhodry and Amanda had built for their growing family. The thought brought a welcome bit of remembered joy, that he'd soon have two tiny, new shifter cousins living within Clanhome. Rhodry was like a brother to him, and his sons would be more than cousins.

When the house came into view, Rhodry was already on the balcony, waiting, his gaze catching sight of Aidan and following his movements. Amanda stood next to him, but she backed up into the house, making room for the three big shifters to land next to Rhodry. Gabriel and Aidan shifted form as they landed, but the third shifter launched himself almost immediately back into the trees, heading for Clanhome's version of a Guild hall. Every shifter patrol from Clanhome was dispatched out of there, and, like the Guild hall in the city, many of the unmarried shifters chose to live there rather than in their family homes. If a shifter force was going to be rallied out of Clanhome, it would be organized out of the Guild hall.

Aidan crouched on the balcony floor, catching his breath and relieved to remain in one place for longer than a few minutes. He'd run nearly nonstop for well over a day. He'd endured longer journeys before, but never without food and water, even if it was on the run.

A bottle of water appeared in front of his face. He drank it down, took a second bottle, and drank that one, too. A nutrition bar showed up next, already unwrapped. He smiled as he chewed and ate the tasteless thing. It came from Amanda's stash and held far more nutrition than the Harp version, but he smiled because it reminded him of Rachel. She'd have preferred the Harp version.

A folded pair of pants landed next to his foot. "No hurry," Amanda said from somewhere behind him.

Aidan chewed and swallowed, then sucked down half of a third bottle of water before grabbing the pants and pulling them on as he stood.

"Let's take this inside," Rhodry said, gripping his shoulder. And for the first time, Aidan noticed that Rhodry was wearing nothing but a pair of loose trousers, as if he'd just recently come in from a run. "The trees have been whispering about you for hours, or about someone. We didn't know it was you until you hit the outer perimeter. Where's the woman?"

"Rachel," Adrian said, grinning his thanks to Amanda who shoved him onto a chair and placed a platter of bread, meat, and cheese at his elbow, along with a glass of fresh fruit drink that he knew would be loaded with sugar. "Her name is Rachel. She's a xenobiologist and veterinarian, if you can believe it, with some other degrees, too. Wolfrum hired her—"

"Wolfrum?" Amanda interrupted. "What's he got to do

with this?"

Aidan swallowed a mouthful of food, took another drink of fruit juice to wash it down, and said, "That's why I'm here." He turned to Rhodry. "Wolfrum's the traitor, and worse, there's a second ship."

Everyone spoke at once until Rhodry's voice shouted them down. "Everyone shut up!" he roared, then nodded for Aidan to continue.

"Two separate ships, each far from the city, but close enough to Clanhome to ensure at least one shifter would come check it out. But we were wrong about what they wanted. Rachel believes Wolfrum knows about shifters. That he didn't set out to capture a big cat for the zoo. He wanted shifters for someone's lab."

Stunned silence greeted his words this time. It was every shifter's nightmare, Harp's biggest secret. Rhodry's hand drifted to rest on top of Amanda's where it lay protectively over their unborn sons.

"We knew it was bad," Rhodry said quietly, "but this… How the hell did Wolfrum learn about shifters?" He shook his head.

"He married on-planet," Amanda reminded him. "Julia. I don't know her family name."

Rhodry nodded. "Aaron Regan's youngest daughter. She must be the one who told him about shifters, or at least confirmed what he'd guessed. Though I hope to God she didn't know what he'd do with the knowledge. If she did—"

"If she did, then her treason is even greater than his," Amanda said harshly. It was easy to forget that she was a Guild member—with her long blond hair and softly pregnant form. But she'd passed the harshest trial that any candidate had ever endured, and she'd done it in the face of active opposition from almost every shifter in the Guild. Opposition that had included an attempt on her life. Amanda was tough as nails. If anything, her pregnancy had made her tougher, because she now had children to protect. And there was only one punishment for treason on Harp. Death.

"Agreed," several voices said at once.

"You know where the damn ship is?" Rhodry glanced at Aidan.

"Near that old hunting lodge that Cristobal's grandfather built in the middle of nowhere."

He frowned. "Damn it. There's a hunting party out there."

"Who?" Aidan asked, alarmed.

"Cristobal."

"Damn. How many are with him?" Aidan growled.

Rhodry shook his head. "His usual six guards plus Cristobal and his son Fionn."

"Is Wolfrum stupid enough to attack the Ardrigh? And all those shifters?"

"Only one way to find out." He turned to Gabe. "What's the status at the Guild hall?"

"They've been ready to hunt since this one got himself caught," he said, punching Aidan's shoulder. Just give the word."

Rhodry nodded. "We leave in twenty."

Gabriel nodded sharply and turned to leave, but Rhodry's voice stopped him.

"I don't have to tell any of you… Amanda's pregnancy…" His arm tightened around her shoulders. "That's off-topic for anyone from off-planet, including Wolfrum."

"I'm sure he already knows," Amanda commented. "I see him in the city all the time."

"That was before he conspired with Harp's enemies. And we still don't know what he was after." He nodded to Gabriel. "Go," he said, then watched as his cousin shifted, jumped from the balcony to the trees, and was gone.

Rhodry turned a very unhappy look on Aidan. "Amanda and I are going back to the city. With Cristobal and Fionn both gone, maybe even injured, someone has to be there to coordinate a response. Looks like it's me, at least until Cristobal gets back. Cullen's going with us, too. I'll need to move around the city, and I don't want Amanda alone until every invader *and* Wolfrum is confirmed dead."

Amanda gave a disgusted sigh. "I keep reminding all of you that I'm a Guild member, too. I'm not entirely helpless."

"I know," Rhodry said, pressing a kiss to her temple. "But it never hurts to have backup." He turned to Aidan. "I want you in charge at the second ship site. You know more about this threat than anyone. But if you're not up to leading—"

Aidan's sharp response was cut off as every shifter in Clanhome froze to listen. The trees' song, which had been a steady, but non-specific uneasiness, suddenly blared to life with an alarm they all dreaded. Fire. A bell sounded over Clanhome, alerting non-shifters to a danger that threatened everyone. Fire spread easily in the Green. Distant flames could be at your door in minutes, and with no warning.

Rhodry gave Aidan a tortured look. "Go," he growled.

• • •

Amanda saw the look on Rhodry's face and knew he hated sending clan shifters off to face danger without him. Just as she hated to admit she was glad they were going back to the city because she wanted him with *her*. She stroked her belly, soothing her tiny shifters as they, too, reacted to the urgent tree song.

Rhodry knelt next to her, one of his big hands covering hers, his deep voice joining hers to reassure the twins. "You ready for this?" he asked, raising his gaze to meet hers.

"I'm not exactly in fighting shape."

He gave her a hard kiss. "No, you're something far more dangerous—a momma protecting her kits." He held out a hand to help her to her feet. "Let's go."

. . .

Aidan was standing outside the Guild hall, watching as shifters disappeared into the trees. He glanced at Gabriel, standing next to him. "Fire's definitely coming from the same area where that damn ship put down."

"Figured that. Where's your girl? Might be handy to have her on-site once we grab Wolfrum."

"Her name's Rachel, and she's on her way there. I ran ahead to get word to Clanhome. Sent Santino to escort her, but she won't have waited for him. She's pissed enough at Wolfrum that she'll march right up to that fucking ship and force answers out of him."

They watched the last group of hunters leap for the trees. "That's it," Gabriel said. "You want to race the pack? Show 'em who's alpha?"

"Let's do it."

Chapter Fourteen

Rachel remained alert, her senses wide open. It would be too easy for her to fall into the habits of the last two weeks, when she'd had a big, bad shifter by her side. She didn't need to be told that Aidan's presence had kept most of the Green's deadly inhabitants away. Other than in the swamp—where it seemed the denizens feared nothing and no one—having him roaming above and around her kept all but the most vicious predators off their backs. With Aidan gone, she needed to be hyperalert, but not so much that she made herself a nervous wreck. That kind of anxiety could be just as fatal. She simply had to remember that before she'd arrived on Harp, *she'd* been the big, bad presence on her treks.

The thought made her smile, and she reminded herself to tell Aidan about it when they met up again. Which shouldn't be too much longer. Admittedly, she didn't know the Green the way a native would, but she was confident in her map skills, and she'd been verifying her position several times a day to avoid getting off track. Navigating by the sun wasn't as reliable as a good old-fashioned compass, or even the stars. But of course, a compass wouldn't work, and she wasn't familiar enough with Harp's night sky to use the very distant stars, even if she'd been able to see them above the canopy. The sun, on the other hand… One didn't need to see the orb itself to know where it was. She'd also climbed to the treetops once or twice to take a look around and judge her position relative to geographic features on her map. But the effort involved in getting up that high and then back down again was substantial, so she limited herself to once a day, at the start of her morning.

She glanced around, noting the growing shadows under the trees. She'd have to stop soon. She'd taken to sleeping in the trees. It gave her a solid trunk at her back and reduced the number of attack vectors she had to worry about, plus not everything on Harp lived in the trees. She sighed. Damn, but she missed Aidan.

She'd just begun to study possible nighttime perches when the forest went perfectly quiet. Experience told her what that meant. There was a predator in the area, something big enough to scare everything else into silence. Her first thought was Aidan, but he was far away by now. Eventually, their paths would converge at the second ship, but not yet.

She came to a slow stop, unhooked her crossbow from the loop on her backpack, and nocked a pair of bolts. Putting a broad tree trunk at her back, she scanned the branches overhead to be sure there was no obvious threat from above, then shifted her attention to the surrounding area.

"Don't shoot," a male voice called.

She frowned. In her experience, bad guys didn't typically announce themselves. And in the Green's deep forest, with shadows all around and the thick foliage overhead, it made no sense, especially since her unseen visitor was probably a Harp native, which immediately gave him the advantage. On the other hand, with that second ship out there somewhere, she wasn't going to take any chances. "Show yourself. Slowly," she added.

A crashing of branches several yards ahead of her told her he was coming from overhead and dropping fast. As fast as Aidan did, although with a lot more noise.

Keeping her finger on the trigger of her crossbow, she watched as a tall, muscular young man emerged from the forest, dressed in loose clothing and filled with the same cocky confidence that Aidan wore like a second skin, although he was quite a bit younger and so on him it was adorable, rather than devastating. Or maybe Aidan had just ruined her for every other male in the universe.

"Santino Devlin, at your service. You're Rachel?"

He didn't offer to shake hands, which spared her the need to refuse, since she wasn't giving up her weapon yet. "Aidan sent you?"

He nodded. "We're cousins."

"Seems like you all are," she said, though she hadn't actually met anyone other than Aidan. She'd just seen them from a distance during the attack on the first ship, and she really didn't want to talk about that. Deciding to skip ahead, she said, "Is Aidan okay? He had a long way to go."

He gave her a flat look. "He's a shifter. He can handle a run like that and more when he has to. And from what he tells me, it doesn't get more serious than this." He cocked an eyebrow at her. "He also said you were supposed to wait for me at the hut."

She snorted dismissively.

"And he said you wouldn't. Which is a good thing, because we have a problem."

Rachel stiffened at the serious note in his voice. "Did something happen?"

"There's a bad fire in the Green. I got word of it after I started after you, but from what Aidan told me, it's right where we're headed."

She took her finger off the crossbow's trigger, lifted the bow, and un-nocked the bolts. "Fire," she said solemnly, thinking about the tactics Ripper and her crew had used to lure Aidan into the open. "It's got to be connected. Can you show me where…" She stuck a hand in the outside pocket of her pack. "I have a map."

"Once I see where we're going, we won't need a map."

"Talking to you is just like talking to Aidan."

"Thanks."

She hadn't necessarily meant it as a compliment, but then, from the smirk flirting around his lips, she was pretty sure he knew that. "Whatever. Look, the sun's setting, and I don't see as well in the dark as you guys, so we either have to check the map right now or wait 'til morning."

"Let's do it now. You have one of those cool little LED flashlights like—" He cut himself off, but Rachel caught it.

"Like Amanda's, you mean?" she asked, trying to sound like it was no big deal. "Yeah. Probably exactly the same. They haven't changed much in the two years she's been gone."

He didn't bite. "Let's take a look at the map then decide what to do. I'm guessing you don't travel well in the dark."

"I can, if the moon is bright enough."

Santino shook his head. "No more moon for a while. Are you hungry? Do you need a fire?"

"Not unless you do. I cooked some fish before I left the Leeward Stream. I've been eating cold and sleeping in the trees."

"You have trail experience. Aidan told me."

"He's way chattier with you than he is with me," she muttered.

He shrugged. "Not really. He just had to pass on a lot of information in a short amount of time."

"Okay, hunker down here, then." She dropped her pack

to the ground and pulled out the map, which was beginning to show the wear and tear of the last few days. He crouched next to her and immediately realigned the map, just as Aidan had done that first day. She grimaced but was happy, at least, to see that she wasn't that far off, which meant she hadn't been going in circles since Aidan left her. "This is where we're going." She pointed at the second ship site.

Santino made a wordless humming noise, then said, "Your map's missing a lot of detail."

"I know," she admitted. "It was the best I could get on short notice." She glanced up at him. "You know how to get there?"

"Of course," he said absently, his gaze on the map, before he glanced at the darkening sky. "We'll hunker down here for the night, then start first thing in the morning. You want dinner down here, or"—he pointed at the tree over their heads—"up there?"

"Might as well climb while there's some light."

He gave her a curious look. "You weren't joking about that? You really can climb?"

Rachel *tsk*ed in disgust. "Like shifters are the only people capable of climbing a fucking tree," she muttered.

"They are on Harp."

"I bet your loggers can climb."

"Not the women."

"You're digging that hole deeper and deeper. Just remember, I'm armed, and you have to sleep sometime." She secured her pack and started climbing the tree.

• • •

The next day was significantly cooler, with gray clouds looming too far in the distance to give any real hope of rain. Rachel didn't know the statistics for Harp, but a lush forest like the Green didn't get that way without a lot of water. Santino had shifted the previous night, just before making one of those jaw-dropping leaps from the ground straight up into a tree. She almost teased him about shifters' seeming inability to climb in human form but thought better of it. For all she knew, they *could* climb in either form, and, besides, why the hell would they bother with hands and feet when they had paws and claws.

A cup of hot tea would have been welcome against the cold, but that would have meant delaying long enough to light a fire, and she was too aware of time running out. No one knew what or who had caused the fire they were running toward, at least not that they'd told her. She was sure Santino would have learned if they knew more, via whatever telepathic or other unusual link shifters all seemed to share. Another secret Aidan had kept from her. But she wasn't blind or stupid. It was obvious they had some form of communication.

She feared the crew from the second ship was using similar tactics, only with fire as their weapon this time. But even if the fire wasn't part of their plan, the attack had to come soon. There might have been a delay in Wolfrum discovering that the first ship had been destroyed, depending on what manner of information transmission the two ships had been using. Maybe he didn't know anything about the first ship. Maybe the plan all along had been for each of the ships to attack independently. He had to have known going in that they had a limited timeframe. On a planet as sparsely settled as Harp, the invaders' plan had been too "loud" to escape notice for long. Even if it had worked perfectly, which it obviously hadn't.

She'd packed up her gear, taken her usual morning read on the sun's position, and started walking, not waiting for Santino, who she figured was up in the trees somewhere and would make himself known eventually.

They'd been traveling most of the morning, and she was reaching for one of Aidan's trail bars, when every tree seemed to move at once. She stopped and leaned back to study the dense canopy. This was the first significant wind she'd experienced on Harp, and given the clouds and humidity, she thought they might be in for some rain. But then she caught a ripple of movement, darker against the gray sky, and recognized it as birds taking silent flight. She watched, more curious than alarmed. In all her travels, she'd never visited a planet with such silent birds. To be sure, prey animals everywhere went quiet at the first sign of a predator, but avians frequently had a warning system with at least one guard cawing to alert the others before they all took off in a noisy flurry of wings. She was thinking she'd love to do a necropsy on one of Harp's birds, when an eerie wail shattered the silence, repeating over and over, calls coming one on top of the other. It was obviously a troop of whatever predator had sent the birds into flight.

She dropped her pack and swung her crossbow into position, nocking two bolts and sliding two more into a side pocket for easy reach. The animals weren't in sight yet, but there were a lot of them, and Harp had already taught her to expect the worst. She'd just backed up to one of the Green's hugely thick trees when the distinct yowl of a hunting cat cut through the noise. The eerie wailing changed abruptly, some of the calls remaining the same, while others changed pitch completely, becoming deeper and more aggressive to her human ear.

Santino appeared a moment later, dropping to a branch that was close enough and low enough for her to see him. He shifted in a whirlwind of golden sparks, his gaze intent and his voice mostly a growl when he nodded at her crossbow and said, "Can you use that?"

"Yes. What are they?"

"Banshee. Like Earth monkeys but much more deadly. Shoot to kill, and don't miss." He met her eyes, as if wanting to be sure she understood. "They'll see you as the weak link. Prove them wrong."

She gave a sharp nod.

He gave her a final penetrating stare then shifted and was gone in three seconds flat.

Rachel didn't waste time trying to follow his progress. Her heart was thundering, adrenaline flooding her veins, but her hands were steady, her thoughts clear. She and Aidan had survived that damn swamp to get this far. There was no way in hell she was going to let Harp defeat her before they took down fucking Wolfrum and his gang.

She stood with her back to the broad base of the tree, her pack close, but around to one side, to avoid tripping over it. The wailing had all but stopped, which should have been reassuring, but she wasn't fooled. Maybe Santino had the pack on the run, maybe he'd killed the pack alpha, and the others had scattered. But she didn't believe in fairy tales, and she wasn't going to bet her life on "maybe."

She was concentrating on everything and nothing at the same time, trying not to focus one sense so hard that she blew out the others, and she nearly missed it. The banshee came down nearly on top of her, dropping out of the tree she'd been standing against. Some sixth sense warned her at the last minute. She spun, taking a quick step away from the tree, cutting it so close that his swiping claw scraped over the top of her head like an iron bar, cutting into her scalp and scraping bone. She ignored the pain, her crossbow already in motion, her finger on the trigger. The banshee was dead before it hit the ground, but Rachel didn't stop to admire her kill. Experience with pack animals had her spinning around, her back to the tree once more, just in time to catch the next animal coming at her from one tree over, leaping from high up, deadly claws distended, ripping teeth bared in a feral snarl. She shot it in the chest, then stepped away and grabbed two fresh bolts. Two bolts down, two left. She hope it would be enough.

Back against the tree once more, she fought for focus against the pain pounding in her head, the warm trickle of blood down her cheek. Santino's howl broke through the roar of noise in her head. She turned toward the sound, knowing she was moving too slowly. She had to stay sharp, had to fight the pain, the blood loss. She could do it. She'd done it before. A high-pitched wail, louder than the others, sinister, undulating... Too close. She twisted as the third beast rushed her on the ground. The animal was too close and her aim too high. It braced itself to leap. She kicked it in the head and then spun one more time as a much larger, obviously male banshee made a twenty-foot jump heading straight for her, only to be struck and knocked out of the air by a blur of shifter fur and fangs. Santino landed on top of the stunned animal, enormous claws digging into the creature's chest, flipping him over, before his fangs closed over the banshee's neck and tore out its spine.

There was nothing but silence for a frozen instant, and then Santino shifted, just as Rachel put a crossbow bolt into the head of the banshee she'd kicked. She didn't know how resilient these fuckers were, and she wasn't taking any chances.

"You're bleeding."

She lifted her hand to the blood on her cheek, then up to her head. "Yeah," she said, fighting the urge to vomit or maybe pass out. Neither would do her reputation any good.

He walked closer. "Sorry about the clothes—"

She waved that away. "No offense," she added as an afterthought.

He grinned then reached out and took the heavy

crossbow out of her hand. "You should at least let me clean it some. You have antibiotics in that big pack of yours? I'm told you Earthers don't have any resistance to our bacteria."

"Yeah," she said and would have bent to pick up her pack, but he stopped her.

"Sit down, Rachel. Aidan would never forgive me if something happened to you." He grimaced. "Well, if something *else* happened to you. Not even my cousin would hold me responsible for a banshee attack." He brought her pack over. "Sit," he repeated.

Rachel unzipped her pack and handed him the spare set of clothes she'd stashed in there for Aidan. Santino took them from her with a small laugh, pulling them on before crouching down next to her once more. "Okay, your virtue is safe. Now let me take care of this. Head wounds bleed like a motherfucker." His gaze jumped to her, his eyes wide.

Rachel laughed, then groaned. "I've heard the word," she whispered. "In fact, I'm pretty sure it came out of Aidan's mouth."

"Probably. His mother despairs of ever making him into a proper gentleman."

She gave him a cynical look. "And you?"

"I'm young. I'm still growing."

She smiled, then winced when Santino sprayed antiseptic on her wound. "Fuck."

His eyes crinkled with amusement. "No wonder you and Aidan get along."

"Just slap a bandage on there, kitty cat. Tell me something, was this attack typical banshee behavior?"

"You taking notes?"

"Something like that. I study animals, and Harp is unusual."

"You can't take any scientific notes with you when you leave Harp. The fleet embargo won't permit it. And even if *they* would, *we* won't."

"So maybe I'll hang around until I've learned everything there is to know. There's no law telling me what to remember, is there?"

He shrugged. "Don't know. You'll have to ask Aidan, or maybe Rhodry."

"Rhodry, your clan leader."

"Aye, and my cousin."

"Of course. Everyone's a cousin. You about finished—" She hissed as he placed a pressure-sensitive bandage on the cut and, well, *pressed*.

"We should really shave your head."

"Try it and die."

"I figured that. About your question, though…the banshee behavior. No, that's not typical. They're carnivorous, and they will attack lesser prey, but my presence should have kept them away."

"You said they'd see me as a weak link. Maybe that's why."

"Maybe. You smell a lot like a norm, and you're female. But four separate animals attacked you. That's not typical. I'd have expected their survival instincts to kick in and send them running after you'd killed two at most, especially in a coordinated attack—"

"They do that? Coordinate their attacks?"

"Sure. But the point is, they should have stopped once you'd proven you were a threat. One of the first to attack was almost certainly the alpha female. When you took her down, the others should have turned tail and run."

"So, what do you think's going on?"

He leaned back on his heels, clearly considering what to say. "I think whatever that ship is doing out there?" He jerked his head in the direction of the second ship. "It's got every animal in the Green running scared."

Rachel met his eyes, her gut twisting with fear over the lives that could be lost, the damage done. And with guilt, because she hadn't seen through Wolfrum's twisted scheme soon enough. "I can walk, Santino," she said firmly. "There's no reason to delay here."

"Rachel, you lost—"

"Blood, I know. And I've got this to help me recover." She held up a small vacuum-sealed pack of nutrients that were designed to aid short-term survival after traumatic injury. "We can make another two, three hours before dark. I'll rest then."

He gave her a doubtful look, but she could tell he was wavering. He wanted to be where the danger was, wanted to be standing with his cousins to defend their world, not escorting Aidan's woman.

"Okay," he said finally. "But if you start to feel weak—"

"If I'm too weak to walk, you'll know when I'll fall over."

"I get why Aidan likes you. All those city women are no challenge. But you—"

Rachel was curious about Aidan's many city women, but that would have to wait. She raised her hand when Santino stood, letting him pull her to her feet. She hung on for a moment, not too proud to let her head stop spinning. She had no desire to fall over before they ever got started.

Chapter Fifteen

Aidan was speeding along the tree road once more, but he wasn't alone this time. An entire troop of shifters flowed through the trees along with him, silent but for the slight breeze of their passage. They had no need to call out to each other, no need for communication beyond their shared sense of the trees' song and what it told them. The forest around them was equally silent, and not only because of their presence. They'd all noticed the unusual flow of animals away from the ship site, animals that went to ground while the shifters passed and then continued their evacuation. It reminded him of how various creatures reacted to a fire in the Green, except this time the Green was warning them to run before disaster struck.

Aidan heard it and knew his fellow shifters did, too. He didn't know if the Green was taking its cue from their reaction to the ship's danger and their headlong rush to confront it, or if something was happening on-site that the Green found imminently threatening. He did know that the sense of doom had grown with every hour of morning light.

He had wound his way to the very top of a grandfather tree and was sorting through the threads of emotion and information that he could sense in the trees' song, when he was suddenly blasted by a sense of danger so powerful that it nearly knocked him from his perch. He dug his claws into the bark, struggling to identify where the warning had come from and what it meant. Before he could even begin, his senses were assaulted by a new blast of sound and fury, but this one was real. Hot air rushed through the treetops, carrying the scent and taste of explosives, and leaving the Green reeling in agony.

He leaped back into action and ran.

• • •

The sun was almost directly overhead by the time Santino dropped down to stand directly in front of Rachel. Her head ached, but she'd dealt with much worse injuries and kept going. Nothing was greater than her need to reach that ship before Wolfrum and his crew did something monstrous. She didn't know what she thought she could do, how she thought she could stop them. But if nothing else, she could be there to help Aidan and the other shifters, whether it was taking part in the fighting itself, or telling them what she knew about the ship's operation, or simply patching up the wounded. She had to be there.

She was so focused on going forward, all of her attention on putting one foot in front of the other, not tripping over the many hazards on the small animal trail she was following, that it took her a moment to realize Santino was standing directly on the path, several feet in front of her.

She stopped. "What's happened?" she asked, knowing from the look on his face that there was something.

"The Green," he said, his face twisted almost in pain.

"It's…terrified. The warning is so loud that it *hurts*."

Before she could formulate a reply, the ground shook, a hard jolt that would have knocked her off her feet if a sturdy sapling hadn't been close enough for her to grab. The sound came next, a huge rumbling explosion, followed by a blast of wind that shook the treetops like a giant had them gripped in its fist.

Santino shifted, his legs coiled to leap for the trees, to race toward whatever disaster had struck. At the last minute, he stopped and stared at her in tormented indecision.

"Go," she shouted. "I'll catch up."

He hesitated a fraction of a second more, but then he was gone, and Rachel was running, not for her life, but for the lives of people she cared about.

Everything was chaos and smoke by the time Rachel made it to the site. She'd had a moment's concern that she wouldn't find her way, but the tide of fleeing animals had told her which direction to take, and the stink of burning flesh—the animals not lucky enough to have escaped the carnage—had done the rest. She'd been terrified at first—fearing for Aidan's safety, for Santino's—but reason argued that the smell couldn't be any of the shifters, that they were too fast and too smart. Weren't they?

She'd run even faster after that, but now that she'd finally arrived on scene, the reality was even worse than she'd feared. She forced herself to calm down and take stock. Triage. She hadn't trained in human medicine, but veterinary medicine wasn't all that different, especially when it came to trauma care. And she *was* a certified medic for the treatment of humans, which was required in order to hire out as an exotic destination guide. She understood the concept of triage, although it didn't look like anyone else here did.

Fire flickered in the distance, and the air was filled with smoke. It was already affecting her, and she could hear others coughing. It would be especially dangerous for anyone who was injured.

She scanned the clearing, looking for Aidan, figuring he'd listen to her while the others might not. The smoke shifted abruptly, and she turned, only to stop and stare. The ship was nearly identical to the one that had brought her to Harp, except that this one was crawling with vines and other greenery. And she did mean "crawling." She'd been on other planets, in other tropical forests, had seen how quickly they could take over every obstacle in their path. But she'd never seen anything like this. This was the Green fighting back, a counterattack that must have begun as soon as the ship landed for it to have grown to such overwhelming heights. Enormous ropes of growth, some as thick around as her thigh—hell, as thick as *Aidan's* thigh—slithered up and over the ship, poking into every vent and valve, choking off sensors until anyone inside would have been blind and at least partially deaf to what was happening outside.

Even worse for those on board, all manner of external equipment had been destroyed, completely ripped from their mountings by the twisting greenery. She wondered if the crew had managed to fight back at all before the accelerated growth around them had taken over. From where she stood, she doubted the ship was even capable of lift-off at this point. But then, she wasn't sure there could be survivors to try. If this ship had landed at roughly the same time as her own, if they'd been smothered by the Green with the speed it appeared, their oxygen must be running down, and with so much of the external equipment clogged or destroyed, they'd have been using battery power for who knew how long. She felt no sympathy, however. She didn't care that she'd shared the same mission with these people once upon a time.

As she drew closer, she saw evidence that someone, at least, had survived. An enormous hole had been torn into the enveloping vines as if something had burst from the ship outward, and she knew the explosion they'd heard had been the result of a large weapon being fired from inside the ship. Trees were flattened and destroyed in a ninety-degree arc around the ship, with the ones closest to the vessel reduced to little more than piles of ash. Dead animal carcasses littered the devastation as the eye moved away from center, and shifters in both human and cat form ranged over the disaster zone.

Damn Wolfrum, she thought. He *had* gotten word of her ship's failure, but instead of acknowledging the futility and immorality of his venture, he'd instructed this second ship to use even greater force.

"Rachel!"

She spun in relief at the sound of Aidan's voice. He was in an area of intense activity near the edge of the blast zone. There was a medium-size structure there, or there had been, before it'd been blasted to hell and back. It had been a wood construction, built of thick, sturdy logs. They were shattered now, broken like huge matchsticks and tossed into haphazard piles. Aidan and the other shifters were working feverishly, moving the enormous logs and destroyed trees, tossing them aside as if they weighed nothing.

Rachel raced to join him. There must be someone trapped under all that wreckage. Why else would they be digging so fiercely? She couldn't lug huge trees around, but she could help whoever was injured.

"Rachel." Aidan's voice was full of the same relief she was feeling.

She gripped his arm, not fully realizing until she saw him whole and healthy how worried she'd been. "What's going on? What can I do?"

"The bastards attacked the Ardrigh and his guard, using the same tricks they tried on me. All but two of the invaders' party were killed in the fighting, both of those badly wounded when they retreated to their ship. The Green fought back its own way." He gestured at the overgrown ship. "But they must have grown desperate."

"They'll have no power and no way of generating more with everything overgrown like that," she said. "That means no oxygen, except what's in portable tanks. If this ship is like the other one, it's not supplied for hostile environments."

Aidan nodded. "Yeah, well. The fire they started to lure in shifters was already out of control when they retreated to their ship. It's been expanding away from this clearing. But now...you must have heard the explosion just now. They targeted the lodge with a laser weapon. Those things are forbidden on the planet for a reason. It blasted through the overgrowth on the ship, completely destroyed the lodge, and did all of this." He gestured around the devastated clearing. "They already needed to die for what the first ship did, but this put the seal on it. This blaze is spreading on four fronts, completely out of control. The best we can hope for is rain because we sure as hell can't put it out. We're trying to evacuate our people, but when the lodge collapsed—"

Rachel nodded grimly. "Are there injured?"

"Yes. Come on." He took her hand, pulling her forward while he kept talking. "The Ardrigh and all of his party were inside. They're all shifters, so some got out unscathed. Others were hurt but have already managed to shift enough to heal." His hand squeezed around hers. "But Cristobal... He's severely injured, trapped. He can't shift because there's too much weight on him. We're digging him out, but we're afraid that even once he's freed, he might be too badly—"

Someone shouted, interrupting whatever he'd been

about to say. Rachel couldn't make out the words, but Aidan immediately raced ahead to where the rescue work seemed most intense. She followed, catching up just as a blond man approached Aidan and started talking rapidly. He was plainly stressed, covered in cuts and bruises, with blood coating every inch of his bare skin and soaking his clothes, dried in some places and still fresh in others. He shouldn't have been walking at all, but his sheer size and the golden sheen covering his blue eyes told her he was a shifter.

"We've lifted most of it away, but he still can't seem to shift," he was telling Aidan, sounding harassed, as she caught up. "We think he might be too injured, but he's in and out of consciousness, and even when he's conscious, he's not making any sense." He was becoming more agitated with every word. "We need a doctor. The city's too far, but there must be someone at Clanhome who—"

"I can help," Rachel interrupted. "Aidan, I can—" She stumbled backward when the big blond shifter lunged at her, his eyes going completely gold, teeth bared in rage.

"What the fuck!" he snarled. "She's one of—"

Aidan stepped between them, cutting the furious shifter off and blocking him with his body. "Fionn. Stop," he growled. "This is Rachel."

"I don't care who she is. She's one of them and doesn't belong here."

Aidan bristled. "She's not like the others. She saved my life."

Fionn sneered. "You just wanna fuck—"

The sound of flesh hitting flesh cut off his words, but Rachel wasn't paying attention anymore. She was already kneeling at the injured man's side, dragging her backpack over and digging down for her first aid supplies. She could tell at once that he needed more help than her kit could offer, but he was a shifter. If she could stabilize him enough to shift, he could begin his own healing.

"Hey," she said softly, addressing her patient. "My name's Rachel."

His eyelids flickered up at the unexpected sound of her voice. He had Fionn's eyes—turquoise blue with gold flecks—and his age made it likely he was either father or uncle. Her brain filed away that detail automatically before her thoughts stuttered to a halt. Aidan had said it was *Cristobal* who was badly injured. This wasn't just any shifter, he was the Ardrigh.

She glanced down the length of his body and saw that his lower legs were still buried in rubble. The shifters who'd been working on clearing the debris had stopped, more intent on watching *her.* As if *she* was the greatest danger here.

"You need to get the rest of that weight off him," she ordered, then turned back to her patient, only to have Fionn push through the crowd to kneel on the Ardrigh's other side.

"Are you a doctor?" he demanded, while taking Cristobal's badly broken hand and holding it with a care she wouldn't have thought possible, given his abrasive words with Aidan.

She hid her grimace but went with the truth. "I'm a xeno-veterinarian, but—"

"My father is not a fucking animal!" he roared and lunged at her again, throwing his arm out.

But whether he'd intended to shove her away or punch her, she never knew, because Aidan intervened once more, this time with the help of one of his cousins. The two of them held Fionn at a standstill but didn't pull him away.

"The physiology is the same," she said calmly, looking up at the furious shifter, "and I'm also a fully qualified medical technician, if that makes you feel better. Now, if you don't want your father to die, you need to shut up and let me help him."

She turned back to Cristobal then, trusting Aidan and the

others to keep Fionn under control. She couldn't blame him. This was his father, and he didn't know her. But she couldn't let him stop her, either, because she hadn't exaggerated. Cristobal was going to die if she didn't do something soon.

She did a quick field examination, running her hands carefully over his skull, then his arms and thighs. There were no signs of a concussion, no head injuries, other than some minor cuts and bruises. The rest of him didn't fare as well. His right forearm had a double fracture, and his hand and fingers were crushed. With all the weight on his legs, there had to be injuries—bruises, if nothing else. But she could see serious bleeding and malformation on his left thigh and suspected more broken bones there. Saving his chest for last, she pulled an old-fashioned stethoscope out of her pack. There were more modern devices for this purpose, but she hadn't known if they'd work in Harp's weird magnetosphere, so she'd gone old-school. Resting the bell on Cristobal's chest, she noted an accelerated heart rate, which wasn't entirely unexpected, but when she checked his lungs, she frowned. The left lung was moving normally, but the right one definitely was not.

She started digging through her pack. "How resistant to infection are you guys?" she asked without looking up.

"Very," Aidan responded. "Nothing gets to us."

"I hope you're right," she muttered and pulled a writing stylus out of her pack. It was an elegant creation, made of some rare wood and designed to work with a digital tablet, which made it pretty much useless on Harp. But it had one benefit. She chopped the ends off with her knife, which gave her a hollow tube. Using antiseptic wipes from her first aid kit, she cleaned her knife and the tube as well as she could, then used another wipe on Cristobal's bloody skin between the fourth and fifth ribs, hoping that shifter physiology was close enough to regular human for this to work.

She heard a yell and glanced up. The treetops on one side

of the clearing had burst into flames. She swallowed a curse. This couldn't wait. She looked down and saw that Cristobal was watching her, his eyes filled with pain, but alert enough to know what was happening. "You have a collapsed lung," she told him, hoping her voice wasn't as shaky as she felt. She'd been trained in this procedure, but she'd never done it under field conditions like this. "You have air and blood pushing on the lung inside the chest cavity and it needs to get out. I'm going to make a small cut and insert this tube. It's going to hurt."

His eyes crinkled slightly. "Do it," he forced out.

Fionn broke away from Aidan and dropped to his knees next to his father. "Da."

Rachel glanced up at the emotion in his voice, and he met her gaze.

"If you harm him—"

Cristobal's strained whisper stopped him. "Fionn. Enough."

Rachel was no longer paying attention to what was going on between father and son. Her focus was narrow and absolute. She had to get this right. She pressed her fingers against Cristobal's side. There was no fat on him, just taut muscle and skin. And air that shouldn't be there. She could feel it popping beneath her fingers.

"Hold your breath, please, sir." Then, holding her own breath, too, she slipped her knife between his ribs, made a small incision, and immediately slid her makeshift tube into the resulting hole. She was close enough to hear the air immediately begin rushing out, followed by a gush of blood. Normally, the procedure would be performed with a drainage tube, which certainly wasn't included in her first aid kit. She did the best she could, wrapping tape and gauze around the opening, stabilizing the tube as much as possible, and packing the wound with as much material as she had. Hopefully, that super shifter metabolism would make up for her lack of supplies. A quick check of his heart and lungs verified that he was improving, but she didn't know what would happen next. Cristobal almost certainly had internal crush injuries. That blood had to have come from somewhere, but she was no surgeon, and there wasn't exactly a med bay or emergency hospital a few minutes' flight away.

Aidan had told her that shifters healed faster, that the shift itself could deal with just about anything. So maybe she only needed to get Cristobal stable enough that he could shift. But she had no idea what that meant.

She glanced down and met his gaze again. "Does that feel better?"

He nodded. "Thank you," he mouthed, but the lines of pain were still etched on his face. If anything, they seemed worse than before. Were there more injuries that she couldn't see?

She forced a smile and began gathering her things. "Okay, guys. Let's move him. Careful, please," she said, shoving her supplies in her pack. She stood, still feeling shaky, but with relief this time, until she saw what surrounded them. The fire had grown in the short time she'd been working on Cristobal. What had been a small, concentrated area of flames had jumped dramatically, igniting treetop to treetop. More than half the trees circling the blasted area of destruction caused by the Earther ship now burned like towering torches, the shorter trees around them quickly becoming completely engulfed in flame.

Rachel stepped back slowly, staring at the fire, and nearly went down when her foot slipped into a pothole beneath the debris. Aidan grabbed her arm, and she leaned into him, soaking in some of his heat and strength. But only for a moment. She understood human psychology well enough to know that she couldn't afford to show weakness in front of this crowd. She *wasn't* weak. She'd just saved their leader's life. A few minutes more and, shifter or not, Cristobal would have been dead.

She gave Aidan a grateful nod, then shouldered her pack and straightened. "What about the people in the ship?"

"All dead. There's a reason lasers are forbidden on Harp. When they fired their weapon, it exploded inside the ship. Two of the Clanhome hunters dug their way in through the rupture. There's no one alive in there."

"Wolfrum?" she demanded.

His mouth tightened and her heart sank. He didn't want to tell her what they'd discovered, which meant it wasn't good. "One of them who knew Wolfrum by sight says the bastard wasn't among the bodies. But he might be wrong. They were in bad shape."

Rachel's eyes closed briefly. She'd wanted to face Wolfrum down, to demand answers. But this… It would have been better if he'd died with all the others. Now, the hunt would go on, and who knew what other crimes he'd commit? A desperate man was far more dangerous, and he'd already inflicted so much pain and loss.

She drew a deep breath and opened her eyes. First things first. "Can they outrun this fire?" she asked, jerking her chin at the shifters now carefully lifting Cristobal out of the wreckage. What she really meant to ask was could *any* of them escape the flames? Aidan would know his forest far better than she ever could. But when she looked up at him, she found lines of pain that mirrored Cristobal's. "Are you hurt?" she demanded, running her hands over his arms and chest, searching for injuries.

Her grabbed her hands. "It's not that." His voice was tight with pain, but he didn't meet her eyes, glancing aside almost guiltily. "I'll explain later. Right now, we have to move. Can you run?"

"Hell, yes, but Cristobal—" She stopped mid-sentence, abruptly aware that all the shifters around her wore the same look of pain as Aidan. Some showed it only in the lines of stress on their faces, but others were bent over, panting with effort, while a few of the younger ones were retching in misery. She frowned, angered and concerned in equal measure. It was possible the burning trees were releasing a toxic spore. But since she wasn't affected, and since no one else seemed surprised at the shifters' nearly uniform distress, she assumed this was another of Harp's secrets that Aidan wouldn't discuss with her, at least not in front of the others. But she couldn't just ignore it. She drew a deep breath and regretted it instantly as she coughed, tasting nothing but smoke.

"Aidan," she said, drawing his attention from where he'd been supervising the construction of a makeshift stretcher to carry Cristobal. "Is it the smoke? Does it bother you all more?"

His eyes shuttered, and his expression went oddly blank before he said, "Something like that. You should go ahead. We'll carry Cristobal and catch up to you."

She tilted her head studying him. He was lying. But why would he lie about something like toxic smoke? "I don't think so," she said slowly. "Not this time. You're all in worse shape than I am."

He opened his mouth to argue, but she stepped right into his space and met his eyes. "I don't know what's happening here, but you know I'm right. Get these others going. *I'll* help with Cristobal."

He swore savagely, but spun on a heel and strode away, calling orders to the various groups of shifters, getting them all moving in the same direction.

Rachel dropped back to oversee the five who'd hung back to carry Cristobal, including Fionn. She studied each of them in turn, wanting to be certain they could handle their task. But while they all seemed to be suffering the same pain, none of the four had more extreme symptoms.

She was most worried about Cristobal, however. He was still critically injured. If not for his shifter metabolism, he'd probably be dead. But whatever toxins were making the others sick would have a far stronger impact on his weakened physiology.

"Sir, how are you feeling?"

"Pain," he said, meeting her gaze steadily, and somehow she understood he was talking about more than himself. He was telling her that it wasn't some toxic smoke effect that was making the others so sick, it was pain. But what—

A huge cracking sound filled the air. Someone shouted a warning, and then one of the giant trees came crashing down, smashing through the forest, tearing off branches and shoving weaker growth ahead of it as it fell, burning.

"Fuck," someone swore softly.

"We need to move. *Now*," Aidan snapped.

The other shifters, even Fionn, responded with an alacrity that she associated with military discipline. But before she could think about that, she was receiving her own orders.

"Rachel," Aidan growled. "Get over here."

She spun back and saw him gesture at the head of the stretcher they'd rigged up for Cristobal. She could tell from the distribution of weight that she wouldn't be carrying as much as the others, but she didn't protest. They were all taller and stronger than she was. But she was no weakling, either. This wouldn't be the first big man she'd helped evacuate under less than ideal conditions. She could carry her share of the weight.

Taking up the position Aidan indicated, she got a good grip on her section of stretcher and waited.

"Up," Aidan ordered.

She lifted with the others and started forward. The fire was a steady heat at their backs, the smoke everywhere, already thick enough to fill her lungs and burn her eyes. She could only imagine what it was doing to the shifters with their mysteriously heightened susceptibility. But she didn't waste breath asking how they were. There was nothing they could do about it, except get away as fast as possible, and they were already doing that.

She freed one hand to reach for her canteen, wanting to refresh the cloth someone had placed on Cristobal's nose and mouth. Her muscles strained to support her share of the stretcher's weight with one arm, until Aidan saw what she was doing and called one of the others back to take her place. Giving him a grateful smile, she stopped long enough to pour water over the cloth, then caught up, and placed it over Cristobal's lower face again. Letting her canteen slip back to its position on the outside of her backpack, she tapped the other shifter's arm and resumed her position carrying the stretcher.

"How long will the fire burn?" she asked. She'd seen other wildfires like this and knew they were nearly impossible to fight. Especially without air support, which Harp didn't have.

"The Green has natural defenses," Aidan told her, his voice gritty with strain, not from the weight, she knew, but from pain. "It will burn itself out eventually."

They were nearing a river, and the path was becoming both overgrown and strewn with rocks. "Are we crossing the river?" she asked.

He grunted affirmatively.

"Will the river—?"

"Rachel," he snapped, then bit back whatever he'd been about to say and softened his next words. "Are you getting tired?"

She flashed him a disbelieving look. "Hell no, I'm not—"

"Then questions later, woman. Now, move." He shouted a single word that she didn't understand, but the others immediately started running.

Vowing privately to pay him back for the *woman* thing, she kept pace, spurred on by the sound of flames that were now roaring like the very fires of hell behind them. She spared a moment's thought for the men who'd been trapped in the invading ship, slowly suffocating to death. But it was no more than a moment. They'd written their own fates when they'd signed up to sell human beings.

. . .

"Rachel."

She didn't know how much later it was when she turned at Aidan's call, barely aware that they'd stopped walking. She was exhausted, her hands sore, her clothes and everything else filthy with soot and soaked from a rain that had begun falling not long after they'd begun their escape. They'd stopped once to wet down throats parched from smoke and exhaustion. She'd taken the opportunity to check more thoroughly on Cristobal, to give him water and take a look at his wounds. He hadn't had a chance to shift yet, and he'd lost a lot of blood, but even so, his wounds had already begun to heal. The researcher in her was intrigued by the potential for medical science, but the woman who'd saved a big cat's life and lost her heart to a shifter saw only the twisted motives that would drive a man like Guy Wolfrum to sacrifice shifters on the altar of his own profit.

Apparently having decided they'd reached a safe distance from the fire, Aidan had called a halt in an area surrounded by trees, but with a relative flat center of short grass and moss. He took over her share of the makeshift litter, working with the others to set Cristobal beneath a big tree on the far side of the small clearing. Aidan stopped her when she would have gone to the Ardrigh's side. "Watch," he said quietly, as Fionn and another man cut away Cristobal's clothes, with much grumbling from Cristobal himself.

She saw the telltale shimmer, and then it was no longer Cristobal lying there on the ground. It was a giant hunting cat, looking ready to pounce, with a mouth full of teeth and a predator's golden eyes. He bared those teeth at her now in what she supposed passed for a smile, and then he lifted his head in a cry that was answered by every shifter, including Aidan, whose not-so-human vocal cords managed to produce a serrated yowl that chilled her bones. It didn't matter that she knew him, that she'd had sex with him. Her earth-born hindbrain recognized the danger in that sound and sent shivers of fear trembling over her skin.

As if he understood, Aidan wrapped his arms around her, pulling her back to his chest, and putting his mouth against her ear. "Don't worry, sweetheart. I'll protect you."

She reacted to the laughter in his voice and shoved an elbow into his side. "I'll protect myself, asshole," she muttered. She couldn't help smiling when he laughed again, but she sobered quickly when Cristobal seemed to collapse back to the ground. She started for him, but Aidan held her back once more.

"He needs to shift again," he explained.

Rachel held her breath, almost hurting for Cristobal as he shifted back to his human form in a storm of golden sparks. There was no way that shift wasn't painful. He knelt on hands and knees, breathing hard and deeply, like a man exhausted from running a race. The tube she'd inserted was long gone, his side completely healed where she'd cut it. He didn't look at anyone, just knelt there, panting, head hanging low. Fionn crouched nearby, murmuring words too low for her to catch. But the look on his face said he was offering what comfort he could. The idea that a man could heal himself by shifting back and forth was beyond her experience, though it made some sense from a scientific standpoint. There had to be some cell regeneration involved in the shift process. An animal's lungs weren't exactly the same as a human's, and neither were the muscles and bones. Although she'd be willing to bet that if she took tissue samples of a shifter in his human form, she'd find that they weren't entirely human norm, either. It simply couldn't work any other way. She didn't know who'd done the genetic modification on the original shifters, but they were geniuses. It would be a tragedy if their records really had been destroyed.

"I know what you're thinking," Aidan murmured.

"No, you don't."

"You want a look at our medical records. Maybe even the original science logs."

Rachel knew the surprise showed on her face, and so she was careful not to look at him. But she was struck again at his intellect, and that of the other shifters, too. It must have been part of the original DNA sampling for the modification process. They weren't only strong and able to shift—they were also unusually smart.

"Forget about it," Aidan said in a voice that held more than dismissal. He was warning her. "I told you. The records don't exist."

But the way he said it… They clearly did exist, just not for *her*. She was about to ask why, when Cristobal shifted back to his animal form again. He seemed inclined to stay that way, as Fionn stood and walked over.

"We haven't met," he said, somewhat surly, but with an abashed note.

"Rachel Fortier," she said, offering her hand. He shook it briefly, and she felt the same calluses on his fingers and palm as she'd felt on Aidan's.

"Fionn Martyn. You arrived with *them*?" he asked, jerking his head back the way they'd come.

"Not precisely. I was with the other ship. You know about that, right?"

He nodded impatiently.

"I didn't know..." She drew a long breath, her mouth pinched unhappily. "I had no idea what Wolfrum planned to—"

"Wolfrum," he repeated, suddenly dangerously intent. "He's behind this?"

She felt Aidan move up behind her, close enough that she could feel the heat of his body.

"I think so," she said. "He planned the mission. He hired me. I knew this was a closed planet, but he said he'd obtained permission from the Ardrigh"—she nodded in Cristobal's direction—"to conduct research. He told me the plan was to study a race of big cats, not to capture, but just to observe. Nothing more. He never said anything about you being shapeshifters, much less human. And he sure as hell never mentioned that this mission was for the fleet research labs. I'd never have agreed to be part of it, which he obviously knew." She unclenched her jaw and asked the question that had been haunting her. "Am I right? Does Wolfrum know about shifters?" She felt the air leave her lungs as she waited for the answer.

Fionn exchanged a look over her head with Aidan. "He wasn't supposed to," he growled. "But he's lived here for two years. Hell, he married a Harp woman. It would be impossible to keep it from him."

"But that's...monstrous," she whispered.

"No kidding," Fionn snapped, then glanced at Aidan again. "Did you kill him?"

Rachel answered before Aidan could say anything. "He was never with the ship I came in on. We thought he was here, with the second ship, but now—"

"Two of the lads checked inside," Aidan said. "All dead, but no Wolfrum."

Fionn swore. "He was in the city when we left. No way he got here before us."

"In the city?" Aidan repeated. "Fuck. He's probably been hiding in there the whole time, was never out here at all. We need to let Rhodry know. He and—"

Aidan's words suddenly cut off, and she looked up to see Aidan and Fionn sharing a secretive look. She remembered Santino suddenly clamming up at the mention of Amanda Sumner and gave Aidan a shrewd look. "I know about Amanda," she said impatiently. "*Everyone* does. So, what's going on?" she demanded.

Chapter Sixteen

Ciudad Vaquero, capital city of Harp, aka "the city"

Amanda was outside again. The twins seemed to rest better out among the trees, and they'd finally quieted down after a bad morning. Fire was still burning in the Green. Fires didn't happen often on Harp, but when they did… Everything that affected the Green affected shifters, including her twins. She'd hoped their umbilical connection to her would blunt the worse of the pain. She could hear the trees' song, but she wasn't tied into the Green at the cellular level the way shifters were. Despite all of that, however, she could feel their stress and knew their little shifter minds were feeling the Green's pain. There was nothing she could do about that, except give them every ounce of love and comfort she had.

The saving grace had been that the fires were far away, and that a rain storm finally had moved in to help douse the flames. Rhodry had told her the fire was connected to whatever the second ship was doing, and he'd gone over to the Guild to dispatch a team of shifters to reinforce Aidan's group.

She heard the door open downstairs but didn't move. She could tell it wasn't Rhodry, and she wasn't prepared to risk disturbing the twins for anyone else. She heard Cullen's deep voice, and then…her mom, laughing. Amanda wiped her cheeks, wanting to erase any sign of tears. She pushed her awkward body out of the chair and turned toward the open doorway.

"Did you come to visit Cullen or your grandchildren?" she called.

Elise stepped onto the main level at that moment, her sharp gaze lingering over Amanda's puffy eyes, before scanning the rest of her body. Her expressive face tightened briefly, then she smiled and said, "I've told you, sweetling. I'm much too young to be a grandmother. Now, how are my babies?"

"*Your* baby is swelled up like a balloon, thanks to *my* babies," Amanda said, walking over to close the patio doors before sitting on the couch. "Where's the Vice?"

Her mother was "dating" Vice-Admiral Randolph Leveque, a relationship made easier by the fact that they were both assigned to Admiral Nakata's fleet. Leveque also happened to be the son of one of the wealthiest industrial families on Earth, which meant he could claim any assignment he wanted. And since what he wanted more than anything was Elise, he could make sure they stayed together.

On the other hand, Leveque wasn't entirely fond of Amanda, since she was living proof that Elise had, at one time, chosen another man over him. But Amanda and the Vice had reached an accord of sorts, since they both loved Elise. As long as Leveque took good care of her mother, Amanda could get along with him just fine. Not that Elise needed taking care of, but Leveque did it anyway.

"Randy's in orbit for now. We have the pinnace," she

said, referring to Leveque's private ship, which was far more elegant than anything the fleet could provide. "He's getting some work done, but he'll be down to visit soon. Never worry."

Amanda scoffed privately. As if she was worried about *Randy* visiting.

"And Rhodry?" her mom asked, leaning over to kiss her cheek as she sat next to her.

"He was called away this morning, but he'll be back soon. Um, Mom…" Amanda bit her lip. The timing sucked, with the Wolfrum situation still going on, but she had to tell her mom about shifters. Rhodry had assured her that while the babies would be born in their human form, they'd start developing shifter traits while still in the womb. Hell, Amanda was already feeling tiny claws, even though he'd assured her they wouldn't begin shifting fully until they were at least a month old. But how do you tell your mom that her grandchildren would be kittens? And not just any kittens, but little shapeshifters who could bounce between baby and kitten at will? And what about the Green, with its special connection to shifters and its singing trees? Her mom didn't need to know all of Harp's secrets. It wasn't safe. Wolfrum's horrendous scheme had proved that much. But she needed to know about shifters. Even Rhodry had agreed with that much.

"Amanda?" her mom asked now, leaning over and cupping her cheek in one soft hand. "Baby, you look so tired. Is something wrong? Are you and Rhodry having—"

"Of course not," she said quickly. "We're fine. He's fine. Well…" She laughed. "He's terrified, but otherwise fine."

"Then, what is it? Come on, you're scaring me. Just out with it."

"Okay. First, and this is really important, you can't tell anyone what I'm about to tell you. Not even the Vice. Not anyone."

Her mother frowned. "All right."

"There's something about Harp that you don't know."

"I'm sure there are many—"

"No, Mom, just listen. Harp's…unusual." She was making a mess of this. She needed to simply come out and say it. Her mom was a scientist. She'd understand. "All right, look. Everything on Harp is connected, like a single organism. I know, I know," she said, raising a hand to stop her mom's predictable protest. "I'm simplifying, but if you let me finish, you'll understand."

Elise's lips tightened into a flat line of disapproval, but she gestured for Amanda to continue.

"Life was incredibly harsh for the survivors of that original crash. It was as if the entire planet was against them, from the smallest plant to the biggest and deadliest predators and everything in between. The colonists were desperate, so they took a chance. They needed people who would be part of the Harp ecosystem, people the planet would recognize as its own, so it would stop fighting them at every turn. Which meant genetic modification, right? No big deal, but…and this is where it gets complicated.

"Every trace of data from the original experiments was destroyed—maybe intentionally—so there's no record of exactly what their geneticists were thinking or what they did. I do know that it was a last-ditch effort. They were running out of everything. Even their genetic samples were in danger because they couldn't generate the power necessary to store them properly. And, the equipment, well—"

"You're telling me they succeeded," her mom interrupted with forced patience. "That Rhodry is a product of this genetic modification, which means the twins are, too. And that's *fine*, Amanda. It's not exactly rare these days. So, what's the problem?"

Amanda smiled at her mother. "It's not a problem. It's

the most remarkable genetic modification I've ever seen. But first…"

She crossed over and opened the stairway door just as Rhodry loped into view. He grinned up at her as he climbed the steps, taking them three at a time. He normally would have come in over the balcony—shifting and leaping in from the trees—but he'd known her mom was there and taken the stairs instead. She grinned back him.

"*Missed you,*" he murmured as he came even with her.

She went up on tiptoe, her arms around his neck as she kissed him. "You, too." His hand stroked her belly, and the babies bounced happily. "We all did," she said dryly, lifting her head to smile at Cullen, who'd come up behind Rhodry. "What am I missing over at the Guild? Any news?"

"Everyone's on their best behavior what with—" Rhodry bit back what he'd been about to say, glancing over Amanda's shoulder where Elise was sitting, probably listening to every word while pretending not to. "The fires," he finished instead. "Report came in while I was there, says the rain is doing its job, so everyone's breathing a sigh of relief."

"They'll no doubt be at each other's throats again by morning," Cullen agreed.

"Not if I—" Rhodry started to comment, but Elise was tired of being ignored.

"Rhodry," she drawled. "How lovely to see you."

It was her mother's way of saying they were being rude, mostly aimed at Rhodry. But it took more than that to get a rise out of him. He corralled an entire Guild of alpha male shifters every damn day, and when he wasn't doing that, he was wrestling with unhappy clansmen who weren't exactly known for their willingness to compromise. One unhappy mother-in-law was a piece of cake.

"Elise," he said easily, strolling over to kiss her raised cheek. "It's great to see you. Amanda's glad you're here."

"But you're not?" she responded perceptively.

"Whatever makes Amanda happy. Where's the Vice?" He'd taken to using Amanda's nickname for Vice-Admiral Leveque.

"Upstairs," Elise said, using fleet parlance for in orbit. "He'll be down soon. In fact, Amanda, darling, maybe you should hold off on your big secret until he's here?"

That got a rise out of Rhodry. He turned his head sharply to regard Amanda, his eyes wide in a question.

"I knew you'd be home soon, so figured I'd get the preliminaries out of the way."

Elise had been listening to every word and now tipped her head thoughtfully. "Telepathy?" she guessed. "Is that it?"

Amanda smiled nervously. "Not quite." They were going to have to demonstrate. She could talk science and historical necessity until she was blue in the face, but in the final analysis, someone was going to have to shift. Rhodry had insisted that he be the one. These were *his* children, and Amanda was *his* wife. And he didn't care *what* Elise approved of.

Of *course he doesn't*, Amanda thought fondly. His alpha male perfection wasn't limited to physical beauty. He had all the confidence and arrogance to go with it. He only cared that Elise's reaction not hurt any of the people he loved, which meant he had to control the scene. He had to be the one shifting.

Amanda wasn't quite as sanguine about it. Elise still resented the fact that her only child had chosen to remain behind on Harp instead of continuing with the fleet and life among the stars. And she blamed Rhodry for Amanda's decision. A lot of that blame was just Elise projecting her own preferences onto Amanda, with a little bit of personal history thrown in for good measure. Amanda's father had chosen his planet over Elise, way back when. He was perhaps the only man in her life whom she hadn't been able to charm into doing what she wanted, and she still held a grudge, even though she admitted she'd once loved him. Or maybe it was *because* she'd loved him. Either way, the parallel between Amanda's father leaving and Rhodry taking Amanda away from her to remain on Harp was just too obvious. So was Elise's transfer of blame, but her mother couldn't see that part of the equation.

For her part, Amanda was worried about Rhodry being Elise's first exposure to Harp's shifters. He was spectacular, even when compared to a shifter population filled with gorgeous masculine specimens. He was beautiful in either form, but his cat form was also huge and threatening. And Amanda didn't want to give her mom another excuse not to like him.

She looked up at Rhodry and found him watching her. "You ready?" she asked.

The look he gave her was full of his usual love, but also confidence that they were doing the right thing. "Aren't I always?" He gave her a roguish wink.

Amanda smiled, unable to do anything else when he looked at her like that. She drew a deep breath and turned to face Elise. "Okay, Mom. We can discuss the science later, at least what little anyone knows, but it's easier just to show you."

Elise rolled her eyes but patted the cushion next to her and held Amanda's hand once she lowered herself to the couch. "Cullen, you want to join us here for the show?" she asked cheerfully.

"I'm good here, Elise," he responded from where he was leaning against the wall, watching Rhodry with an unreadable smile on his face.

Elise noticed the smile and frowned. A moment later, she was too busy staring in disbelief to worry about Cullen. Because Rhodry didn't wait, didn't give any indication that something was about to happen. He'd already slipped off his shifter-style soft boots, and now he simply pulled off his shirt and shifted.

With a soft growl, he prowled over to Amanda's side, rested his big head right up against the swell of her stomach, and started to purr. She stroked her fingers through his soft, black fur, tears spilling down her cheeks—damn hormones—when she felt the gentle hum that was her babies purring back for the first time ever.

And then she remembered her mother.

She turned, not knowing what to expect, but Elise was just staring, her mouth open in a silent "oh" of surprise.

"He's a shapeshifter," Amanda explained unnecessarily. "Or just a shifter. That's what they're called here on Harp."

"How…" Elise breathed, and then paused to stare some more.

"I told you, the records were lost. We don't know—"

"No, no. Not that. How many of them are there?"

Amanda blew out a breath. "Well, there's Cullen."

Elise's head spun to where Cullen had straightened from the wall, hands spread wide as he shrugged. "Are you all…? Good God," she said, "I don't even know what question to ask first. I need to contact my assistant—"

"No," Amanda said instantly, even as Rhodry's head came off her lap to aim a golden stare at Elise. "Remember, Mom, I told you. You can't tell *anyone.* Not even Leveque."

"But, Amanda, this is remarkable. It would be worth a fortune to…" Her words trailed off as she suddenly understood. No one had ever accused Elise Sumner of being slow-witted. "They'd never leave you alone. Even worse, they'd try to claim you're less than human in order to assert control, deny your basic rights. It won't even matter what the genetic reality is, they'd tie you up in the courts for centuries, while they… You're right, Amanda. No one can know of this. Can you shift back as easily?" she asked Rhodry, her expression grim.

Amanda felt the shift the moment it began. She lifted her hand, and when she put it down again, it was Rhodry sitting on the floor next to her, not his cat. Cullen shot a pair of pants over their heads, which Rhodry donned quickly in deference to Elise. He then stood, lifted Amanda as if she weighed nothing, and sat down again with her on his lap.

Elise watched the whole thing, and Amanda knew her mother didn't miss the ease with which he'd lifted her. Or the ease of his second shift, either.

"The twins?" her mother asked simply.

"Our sons will all be shifters," Rhodry explained. "Our daughters will be strong and beautiful, like their mother. But not shifters."

Amanda rested her head on his shoulder, feeling all squishy at his casual reference to their sons *and* daughters.

"The gene is sex-linked. Of course," Elise murmured. "What about development? How much control do infants and children have over their form?"

"They'll appear human enough at birth," Rhodry answered. "But they'll have little control over the shift for the first six months. In fact, most shifter babies prefer their cat. It's easier. After that, it's more a question of whether they *want* to control it or not. Their cat develops much faster physically, which gives them much greater mobility at a younger age."

"I wouldn't look for much cooperation from the twins on that front, Elise," Cullen chimed in. "Rhodry's mother still has tales of his harrowing escapes as a babe. Him and Aidan, both."

Amanda could have hugged Cullen for injecting that much needed note of humor. It made even Elise smile.

"Aidan?" Elise asked Rhodry. "You have a brother?"

"As close as, but Aidan's a cousin by blood. We were

born minutes apart and raised together. We're brothers in every way that counts."

"I see. I'll want to consult with your physician here on Harp, Amanda. I assume you've spoken with them, so they know I'm—"

"They know you by reputation, know you've been Chief Medical Officer with the fleet for several years, and have read everything you've written. They're excited to work with you."

"Well, it seems I'll be working with *them*, rather than the other way around. Hold on to those babies for another few weeks, if you please, so I can get up to speed." She paused, thinking. "I'll tell Randy I'm staying on-planet for a bit. He won't question it. He knows how I feel about you—" Her mouth tightened on whatever she'd been about to say. "How I feel about you," she said finally. "He has other business he needs to handle, anyway."

Amanda leaned over and took her mother's hand, recognizing her rambling talk for nervous energy. "It's okay, Mom," she said quietly. "The twins and I are healthy, and we're going to stay that way. Women have been delivering and raising shifters for nearly as long as humans have been on Harp. And that thing I told you? About how the planet knows its own? Well, Harp loves its shifters, especially the baby ones. And we have Rhodry to take care of us, and all his cousins, too. We're safer here than we would be anywhere else in the universe."

Her mother drew a discreet breath and then swallowed, while squeezing Amanda's hand hard enough to hurt. "It's a lot to take in. The twins, of course, but also the scientific accomplishment. My God, think of the conditions they must have been working under. Genius doesn't begin to describe it. But don't you worry," she hurried to say. "Those are my grandbabies in there, even if I'm not old enough to be a grandmother," she added primly. "There is no one in this universe more important to me than them and you. No one hurts my babies. I'll kill anyone who tries."

Rhodry jerked a little, stunned at vehemence of Elise's last proclamation, but Amanda wasn't surprised. People tended to underestimate Elise. They saw the delicate beauty and never realized that it hid an iron will and a protective streak a mile wide when it came to those she loved. Rhodry took it for granted that he'd defend his family. Well, Elise did the same.

"I've made up the guest room," Amanda told her mom. "You know where everything is. But if it's all the same to you, these two wore me out this morning. I need a nap."

"I'll join you," Rhodry said predictably. Amanda knew he wasn't tired. He just wanted some alone time with her, and she'd sleep a lot better with him next to her, anyway. The twins were always quieter when he was around. The little fiends.

Rhodry stood, lifting her easily and setting her on her feet.

"I'll see you in a bit, Mom," she said, leaning over to kiss Elise's cheek. "Thank you for coming."

"I wouldn't miss it for the world. Rest well. Cullen," she said, switching her attention, "carry my bag into the guest room, would you?"

Amanda watched them go, with Cullen giving her a reassuring wink over his shoulder before disappearing down the hall after her mom. The guest quarters were at the opposite end of the house, in their own separate wing, so that everyone could have privacy.

She almost sagged against Rhodry once they were gone. He caught her automatically and held tight. "Hey," he said in concern. "You okay?"

She nodded as she turned into him. "I'm so relieved that's over with."

"She took it better than I expected."

Amanda chuckled. "Cullen said she'd be fine with it, and he was right. You think the Vice should be worried about how close Mom and Cullen are getting?"

Rhodry shuddered. "Don't even think it. She'd eat my baby cousin alive, and then I'd have to explain to the family what happened to him."

"She's not that bad."

He snorted. "She's every bit that bad, *acushla,* and worse. I'm softening the truth because I love you."

She laughed. "Do you? Come prove it then. The doctors say sex is good for me."

"That makes me feel a bit used."

"Poor baby, I'll make it worth your while."

"You make my *life* worthwhile. Do with me what you will."

Chapter Seventeen

"What does Amanda have to do with this?" she persisted, switching her gaze between Aidan and Fionn. As one, they turned to stare at her with more than a little suspicion. Seeing the distrust in Fionn's gaze didn't surprise her, but from Aidan… Her heart cracked just a little bit. He shouldn't have had the ability to hurt her like that. He *didn't* have that ability. She wouldn't allow it.

Fionn gave Aidan a glance filled with meaning she didn't understand and wasn't meant to. And then he walked over to where Cristobal was recovering from a fast shift back to human.

She looked after him, not really wanting to hang around Aidan. "Whatever," she said dismissively. "I need to check on Cristobal's—"

"He's fine," Aidan interrupted. "With every shift, his body will heal a little more. He'll be tired after each one, because his injuries were severe. But with enough food and some rest, he'll be back to nearly full strength by morning. Sooner, if the situation demands it. He's a strong shifter."

"All right. So, I guess we're making camp here. I'll find a—"

"Rachel."

"—spot where I can set up. I know you all prefer privacy, so—"

"Rachel," he repeated, taking her arms and turning her to face him. "There's no rush to set up camp. We'll wait until Cristobal recovers enough, and then it's up to him."

"What's up to him?"

Aidan shrugged. "Some of us will probably race ahead to the city to warn the others. If Wolfrum is still at large, there's no telling what he'll do."

"But you think there's some danger to Amanda. From me. Why?"

His gaze went carefully blank, as it had before, but this time, it was just the two of them, and her reaction was more anger than hurt.

"For fuck's sake, Aidan. I've read the First Contact reports. Hell, Amanda *wrote* some of them. It's no secret she stayed behind, or that she resigned her commission after only a few months to remain here."

He stared back at her with no expression, and she could practically see the shutters sliding over his eyes, concealing his thoughts, his emotions…and whatever truth he and Fionn held between them.

Her heart squeezed a little harder. "Fine. As long as we're waiting on Cristobal, I'm going to take a break. You all might not need it, but I sure do." She turned away without waiting for his response. Whatever it was probably wouldn't be the truth anyway, so what did it matter?

"Rachel."

She stopped walking and turned her head just enough

that he'd know she was listening.

"Don't go far. It's not safe for you."

She smiled a little. She already knew Harp wasn't safe for her. She'd known that going in. What she hadn't known was that the greatest danger would be to her heart.

. . .

Aidan tracked Rachel as she disappeared into the thick brush, even tuning in to the murmur of the trees as they responded to her presence. It wasn't the same as the way they were with Amanda. Rachel couldn't hear their song. But the trees didn't react to Rachel as they did to most Earthers, either, like the fleet techs who staffed the science center in the city, for example. Or Guy Wolfrum.

"You and Rhodry marching in step again?" Fionn asked, his voice low and not meant to carry.

Aidan turned. "I don't know what you mean." That wasn't true. He knew exactly what Fionn meant.

Fionn snorted dismissively. "First, Rhodry and Amanda, and now you and Rachel. You've both fallen for Earthers. Mind you," he hurried to add before Aidan could protest, "I'm half in love with Amanda myself, or at least I was, before she started making little shifters. Now, I'm fully in love with her," he added, laughing. "She's a remarkable woman, just like that one." He nodded in the direction Rachel had disappeared. They couldn't see her any longer, but Fionn probably knew just as well as Aidan how far she'd gone and what was happening around her. "I wonder if they breed them that way on Earth. Do you think it's the fleet training? Or something in the water?"

Aidan followed Fionn's gaze. "It's neither one. Amanda was never on Earth, and Rachel was never fleet. It's just... *them*."

"See, that's what I thought. You're as far gone as your cousin."

Aidan spun to face him, deliberately turning his back on Rachel's path. "Was there something you wanted, Fionn? Something other than fucking with me, I mean."

Fionn chuckled. "Totally gone, my friend," he repeated, but sobered quickly enough. "Rhodry needs to be warned that Wolfrum's still at large."

Aidan scanned the shifters moving around their makeshift encampment. Cristobal's personal guard were there, all of them fully healed and functional. But they were outnumbered by clan shifters. "I'll send word."

Fionn tilted his head curiously. "You're not going yourself?" The question was serious enough, but there was a light in his eyes that told Aidan the real reason for the question.

"No, you ass, I'm not going myself. But I'm sending cousins who are sworn to Rhodry by both blood and oath, and who'll get the warning there or die trying. And in the meantime, I'm going to make sure that Rachel reaches the city alive, so she can confront Wolfrum and we can get the truth out of him. I want everyone to know him for the belly-crawling zillah he really is."

"Wolfrum has a Harp wife. She may want to speak for him."

"And I'm the one who was captured and caged like a fucking animal by his personal militia," he growled viciously. "I'll have something to say, too."

Fionn blinked in surprise. No one except Aidan's fellow clansmen—the ones who'd taken down the first ship and who'd been at Clanhome when he'd arrived—had known about his capture.

"Fair enough," Fionn said. "Dispatch your cousins to Rhodry. I'll tell my father."

"Fionn," Aidan said, when the other shifter would have turned away. "You know who got me out of that cage?"

Fionn shook his head. "I'm assuming it was Rhodry and—"

"It was Rachel. She risked her life, walked away from everything she knew, to save the life of a *cat*. She didn't even know shifters existed."

Fionn's eyes lit with understanding. "With your permission," he said, tipping his head to emphasize the request, "I'll make sure the Ardrigh knows the full story."

"Of course. And I'll go find Rachel before something eats her."

• • •

Rachel sat back against the trunk of a big tree—possibly the biggest she'd seen in her many travels—and watched Aidan wind through the trees toward her. She scowled, knowing that if he'd wanted to he could have shifted into his cat form and crawled down the tree right on top of her head. She was incredibly jealous of that. How great would it be to be able to shift into something as beautiful and deadly as a giant hunting cat? Or anything else, for that matter. Maybe not that rat-like creature that they called a rabbit here on Harp. It wouldn't be good at all to turn into something that people ate for dinner, and Santino had cooked a few of those the night they'd fought off the banshee pack. No, it would have to be something big. A predator for sure.

"Are you just going to ignore me?"

His voice interrupted her musings on the best shifter animal to be. She glanced up, moving only her eyes. He was standing right in front of her. "Is there a problem with Cristobal?" she asked, mostly to piss him off. But he'd pissed her off first. Or rather, he'd bruised her heart, but she'd never admit that. "Or does one of the others need something?" she asked, adding some frosting on the cake of his anger. His eyes narrowed predictably.

"Come back to camp, Rachel. It's not safe for you to be alone out here."

"You all keep telling me that. And yet here I am, still alive and well. What's the plan? Are we staying here for the night or moving on?" She could see his jaw clenching. It was almost entertaining.

"We're staying. We'll get an early start in the morning."

Rachel stood, ignoring the hand he held out to help her. She didn't need Aidan Devlin's help to stand up, for fuck's sake. "Good," she said briskly. "I'm going to wash up. If there's anything I can do to help set up camp, I'm willing to work. Just let me know." She turned her back on him and started for the river she'd been hearing for the last couple of hours. They'd been following its path, but the banks were so dense with growth that she hadn't yet seen the water.

"Goddamn it, Rachel."

She raised her eyebrows at Aidan's outburst but kept walking. He'd made his position clear. He didn't trust her with whatever big secret everyone else knew. Something to do with Amanda. Was she dead? Was that it? Had she contracted some awful Harp disease that her Earth-born immune system couldn't fight? Whatever it was, Aidan didn't trust her with it. So what the hell did he expect from her? Did he think she was going to continue fucking a man who so patently distrusted her? And maybe she would have if he'd been someone else. If they'd been some*where* else. But they weren't. She'd *earned* his trust. She'd saved his life. She'd betrayed her fellow Earthers to help him, and it didn't matter that they'd been scum-sucking lowlifes. She'd left behind everything she knew to help Harp—human, animal, and everything in between—and he didn't trust *her*? Well, fuck him. And not in the literal sense, either.

He grabbed her from behind, spinning her around and trapping her against his chest when she tried to fight back. She hadn't even heard him coming.

"Let go of me."

"Not until you listen."

"Let go of me, Aidan," she said again, wishing she'd had the foresight to load a syringe with something nasty, something she could shove into his thigh. The same thigh that was sliding its way between her legs.

Oh hell no.

"Listen to me," he insisted. Like she had a choice. "Shifters have good reasons not to trust people."

"Bullshit," she snapped. "You guys run the fucking planet. You think I haven't figured that out?"

"You have us all figured out, then? Based on what? A few days in the Green? We were all born on Harp, shifters and norms both. We've lived and died here for more than five hundred years. Raised families, fought to keep them safe."

That caught Rachel's attention. "What aren't you telling me? What are you afraid of?" She leaned back to see his face and saw his expression shut down yet again. What little warmth had been left in her heart cooled to ice. "Nice chat," she snarled. "But you know what? Never mind." She flexed her arms and pushed against his iron-hard chest. Or she tried to. "Let go of me."

"Listen to me," he demanded. "You think that just because you saved my life, saved *Cristobal's* life, that you have the right to know everything there is about us? You think you deserve our blind trust?"

"No," she said softly, meeting his beautiful eyes. "Not because I saved anyone's life. But because I survived that damn swamp with you, because we fought side by side to get this far, because we… I don't think I deserve blind trust. But

I know I deserve more than a fucking cold shoulder. Let... *go* of me."

His arms tightened briefly. Long enough that she began listing the options in her head of what weapons she had handy and how to get to them. But then his arms opened, and she almost stumbled as he turned and walked away from her.

Rachel focused on breathing as she filled her canteen with icy river water, then settled for a quick wash of her face and neck, her arms and hands. It was far too cold for anything else. Running wet fingers through her hair, she re-braided it tightly, then headed back to where the others were setting up for the night. As she walked, she repeated a mantra in her head. *Breathe in, breathe out. And whatever you do, don't let him see the hurt on your face, the pain in your heart. Don't give him the satisfaction.*

By the time she reached the main camp, she was back in control. She had more important things to worry about than Aidan. Wolfrum was still out there, and everyone seemed to agree that he'd returned to the city. She wasn't sure he'd ever left. It was possible he'd sent his goon squads out to do the dirty work and was still waiting for them to report back with their captives, so they could all rendezvous and leave Harp together. That would explain how he'd known about the first ship, despite Harp's comm issues. Population-wise, Harp was a small place, and as with all such communities, gossip was probably a competitive sport. No matter how hard Aidan and the others had worked to keep a lid on the arrival of the invaders, it would have gotten out. These things always did.

But now, she considered the logistical problem Wolfrum would have faced in getting not just himself, but his two crews and their captives off-planet. She and the rest of the crew from her ship had piggybacked on a big transport for most of the journey here. Which meant that Wolfrum must have made some similar accommodation for their departure with the captured shifters. In fact, it would have been even more crucial to his plan at that point, because he'd be sneaking *unwilling* captives *off*-planet. She scrolled back through her memories of the commercial vessel that had brought them here, but there was nothing. No hint of to whom it had belonged, no logos, no stray cargo stencils. Whoever it was had been very careful to keep her and the rest of her crew locked up on their own little shuttle.

For now, it seemed she'd have to settle for stopping Wolfrum, and maybe getting him to spill his guts. But despite whatever he told them, she'd investigate the rest of it herself once she returned home. He'd lied to her from the very beginning. She wasn't inclined to believe anything he said at this point. But once back on Earth, she'd have the full resources of a major university at her disposal. It would be much easier to discover Wolfrum's industrial backer, then. And her brother would help her, too. He was a genius at uncovering all sorts of records that people tried to hide.

It suddenly hit her that she'd be going home after this. In the past, after an arduous trek through some dangerous environment, those words had always made her heart feel lighter. She was sure the feelings would come this time, too, once her task was complete and Wolfrum had been stopped. She'd feel better about all of this then. She was sure of it.

She happened to glance up and see Aidan on the other side of the fire, conferring with Fionn and Cristobal, who was looking remarkably well, albeit not yet at full strength. All three men looked over at her at the same time, and she stared back at them, refusing to be cowed by their alpha stares. Cristobal smiled and said something to Aidan that made him scowl, even as Fionn shot her an amused grin. It was possibly the first time he'd ever looked at her with anything other than a snarl on his face.

Whatever. She was so done with these guys.

. . .

"God knows I'm no expert on women," Cristobal said cheerfully, "but I think she's pissed at you, Aidan."

Great, Aidan thought. Now the whole damn family were sticking their noses into his love life. He caught Fionn grinning over at Rachel as if they were sharing the greatest jest of all time. Asshole. He'd almost taken her head off when she'd tried to help his father, and now suddenly they were best friends.

"Yes, sir," Aidan said, tired of being the source of Fionn's amusement and pissed that Rachel had put him in this position. She wouldn't even *try* to understand. Not that he'd done much explaining. He believed in his heart that she could be trusted with the truth about Amanda's pregnancy. But it wasn't his decision. Was it? If Rachel was his, wasn't it his choice whether to trust her or not? And if he didn't take that step, wouldn't he lose her?

"There's no reason for everyone to take the slow route back to the city," he told Cristobal. "You and your guard can take the tree road, travel at your own pace. I've already tasked several clansmen to race ahead and warn Rhodry that Wolfrum's still at large. The others will return with word for Clanhome, and I'll bring Rachel to the city. She travels fast for a norm, so we won't be more than a day or two behind you."

Privately he was thinking he could use the time to bring Rachel around, to make her understand… He glanced over and saw Santino being a little too helpful. What the hell?

. . .

"You should set your bedroll over here."

Rachel looked where Santino was pointing and saw that

the area that had been cleared of the worst bits of loose forest debris, the kind that could torment even the most exhausted traveler's sleep and leave them with some nasty bruises.

"Take the spot nearest the fire. You'll need it more than the rest of us will," he said.

She saw him wince, as if wishing he could take the words back. After all, if she'd still been Aidan's lover, she'd have been bedding down with him. Warmth wouldn't have been an issue. "My cousins and I will be leaving during the night," he hurried to add. "A couple hours' rest and we can travel straight through to the city."

"That's where I'm heading, too," she said casually, taking his advice and spreading her bedroll close enough to the fire for warmth.

Santino grimaced. "I'd let you come with us, but we'll be moving nonstop and full speed. I don't think—"

"No, that's okay," she assured him. "I know you're all worried about Amanda."

He snorted. "Rhodry's crazed enough about her safety. The last thing he needs is that fucker Wolfrum stirring up more trouble."

A sudden unwelcome thought made Rachel's breath catch in her throat, but she strove to keep her response casual, her movements easy. "I hear that."

Santino suddenly glanced over her shoulder and grinned. "Looks like someone wants a word," he said and strode off to join a pair of shifters who welcomed him with low words and jabs at his shoulders that would have felled an ordinary man. Rachel's gaze slid sideways and wasn't surprised to see Aidan strolling around the fire.

She watched him, unable to do anything but admire the easy play of muscle and grace as he moved, avoiding every obstacle in his path as if it wasn't there. If they'd been on a space station, or somewhere with an artificial gravity, she'd have suspected he'd been artificially enhanced. But Aidan's grace was owed to a shifter's inborn strength and prowess, which only made it more appealing, not less.

"Trying to suborn my cousin?" he inquired.

"He was just being friendly, showing me where to drop my stuff. We spent two days traveling together, you know."

Judging by the look on his face, that didn't make him happy. Too bad. They had more important things to discuss. "Tell me something." She stared up at him, daring him to lie. "Is Amanda married to Wolfrum?"

His reaction was immediate and very telling. "What? Fuck, no!"

She tilted her head thoughtfully, remembering Santino's comment about how Rhodry was "crazed" with worry for Amanda. She met Aidan's gaze. "She's married to your cousin Rhodry, isn't she?"

His expression tightened. "I'm going to kill Santino."

She shook her head dismissively. "Santino didn't say anything. He didn't need to. You're all tiptoeing around Amanda so carefully. You won't even say her name. It was obvious she's more to you than just some novelty Earther."

"She's a member of the Guild. That alone gives her status on Harp. It's the Guild who keeps everyone safe, and does most of the hunting, too."

Rachel hummed wordlessly. "Maybe," she conceded. "Or maybe it's just that she's female. Are all shifters such asshole dominants?"

Aidan's eyes flashed. "You weren't complaining about dominance when I got you through the damn swamp."

"That's because you didn't," she said sweetly. "I seem to recall killing a snake that was trying to eat you. Maybe I should have let it."

"What the hell, Rachel?"

She gave him a narrow stare. "The hell is that after

everything we went through together, after—" *No*, she thought. She wasn't going to bare her soul like that. Wasn't going to tell him how she'd thought they were building something between *them* that had nothing to do with anyone else. And she sure as hell wasn't going to admit that she had *feelings* for him. Feelings that, in her most private of private thoughts, she'd been ready to admit might be…love. But you didn't lie to someone you loved. If there was something he didn't want to tell her, something he maybe *couldn't* because it involved more than just him, a secret crucial to Harp's safety, even—*that* she'd understand. Every state had its secrets. Harp probably more than most, given its history. But why couldn't he just come out and *tell* her that's what it was?

"Never mind," she said now. "I'll stay out of your way until we get to the city. And then I'll do everything I can to help you catch Wolfrum and prosecute him, or however Harp handles it." A new possibility hit her. "If you're worried about the fleet or Earth authorities or whatever, don't be," she assured him. "First of all, they won't want anything to do with his scheme. Not publicly, anyway. But, more important, the crime happened on Harp, against Harp interests, which means it's subject to your laws. That rule goes back to the original colonies, probably about the same time as your ancestors took off from Earth."

Aidan was watching her, but he seemed impatient. As if he was being polite, rather than interested in what she was saying. When she finished, he studied her a moment longer then took her arm and said, "Let's take a walk."

She started to pull her arm away, but he tightened his hold, and she didn't want to make a scene, especially since she didn't have a chance of breaking away if he didn't want her to.

"Why are we walking?" she demanded in an angry whisper.

"Because you need to know some things, and we need privacy for this conversation."

She glanced over to see his jaw clenched as he stared straight ahead. "You could have asked," she muttered, but stopped struggling.

"Please," he said insincerely.

Rachel wanted to tell him to shove it, but she wanted to know what was going on even more, so she held her silence and kept walking.

...

Aidan had made his decision, but it hadn't been easy. His loyalty to Rhodry, to family and clan, was in the very blood that ran through his veins. But Rachel...she was important, too. It was new to him, these *feelings* he had for her. It had never happened with any other woman. But his gut, and maybe his heart, was telling him she was just as important as those other loyalties. It wrecked him to know that she didn't think he cared, that she thought she didn't matter. And he wasn't willing to let that go. He'd lived this long by trusting his instincts. He knew Rhodry would understand.

They finally stopped in the deep shadows beneath an ancient grandfather tree, the branches so heavy that they drooped almost to the ground. Aidan pulled Rachel into the quiet beneath that canopy and pressed her up against the trunk. She gave him a hostile stare, but didn't try to get away, which he took as a positive sign.

Resting his forearms against the rough bark to either side of her head, he leaned close enough to feel her breath on his skin, to feel the humming tension in her stance. "I know you think we're secretive, probably too much. But Harp has good reasons for that. You've seen what would happen if news of our existence got out."

"You mean shifters," she said quietly, her eyes reflecting horror at what the invaders had tried to do to him. "I'd like to say it was an aberration, a few Earthers willing to undertake unspeakable activities for money." Her eyes closed briefly as she shook her head. "But it wasn't. It they'd succeeded…"

"But they didn't," he reminded her. "Because of you, and because we don't tolerate invaders of any kind, but especially not those who mean us harm."

"I get all of that, but what's it got to do with Amanda Sumner? I know she's here, for Christ's sake. What's the big deal?"

"The big deal, as you say…" He paused, knowing his decision was the right one, but still struggling with going against Rhodry's last position on the matter. "She's pregnant," he snapped out, and felt an odd rush of relief. "Amanda's pregnant."

Rachel stared at him, her heart beating faster against his chest. "Pregnant?" she whispered. "How far…"

"A few more weeks, if she holds out that long."

She swallowed audibly, but her words were dry, as if she needed water. "Is it a boy? A shifter?"

"Here," he said, offering her water from the canteen on his belt. "Drink."

She shook her head but took a long sip, swishing the water around in her mouth before swallowing. "Answer the question," she said, sounding even more stressed than she'd been before.

He studied her a moment, but decided what the hell? He'd already given away the most critical information. "Twins. Both boys."

"Oh no," she murmured, lowering her head, eyes wild, as if faced with a terrible choice.

"What? I don't get it. A pregnancy is good news. And twins, double that. Especially twin shifters."

When she looked back up at him, he'd have sworn the dark gold of her skin had lost a full shade. "You don't understand. Those babies, and Amanda, too, are terrible danger if Wolfrum's still alive. Especially if he really is in the city. Wait. Where's Amanda?"

"In the city, but she's with Rhodry and Cullen, not to mention a whole damn Guild hall full of shifters."

"Maybe," she said, nodding rapidly. "That might be enough. But you have to tell them, you have to let Amanda know."

"Know what? Explain," he demanded.

"Wolfrum will go after her!" she practically shouted, as if he should have figured that out already.

"After Amanda? But— Oh shit. The twins." He grabbed her hand and started pulling her back to the main camp.

"The babies are shifters, but they're gestating in *her* body, and she was *born in space,*" she continued. "She's the perfect incubator. They'll have all her adaptations to space travel, which means they might even travel better than you would have." She almost tripped. Aidan caught her but didn't slow down. Rachel kept talking, to herself more than him. "But Amanda's well connected. That might save her," she muttered. "Her mother's way up in fleet and all but married to Vice-Admiral Leveque. Rumor has it he's a good guy. Difficult to work with, but honest. Which is saying something, coming from that family."

They'd reached the camp now, though she didn't seem to realize it. Her attention was all for Aidan, who was staring at her, hands scraping long hair back from his face, eyes flashing from blue to gold as his body fought the urge to shift in the face of a danger he couldn't yet attack.

Rachel lowered her gaze, her expression blank, as if she were processing her own thoughts. She glanced up. "Does Wolfrum know she's pregnant?"

Aidan shrugged. "I'm sure. Everyone knows."

"He has to have a ship waiting. Nothing else makes sense. He had to have a way to get off-planet. And now that he's failed to capture one of you...he'll go after Amanda. And if he gets her on a ship, she'll disappear with her babies, and you'll never see them again."

. . .

Ten minutes later, Rachel watched the camp dissolve around her. The fire still burned, banked to white-hot embers for the night. But nothing else was the same. No one was getting ready to sleep anymore. She'd noted the departure of Santino and a few of the others a while ago, foregoing even the two hours' rest they'd planned. Everyone in camp was on the move, either stripping down and shifting, or already shifted and prowling the campsite restlessly, as if waiting for the order to depart.

She felt Aidan's presence behind her. "What's the plan?" she asked without turning. He seemed to be the only person, other than her, who wasn't getting ready to leave.

"I've sent all the cousins to the city to warn Rhodry and to hunt down that fucker Wolfrum, if it comes to it. Cristobal and his guard are leaving in a few hours. They'll take the tree road, too, but he won't be able to match the cousins' pace. Not at first, anyway."

She knelt and silently began gathering her things. If everyone else was leaving, she might as well, too. She couldn't keep up with them and didn't intend to try. But if Wolfrum was in the city, then that's where she needed to be. The evidence was piling up against him, but she wanted to hear it from his own mouth.

"We don't have to leave yet, Rachel," Aidan said. He hadn't moved from where he'd been standing. "You can't keep up with Cristobal's group anyway."

"Thanks for reminding me." *Again.* She ignored everything else he'd said and tied her bedroll to the bottom of her pack. Her other gear was already inside. She did a quick check of her weapons. She'd retrieved the crossbow bolts she'd fired at the banshees. Two had been slightly warped, which would affect accuracy, but at short range, they'd work, and she still had all her knives. That was the good thing about knives, they were always ready. She also still had the tranquilizer gun she'd used in getting off the ship—it seemed like months ago, not weeks—and plenty of tranq darts.

Her canteen was full from her earlier trip to the river, and before he left, Santino had topped off her supply of Harp-style trail bars, along with some dried meat from the provisions brought by his Clanhome cousins. She'd decided it was a hard, four-day walk back to the city for her. She could shave that closer to three if she hustled, and if nothing ate her in the meantime. Cristobal and his shifter guard would make it in half that time, Santino's group even faster. But she wasn't trying to compete with them.

She shouldered her pack and walked around the fire pit to take off in the direction she'd seen Santino go earlier, with the river on her left. Since she had no knowledge of the surrounding terrain, she'd have to stick to the tried and true method of following the river, which ran all the way to the city. She knew it wound around before getting there, but hopefully not too much. Her map didn't give enough detail to know for sure.

"Where are you going?" Aidan demanded.

"To find Wolfrum," she said without looking back at him. "Make sure you douse the fire before you leave. I think you're the last one here."

"Goddamn it," he growled.

Rachel grinned viciously when she heard the crack of

big rocks and the swish of dirt as he buried the fire before starting after her.

"Stop, Rachel."

She kept walking. Yes, he'd told her the truth about Amanda, clearly going against his clan in doing so. She had to give him credit for that. But anger would give her a much-needed burst of energy, so she'd decided to nurse it a while.

Of course, he caught up with her in about two seconds, but he made no attempt to stop her or make conversation. So, she did the same, focusing instead on heading in the right direction.

. . .

It was a silent march through the Green the first night. Rachel was forced to stop after only a few hours. She'd been on the move with Aidan for weeks getting through the swamp, finally reaching the site of the second ship, and then the adrenaline rush and stress of dealing with Cristobal's injuries, and the fire and smoke on top of that. She'd have run all the way back to the city if she could have, but her body wasn't going to cooperate. She needed sleep, and she needed food. Or, at least protein. The dried meat took almost as much energy to chew as it provided in nutrition, but the trail bars were sticky and sweet, and the river provided plenty of water. She'd been ready to share her food with Aidan, her anger long dissipated. But he'd shifted soon after they left the camp site and had remained up in the trees the entire time.

She didn't fool herself into believing his presence wasn't making a difference, and she was grateful for it. She sensed the difference in the forest as they traveled. It was a pocket of silence that followed everywhere they went, while thirty or so feet beyond them in any direction, the Green was still alive with the sounds of nocturnal hunters and their prey. It was an odd sensation, but comforting, too. When she slid into her bedroll, she missed him for all of two minutes, before she fell deeply asleep.

She woke with the sun the next morning, feeling its heat on her back, soaking it up...before her brain kicked in and reminded her of the hard facts, which were confirmed by other hard things that were pressed up against her body. She slowly extricated herself from Aidan's clutches, which wasn't easy. Generously, one could say he was a cuddler. One could also say it was simply more evidence of his domineering personality. But whatever description she used, he was all over her, with one muscled leg hooked over both of hers, and a heavy arm draped over her waist. The fact that she was cocooned in her bedroll, with that fabric between them, only made escaping him more difficult. Especially since he wasn't inclined to help.

She finally gave up on subterfuge, jabbed an elbow into his gut, and sat up. "Aren't you ever cold?" she asked, noting he wore nothing but the usual drawstring pants. She was surprised he'd put on that much. He stretched behind her, and she caught glimpses of golden skin over muscle but refused to turn and look.

"If I was cold, I'd shift."

"Give me ten minutes to freshen up, and I'll be ready to go. There's trail bars and dried meat in my pack, if you want. She turned finally to look at him, focusing on his face, which was distracting enough. "Do you need to hunt?"

He gave her an indecipherable look. "No. Be careful when you go to the river. The banks are steep in this area, and we're in the middle of spring run-off. The water's high and fast."

She didn't really need his warning. She'd heard the difference in the sound of the river for herself last night. It had kept her from attempting to get down there in the dark.

This morning she could see the incredible pounding of whitewater as it slammed its way through a series of narrow rock formations. She had friends back home who lived for the adrenaline rush of riding high-risk whitewater like this. She'd even accompanied them on a few of their trips. But she doubted even they would take on this one. The banks were high and steep, just as they'd been near the hut where they'd stayed, but this part of the river was cluttered with jagged rocks and far too narrow for even the most daring of risk-takers.

Lying on her stomach, she scooted forward until she could stretch her arms down to the water just as she had before, settling for another quick splash of her face and hands. She filled her canteen, then rinsed her mouth quickly, the water so cold that it made her teeth and entire face ache.

She inched back and climbed to her feet, brushing away the dirt and bits of detritus that clung to her clothes. It was more from habit than anything else. She wouldn't be clean until they reached the city and she could finagle a hot shower. If nothing else, there was a fleet science center there, with a small contingent of live-in techs. There were no more than two or three of them, but enough that they'd have all the amenities, and bunks for visitors, too. She wondered if that was where Wolfrum was hiding. Could he be that stupid? Someone at that center must have looked the other way when the two ships landed. And fleet center or not, if the shifters wanted Wolfrum or whoever had helped him, they'd walk in and take them.

Aidan was waiting when she returned to their cold camp. "I'm ready," she said. She hooked her canteen onto her pack, broke off half a protein bar and zipped the rest into her pack. She then swung the pack onto her back and eyed Aidan expectantly, waiting for him to give her a direction.

Instead, he pulled the drawstring on his pants and let

them drop to his ankles, giving her an almost challenging look with eyes gone completely gold, and then he shifted.

Rachel sighed. Asshole or not, he was still a beautiful sight.

He leaped into the trees and raced a few yards along the branches, remaining low enough that she could get a bearing before he disappeared into the Green's impenetrable canopy.

"Right," she muttered, then, out of habit, folded his pants into her pack and started walking at a rapid, but sustainable, pace.

The morning was oddly peaceful. Again, she was sure that this was Aidan's doing. More than once—in fact, several times—she saw signs of small animal habitation that she normally would have stopped to study. But her only goal right now was to reach the city. With luck, she'd have a little time to explore the Green before she left Harp. When she wasn't running for her life or anyone else's. A surge of sadness swept through her at the idea of leaving, but she told herself it was simply the scientist in her that was reluctant to leave such an unexplored treasure trove of life-forms.

She'd just convinced herself that's what it was when she heard the soft scratch of claws on bark and the even softer thump of padded feet on the forest floor, telling her Aidan was on the ground. She supposed it could have been some other shifter, but anyone else would have approached silently, while Aidan wanted to give her warning. And besides, he'd never have let anyone or anything else get that close.

"You never asked why," he said from behind her.

She frowned as she kept walking. "Why what?"

"You claim to be a scientist, but you never asked why we're so reluctant to trust. Why *I'm* so reluctant."

Rachel shrugged. "I didn't think you'd tell me."

Silence. And then, "Fair enough."

They traveled another fifty yards before Rachel finally

surrendered. Still without turning, she asked, "So, why *are* you all so short on trust? I mean, I know about the explosion when the fleet was here the first time, but honestly, I think I've proven I'm not like those idiots. And the habit is too ingrained to be a recent development. It has to be something older."

"See, you're a scientist, after all."

Rachel refused to ask again. He'd brought it up, so it was up to him to keep the ball rolling. A strong arm snuck around her waist, stopping her forward progress by simply lifting her off the ground.

"Put me down."

"Stop, sweetheart. Take a break and talk to me." His voice was a low purr of sound in her ear that made every feminine nerve in her body stand up and take notice. Especially since his pants were still in her pack.

He put her back on her feet and turned her to face him.

She looked up and met his gaze thoughtfully. The last thing she needed was more vague answers and stonewalling. On the other hand, she could use the break to hydrate and eat another trail bar. "All right. We'll talk. But put these on first." She retrieved the pants and shoved them at is chest.

He gave her a knowing smirk but put them on. "We've been isolated here on Harp since its founding," he began. "The original colony ship was intended to land on a habitable planet and never leave. It wasn't designed to escape atmosphere. It wasn't even built in atmosphere back on Earth. But even if it had been, it was already damaged before the landing, which was how the colonists ended up here in the first place. This was the only suitable planet they could find that was close enough for a controlled landing. Although, in the end, it was more crash than control. But all of that's probably in your fleet's First Contact report."

Rachel nodded. "It took some work, but the contact ship

managed to extract the colony ship's technical data from the beacon. I'm not an engineer, but I studied the report in preparation for this mission, so I know the ship was beyond recovery. It's a miracle they managed to land safely at all."

He nodded, then took her hand and tugged her over to sit on a fallen log that was completely overgrown with vines. She eyed it carefully—all sorts of little beasties could be hiding in there—but she finally decided it was probably safe enough to sit since Aidan had suggested it.

"Right, so you don't need me for a history lesson," he continued, "and that's not the point, anyway. What you need to know is that as catastrophic as that crash was, between the recovered databanks and the oral histories of the colonists, much of human knowledge up to that point survived intact. So, while Harpers have been isolated, we know the full history of human expansion into space, including all the genetic modifications designed to make space exploration, and eventually life itself, possible in many of the artificial environments created to support that expansion. And we also know how those genetically modified people were treated. Hell, it's how they're *still* treated…like machines rather than people. And what happened here? With Wolfrum betraying us, trying to kidnap a few living lab specimens for *money*? That's *exactly* what we're afraid of. It's the real reason that we insist on Harp remaining a closed planet."

"I get that, Aidan. I really do, but I already knew about shifters. Hell, I didn't even question your decision that everyone on that ship had to die. You think I don't *know* that the only way to keep you safe, to keep *everyone* here safe is to make sure shifters remain a secret? After everything we've been through, did you really think that I'd betray Amanda and her babies? Or did your cousin plan to make sure I *couldn't*?"

His head shot up. "Never," he snarled, then added.

"Rhodry wouldn't do that."

She gave a little laugh, not believing him. She didn't even know cousin Rhodry, but she believed he'd do whatever he felt necessary to protect his family. She couldn't even blame him for it. "Forget it. Let's just go."

"Rachel."

She ignored him, standing and shrugging her pack into place. "We need to pick up the pace. I can't keep up with the rest of you, but I can make better time than this. And I'd like to reach the city before Wolfrum's dead."

Aidan stood and stared down at her. "All right. How fast can you travel?"

"As fast as I need to. It doesn't matter if I'm half dead myself by the time we get there."

His eyes shifted all the way to gold, narrowed with irritation. "It matters to *me*," he said abruptly, and then he pulled her close and kissed her. Not a fast kiss, either. It was deep and long and wet. When he finally released her—pulling his mouth away then gently licking her lips and brushing a final touch of his lips over her mouth—Rachel's body was aroused and confused in equal measure, tossed between the adrenaline rush of their decision to hurry back to the city, and the scorching desire that only Aidan had ever stirred in her.

"How long can you go without rest, and how much do you need?" he asked. He was still holding on to her arms, bracing her against the aftereffects of their kiss. And for once he wasn't being smug about it.

She blinked, focusing on what mattered. "I can travel straight through today and most of the night. Four hours rest before daybreak, and it'll keep me going until we hit the city." She didn't tell him she'd be using stimulant tabs to make that pace possible. She rarely used the little white pills. They were just short of an adrenaline shot to the heart and had originally been designed for battlefield use. But there was no way she was going miss Wolfrum's takedown.

"Right, then. We should be there tomorrow night," he said, then leaned back to study her face, "Are you sure about the pace?"

"I know my limits. I'm sure."

"Good enough. One rule—you don't fight me. I'm going to be helping you run a good part of the way, picking you up on the fly when necessary to jump over obstacles. If you fight me, we'll both get hurt. Understood?"

"Understood, but I have a rule of my own. When we get close to the city, you leave me behind. If your cousin has everything under control, then great. But if not, you'll be there for him."

"Stubborn woman. Define close."

"Right, *I'm* the stubborn one. Within a day's walk of the city. *Your* pace, not mine."

"Damn you. All right. Let's move."

. . .

Ten hours later, they were flying low to the ground, with trees speeding past, along with bushes and rocks and everything else Rachel could imagine. She was mostly running; he wasn't carrying her. Her legs were pumping, and her feet touched the ground, but Aidan's strength was all around her, gripping the strap of her pack, or her arm, leaping over some obstacles and running over others, his arm sometimes circling her waist when they jumped higher than she would have thought possible. It was exhilarating, but also chilling once the sun faded and shadows took over. Then it became something entirely different, beyond terrifying.

Aidan didn't seem to notice. He ran easily, smoothly. His breathing was unstressed and even, his eyes twin sparks of gold, gleaming in the night and seeing everything. His arm around her grew tighter, knowing without being told that she was practically blind. But she kept running, kept pumping her arms and lifting her knees. She refused to be a burden, refused to be the weak link.

It took her a moment to realize when they stopped running. Like a person leaving a boat for dry land, her brain needed some time to catch up to this new reality.

"Okay?" Aidan asked, holding out her canteen. "Drink."

Rachel nodded wordless thanks. Taking the canteen, she drank slowly, small sips. Anything else and she'd just throw it up when they started up again. She frowned when he slipped his hands under the straps of her pack and pulled them down her arms.

"Wait," she protested. "I need that."

"Not right now, sweetheart. It's time to rest."

Oh. Right. They'd discussed this earlier. It felt like a year, maybe two, but it had been only hours, though she couldn't really say exactly how *many* hours.

"Already?" she asked.

He smiled. "Already."

She watched sluggishly as he untied her bedroll and spread it out on a smooth patch of loam-covered ground.

"Come on," he said, guiding her to the bedroll and pulling her down with him. "It's a few hours until dawn."

How did he know that? Had he memorized the Farmer's Almanac? Did they have that out here? And why the hell was she worrying about it?

"Sleep," she murmured and curled into his heat, her head pillowed on his chest.

• • •

The weather changed while they slept, becoming colder, with

a touch of moisture that told him it would rain by morning. It wasn't what they needed. He could run for days more, but Rachel was already using all her strength just to keep up with him. She hadn't said a word of complaint, but he could feel the twitches in her muscles as she slept that told him her body was draining its resources for the effort.

She had no way of knowing—and he was beginning to think he should have told her—but ever since she'd told him about the possibility that Wolfrum would go after the twins, he'd been sending a warning through the trees, using the unique connection to the Green that only shifters could tap into. He knew from Amanda that the trees felt a special bond with Rhodry's unborn sons, and he was confident that the message would get through. Hell, there were more shifters in the city right now than in all of Clanhome, and every one of them would die to protect a child. Any child, but especially one of their own.

That didn't stop him from wanting to get there himself. The drive to protect was in his DNA, the belief that no one could safeguard those he cared about as well as he could. But for the first time in his life, he was conflicted. Rhodry was his brother, his children like Aidan's own. But Rachel was *his*. He pulled her closer, keeping her warm. A body could chill easily under wet conditions like this, and he didn't want to risk it. Plus, he liked the way she felt in his arms. He stroked a soothing hand over her back, brushing the side of her breast with one thumb as his fingers molded to her waist before resting possessively over her hip.

She murmured in her sleep, and stretched against him, her arms slipping around to hug him tightly. Soft breasts pushed against his chest, her nipples firm and plump enough that he wondered what she was dreaming, and if he was included. She hummed softly as her breath brushed his neck, a moment before her lips coasted over his skin, her mouth warm and wet.

He slipped his hand over her back to the curve of her ass and pressed her against his fully aroused cock.

She sucked in a breath. "I'm sorry. I didn't mean to—"

He chuckled. "Don't worry, it'll keep until everyone's safe. But then...you're mine, sweetheart." He rolled her, putting her back to his chest. "Now, sleep. Tomorrow will be even tougher."

Chapter Eighteen

"You sure you'll be all right?" Rhodry's golden eyes were laughing as he rubbed Amanda's swollen belly with one hand while the other was hooked around her neck to pull her closer. He kissed her gently, a very proper kiss, except for a quick swipe of his tongue to remind her of their recent "nap." There'd been nothing proper going on there, and very little napping.

She swatted his chest, but let her hand linger to appreciate the solid muscle. Looking up, she met his smile. "You're going a couple hundred yards to the Guild Hall, to meet with some shifters, not the other side of the planet. We'll be fine."

"Cullen will stay with you."

"And don't forget, Mom's here. She's vicious when riled."

"I believe that," he muttered. "All right," he said, stripping off the pants he'd donned just in case her mother decided to join them in the living room. "I'll be half an hour, no more." He gave her a final hard, quick kiss, and then shifted. His cat was huge and sleek and pitch black, his cat eyes the same solid gold as in his human form, but with the enhanced vision of his animal. He wrapped himself around her legs, butting his head at her hand.

"Yes, you're beautiful," she crooned, stroking his thick, silky fur. She bent over and petted him thoroughly. "Go," she whispered. "So you can come back sooner."

He let out an animal groan that made her laugh, then licked her face—starting at her neck, over her cheek, and ending at her ear—and opened his jaw in a feline grin that displayed a mouth full of deadly teeth.

"Blech," she protested, pretending to wipe her cheek before kissing his nose. "Go."

He wound his body against her leg one last time and then ran through the open doors, going from the balcony to the trees with a soundless leap that belied the power behind his movement.

Amanda watched him go, admiring his graceful strength at the same time she longed for the ability to move through the trees as easily as he did. Someday, her sons would be jumping from tree to tree just like Rhodry, and she'd be the only one stuck on the ground. She sighed and heard the song of the trees trying to soothe her. It made her smile. She heard her mother's footsteps coming down the hall and looked up. "Hi, Mom. Did you rest well?"

Elise came over and sat next to her. "It's very quiet here. Almost too quiet. I'm so accustomed to the sub-audible hum of engines that I miss it when it's gone. Like a lullaby."

Amanda flicked her eyebrows up and down but didn't comment. She'd never thought of the noise on a starship as a lullaby. She preferred the wind in the trees outside her window.

"Where's Rhodry?" Elise asked, leaning back into the comfortable couch.

"There was some business at the Guild Hall. He won't be gone long."

"And Cullen?"

"Your favorite shifter is downstairs. Diligently on guard as always," she said. She started to chuckle, but was almost instantly on her feet, all traces of humor gone. The trees' song had turned abruptly discordant, like a symphony played in the wrong key, and with every instrument doing its own thing. It was a warning. Danger was lurking, but she didn't know where.

She listened for Cullen's footsteps on the stairs. He would have heard the same warnings she did, and being Cullen, his first reaction would be to check on her. "Cullen?" she called softly, knowing his shifter hearing would hear her easily if he was anywhere near. And with Rhodry gone, he'd definitely be near.

"Amanda?" her mom said, picking up on the heightened tension, but not knowing what was going on. "What is it?"

"Something's wrong, and Cullen's not answering."

Elise started for the door, saying, "Are you sure he can hear—"

"Mom. He's a shifter. He'd have heard me."

Elise shot her a penetrating look, and Amanda could tell it was on her tongue to ask what the hell was going on. But her mother had lived most of her life in space, and out there you followed your instincts, or you died. She immediately turned around and headed for her room, saying, "I'll get my gun."

Amanda should have been shocked that her mother the doctor, a saver of lives, had a gun, but she wasn't. Elise Sumner was a fleet officer.

As her mother disappeared down the hallway, someone knocked on the upstairs door, which only confirmed that something was seriously wrong. Cullen would never have knocked, and he *never* would have let someone climb those stairs without warning her.

Walking to a side cabinet, she slipped a small knife into the pocket of her oversize shirt then crossed to the stairway door. Without opening it—she wasn't a total idiot—she called through the heavy wood, "Who is it?"

"It's Guy Wolfrum, Amanda. I heard Elise was visiting and came to say hello."

She recoiled in surprise. Guy Wolfrum should have been dead by now. Or, if not dead, then at least taken prisoner along with any of his surviving crew. How had he managed to evade capture and get back to the city before any of the others? And did Rhodry know?

She answered her own question. No, of course, he didn't know. He'd never have left her alone if he did. There were limits to the information that could be passed through the trees. They conveyed emotion, not words. And even if Wolfrum had somehow escaped capture in the chaos between fighting the fire and dealing with the invaders, the threat would have been drowned out by the danger already presented by the fires.

"Amanda?" Wolfrum knocked again. "Are you all right?"

"Yeah," she called. "Sorry. Just pulling on some clothes. I was taking a nap." She glanced over and saw her mom standing in the opening to the hallway. Elise's expression reflected her confusion. She hadn't been briefed on the Wolfrum situation. There hadn't been time. But taking her cues from Amanda, she gave a slight nod and stepped back into the hall so she couldn't be seen.

Amanda opened the door slowly, intending to say just enough to send Wolfrum on his way, so she could let Rhodry know his whereabouts. But Wolfrum didn't wait. He pushed the door open, forcing her to stumble backward to avoid being knocked over. Staring at his back, she took a moment to scan the stairwell, but it was empty. No sign of Cullen. She was worried about him, but right now she was more worried about what Wolfrum wanted from her. Maybe he knew Elise was on-planet and simply hoped for a free ride off-planet. But that didn't explain why the trees were continuing to scream of danger. Was it Wolfrum? What could he want with her or... Understanding struck, and she felt a rush of such intense rage that it stole her breath away.

"Where's Elise?" he demanded, searching the room.

She turned to study him carefully. He looked awful. He was a big man, but he looked as though he'd lost weight recently. His clothes were loose and disheveled, as if he'd been sleeping in them for days. His eyes were bloodshot and puffy, and the hand he raised to wipe his forehead trembled.

He lowered that same hand to his pocket and pulled out a tranquilizer gun which he pointed at Amanda. "I said where's Elise?" His voice was scratchy, his eyes continuing to dart around the empty room.

Amanda pointedly ignored the gun. "She's resting. Would you like to leave a message? Or you can come back later. Maybe without the tranq."

"You think you're so special," he sneered. "Living with one of those animals, fucking it," he spat, gesturing at her belly. "What about me?" he shouted suddenly. "Two years and these people *still* treat me like an outsider, an *Earther.*" He said the word as if it was a curse. And maybe it was on Harp. "But you know the worst of it? The very worst?" He didn't wait for her response, just kept up his whining. "Shifters," he snarled. "I know they exist. I'm a xenobiologist, for fuck's sake. Did they think I wouldn't notice? I've seen them in the forest. I've seen them *shift.*" His bark of laughter had a hysterical quality that had her taking a step away, edging toward the big chair near the fireplace. She wanted something besides skin between her babies and that tranq gun.

"Don't move," he snapped. "You think I'm stupid?"

"Well," she hedged, as she kept moving, putting more distance between them, buying more time for Rhodry to return. Because he would have heard the danger in the trees just as she did. He was on his way. "I'm not sure, Guy. I mean, you did barge into my home with a gun, even though you've just admitted you know my husband's true nature, so…"

"You smug bitch. You won't be laughing when I'm through with you. You *and* your brats. I'm not returning to Earth with nothing. I told them we needed real soldiers, not rejects who couldn't cut it in fleet. But they didn't listen. And now it's all gone to hell. Well, fuck that. I didn't give up my commission, my job, my fucking *reputation*, for *nothing*," he screamed the last word at her, jaw straining and eyes crazed.

"They're all dead now," he continued conversationally, suddenly as calm as if they were discussing the weather, as if he hadn't been bulging-eyes crazy only a moment before. "But *I'm* not, and I started thinking—where else could I get the specimens I'd promised to deliver? And how could I do it alone? And then, it hit me. There are two of them right here in the city. *Perfect* specimens that don't require a small army to capture, and that come with a live incubator who's already adapted to space travel." He grinned, so very pleased with himself. "Those twins of yours are going to make me a fucking fortune."

"Over my dead body," Amanda said calmly, although there was nothing calm about the fury burning in her gut. She was going to kill this motherfucker.

"You always were an asshole." Elise's quiet words had Wolfrum spinning in surprise to see her standing in the hall with an ancient pistol pointed his way.

He cast a hate-filled glance at Amanda. "Bitch," he snarled. And then, moving faster than she would have thought possible, he reached out and grabbed her arm, slamming her into the hard corner of the chair as he yanked her past it and against his chest, placing her body between him and Elise.

"If I'm killed, the babies die, too," she said reasonably, belying the sheer terror squeezing her heart.

"Not if I keep you alive long enough to cut them out of you. Besides, she won't shoot."

Amanda knew that was true. Her mom would never risk her or the twins. But was Elise a good enough shot to do anything else? Could she shoot Wolfrum in the kneecap, for example? Or, hell, just pop the asshole in the brainpan and get rid of him. He deserved to die. He *would* die for this. He'd threatened her children. She fingered the knife in her pocket, waiting for an opportunity.

"So what's the—" Her words were cut off as a spasm tore through her body, rippling through her abdomen like a wave. She staggered, yanking away from Wolfrum as she fell to her knees. "Mom," she cried, her terrified gaze on Elise.

Her mother rushed forward, just as Wolfrum grabbed Amanda's arm, trying to drag her back to her feet. "Let's go. I want those little bastards born off-planet."

"It's too soon," she gasped.

"All the better. Stay back, Elise. I don't need—"

The furious roar of a hunting beast filled the air, making the entire house tremble and bringing a smile to Amanda's face.

· · ·

Rhodry landed silently in the tree next to their balcony just in time to see Wolfrum, gun in one hand and yanking at Amanda with the other, trying to drag her to her feet while she knelt on the floor, curled around her stomach.

And he lost all reason.

Launching himself through the open window, he roared with a fury that had every shifter in the city jolting up in alarm.

The coward screamed and ran for the door to the stairs, dropping the gun in his terror, his cries reaching a fever pitch when Rhodry's paw caught the back of his leg, ripping into muscle and tendon. The man went down, and a rumbling cough sounded from Rhodry's throat, the satisfied growl of a hunter. The cat liked nothing better than to toy with its prey before the kill. He pounced again as Wolfrum crawled to the door, the man sobbing in relief when he managed to drag it open, only to shriek in agony as Rhodry's claws raked down his back and buttocks, digging into flesh. He prowled closer, ignoring Wolfrum's pleas, bunching his muscles for a final attack, and… Amanda's soft cry had him spinning in mid-leap, the need to respond to her pain more powerful than any instinct he possessed. This was his mate, his sons. *Nothing* was more important than that.

He shifted to human, aware of Wolfrum falling down the stairs in a bid to escape, but he didn't care. Wolfrum could wait. He wouldn't make it off the block, much less the planet. Every shifter in the city was closing on his location. Harp held no sanctuary for Guy Wolfrum.

Rhodry spun in an instant, then raced over and skidded to his knees next to Amanda, wrapping her in his arms. "What do I do?" he asked, fear tinging the question with the growl of a cat.

It was Elise who answered. "Can you carry her to"—Rhodry gathered Amanda in his arms and stood—"the bedroom, please. I'll get my bag."

"It's the babies," Amanda said softly.

His lungs seized up as every breath in his body fled. It was too soon. Shifter babies matured early, but not this early. If she went into labor now… He held her closer, willing his body to lend her some of his strength, to take the pain. And he forced himself to keep moving, to carry her into their bedroom with the big bed where they'd made love just a few hours earlier because Amanda had joked that sex was good for her.

Rhodry knew about birthing. He'd waited plenty of times while cousins or cousins' wives gave birth, standing down the hall or in the garden while the woman cried in pain. But those were nothing compared to this. This was Amanda, the woman who made his heart beat, who put the breath in his lungs.

"I'm okay," she reassured him, touching his cheek as he laid her down on the bed. "Don't cry." He stared as her fingers came away wet, aware for the first time that he'd been crying. "*We're* okay. Your sons were just angry."

Rhodry froze, then placed a hand over her abdomen and listened. The rush of relief was so strong that he nearly started crying again. He looked up and met Amanda's smile with a grin of his own. "They're pissed as hell."

She nodded. "They knew you were coming and wanted you to *hurry*." She laughed just as Elise rushed into the room.

"I'll examine her," Elise was saying briskly. "You go…" Her voice trailed off as she registered her daughter's laughter and the smiles all around.

"It's okay, Mom," Amanda said, sounding tired but nothing else. "It was my back, not the babies."

Elise stared then seemed to sag in place. But only for an instant. Her head came up, and she said, "We need to get your doctor over here. You," she said, pointing at Rhodry, "put on some damn clothes."

Rhodry bit back a grin. He was naked, but then, shifters were always naked. He glanced down and met his wife's laughing eyes. The laughter disappeared a moment later. "You need to check on Cullen," she said urgently. "Wolfrum must have tranqed him. You know he'd never have let that bastard up here, otherwise."

Rhodry stood at once. "I'll be right back, *acushla*." Striding to the closet, he yanked on a pair of pants. Chances were he'd be shifting in the next few minutes, but if Cullen was injured, he might be concealed on a side street, and nudity was frowned on in the city. He'd no sooner hit the street below the stairs than a familiar scent hit his awareness, his nostrils flaring to take it in and "taste" it. He relaxed minutely, recognizing Cullen, but then he frowned. His cousin's scent wasn't quite right. He rolled it over the back of his throat. Amanda was right. Cullen had been dosed with something.

A moment later, he found him, just beginning to sit up, one hand to his head. Rhodry felt Cullen's energy change and knew he was about to shift. He knelt next to him quickly.

"Amanda's fine," he said immediately, knowing what was driving his cousin. "And Wolfrum's got every shifter in the city on his tail by now."

"I'm sorry, Rhodi. No excuse. But that bastard came around the corner shooting two guns at once. He hit me with a half dozen tranqs. You're sure about Amanda and the twins?"

Rhodry grinned. "Amanda's pissed and my sons want to join the hunt."

"Tell the bairns the hunt is on, and they've got company," a third voice chimed in.

Rhodry didn't even turn around at the sound of his cousin Gabriel's voice.

"The Devlins are here now," Gabe said. "We'll trap the bastard, don't worry."

"I wasn't," Rhodry said, turning. "I'll be staying here with Amanda."

"Understood. What do we do with the coward when we

catch him?"

"Keep him alive. After today, he belongs to the clans, but I'll let Cristobal reach that decision on his own."

Gabriel snorted a harsh laugh. "He damn well will. I'll keep you informed."

Rhodry scented the change in the air as Cullen shifted, heard the nearly silent slide of giant paws as his cousin stood. He looked up and met Rhodry's eyes, then raced to follow Gabe down the street. The hunt was well and truly on.

Chapter Nineteen

Aidan ran without thinking. It was second nature for him to move swiftly through the Green, his body swerving and jumping without conscious thought. He could have traveled much faster on his own, but he had to admit that Rachel was far more skilled, more determined than he'd expected, even after all they'd survived together. He'd set a punishing pace and had kept waiting for her to demand he slow down. But she was tough. She'd not only kept up, she'd done it without a single complaint, not even on the two occasions when she'd fallen and sustained significant injuries. She'd simply bandaged her bloody leg the first time and insisted they keep going. The second had been an injury to her hand that he was sure included a broken finger or two. She'd barely slowed, binding them together on the move and signaling him to keep running, that she'd catch up. He hadn't, of course. He wasn't letting her out of his sight, and not only because Cristobal wanted her to testify. He'd told her she mattered to him, and she did. More than he wanted to admit.

But now…the closer they got to the city, the more convinced he was that something major was going on. The trees were no longer blaring an alarm, the way they had earlier. They were whispering of a hunt, instead. All around him, the smaller animals were digging deep into their burrows, and even the predators—the ones who feared only each other and shifters—were racing for cover.

He raised the "volume" on the part of his shifter brain that heard the song of the Green. Most times it was background noise, a steady hum of information that his brain processed without conscious input from him. But now, he was listening, because there was a *feeling* to the Green, a sense of *vengeance* that he'd never before detected.

Shifters were moving through the trees, herding prey before them, and their hunt was heading directly for him and Rachel.

· · ·

Rachel raced next to Aidan, his arm around her waist lending her speed like she'd never have managed on her own. It was terrifying. It was *exhilarating*. Turning and weaving to avoid trees, rocks, vines, and every other kind of obstacle in a forest filled with them. Aidan seemed to have a sixth sense, flowing around and through the dense growth like those rapids she'd seen foaming around rocks in the Leeward Stream.

They were moving far too fast for him to be eyeballing their path. She figured it had to be part of his shifter DNA, some long ago adaptation for survival on Harp that had made the leap to shifters during the genetic modification. She stumbled and reached out a hand to brace herself without stopping, reminding herself to focus on the present. She wasn't as good as Aidan, but she had learned some things. Enough to know his pace had changed as they'd drawn closer to the city. She would have expected him to speed up with their goal in sight, but, instead, he'd begun to slow, to pay more attention to their surroundings—the wind through the trees, the movement of unseen animals.

"Rachel."

His voice broke into the almost meditative state she'd adopted to keep up with him. She braked to a stop, and stood there, swaying, as she blinked up at him, forcing her brain into this new mode.

"You okay?" he asked and took hold of her upper arm to steady her.

She nodded, then licked her lips, and said, "Is something wrong?"

He pulled her off the animal trail they'd been following and under the branches of one of the biggest trees she'd ever seen, even in the Green. The branches hung low to the ground, doing a good job of hiding them from anything looking down from above, but still left them a good line-of-sight all around. She'd noticed that about Aidan. He always thought tactically.

Deep in her heart of hearts, she wondered if she was nothing more than one of those tactical considerations. Keep the Earth girl happy. Keep her satisfied and sated. She's a witness to Wolfrum's atrocity, to the fleet's immorality—at least the part of fleet that funded Wolfrum. Assuming they had. But if not them, then some other Earth-based organization. Either way, it was in Harp's interest for Aidan to gain her loyalty, even her love, so she'd testify on Harp's behalf.

The bitch of it was… Harp already had her loyalty and her love. And so did Aidan. And she was a fool.

"Are you listening?" Aidan's voice betrayed impatience, which told her she'd zoned out again.

"Yes, sorry. I'm listening."

He studied her for a moment, staring into her eyes. "We're almost there," he assured her. "Only a little farther."

She nodded. She already knew they were close.

"But something's going on," he continued. "I know this part of the Green nearly as well as the forests of Clanhome. And something's not right. Or it's *very* right. I can't tell from down here. I need to go up, and you need to hide."

"Hide from what?"

"That's what I don't know. You can shelter here on the ground or climb up a ways. Either way, you'll be safe, because it seems every animal in the forest is running away from whatever's coming."

Aidan looked like he expected her to argue, but he should have known better by now. These were his forests. If he said there was danger coming, she believed him. "I'll climb," she said and skimmed her hand up the thick trunk, looking for fingerholds.

"Let's do this the easy way." He cupped his hands and held them low, offering her a boost into the tree. Without a word, she put her foot in his hands and her hand on his shoulder, barely reacting when he tossed her up through the lower branches to a sturdy, straight roosting spot.

She looked down in time to catch his shift. No matter how many times she saw it, it was still beautiful and magical, and faster than her eye could see. One moment there was a gorgeous man, and the next a magnificent cat was leaping through the branches to land next to her, his golden eyes revealing the sheer joy he felt in this form, the freedom. Seeing it, she felt guilty that he'd had to remain human to get them both to the city.

She stroked a hand over his big head, digging her fingers into his fur like she knew he liked. Aidan twisted his head to push into her hand and made a short, purring noise.

She laughed. "Go," she told him. "I'll wait here."

He lifted his head to rub his cheek against hers, whiskers scratching her skin, and then he was gone, winding up into the tree so easily, it was as if he had no bones to contend with.

Rachel sighed and settled as comfortably as she could in the vee of the big tree, using her pack as a pillow. Another thing she'd learned in her years of wilderness experience— you had to take your sleep when you could. If Aidan said it was safe, then it was safe. She closed her eyes and slept.

• • •

Aidan climbed as high as he dared, which was pretty damn high. He and Rhodry had always loved racing through the trees, competing against each other. He slowed and finally stopped, reminding himself that this wasn't a fun romp through the Green. Lifting his nose to the wind, he drew in the scents of the forest, turning his head when he caught one that was very familiar. Cullen. He immediately set off along the tree road on an intersect course.

As he drew closer, he wasn't surprised to detect several other familiar scents. Gabriel, Santino, and the rest of the cousins had arrived, but what were they doing out here? He gave a coughing roar to let them know he was coming in, then dropped down to find Cullen already shifted and waiting for him on the ground with the fierce gleam of rage in his eye.

Something had happened to bring that furious spark to his cousin's eye. Cullen was one of the biggest Devlins, but he was an amiable man, and most people never saw the hunter side of him. In point of fact, Cullen's hunting skills rivaled even those of Rhodry and Aidan. Once the scent of prey was in his nose, he was deadly and single-minded in pursuit.

Aidan made the final jump, shifting between the tree and the ground. "Cousin," he said, clasping arms with Cullen.

"Talk to me."

"We're after Wolfrum. We've got him corralled, and we're just toying with him now. Wearing him out before the game really starts."

"Amanda?" he asked sharply.

"Fine, though the bastard went after her and the twins." He spat disgustedly. "What kind of man does that?"

"Not much of one. Where's Rhodry?" Aidan was surprised his cousin wasn't leading the hunt.

"With Amanda. Our newest cousins didn't like Wolfrum scaring their mum. They got a mite pissed off and gave her a fright. But she's all right now."

"Good for them. Let's bring them a reward, shall we?" he added grimly.

Cullen nodded. "That's the plan. You want in?"

"Oh hell, yes. Those bastards locked me in a cage."

Cullen grinned. "Heard they had plans for you. Glad to see you in once piece."

"Very funny," Aidan grumbled. "Listen, I've got Rachel waiting about a mile in—"

"Rachel. That's the Earther who got you *out* of that cage?"

"The same. She's also our best witness against Wolfrum, proof of what he intended. Let's drive him in her direction, let her talk to him, make him think he has a chance. We still don't know his escape route. Maybe he'll let it slip."

"You willing to risk her life on that? If he knows she betrayed him…"

"He'll never get close to her," Aidan growled. "But it's her decision. Keep driving him the way you are. I'll talk to Rachel. If she wants a chat, she'll be in his way. If not, then the rest of us will play."

• • •

Rachel woke all at once, her heart pounding as instinct kicked in, her brain trying to process what had woken her. Where was the danger? The tree was trembling beneath her, as if some enormous creature had… *Well, fuck.*

She twisted around to glare at Aidan, who was sitting on the branch next to her like a giant house cat, licking his paws one at a time. "That wasn't funny."

He shifted in a whirlwind of gold sparks. "Better me than a banshee scout, or worse. Sleeping like that…it wasn't smart."

She wanted to tell him where he could shove his lectures on *smart*. She'd woken, hadn't she? But she wasn't going to argue. He'd only win. "What'd you find out?" she asked. "Who's out there?"

"Half of clan Devlin, for one. Wolfrum went after Amanda—"

"Is she hurt?" Rachel demanded.

"She's fine, and Wolfrum's on the run."

"I'm surprised he survived."

"Rhodry was more worried about Amanda than chasing Wolfrum, but the cousins arrived soon after, and they've been on the bastard's tail for the better part of two days. They've been holding back, having some fun with him, but also hoping to discover his escape plan. He has to have one. If we can learn that, we might know who paid him."

"The shuttle my crew arrived in was FTL capable," she said. "So was the second one. If they'd managed to capture any shifters, they could have simply left the planet the same way they arrived. Although, my guess is they were supposed to have rendezvoused with a faster transport back to Earth, or whatever their final destination."

"Yeah, but we now know that Wolfrum wasn't on either of those two ships."

She frowned. "If things had gone smoothly, no one would

have known he was involved. There'd have been no reason for him to leave Harp."

"Not right away, maybe. But he couldn't enjoy his millions if he was stuck on Harp."

Rachel thought about it. "Even if he has an ally off-planet, his plan failed. I can't see anyone risking much to save him. Certainly not right away. So, he has to hide, wait, and hope his ally still sees enough of a future here to bail his ass out. But the Green isn't a very friendly hiding place. So, where does he go in the meantime?"

"That's where you come in."

"Me?"

"Wolfrum has to know he's being hunted, but he doesn't know he's already caught. If one of *us* confronts him, he'll know that his scheme—hell, his *life*—is over. But if *you* show up instead…"

"He might think I'm running from the same fuck-up, maybe even looking for *him*. You think he'll talk to me."

Aidan gave a little shrug. "It's worth a shot. But only if you're willing. And you won't be alone. We'll all be there. He just won't know it."

Rachel stood on the broad branch, pulling her backpack up with her. It was too far to the ground to jump. She'd have to climb. She checked her weapons, and turned to begin her descent, but Aidan's hand on her arm stopped her.

"You'll do it, then?"

She gave him a curious look. "Did you think I wouldn't?"

He grinned. "Never. You're as fierce as a shifter when you put your mind to it."

"I'll need you to point me in the right direction. I don't have your nose."

Before she knew what was happening, he had her pressed against the solid muscle of his naked body, one arm banded behind her like an iron bar. He gave her a quick but thorough kiss. "I'll be a heartbeat away."

Rachel threaded her fingers through his long hair, brushing it over his shoulder. She cared way too much about this man. Leaning into his embrace, she touched her lips to his, letting her tongue glide along his lower lip and between his teeth until he growled and gripped her even tighter. And the kiss became something more. Passion and heat and possession. Until her arms were wrapped around his neck and the hard length of his cock was nestled between her thighs.

Aidan broke away with a hissed breath. "Fuck."

Rachel could only nod her agreement. She hadn't meant to take it this far, but Aidan was temptation itself all wrapped up in golden skin and muscles. "I should probably—"

"Yeah," he agreed, still holding her close. "Half the clan will be here soon, and…"

He didn't need to finish that sentence. She could still feel his erection like a brand, hot and hard and dangerous as hell. And probably embarrassing if his cousins showed up.

"I'll just…" She gestured toward the ground.

"I'll go first and spot you."

"You sure?" She pulled back enough that their bodies were no longer touching, but they were both aware of his cock between them. She gave him a doubtful look, and he gave her a narrow glare in return.

"It'll go away when I shift."

She bit back a laugh then patted his chest and stood back even farther. "Let's do this."

With a low growl, he brought his mouth to hers one more time. But instead of a kiss, he bit her lower lip and licked away the pain. "Bad girl," he whispered, then released her all at once and leaped to the ground, shifting in midair.

"Very pretty," she murmured, smiling from her perch in the tree when he growled up at her, pretending to object to the compliment. And it *was* pretense. Aidan was feline to his core. He loved being petted and admired.

A sudden noise in the distance had them both turning to listen. When she looked back at Aidan, his golden eyes were glittering with anger and intent. There was no more time for kisses and quips. The hunt was coming their way, and she had a job to do.

Settling her pack over her shoulders, she started downward, descending nearly as fast as a shifter could have. The minute her feet hit the ground, Aidan was there, stroking the full length of his big cat body against her leg. He stood like that for a long moment, perfectly still, his attention focused on the path to the city. Rachel knew he was hearing and seeing things she'd never be able to, no matter how long she spent on Harp. He moved suddenly, turning to match gazes with her a moment before he took off, disappearing into the trees with an astounding leap at least twenty feet straight up. She heard the slight scratch of his claws on the bark, a signal to her of his presence, and then nothing.

She looked around. This area of the Green was a riot of growth, with trees so close together in some parts that she could barely distinguish one from the other. Far overhead, crisscrossed branches closed off most of the sunlight, which should have made it cool on the ground. But instead, it was warm and humid, with the canopy preventing even the slightest cooling breeze from penetrating. She was tempted to remove her long-sleeved top, but she knew better by now. This was the Green, where everything that moved could be deadly.

Reaching around, she grabbed her canteen for a long drink of water and then set off toward the city, exaggerating the limp from her bandaged leg, letting all of her exhaustion show. If Wolfrum was watching, she wanted him to see a woman who'd been hiking for days, who'd made her way through a deadly forest with more than one dangerous encounter and was eager to reach the safety of the city.

As she walked, she was aware on a subliminal level that she was being stalked. It was the same instinct or awareness that made her such a successful wilderness guide. The shifters didn't make a sound, but she knew they were there, high overhead, circling around and out as they drove their prey in her direction.

It wasn't long before she heard something, or someone, crashing through the brush ahead of her. Taking nothing for granted, she readied her crossbow, and was perversely disappointed when the approaching figure turned out to be Guy Wolfrum. Or at least someone who resembled him. She'd only met the asshole that one time at a formal reception, where he'd been wearing a dinner jacket and bow tie. She hadn't expected him to look like that, obviously, but she hadn't expected the human wreck who confronted her, either.

Every inch of visible skin was scratched and bleeding, his eyes wild with fear, his clothes torn and disheveled. He carried no pack or weapons that she could see. And when a cat's serrated yowl had him spinning around to study his back trail, Rachel gasped out loud at the state of his back and legs. Only fear could have kept him upright. It looked like a wild animal had attacked him. Or a shifter. After hearing Aidan's report, she had a fairly good idea of which one it was.

"Dr. Wolfrum," she said urgently, running to meet him and playing her part. "What in God's name happened to you?"

He spun around in shock, eyeing her suspiciously for a long time before recognition seemed to click in. "Rachel Fortier," he said. "I'm sorry, *Doctor* Fortier."

She nearly laughed out loud at the ridiculous formality. "Rachel is fine, sir. Please, you're wounded, let me help you."

The life seemed to drain out of him all at once. He

slumped downward, his shoulders drooping, head falling to his chest, and then he was crumpling to the ground as she hurried to brace him.

"Here," she said, placing her canteen against his lips. "Drink. Where's your kit? Your water and the rest of your gear?"

He gulped from her canteen and would have taken more, but she stopped him. "Not too fast. It's not good for you."

He licked his lips, sucking up every bit of moisture as he nodded his head. "You're right, you're right. It's just…" His eyes were still wild with fear. "It's been a nightmare, Rachel. You don't know this place, these people. They're frighteningly primitive."

She nodded. "They attacked the ship, sir. I was outside, gathering samples, when… It seems fantastic, I know, but I saw it with my own eyes."

"What? What did you see?"

"A pride of huge predator felines. They acted in unison, clearly following well-honed hunting techniques, probably learned behavior, passed from mother to cub, like the lions of—"

"Rachel, please," he impatiently interrupted her scholarly recounting of the attack. "What happened?"

"Sorry, sir. I get caught up sometimes. Just fascinating… Uh, right. They attacked the ship and…" She drew a deep breath, letting tears fill her eyes, before leaning forward to whisper, "They killed everyone." She wiped a rough hand over her eyes. "I only survived because I was outside the ship."

He seemed to stop breathing when he stared at her. "Ripper? The others? They're *all* gone?"

She nodded. "I went onboard after they were gone— the cats, I mean, thinking I could help the survivors, but… they weren't just dead, sir. They were torn apart. There was nothing I could do."

"Of course not," he reassured her faintly.

"I tried, but couldn't raise anyone on the radio, too much interference, and I was terrified the beasts would come back. So I packed my gear as fast as I could and headed for the city, looking for you. I didn't know what else to do."

All at once he seemed to recover his pompous self, sitting up and tugging at his clothing as if that would make it better. "You did the right thing, Rachel. In fact, it was quite brave of you. I'm impressed. But now"—he gripped her arm and stared, pulling her gaze to his—"we need to escape this place. Fleet needs to know what's really going on here. They have to be warned."

"Fleet? The cats are wild, sir. I'm sure the local—"

"Cats? You think that's all they are? There was a second ship, did you know that? They killed everyone there, too, and destroyed the ship. This forest…" He studied the greenery all around them with such fear in his eyes, that for a moment she thought he was going to succumb to terror all over again. But then he shuddered and said, "It's unnatural."

"Second ship?" Rachel said, playing dumb. "There were two?"

Wolfrum sucked in a breath, as if aware he'd said too much. "I forgot," he said finally. "You were confined onboard for most of the journey. It was a matter of mission security, you understand. You couldn't reveal to others what you didn't know."

She frowned. "But I thought we had permission—"

"I told you this is a primitive place. Their so-called Ardrigh rules nothing beyond the city limits, certainly not in the areas where we needed to land in order to complete our studies. We had fleet permission, which is what matters."

"Of course. Were you with the second ship, sir? Is that where you were injured?"

"Exactly."

"I should look at your wounds. In this environment, infection—"

"There's no time. We have to keep moving."

"But, sir…" She frowned in confusion. "There's nothing out here. Nowhere to go. We should return to the science center in the city and get you the help you need. We can contact fleet from there."

"Right, right. But it won't be fleet that comes to save us. They can't be openly involved with this. You understand."

"But if not fleet, then—"

"A private investor, of course. One with fleet contacts and enough money to buy off the right people."

Rachel tilted her head. "Is it Leveque? Amanda Sumner's mother must visit here, and she's—"

"Not Leveque. He's far too proper. But not everyone in his family suffers under the same scruples, and they all have access to the necessary transport. It's good that you reminded me about the science center. I've been so rattled since the attack. But I can arrange a pickup from there. And in the meantime, the center is still fleet property. We'll be safe there while we wait." He spun in a circle, slapping a fist into the opposite palm as if it helped him think. "We can't chance it in daylight. They'll try to stop us."

"Who'll try to stop you? Who's chasing you? I think we should—"

"I don't care what you think!" he yelled, suddenly furious. "You're nothing but a glorified tour guide with some academic credentials to your name. You don't have the right to question me. I've been with fleet for decades. I've sacrificed and scraped and for what? So that I could die on this dirtball of planet with a bunch of freaks? Not in this lifetime. Now help me up or get the fuck out of my way."

"But where will you go until you can reach the center?"

she persisted. "It's not safe out here."

Wolfrum stilled as he turned to stare at her. "You know about them, don't you?" he whispered. "You've seen them."

Rachel stared back at him then admitted. "If you mean the shapeshifters—" She shrugged. "I couldn't believe it, but yes, I've seen them."

"Rachel," he said urgently. "You're a scientist. You must see their potential, their *value* to fleet, to humanity."

"But what about their value as people? To their families? They're human. You can't just sell them to a lab somewhere."

"Human? You saw what they did to Ripper and the others, how they tore them apart. Is that human?"

"Yes," she said calmly. "I saw what they did. But I also saw what Ripper did, and what she *would* have done if she hadn't been stopped. The shifters defended themselves, just as people have since the beginning of time. War is hell, Dr. Wolfrum. All those years with fleet must have taught you that, too."

His lip curled in a sneer as he studied her. "They've already brainwashed you, haven't they? Are you fucking them yet? *That's* why they let you survive, you know. You and that Sumner bitch. Thinks she's so superior to the rest of us because she survived a damn camping trip. But you're both fools. You're nothing but incubators for their offspring. Fresh blood for a dying race. It must be a pheromone," he muttered to himself, and then suddenly spun, pulling a knife from the folds of his filthy clothing. "Out of my way, or I'll gut you where you stand."

Rachel gave him a disgusted look, as if he actually had the skills to defeat her. But she pretended to comply, stepping out of his reach…and pulling her tranq gun.

He eyed the weapon and laughed. "A tranq gun? You don't even have the balls to *kill* me. At least Sumner tried. But I killed her filthy brood instead," he snarled. There was such hatred in his eyes that Rachel took an instinctive step back.

"Amanda's babies aren't dead," she said mildly. "But, you're right. I'm not going to kill you." She fired the tranq gun, hitting him in the neck. He fell to the ground, paralyzed, eyes wide open in confused fear. Rachel leaned over him, grinning. "Special formula of my very own. Something I invented during my glorified tour guide days to deal with cowards like you. You can't move, but you can feel. It's what you planned for the shifters, isn't it?" She straightened and backed away. "I want you wide awake for every minute of your trial, for every second of whatever punishment they choose to inflict upon you. And I think we both know what their version of justice looks like, don't we *Doctor* Wolfrum?"

The small clearing was suddenly filled with cats—in the trees, on the ground, on every branch overlooking Wolfrum where he lay on the ground, helpless, his eyes rolling white with terror.

Rachel caught the golden shimmer of a shift from the corner of her eye, and then Aidan was touching her back. "We've got it from here, Rachel."

There was something in his voice that had her turning to study him, something that suggested she needed *handling*. She grinned in sudden recognition. "You thought I was going to kill him, didn't you? You thought I'd gone over the edge."

His face relaxed into a smile. "I'll admit, you scared the hell out of the cousins with that bit about him being paralyzed, but able to feel everything. That's a fine torture technique you've developed there."

"But you weren't worried at all?" she asked skeptically.

"Of course not. Though, for the future, I will remember you've a bloodthirsty streak."

She laughed, then toed Wolfrum's paralyzed form. "You'll get this thing back to the city?"

"The others will. You and I will be taking our own path."

"Yeah? Is there a hot bath at the end of it?"

"A hot bath and more," he murmured, nuzzling her ear.

She sighed in relief. She was more than ready for this adventure to be over with. "Let's go. Wait," she said, digging into her pack and producing a pair of the drawstring pants the shifters favored. "Put these on first. We don't need any more embarrassing displays for the cousins."

"Shifters don't get embarrassed."

"That's not what you said an hour ago."

"That wasn't embarrassment, sweetheart. I just didn't want them to feel inadequate."

She laughed at the chorus of groans that met his statement, not to mention the expertly targeted pieces of fruit and less savory bits that pelted Aidan while missing her entirely.

"Come on," she said, grabbing his arm. "I'll protect you."

"A few days ago, I would have laughed at that," he said, draping an arm over her shoulder. "But not anymore. Let's go home."

Chapter Twenty

Two weeks later

It was the biggest scandal Harp had ever seen. Hell, it was very possibly the *only* scandal of any note. Harp wasn't a perfect society. There was no such thing in human or any other history. But it was a small planet with a population that had fought together for generations just to survive. The idea of selling each other out simply didn't compute.

Guy Wolfrum's plot to capture shifters for experimentation, and then his desperate attack on the pregnant Amanda, had drawn a great deal of attention from the Shifters Guild, which understandable. But the mountain clans, who typically ignored what was going on in the city, were also deeply involved this time. Not only because Aidan was one of their own, but because it was Rhodry's pregnant wife who'd been attacked. Rhodry was the de Mendoza clan chief, which made him overall leader of the mountain clans. His sons were the future leaders of de Mendoza, and his people were taking Wolfrum's attack very personally. There were more Devlins, de Mendozas, and every other kind of clansman in the city than anyone had ever seen at once, all there to support their leader.

They'd had to wait two weeks so Wolfrum could heal from the damage Rhodry had done in defending his family. It wouldn't do for him to face Harp justice with a bad leg, after all. But the time had finally come, and Cristobal had decided to hold the hearing in the palace's grand ballroom, so that all interested parties could attend. A room which normally saw elegant parties with ladies in gorgeous gowns and men in formalwear was now filled with row after row of people who'd never seen the inside of the Ardrigh's palace before today, unless it had been as part of a children's tour when they'd been in primary school.

Aidan stood in the back with Rachel and most of the Devlin cousins. There were chairs up front, but he was too tense to sit. It was everything he could do not to pace back and forth liked the caged animal that Wolfrum and his cohorts had tried to make of him. Rachel slid her fingers into his at the same moment that Rhodry's heavy hand fell on his shoulder. His cousin was standing next to him, with Amanda sitting in the last row, right in front of them.

"Don't worry, cuz," Rhodry murmured close to his ear. "We'll have justice one way or another."

Aidan had never doubted that was true. He believed Cristobal would come through, that Wolfrum would be punished in a way that fit his crime, with no regard for fleet or any laws other than Harp's. But he knew with a certainty born of shared blood that if the clans didn't like Cristobal's justice, then they would simply take their own.

The crowd settled as Cristobal entered the room with his son, Fionn, as well as his wife and daughter. Several advisors entered at the same time, but Cristobal climbed the short dais alone. The Ardrigh had the sole power to pass judgment.

There was a stir to one side as Wolfrum was brought in flanked by two of Cristobal's shifter guards. Wolfrum wasn't a small man by any measure, but the two shifters dwarfed him as they strode into the room, escorting him between them. Wolfrum entered with his head held high and nose in the air, seeming unaware of the mood of the crowd.

"Guy Wolfrum," Cristobal said, addressing the prisoner. "We all know why you're here. But to be fair, do you require a listing of your crimes?"

Wolfrum glared first at Cristobal and then at the assembled Harpers. Aidan was reminded that this was a man accustomed to power, that he'd held a high rank in fleet, and been honored as one of Earth's most esteemed scientists.

"Let's not waste time, Cristobal," Wolfrum rasped, ignoring the Ardrigh's title. "I have rights as an officer of United Earth Fleet, as a ranking member of the Earth Science Academy, and as a citizen of Earth, all of which have been violated by my illegal detention. There's a shuttle leaving tomorrow, and I intend to be on it."

Cristobal's mouth curved into a faint smile. "While I hesitate to remind someone with your lofty accomplishments of such basic facts," he said in a tone which made it clear that he didn't mind it at all. "You must surely recall that you swore an oath as a citizen of Harp. That oath confers both privilege and obligation, including the observance of Harp law, which prohibits kidnapping, enslavement, assault, attempted murder, and, of course, treason."

"Treason!" Wolfrum shouted. "I never—"

"You conspired with a member of the fleet science center—a man who *is* scheduled to leave on that shuttle tomorrow, under the arrest of fleet authorities—to facilitate the invasion by not one but two hostile forces. *That* is treason against Harp."

Aidan could hardly withhold his snicker at Cristobal's

careful wording regarding the science tech's departure. Yes, he was *scheduled* to depart. But he wouldn't be on that shuttle. No one who'd had a part in the plot could be allowed to leave. Poor lad was going to make a break for it tonight, never to be seen again. The Green was such a dangerous place for the uninitiated.

The clan's only disappointment, a sense of justice delayed, had to do with Wolfrum's employer. The one who'd hired him to capture shifters, in the first place. Whoever it was had gotten wind of the mission's utter failure, along with Wolfrum's capture, and had made no attempt to contact him, much less send a rescue mission. It wasn't difficult to figure out how they'd found out, especially not once fleet started asking questions about the laser weapon fired by the second ship. The laser's energy signal, magnified and distorted by Harp's odd magnetic field, had been picked up by a passing fleet armada. They'd rushed to Harp, expecting to find some cataclysmic event had occurred and prepared to render aid, only to discover Wolfrum's crime and the collusion of one of their own.

Unfortunately, their timely response had scared off the corporate conspirator before Wolfrum could be forced to send a rescue request to them, and well before they could become curious. That part was frustrating, but shifters had long memories. They'd discover the truth eventually, and when they did, they would act according to their own laws. But in the meantime, they had Guy Wolfrum, whose crimes were heinous enough.

Wolfrum was speechless in response to Cristobal's litany of charges, but only for a moment. "Then, as a citizen of Harp, I assert my right to Ardrigh's justice," he said arrogantly.

Aidan couldn't believe his ears. And from the reaction of the crowd, neither could anyone else. He glanced over at Rhodry and found his cousin giving him a predator's grin of victory.

"Very well," Cristobal said mildly, ignoring the crowd. "I've heard testimony from many of those who witnessed or were injured by your actions, including Dr. Rachel Fortier whom you yourself hired to assist in your monstrous scheme, albeit without her knowledge, and who witnessed the capture and torture of Aidan Devlin. I also received and considered your own statement as to the facts. However, there is one more citizen who has asked to address this public hearing." He looked over and nodded to his left, where a young woman stepped into the room from a side door. She was pretty, with the fair hair and golden skin which was so common on Harp, a combination of the Spanish and Irish heritage of the original colonists.

Aidan had no idea who she was, but Rhodry leaned over and murmured, "Wolfrum's wife."

Aidan was shocked. Why would this pretty, young thing have married a zillah like Wolfrum? Rachel buried her face against the back of his shoulder, and he could feel her body shaking with laughter. Either she'd had the same reaction, or she was laughing because *his* reaction was so obvious.

Up front, Cristobal was saying, "Whenever you're ready, Julia."

Wolfrum was regarding his wife with a smug confidence that was clearly misplaced, since Julia was very carefully avoiding looking back at *him*. If Aidan's woman had refused to look him in the face, he'd have known something was wrong.

Turning her back, literally, on Wolfrum, Julia faced the crowd and told everyone what she knew. How Wolfrum had kept pushing her for information on shifters, and how he'd begun keeping secrets, followed by promises of great wealth once they left Harp.

"But you see, my lord." Julia turned to face Cristobal and

continued in her soft voice. "He never asked me if I wanted to leave. I have family here, and friends. Why would I want to go anywhere else?"

"Julia!" Wolfrum snapped her name like a command, but it also revealed shock. Was is that she'd spoken against him? Or that she didn't want to leave Harp, with *or* without him?

"If you wish mercy for your husband, I *will* take your feelings into consideration," Cristobal said kindly.

She drew a deep breath and said, "I have no husband." And then she walked out the same door she'd come in.

The ballroom filled with the hum of conversation as those present speculated about what it all meant for Wolfrum. And probably a good deal of that speculation was about the state of Wolfrum's marriage, both before and after he'd hatched his scheme. The fact that Julia herself wasn't on trial meant that Cristobal had already taken her testimony and was satisfied that she'd known nothing of the plot. Aidan didn't envy her future, however. Harp was a small place, full of gossip. There'd be nowhere she could escape her past.

He looked up when Cristobal stood. The crowd quieted expectantly.

"The facts in this case aren't in question. Guy Wolfrum doesn't deny what he did or what motivated him. But, in any case, the number of eyewitnesses, myself included, are too numerous for any meaningful defense on his part.

"The only question, therefore, is what constitutes justice and who has the right to make that decision." He raised his gaze to look over the crowd, finally settling on Rhodry. "The initial crime happened in clan territory and it was the clans who were the most injured. First, the imprisonment and torture of Aidan Devlin, and then, the unforgivable attack on Amanda Sumner de Mendoza and her unborn children. Therefore, it is right that clan law prevail, and that clan justice determine Guy Wolfrum's punishment."

The room went perfectly still. Everyone there knew what clan justice required in this, or any other case. The person injured had the right to confront the guilty party one-on-one, a fight to his choice of first blood or death. Even Wolfrum seemed to understand what this meant for him. His face, which had paled when Cristobal had made his judgment clear, now looked as if every drop of blood had left his body. He would have fallen if the guards hadn't been holding him up.

And why not? Rhodry, who'd been half slouched against the wall like a big, lazy cat, had straightened to his full height and now stood, legs braced, staring at Wolfrum with golden eyes gone half cat and gleaming, his teeth bared in a vicious grin. When he spoke, his voice was little more than a growl.

"The clans accept your judgment, Ardrigh, and thank you for this opportunity to avenge the wrongs done our people." He took a moment to scan the assembled crowd. "The only question before me, as leader of the clans, is who among the many clansmen and women injured by this criminal should have the right to confront him in the circle of justice?"

His look turned sly as he stared at Wolfrum over the heads of the crowd. "I could do it myself. After all, I represent every clansman, and it was *my* wife the coward tried to kill, *my* sons he thought to kidnap and take off-planet—" His voice dropped to an even lower register, the words barely understandable for the deep snarl surrounding them. "—to be *experimented on,* their lives spent in cages.

"Or," he continued speculatively, "I could let my wife, Amanda, fight for herself."

Wolfrum's expression brightened with hope, which showed just what fool he was. It might gain him a few months' reprieve while Amanda carried to term and recovered. But in the end, Amanda would tear him apart. Forget the attacks on her or even Aidan, the man had threatened her *children.*

But Rhodry wasn't finished. He looked straight at Wolfrum and said, "But, no. As he was the first injured, first justice goes to my cousin Aidan."

Aidan's eyes blazed as gold as his cousin's as he stared at Wolfrum, and there was nothing but death in his gaze.

Wolfrum tried to run. Fool. His shifter guards didn't even bother trying to catch him. The crowd drew back as Aidan leaped over people and chairs, snagging the Earther before he'd gone ten feet. He tried to grab a knife from someone in the crowd, but Aidan batted it aside with ease and began circling his prey.

"If you please, Aidan," Cristobal called. "Could we take this outside? Blood is such a bother on the floors."

Aidan laughed and gave a mock bow, before jerking his head at the shifter guards. They grabbed their prisoner once again and dragged him outside to the wide dirt courtyard where the guards practiced their fighting skills almost daily.

Wolfrum fought their hold, twisting and screaming. To no avail, of course. It was a waste of energy that he should have been conserving to fight for his own life. But reason seemed to have fled the esteemed scientist.

"For a guy who tried to kidnap shifters, he sure doesn't seem to have learned much about them," Rachel said, her breast soft against his arm as she leaned up to speak into his ear.

Aidan started to reply, but Wolfrum claimed his attention. The man had finally recovered some semblance of pride as he pulled away from his guards and stood tall, tugging at his clothing as if to straighten it.

"Is this justice?" he demanded. "A shifter animal against a human?"

There were growls all around at his description, but Rhodry held up a hand and they quieted.

"I have rights, too," Wolfrum continued. "The fight

should be a fair one."

That wasn't true, but Aidan was curious enough to let the fool keep talking.

"He has to remain in his human form."

Aidan waited for something more, some ridiculous demand that the idiot might think would make a difference. One hand tied behind his back, maybe, or blindfolded. But, no. Wolfrum's only demand was that Aidan fight in his human form. He joined the laughter that rippled through the crowd. It was mostly shifters in the courtyard, with norms lining the balconies, away from the blood and violence that was sure to come.

Aidan stepped forward. "I accept," he said, and then took it a step further, stripping away his belt knife, and tugging his shirt over his head to prove he carried no weapons. Handing both to Rachel, he pulled her in for a kiss. "For luck," he told her, winking.

"Wolfrum's fleet," she reminded him seriously. "He'll have at least some skill in hand-to-hand, and don't trust his honor. He doesn't have any."

He nodded and turned to face his opponent.

Wolfrum went into a defensive crouch, looking very smug. Rachel had been right about his training, but it wouldn't make any difference. Aidan was a shifter in the prime of his life. And he was Guild, the elite, even among shifters. He fought and defeated more deadly creatures every week than Wolfrum would in his entire life.

He faced his opponent without fear, but even a coward like Wolfrum could score a deadly blow under the right circumstances. So Aidan stood ready to defend himself—knees bent, weight distributed, arms loose at his sides.

Wolfrum circled, looking for a weakness, more disciplined than Aidan would have credited. But in the end, impatience won the day, as Wolfrum took a quick step closer and launched a sidekick that, had it connected, might have knocked Aidan back. But Aidan saw the attack coming and countered it, grabbing Wolfrum's leg and jerking him closer still, putting him off balance while Aidan's fist swung up and smashed into the Earther's jaw. Even then, he held his punch, not wanting the fight to be over too quickly. The match might be uneven, but he still needed his vengeance. Needed blood and pain.

Wolfrum reeled back, but managed to recover, steadying himself at a safe distance, his eyes wary. He probably knew Aidan hadn't struck with his full strength and was looking for a sneak attack, a cheat of some kind, because that's what he would have done.

When Aidan held out his bare hands, as if to ask what was next, Wolfrum bared his teeth in a triumphant grin. Slipping his own hand into a deep pocket inside his tunic, he pulled out a small pen-like instrument and pointed it at Aidan.

"You remember this, shifter? I took you down once. I can do it again." He squeezed the narrow cylinder.

Aidan moved faster than the human eye could follow. Before Wolfrum could trigger the small tranq gun, Aidan was across the ring, his fingers breaking the man's wrist, crushing the bones into shards as Wolfrum screamed.

"I remember your tranq guns, Earther, and I learned," he growled, squeezing harder, feeling the shards turn into pebbles of bone. "And it wasn't *you* who took me down. Not then, and not now." He threw the shrieking man across the ring to land at Rhodry's feet. "I'm done with him, cousin. What say we let the Green have its justice next?"

· · ·

Rachel hadn't known what to expect. Oh, she'd known that Aidan would wipe the floor with Wolfrum. Her only fear had been that the coward might do something sneaky and inflict some damage, though she'd expected a knife, not a tranq gun. After the fight was over, she'd examined the one Wolfrum had tried to use. It held only one charge, but the dosage was heavy, clearly gauged for a shifter's metabolism. She didn't know what effect it would have had, and she never would. Nor would anyone else. She'd crushed both pen and tranq cartridge beneath her boot, grinding it to dust, much the way Aidan had Wolfrum's wrist.

Was it wrong that she'd taken pleasure in the man's screams of pain? She'd asked Aidan that same question, but he'd only grinned and said, "Nah, it only proves you're the perfect woman for me."

"As if you needed proof," she'd teased lightly.

But now, they were headed into the Green, dragging along a whimpering Wolfrum who remained unresisting other than constant complaints about his wrist, which had been bandaged and braced. He'd also been given a numbing shot for the injury, which was more than she'd have done for him. In fact, she found it curious. Wasn't the point of this exercise to make him pay for his crimes?

"Why tend to his wrist?" she finally asked Aidan as their much smaller group traveled deep into the Green. The courtyard had been accessible to anyone who wanted to watch, but this was something new. No one except shifters ever went this deep into the Green. Well, shifters and her and Amanda, anyway.

"So we don't have to listen to him scream all the way here," Aidan said, his gaze on the trees overhead which were filled with shifters, moving silently from branch to branch.

"Go ahead and shift," she told him. "I know you want to."

He looked down at her and grinned. "Later. First, you'll climb with me for the finale."

She frowned. Finale? He deserved to be staked to an ant hill and covered with honey like in the ancient Earth stories, she thought facetiously. "What will they do to him?"

"You'll see," Aidan said mysteriously. "The Green has its ways."

Well, that sounded ominous—for Wolfrum.

As if by silent agreement, the group stopped in a small clearing where the loam was deep and soft beneath their feet, every inch of it covered with green, from slender trees to low bushes and even lower moss and vines that crawled over everything in sight. The clearing was dominated by one of the huge trees the shifters called grandfather trees. She'd assumed it simply meant old, but she was beginning to think there was more to it.

"Here we go," Aidan said softly and began shedding his clothes, along with just about every other shifter. Even Wolfrum's guards had thrown him at the base of the giant tree and were now stripping naked and shifting.

"Climb, love," Aidan said, indicating a good-sized tree directly opposite the grandfather. No one was climbing that one, she noticed.

She turned to study the tree he indicated. It was old enough that its trunk was craggy with hand and footholds. "How high?" she asked as she drew on her gloves and started climbing.

"Follow me." A moment later he was shifted and twenty feet up into the tree. Damn him.

"Follow me," she muttered cynically, focusing on the next place for her fingers, her booted foot. The last thing she wanted was to topple backward, embarrassing herself and Aidan.

He was waiting for her—a beautiful, golden beast, head on his front paws, purring like a motor, his cat eyes somehow managing to look innocent. She snorted. Yeah, right.

Innocent.

When he didn't shift back to human, she simply settled in next to him with one arm around his thick neck and stared down into the clearing, just as every other shifter was doing now. She noticed Amanda lower down in the next tree, one with plenty of low branches, making for an easier ascent in consideration of her pregnancy, probably with Rhodry's considerable help. She leaned against his huge, black form, while cats high and low faced the grandfather in a three-quarter circle.

Wolfrum struggled to gain his feet, looking around as if suddenly aware he was free, ready to make a break for it. But no matter how hard he tried, his feet and hands kept sinking into the loam, and he couldn't seem to gain enough traction to push to his feet. Finally, he crawled to the grandfather and clung to its trunk, getting one foot beneath him. But he'd no sooner started to rise, than a whip-thin root came out of nowhere, tripping him up and slamming him back to the ground. He fought to free himself from its grip, but with every root he disentangled, another two surfaced to grab hold and pull him even deeper. He was screaming now—incoherently, frantically—as he struggled to escape a tangle of roots that became first a cage and then a straitjacket, until finally a thick band wrapped around his throat and turned his screams into choked shrieks of terror that she could still hear, even after he'd been sucked down and completely disappeared beneath the moss-covered forest floor.

Rachel stared, horrified.

"His crime was against the Green and its creatures first," Aidan said from right next to her. She'd been so caught up in the terror of Wolfrum's death that she hadn't noticed him shifting. "And the Green always takes care of its own. Now you know why the colonists needed shifters back then, and still needs them now."

She nodded wordlessly, her mouth dry. It wasn't that she thought Wolfrum didn't deserve what he'd gotten. He'd deserved that and more. But...what a nightmarish way to die.

"Don't worry," Aidan said, putting his arm around her later. "You're safe."

"I know," she said faintly. They walked a little way together, taking their time. Just a stroll in the beautiful Green...which also happened to eat people it didn't like.

"Does it bother you?" he asked.

She shook her head. "No, not really. I mean, yeah, I'm a little freaked out, but...if you tell me I don't have to worry about being eaten alive, I'll believe you."

He chuckled. "What you saw out there is extremely rare. In fact, it's never happened before in my lifetime. That wasn't true of those first colonists, though. The planet saw them as invaders and fought back. It's why they were so desperate to create shifters."

She cocked her head curiously. "But why shifters?" she mused, half to herself. "I mean, I can see why they'd want to include some Harp DNA in the next generation, but why shifters, specifically?"

He seemed reluctant to answer, and it occurred to Rachel that this might be another one of Harp's secrets. The ones she wasn't allowed to know.

But then he said thoughtfully, "I'd say we were a fluke rather than a plan. I don't think they meant to create what they did. Shifters, that is."

Rachel nodded. Now *that* made sense. Although she'd love to learn more. Even if they didn't have records, they had oral histories. And medical records, although from what she'd seen, it didn't seem shifters had much need of a hospital. Unfortunately, she wasn't going to be around to explore any of that.

"Why so sad, love?"

She shrugged, her shoulders moving under the warm weight of his arm. "The shuttle arrives tomorrow."

He stopped dead, which meant she did, too. "What's that got to do with you?"

"Well… I'll be on it, won't I? I mean, I didn't exactly arrive here legally, and—"

"Do you want to leave Harp?" he asked, and there was a note of vulnerability to his question that she'd never heard from him before. Aidan Devlin didn't do vulnerable. He was big and tough and able to handle whatever life threw his way.

Her heart was a flutter of trepidation clogging her throat, so that she had to swallow before she could answer his question. She met his eyes, once again human blue with no more than sparks of gold. "No," she breathed, daring to hope. "I don't want to leave. I mean, there's so much to explore here, so much I could study."

He regarded her in bemusement. "That's the only reason?"

"Well. Shifters, of course."

"All of us?"

She gave him a narrow-eyed look. Was he laughing at her? "Fine," she admitted. "You. You're the reason I want to stay. Happy now?"

He grinned. "Almost. You want to study me, sweetheart?" His lips nibbled at her ear, his voice a sinful purr that lifted the hairs on her neck.

"Yes," she said breathlessly.

"Much easier to do if you stay close." He slid both arms around her, holding her flush against his body so that she could feel the defined muscles of his chest and arms, the firm thickness of his thighs, and the hard length of his erection. Desire shivered over her body.

"I love you," she whispered, then pinched her lips and slammed her eyes shut. She shouldn't have said that. She meant it, but she shouldn't have said it. She waited for the inevitable rejection. Waited for him to pull away and make an awkward joke.

"I love you, too," he said, so softly that she wasn't sure he'd meant her to hear.

She had to swallow again, but it wasn't fear clogging her throat this time. "Okay." It was the only word she could squeeze out.

He stroked the back of his knuckles over her cheeks, wiping away tears. "Okay?" he said, smiling. "That's it?"

She laughed, half sobbing with emotion. "I guess I'm staying."

"There you go, love." He slung an arm over her shoulders and turned them back onto the path to the city.

Epilogue

Amanda stood in the guest bedroom, watching her mom pack. Elise would be back, but the universe was a big place, and she was still a fleet officer.

"This won't be the end of it, you know," Elise said.

"I know."

"Randy tells me there are certain forces pushing for your recall to active fleet status."

She hadn't known that. "I served my full contract."

"But you're always subject to recall if circumstances warrant. You know that."

"Last I heard, the fleet wasn't at war with anyone," she scoffed. "At least, not anyone big enough to justify the recall of retired officers."

Elise tipped her head in agreement, her eyes never leaving Amanda's. "True, and you could certainly fight it. But they don't need a war to try."

"Why would they bother?" Amanda finally asked, although she knew the answer.

"Because someone in the Admiralty knows about shifters,

or thinks they do. I doubt Wolfrum managed to smuggle any real data out to whoever employed him. You Harpers are too tight with what you share. But he admitted that his employer had at least one contact high up in the fleet—although that was so obvious that a blind man could have called it. And whatever he did pass on made them curious enough to support his crazy plan, and now they're pissed."

"Yeah, well, they can waste time recalling me, if they want. I'm not going anywhere. I know my rights."

Elise nodded noncommittally, but said, "I'll keep looking for whoever was behind this, and so will Randy. He doesn't need to know about shifters to know something happened here. It would be odder if I *didn't* ask him about it. But be careful, Amanda."

She gave her mother a bemused look. "This is Harp, Mom. Careful is how we live." She rested one hand on her belly and turned back to smile at Rhodry, who was carrying Elise's luggage in from the guest bedroom. "And I have a lot to live for."

Acknowledgments

First and foremost I want to thank my editor, Brenda Chin, who never lets me down, and who inspires me to make every book the best it can be. To Liz Pelletier and Heather Riccio for letting fellow Earthers travel the universe with me. And to all the people at Entangled—reviewers, copy editors, cover artists, and everyone else... I may never know your names, but I benefit from your hard work and I appreciate it.

Angela Addams read this manuscript more than once, providing honest and always excellent feedback. Karen Roma did the hard task of reconciling the details from various revisions. Annette Stone handles the myriad details of publishing life, so I don't have to. And my family and friends encouraged me to keep writing my shifters, even when life conspired against me.

This book would never have been written without the enthusiastic and consistent support of readers who loved my shifters and kept pushing for more. A million thanks to all of you for letting me do what I love.

xoxo
DBR

About the Author

D.B.Reynolds is the award-winning author of the popular Vampires in America series, as well as other paranormal fiction. She lives in a flammable canyon near Los Angeles, and when she's not writing her own books, she can usually be found reading someone else's.

Don't miss the series...

SHIFTER PLANET

Discover more Amara titles...

The Rogue King
an *Inferno Rising* novel by Abigail Owen

Kasia Amon is a master at hiding. To dragon shifters, she's treasure to be taken and claimed. But now she can't stop bursting into flames, and there's a sexy dragon shifter hunting her... As a rogue dragon, Brand Astarot has spent his life shunned by his own kind. Delivering a phoenix to the feared Blood King will bring him one step closer to the revenge he's waited centuries to take. But when Kasia sparks a white-hot need in him, Brand begins to form a new plan: claim her for himself...and take back his birthright.

Bitten Under Fire
a *Bravo Team WOLF* novel by Heather Long

The last person Bianca Devlin expected to see was Sergeant Carlos "Cage" Castillo, the member of Bravo Team WOLF that helped rescue her from a kidnapping on her vacation. But there he is, living across the street from the house she just bought. But there's something off about Cage. And how can Bianca manage her growing attraction, when everything she knows about him and his reason for being there, turns out to be a lie?

The Hunt
a *Shifter Origins* novel by Harper A. Brooks

Prince Kael has just lost his father to an assassin, and he's the next target. A murderer is on the loose, the kingdom is in disarray, and Kael is determined to make the person responsible for killing his father pay. But falling for the beautiful Cara, panther shifter assassin and main suspect his father's murder, wasn't part of the plan. He's not at all sure she did it, and he finds himself going against everything he's ever known just to claim her.

Twice Turned
a *Wolves of Hemlock Hollow* novel by Heather McCorkle

Ayra's father is forcing her to marry to make alliances, her brother has gone off the deepened, and her reaper powers have been awakened, something she hoped would never happen. And now? Her old crush Vidar is back, looking hotter than ever and still managing to ring all her bells with just a look. Vidar swears he's the only one who can help her on her journey. But he already left her once...